D0283685

found in translation

AN ALTERED HEARTS NOVEL

© 2011 by Barbour Publishing, Inc.

ISBN 978-1-60260-961-7

All rights reserved. No part of this publication may be reproduced or transmitted for commercial purposes, except for brief quotations in printed reviews, without written permission of the publisher.

All scripture quotations are taken from the Reina-Valera translation of the Bible, 1909 edition.

Song lyrics for "When God's People Come Together," p. 143, and "Wherever There Is Need," p. 144 written by Roger Bruner. Used by permission.

This book is a work of fiction. Names, characters, places, and incidents are either products of the author's imagination or used fictitiously. Any similarity to actual people, organizations, and/or events is purely coincidental.

Cover photograph: © Kathrin Ziegler/Corbis

Published by Barbour Publishing, Inc., P.O. Box 719, Uhrichsville, Ohio 44683, www.barbourbooks.com

Our mission is to publish and distribute inspirational products offering exceptional value and biblical encouragement to the masses.

ecpa Member of the
Evangelical Christian
Publishers Association

Printed in the United States of America.

found in translation

AN ALTERED HEARTS NOVEL

by Roger E. Bruner

with Kristi Rae Bruner

BARBOUR
PUBLISHING

Foreword

During my junior and senior years of high school, I participated in weekend seminars to strengthen my walk with Christ and my evangelistic skills. Two of my favorites were Dare to Share and Acquire the Fire, both of which were connected with Global Expeditions.

The seminars I attended featured Global Expeditions' trips. Hearing the stories and seeing the pictures of all the people who were very much in need of help and evangelism touched my heart. I desperately wanted to go to another part of the world and become involved in any way I possibly could.

I requested information on an upcoming trip where volunteers would build houses for people in a Mexican village and evangelize as much as possible. I ended up taking this trip when I was eighteen, after my senior year of high school. It required a lot of preparation work; I had to take time off from my job, complete a lot of forms, and even get a passport.

The trip lasted seven days, and the participants were a combination of Global Expeditions staff, church youth, young adult groups, and individuals like me. Once everyone arrived, we had orientation and received our group assignments. The twenty- to twenty-five groups consisted of about fifteen people each.

Although I was aware we would be doing construction work, I'd been under the mistaken impression that we would stay in housing—complete with roofs and electricity. So while preparing for the trip, I made sure to pack my hair dryer and flatiron, makeup, a CD player/radio, my cell phone charger, and several changes of nice clothes for group Bible study. I even paid extra money at the airport because my luggage was well over the weight limit.

I flew to San Diego, and then we drove in groups on buses to the area we used as our camp. Camp consisted of a large building (we used that as our meeting area); two different clearings with tents (one for the boys and one for the girls); a kitchen and eating area; and two areas with outhouses and shower stalls.

When I saw the tents we were to sleep in, I was very upset. All of that money spent and trouble getting everything to fit in my suitcase, and it was useless there. All I'd really needed to bring was a sleeping bag and pillow and grungy work clothes. Because of my error in judgment—I failed to take part of the instructions seriously—I ended up sleeping on a blanket and wearing my good clothes for construction. I was definitely out of my comfort zone.

Each day, during the morning hours, we worked on the houses. Although we didn't have a translator, some of the volunteers knew minimal Spanish and were able to communicate with the villagers. In the afternoons we walked around different parts of the town and shared the gospel. Each of our groups had a translator during that time.

While talking to the villagers, we discovered that some people had heard of God and were God-fearing, but they didn't seem to have a personal relationship with Christ. We shared the gospel with them and frequently used the Roman Road. We also gave Spanish Bibles to the villagers.

After the trip was over, I told my parents all about my experiences. They heard about the people I met, the trials of learning to do construction work, and the joys of helping those less fortunate, and they saw how the trip changed my life.

So my dad decided to write a short story about a girl who goes on a mission trip to Mexico and has her worldview changed. That short story turned into an even better novel. (I'd say that even if my dad hadn't been the one to write it.)

I hope you enjoy *Found in Translation*. . .and I pray that it changes your life.

Kristi Rae Bruner

chapter one

Day 1

"What do you mean I missed my connecting flight?"
Never had I raised my voice to my parents—or
to any other adult, for that matter—but I couldn't have
screamed much louder at that forty-something Skyfly Airline
representative if I'd tried. She may have been joking, but I
didn't feel like laughing. I couldn't have missed my flight.

"The plane was here and ready to leave at 1:19. Your
baggage was aboard, but you weren't." Although her voice
remained calm, she resembled a flashing danger signal and
siren that screamed from head to toe, "Kim Hartlinger, it's not
my fault you're the most irresponsible eighteen-year-old I've
ever met!"

"So," she said, "your flight left without you. We paged you
a number of times first, but you never responded."

"Is that what those announcements were?" Curiosity and
defensiveness made me forget my initial irritation. I was too
naive to know how concerned I should have been. "I heard
somebody paging a Kimmy Somebody-or-Other, but nobody
calls me Kimmy—and nobody ever will. If that guy said
Hartlinger, I misunderstood him. His accent was thick, like a
TWI—talking while intoxicated—or maybe like someone who
isn't a native English speaker. Don't tell me announcements
like that are made somewhere offshore."

Telephone support for our home computer was, and I
hated calling there for that very reason.

Oblivious to everything I'd just said, Millie Q.—I'd glanced
at her name tag a moment before—had the nerve to smile,

revealing an excess of leathery wrinkles that wood filler would have smoothed out better than her rainbow of cheap and ill-applied makeup.

I could also see a mouthful of teeth that needed braces so badly I was tempted to refer her to my orthodontist. I doubted, however, that she could handle the commute from the Dallas/Fort Worth Airport to Georgia on a regular basis, even for something as important as making those fangs look friendlier.

Besides, I wasn't in a mood to do her any favors. If she was teasing about missing my flight, her humor was sick and her attitude the ultimate in unprofessional. If she was serious—I was battling hard to reject the niggling possibility that she was—I needed to consider my alternatives. Normally, Scarlett O'Hara and I could put our worries on hold until tomorrow; but I had to reach San Diego early enough today to join the mission team to Mexico or turn around and go home again.

I could have panicked then, but I didn't. Missing my flight would be a minor nuisance comparable to short periods of bumpiness due to mild turbulence. It couldn't be a real problem like a major blizzard closing the San Diego airport in mid-July and preventing the plane from landing.

Although I'd never been on a plane before today, I imagined flying must be pretty much like traveling by city bus. Miss a flight, especially at a large airport like DFW, and another one headed for the same destination will come along any minute.

No worries. I'd be on a plane to San Diego soon enough.

Millie Q. hadn't finished getting her digs in, though.

"They spent fifteen minutes wrestling your luggage off the plane, making that flight late leaving. Very late. One of the baggage handlers ended up in the emergency room with two broken toes after dropping one of your bags on his foot. What do you have in there—bricks?"

She couldn't fool me with her story about the baggage handler, although I couldn't deny that my luggage was heavy. Excessively so.

I didn't regret having to pay seventy-five dollars for the overweight extra suitcases, though. I needed everything I'd packed: a professional-quality hair dryer; enough matching shoes and purses to have a fresh look every day; a treasure chest of my best cosmetics and toiletries; enough clothes to wear separate day and night outfits for the next fourteen days; a steam iron and travel-sized ironing board; and a small, high-power portable karaoke system with dozens of accompaniment CDs and tons of extra D-cell batteries.

Oh, and I'd packed a thick Spanish-English Bible I hadn't taken out of the box yet. I didn't bother bringing a Spanish dictionary, though. After all, we would have translators; and I wouldn't need to communicate with the Mexican natives without one. Besides, I'd studied too much French in high school to feel like learning any Spanish now that I'd graduated.

"Kim," Millie Q. said, resuming what seemed like her current favorite activity—picking on me, "if you'd been here at boarding time, you would be in the air now. You and every one of your bricks." She grinned.

I cringed at seeing those teeth again. *Doesn't Skyfly care about the appearance of your mouth?* Then I smirked without intending to. *Your mouth reflects badly on Skyfly in more ways than one, lady.*

Then I realized what she'd said.

"At boarding time? Look at my watch!" I stuck my left wrist in front of her eyes, unaware that the time display was upside down. "You see that, Millie? It's only 1:00 p.m., and my plane isn't supposed to leave until 1:23." I glanced outside where the plane should have been. "What have you done with my plane?"

Although I'd once seen a magician on TV make an airliner disappear, Millie couldn't shrink my concerns by a single millimeter.

"There's your problem." I heard the implied "you dodo" as she pointed to my wrist. "Your watch is wrong. It's 2:00 p.m. now—actually 2:04. We started talking at 2:01." She failed to suppress a smirk as she pointed to the huge digital clock on the wall behind her without turning to face it.

The next Vanna White? No way.

"I, uh. . ."

No matter how poorly Millie and I had communicated so far, I couldn't argue with the facts, and they all agreed that my time didn't match DFW's. I had too much intelligence to question which one was wrong.

But why weren't they the same?

"Didn't you set your watch to local time when the pilot from Atlanta announced it?"

She didn't grin like the Cheshire cat in *Alice in Wonderland*, but like a demented rat. I might have reacted less defensively if she'd asked a helpful, friendly "Did you. . . ?" instead of what assailed my ears as a nasty, accusatory "Didn't you. . . ?"

"Of course I did!"

I remembered setting my watch. I'd stopped freshening my makeup to do it. I was a hesitant first-time flyer, but I knew having the right time was imperative. Mom and Dad would have been proud of me. No carelessness on my part today. No, sir.

But—oh, no!—I forgot I was wearing a different watch now. When I spilled my makeup on the floor of the plane, I lost the watch I'd just reset and was now wearing the totally inelegant replacement I bought at one of the airport gift shops. Since the new watch was already running after I fought my way into the plastic packaging—it was too cheap to merit a box—I assumed the factory had set it to the correct time.

Duh. The correct time at the North Pole, maybe. So much for "no carelessness" today.

Imagining Mom and Dad shaking their heads as if they'd predicted a disaster like this was bad enough. Just this morning before leaving home, Dad said, "I wonder if the airlines are up to our well-intentioned Kimberly." He barely cracked a smile when he added, "Do you suppose Mexico has special insurance to cover Kimber-quakes?"

He'd been teasing—or so I'd convinced myself at the time. I wasn't so sure now. Either way, I wasn't going to admit any more of my carelessness to Millie Q. than I had to.

"I bought a new watch," I said, as if that explained everything.

"I assumed that." Millie reached across the counter and peeled off a sticker I'd overlooked.

"They failed to set the time correctly at the factory." There. I'd told her my version of the complete truth.

I wished she would stop laughing so hard, though. I was going to have to compromise if I wanted her to help me. "I guess I should have checked the time on an airport clock, huh?"

She nodded, tears of laughter overflowing the dam of her raccoon-look, black eye makeup and giving her face a mildly water-colored streak.

I guess I should have prayed then, but swearing came more naturally under the circumstances.

I couldn't yield to the urge to curse, though. I was desperate to break that habit. If I didn't succeed now, I'd chance being sent home early from the mission trip. Swallowing my favorite four-letter words to keep from saying them aloud was like trying to eat dry, crumbly cheese without a nice mug of diet root beer to wash it down.

"Millie, will you please get me on the next available flight?" I smiled at her as if we'd become best friends. That was tougher than forcing back swear words. "Just book me on a plane that's a lot faster than the one I missed so I can still arrive in San Diego at the original time. Okay?"

Her laughter broke the cosmetic dam that time, leaving her face looking like a little kid had finger painted a hodgepodge of abstract art all over it. I had to keep my eyes focused on hers so I wouldn't crack up laughing back.

I didn't want her to think I was laughing with her.

"Kim, you've never flown before, have you?" She didn't wait for me to shake my head no. "You'd need to rent the space shuttle to reach San Diego that fast. Or maybe ask Scotty to beam you there."

She cackled. I didn't.

Stranded on Gilligan's Island in the middle of a busy international airport, I was starting to despair of Millie Q. even wanting me to get to San Diego on time. More likely, though, she enjoyed torturing me so much she would keep it up as long as she could.

I kept waiting desperately for Mom's voice to say, "Wake up, Kim. We need to leave for the airport in thirty minutes."

But—alas!—I was already wide awake.

Miss Congeniality started clack-clack-clacking away on her computer keyboard without saying anything else. I couldn't tell if she was doing something to help or just ignoring me. Whatever else, she succeeded at annoying me big-time.

Lord, if she doesn't help me now, You will, won't You? After all, this mission project is Yours, and I know You plan to bless my activities in a special way. Don't You have a moral obligation to fix this mess and get me to San Diego in time for orientation?

Perhaps whining, cajoling, and trying to pin a guilt trip on God as if He'd landed me in this dilemma weren't the most mature things for a Christian to do; but I was starting to catch on that this situation far exceeded my ability to control, and that realization made me more than a little queasy.

When God didn't respond the instant I said amen, I looked at Millie Q. She was still clack-clack-clacking—can't you set that keyboard to silent mode!—doing who knows what.

My panic level began inching its way up, like the red column of mercury in an old-fashioned thermometer. But if I'd known what I was facing today—this problem was just one more installment in today's ongoing tragicomedy—I would have begun practicing my panicking months ago rather than my music.

Witnessing to the lost people of Ciudad de Plata—Silver City—with my singing, my testimony, and my modest Southern charm—I'd use that Spanish-English Bible if I needed to—would be the thrill of my young adulthood, especially when we won everyone in Silver City to Jesus in two weeks.

Well, almost everyone. They might not let us visit prisoners, and they might be afraid to let us convert high-ranking government officials.

Of course, I was also looking forward to chowing down on all the authentic Mexican tacos, chimichangas, and enchiladas I could and buying one of those sombreros that's bigger than me. That would look so cool at the community pool back home. Making people walk three feet around me would be a blast.

Although I'd been a professing Christian for just a couple of years, I'd grown up in a Christian home and been heavily involved in church activities almost since birth.

I believed God loves and cares about everyone equally.

"He loved Judas Iscariot as much as He loved Simon

Peter," my parents used to tell me.

So every person in the world should have a chance to hear and respond to His Good News—even that toothy toad across the counter from me.

I hoped God didn't expect me to witness to her, though. Playing Jonah to a Nineveh that welcomed me—that's how I pictured Ciudad de Plata—was one thing, but I almost gagged at the thought of having to be Jonah to Millie Q.

Miss Congeniality's nasal voice brought me out of my daze.

"The good news is we have five flights leaving for San Diego between now and midnight"—*Huh? What's wrong with Skyfly? Only five flights in ten hours isn't one every few minutes!*—"and the next flight hasn't started boarding yet."

I stared at her, unsure whether to get my hopes up. What was the. . . ?

"The bad news?" The expression on my face must have been as legible as handwriting. "That flight is completely full. The next one doesn't have any available seats, either. Neither does the one after that or the one after that." I was glad she didn't say, "I'm sorry." I wouldn't have believed her.

Then she changed to an unbelievably cheery voice that would have sounded more convincing coming from an undertaker talking with a bereaved family. "But switching back to the good news channel. . ."

She glanced to her right and to her left as if expecting a drum roll from somewhere. I rolled my eyes impatiently, but I doubt that she saw me.

"The 10:19 red-eye has one seat left. It's at the very back, but at least it's inside the plane." She paused as if expecting me to laugh. "Shall I book you on that one?"

"But the mission team buses will leave for Mexico without me. They'll reach Ciudad de Plata before I leave Dallas/Fort Worth."

"Oh, you're going to Mexico? Your baggage is only checked through to San Diego, you know. Before you change planes there, you'll have to pick up your luggage at the baggage claim area and recheck it. I hope you have plenty of time before the flight to your final destination. Of course, since flights leaving San Diego after 11:30 p.m. have to pay a hefty fine, practically no airlines fly out that late. So you'll have to wait until tomorrow morning after 6:30 for a flight to Mexico, anyhow."

I seldom cried—I could manipulate boys without having to—but the reality of my dilemma finally hit and hit hard. I was terrified, not just angry and frustrated. I couldn't waste time and energy calming down, and Millie's inattentiveness was making things worse—if that was possible.

She didn't honestly believe she was helping me, did she? Like my dad sometimes, Millie Q. hadn't listened closely enough to grasp the real problem, and she couldn't have misunderstood the facts more perfectly if I'd been speaking a foreign language.

But worst of all, she was a grown woman. She should have been more like Mom than like Dad.

"That's all well and good, Millie, but—as I just explained to you—we're going to Mexico by bus, not plane, and the group I'm going with is not going to wait for me."

I heard my voice rising again, and my favorite expletives began pawing the earth to see which one would break out of the starting gate first. I was cheering for the one that would tell the toad where to take an extended hot vacation.

No, Kim. Don't even joke about something like that. Hell is for eternity, and your goal is to stop people from going there, not encourage them to.

Millie Q. hadn't maxed out on thoughtlessness and insensitivity yet, though.

"So, Kim," she said, just as oblivious to my dilemma as before, "do you want to take the 10:19 flight or not? There's a hundred-dollar fee for changing your unchangeable reservation. We wouldn't charge you if Skyfly had been responsible for your missed flight, but. . ."

She shook her head and shrugged. She didn't need to say, "But we're not responsible."

"Do you have a hundred dollars, Kim?"

As if I could have gotten a refund on the manicure I had an hour ago while killing the time I didn't know I didn't have. Or on all the airport food I'd eaten in the past two hours.

"But I'm not changing reservations. I'm just"—*think hard, Kim!*—"I'm just using my reservation later than I'd intended to."

I didn't realize how featherbrained I must have sounded until I'd said it and heard Millie Q. start guffawing. Passersby were looking at us now—in amused amazement at Millie and in sympathy at me.

She'd be the hit of the break room today with my story. At least I had the satisfaction of knowing nobody would believe one bit of it.

I let an obscenity slip. In fact, I pushed it out. But it was the least offensive one I could think of.

I didn't seem to have any choice about the 10:19 flight, although it meant using the Visa card Mom and Dad had given me for emergencies only—the same one I'd used for the manicure, which I hoped Mom and Dad would view as an emergency. I'd forgotten to have my nails done the day before.

I'd fly to San Diego tonight as if everything was okay and return home tomorrow. I'd explain to my parents that there'd been a problem with my flight—I'd try to avoid admitting that I was the problem—and, by the time I reached San Diego, the team had already left.

That plan sounded better than returning home today and

saying, "Guess what, Mom and Dad? I discovered the funniest thing after killing hours at DFW. Did you know cheapie-watch factories don't set their products to the time zone they'll be sold in?"

Like I could've expected Mom and Dad to make the three-to four-hour roundtrip to Atlanta twice today, anyhow.

Then something caught my eye.

Huh? You're kidding me. You can't possibly be a. . .

chapter two

S ure enough, Millie Q. was wearing a WWJD bracelet. I
used to think the initials meant Walking with Jesus Daily,
but my best friend, Betsy Jo Snelling, laughed and told me
they stood for What Would Jesus Do? I liked my interpretation
better.

I hadn't seen one of those things in ages and never on
anyone as old as her. I was glad she had it on, though. I would
never have suspected she was a Christian, otherwise.

Whew! I don't have to witness to you after all.

Okay then, what would Jesus do in a situation like mine?
Since His only recorded flying experiences—that's how I
pictured His ascension and maybe His trips through locked
doors after the resurrection—were supernatural, He hadn't left
any specific instructions in the Bible that I could recall.

WWJD. What would Jesus do? I kept repeating that
question to myself as if inserting bullets in a gun until the
chamber was full. But when I pulled the figurative trigger, I
drew a complete blank.

Okay, if not Jesus, what would my parents do?

I snapped my fingers in a lightbulb moment. I knew what
they'd do. I'd seen them do it dozens of times when they
encountered bad service, and it almost always helped.

"Millie. . ." I suppose I should have thanked her for her
uselessness so far, but I wasn't that mature a Christian.
"Millie, I need to speak to your supervisor. . . ." I hesitated a
moment before adding, "Please."

I thought I owed her that much, anyhow.

Without responding, she picked up a nearby telephone, punched in several numbers as if driving tiny finish nails into a fragile picture frame with a humongous sledgehammer, and mumbled a few indistinguishable words to whoever answered. They talked for several minutes.

I fiddled with my purse, searching for the cell phone I'd packed in my suitcase because Mom and Dad told me I couldn't use it on the plane. True, but duh, I didn't think about being able to use it the whole time I was at the airport. Although I was experiencing severe Twitter withdrawal, at least my fruitless search kept me from eavesdropping on Millie.

Millie, don't people go over your head frequently? Or am I the first person you've ever failed to help? I sighed. *I hope your supervisor is more helpful than you. Otherwise, I'm sunk.*

An African American woman in her early thirties emerged from an AUTHORIZED PERSONNEL ONLY door I hadn't noticed before. She may have been Millie's supervisor, but she looked so chic and gorgeous in her shoulder-length cornrows and stunningly tailored Skyfly pantsuit uniform that I could have mistaken her for the superstar of some new airplane movie.

"Millie, you haven't had your break yet, have you?" *My word! You know how to express authority through a gentle, considerate suggestion.* "Feel free to take an extra ten minutes. I'll handle things here." *Millie, that means go and go now.*

I could barely hear her when she added, "You might want to freshen your makeup while you're at it." Not everyone would have made such an effort to avoid embarrassing an underling.

From the look on Millie Q.'s face, though, she would have preferred sticking around and defending herself, probably by telling all the truth she knew about me. Fortunately for me, she didn't get a chance to do that.

Her body language spoke now of frustration. Even the back of her head looked defeated as she disappeared through the door her supervisor had used. Maybe people went over her head all the time.

I almost felt sorry for her. She wasn't necessarily an evil person—just one who'd made a career of the most inappropriate job imaginable for somebody with her temperament. Or her intemperament, anyhow.

"I'm Penny Adams," Millie's supervisor said, extending her hand. Her smile was so pleasant her face glowed, giving her a positive, optimistic, I-can-help-you countenance. I already felt better.

Her words matched her countenance. "How can I help you today? I'll do everything within my power to help."

"Thank you, Mrs. Adams." I couldn't stop staring at the diamond ring set on her left hand. "I'm Kim Hartlinger, and I need all the help I can get."

I decided against complaining and getting Millie Q. in trouble. The day had plenty of hours left for some non-Christian to do that. Then, much to my amazement, I caught myself praying no one would.

I took a deep breath.

"I've never flown before today, and I lost my watch on the plane from Atlanta when I dropped my makeup on the floor and I had to replace it—the watch, that is, not the makeup—and I didn't know it—the watch, not the makeup—wasn't set to DFW time until I arrived at the gate for my flight to San Diego and Millie Q. told me I'd missed it, and I've got to get to San Diego as soon as possible or the buses will leave on the evangelistic mission trip to Mexico without me and I'll have to go home to Georgia and tell my parents and my best friend, Betsy Jo, that I messed up big-time and have all of them mad at me, and maybe Betsy Jo will be so disgusted she'll quit being my friend anymore, but at least my parents will still be my parents."

That sentence was undoubtedly the longest, most childishly convoluted one I'd ever spoken, and I'd done it in a single breath. I barely had enough air left to gasp for more.

"Miss Hartlinger—do you mind if I call you Kim. . . ?"

I nodded, meaning that's fine. But then I remembered she'd asked "do you mind?" and I began shaking my head no, hoping I hadn't lost my meaning in the translation.

But after a couple of headshakes to say no, I don't mind, I got mixed up and started moving my head in a circle instead. We both giggled at my confusion, and that was fine. At least Mrs. Adams knew how to laugh with me and not make me feel foolish.

"Kim, let me make sure I understand correctly." I could already imagine Jesus saying, "Peace! Be still!" to the storm at sea. "You're traveling alone today?"

I nodded. I wanted to explain that Betsy Jo was supposed to come with me today, but that wouldn't have been relevant even if I'd regained enough breath to say anything.

"And you're having trouble getting to San Diego after missing your flight?" I nodded. "You're going to be late for a Christian mission trip?"

I smiled. She'd been listening. I wondered if she'd be willing to give Dad lessons, but concluded she had her work cut out for her if she hoped to help Millie Q.

"Yes, ma'am." I took a big gulp of air. "Not just late, but too late. Millie Q. said there are no seats available until ten-something tonight, and the buses will leave for Mexico hours before that."

I spoke earnestly, but not frantically. Mrs. Adams's concern had calmed me down so much I didn't even feel like swearing over my dilemma.

"Technically, Millie may be correct." Seeing my look of horror, she continued without missing a beat. "Technically."

She smiled. "However, she doesn't have the pull I do—the extra leverage—if you follow me."

Huh?

"If you don't mind my asking, Kim—you understand I'm just trying to help—how tall are you?"

Double-huh? The more accurate question would be how short.

"Just under five feet. I look so young and petite, most people don't realize I'm already—"

"The age you are?" she said, winking mysteriously.

"Right. If I ever started smoking or drinking—not that I ever would—they'd probably card me my whole life. Even when I'm old and gray."

"Ah."

Not until she directed her full attention to the computer screen did I realize her "ah" had nothing to do with what I'd just said.

I was dying to know what kind of solution she might have found. Had Millie kept secret from me that the space shuttle actually flew for Skyfly? Or did Skyfly keep a small, supersonic, private jet around for emergencies like this?

Lord, thank You for putting Mrs. Adams on my side. I'm sorry I questioned You.

"When I have a youthful flyer with a problem—"

"I'm not—" I was about to add "that youthful," but she shushed me quietly.

Was she doing what she seemed to be doing? I played along just in case.

"I am a first-time flyer, though, and today has evolved from a problem into a nightmare."

"Youthful, inexperienced flyers merit a little extra consideration, don't you think?" Her eyes had a playful twinkle.

"I think all inexperienced flyers deserve that." I grinned.

She frowned for a moment. "Kim, I can't get you on the next flight. It's severely overbooked, and your luggage probably wouldn't have made it, anyhow. . . ." She looked at the screen again. Although my hopes started crashing to the floor, she caught and raised them again with the magic of her words. "However, I can get you on a flight that leaves at 4:12 p.m. I can't promise that your mission team friends won't leave without you, but at least you'll only be three hours late and not ten."

My spirits soared. I had a fighting chance. I had the name and address of the hotel that was hosting orientation, and it was near the airport. I could take a taxi and find my group—if the meeting just lasted long enough.

If. Just. How can two such short words be so important?

"By the way, Kim. . ."

"Yes, Mrs. Adams?"

"Under the circumstances, I won't charge you for changing your reservation."

"Thank you!" I ran around the counter and hugged her.

"I hope you don't mind flying first class at no extra cost, though. That was the only way I could get you on this flight."

I hugged her again, and she whispered in my ear, "Just think of this flight as a cup of cold water in Jesus' name. Now go to Mexico and use whatever cups God tells you to use."

I will, Mrs. Adams, I will—if I make it to Mexico at all.

chapter three

My flight to San Diego landed on schedule—only three hours and five minutes later than my original flight.

Under normal circumstances, I would have taken advantage of every luxury first-class travel offered. But nothing was normal, and I sank so deep into the mire of practical concerns that I didn't enjoy the flight at all. I couldn't eat any of the filet mignon that looked as if Mom had fixed it especially for me, although I did take a couple of bites from the bacon it was wrapped in before realizing I'd lost my appetite.

What if they lose all my belongings? What if only some of my luggage arrives? Will they bring the rest to Ciudad de Plata when they find it, and how long will that take? Even if my luggage arrives, how long will it take to get it? Will I have any trouble finding a taxi? Will the driver speak English—or even French? If he doesn't, will he take me to the right hotel? If he does, will he? Do taxi drivers accept charge cards? Will the cab be thick with sickening cigarette smoke? Will the team still be at the hotel? How will they react to my tardiness? How angry will Mom and Dad be if I have to spend the night at the orientation hotel? What will they say if they have to come back to Atlanta to pick me up tomorrow?

After going half-nuts over issues like those, I switched to theological and theoretical matters.

Is God punishing me for committing to this mission trip without praying about it first? Or for swearing and talking so abruptly to Millie Q.? How different would things be now if Betsy Jo's parents hadn't changed their minds about letting her come?

Mom and Dad and Pastor Ron had done their best to convince the Snellings that the Mexican border drug wars they'd been reading about on the Internet were many hundreds of miles from where we'd be. We couldn't be safer.

But the Snellings hadn't listened. Especially Betsy Jo's mother. Maybe she was related to Millie Q.

I tried praying myself to sleep in my spacious lie-flat seat, but the words wouldn't come. Neither would sleep. Not even rest. As the first passenger off the plane—Mrs. Adams had arranged that with the flight attendants, who for some strange reason treated me like I was younger than eighteen—I started sprinting toward the baggage claim area.

But my stomach was so jittery with unanswered questions that I had to make a sudden, prolonged, emergency pit stop. I couldn't recall when I'd last been that nauseated, but by the time I emerged from the restroom, I was too weak to rush.

But weakness was preferable to what I'd just experienced. I would gladly live without pizza for two weeks now.

Although the lengthy delay had raised my anxiety level higher than ever, it had its plus side. By the time I found the baggage claim—I turned the wrong direction coming out of the restroom and went miles in the wrong direction before discovering my mistake—my suitcases were the only ones left on the carousel, and no one was in sight to laugh at my feeble efforts to get them off.

Feeble? I couldn't lift those suitcases by myself this morning when I was still feeling okay, and now I could barely fight the pull of the conveyor belt to drag the first bag to the edge and let it fall to the floor, where it just missed my toes.

The carousel had already begun giving my second, third, and fourth bags their own guided tour of the baggage claim area, making me wait several long and restless minutes for its return.

I started thinking about the baggage handler who'd supposedly broken two toes moving my suitcases at DFW. I hoped Millie Q. was exaggerating about the poor guy. Then again, how else would she have known about my bags being so heavy?

I finally got all four pieces off the belt but realized I needed help getting my stuff outside to a taxi stand. Inserting three dollar bills—which way do those stupid heads go?—into the cart-rental machine, I pulled the rearmost trolley free. Only then did it strike me that lifting my bags onto the cart would be more stressful than dragging and dropping them from the carousel.

More stressful and more impossible. Only God could make my luggage fall upward, and I wasn't counting on that kind of miracle today.

If only I'd thought to remove the largest and heaviest items from my suitcases and put them in the trolley by themselves, leaving the luggage manageably light.

But I didn't, so I spent ten frustrating minutes searching for a porter. One who looked strong, compassionate, and disinclined to be sarcastic. I didn't even care what his teeth looked like.

"I can't lift these, sir," I said to the mostly-bald, upper-middle-aged man who'd appeared out of nowhere and was now walking toward me as if God had divinely appointed our meeting. He didn't look like a porter, though. He wore faded jeans, a short-sleeved plaid shirt, and a baseball cap that said GRANDDAD. In one hand, he held a clipboard, a marker or ink pen in the other.

"No?" he said in a restrained tone. I didn't know if there was such a thing as a California accent, but if so, he had one. He flipped through the papers on his clipboard before making what I assumed was a check mark on a sheet somewhere around the middle. "You must be Kimberly Hartlinger, our team's late, latest, and last to arrive."

Hallelujah! I'm not too late!

I threw my arms around his neck and broke out crying—tears of joy and relief mixed with tears of guilt and regret. I didn't care that he didn't hug me back, pat me on the shoulder, or do anything else a Christian grandfather might have done to reassure a youthful damsel that she was no longer in distress.

"My name is Rob White. I'm the senior project director on this mission trip to Mexico."

He handed me a photo ID—his passport, actually—and insisted that I examine it closely to make sure he was who he claimed to be. He was all business, that man. And cold enough to make me feel like shivering.

"Mr. White, am I glad to see you, sir. I was sure you'd leave for Mexico without me."

"We wanted to. We'll discuss that later."

He reminded me a little of my dad the way he said that, but Dad wouldn't have waited till later to talk about it.

"You overpacked," he said with a straight face that was already red from trying to lift the first of my suitcases. It was still on the floor, and he didn't smile at the prospect of having to bend over and try again.

Come to think of it, I hadn't seen him smile yet.

We struggled and strained together then—I'd heard them call it a team lift at my favorite Target Store—to get my bags into the trolley. I hoped the strain wouldn't give him a board-game card reading, GO DIRECTLY TO HEAVEN. DO NOT PASS SILVER CITY. DO NOT BRING KIM HARTLINGER.

"What do you have in here—bricks?"

No! Not two Millie Q.s in one day. Please.

He left me with the carts—we had to rent another one—in the passenger pickup area and returned six or seven minutes later driving a well-worn but otherwise immaculate, boring white passenger van. My arms, legs, and upper body started screaming

"No!" at the thought of having to repeat our team lifts.

But I could have hugged God right then. He had blessed the van with a lift.

Mr. White didn't say one word on the eight-minute drive to the hotel, and I sat on the passenger side looking straight ahead, sweating over what he might say once he unleashed his honest feelings.

chapter four

When we arrived at the hotel, orientation was about to start. I didn't think about the fact they might have been waiting for me or I would have felt worse than I already did.

I took a seat in a vacant row halfway back.

"Welcome to San Diego, my young friends." I hadn't seen this guy before. "For anyone who hasn't met me, I'm Charlie, the second-in-command on this trip. Since we're all on a first-name basis here, I won't burden you with my last name. It's so convoluted I can barely pronounce it myself."

I smiled politely, thrilled to be surrounded by this group of Christian strangers who, I assumed, would soon be closer to me than brothers and sisters. I giggled once. How would I know something like that? I was an only child.

"I'm an experienced builder from Santa Barbara, California, and I'll help organize and oversee your activities. I hate to disappoint you, young ladies, but I'm happily married."

All over the small ballroom, I heard girls groaning in mock disappointment.

The boys cheered, though, perhaps relieved at having one less competitor for the girls' attention. Of course, as an awkward thirty-something, Charlie couldn't have competed with these guys, anyhow; but that wouldn't have kept them from worrying about it. From the hungry looks on their faces, they'd come on a dual-purpose mission trip: evangelism and finding Miss Christian Right.

Several of the boys started eyeing me. I wasn't surprised. Boys usually noticed me.

Many—maybe most—of these girls were on the prowl for mates as well. I could have told them why their search would probably prove fruitless in the long run, but I didn't normally impose my opinion on others without being asked. Especially not strangers I would be in close contact with for the next two weeks.

"This other fellow up here is Rob White. He's our senior project leader. You can thank him for spending the day chauffeuring you to the hotel rather than making you hang around the airport. He also suggested you might prefer spending these past few hours getting to know one another to listening to me preach a sermon."

Applause broke out all over the ballroom. I clapped as hard as anyone. Rob had been my savior with a lowercase *s*, no matter how he felt about it.

"Rob hails from San Francisco, farther up the coast from me. He's a builder, too, but he has experience working on a greater variety of projects, including some that are similar to this one. He's a bit older, as you can see from all the wrinkles he got raising a houseful of teenagers. But he survived that, and he's a great sport; he can dish out the teasing as well as take it."

Yeah? Show me.

"I'm fairly certain he won't put his pet rattlesnake in my sleeping bag for joshing with him."

Sleeping bag? Didn't Pastor Ron say we'd be staying in church members' homes? "In homes" implies "in beds," doesn't it?

Charlie's comment must have been a slip of the tongue or maybe a figure of speech. I dismissed it.

"Rob isn't available, either, ladies. And would you believe his beautiful wife married him just for his hair? He looked exactly like one of the Beatles when he was younger. Ringo, I believe."

He circled his own head with one finger to denote that Mr. White had only a gray ring of hair left. Although he chuckled at his own joke, nobody else seemed to be laughing. Even Pastor Ron would have found this audience tough. I giggled to myself, wondering if he would have recognized any of himself in Charlie.

I giggled again. He would have found Charlie's humor just as tedious as we found his.

"But if you really want to get on Rob's good side, ask him about his grandkids." Rob waved his Granddad cap and smiled. I was glad to see him smiling.

Mock "ooo's" and "ahhh's" came from all over the room at the prospect of having to look through a wallet full of family photographs. I wanted to see them, though. I may not have spent much time around little kids growing up, but I was a sucker for them now—especially after my brief time working with migrant children at the House of Bread.

And if showing a sincere interest in the photographs of Mr. White's—Rob's—grandchildren would help mend our nonexistent relationship, more power to them.

I probably should have wondered why two highly qualified builders were leaders on an evangelistic project, but I didn't. It's not like we needed to have preacher types along.

After all, the purpose of this trip was lay evangelism. Since a Protestant church in Ciudad de Plata was going to coordinate our activities, their minister would serve as our team pastor.

Rob took the microphone from Charlie.

"It's great to see you here today, excited and primed for practical action in the name of our Lord and Savior, Jesus Christ."

I must have had a strange look on my face. As important, as essential, as I thought evangelism was, I'd never heard it described as "practical" before.

"One thing Charlie failed to point out is that neither of us has ever led a mission project before. We got pulled into this one at the last minute. We haven't been trained to do anything like this, but we'll do our best. We'll make mistakes; you can be sure of that. Please be patient. We'll do our best to correct them."

Heads nodded throughout the room, and I felt a tad better about Rob. I hoped that feeling would soon be mutual.

"It's miraculous that all 144 of the young adults we expected today showed up, even though one of them made a wrong turn at Dallas/Fort Worth and arrived a tiny bit late." Although he'd smiled and used a humorous tone on *tiny bit*, he'd placed a conspicuous emphasis on *late*.

Then he looked me straight in the eye—now I understood how I made Dad feel when I did that to him—and I examined the legs of the chair in front of me with equal parts of shame and self-defense. I was roasting from the heat of a hundred and forty-five pairs of eyes searching intently for America's Dumbest Traveler as if I were a dangerous fugitive. I should have been easy to spot, though, for I was the only one in the room not searching for the criminally careless culprit.

I'd spent my whole life in Georgia; and my parents, teachers, neighbors, people at church—everyone—taught me that staring and pointing were rude. Most of these kids were apparently just "Dratted Yankees" who didn't know any better.

I was proud of myself for not even thinking the common wording of that epithet.

I was also criminally crimson by then. As red as my face felt, nobody would've mistaken me for one of the 143 youth who'd arrived on time. Missing my connecting flight had been bad enough, but being totally at fault was worse. My original itinerary had me arriving in San Diego last, anyhow. So my avoidable delay threw the whole day's schedule off by nearly four hours.

That wasn't something to be proud of—and a lot to feel embarrassed about.

Charlie cut in, leaning toward the microphone. He was obviously comfortable speaking before groups. "Because of the delay in starting, we'll cut orientation short—shorter, anyhow—so we won't be too late getting to the village."

I didn't take time to ponder Charlie's reference to "the village." Probably just the name of a Silver City suburb.

I wished I could be that comfortable addressing groups. But instead of having Charlie's fluency, I suffered a form of disfluency that made me repeat my words or get so tongue-tied they came out super tangled. The problem only showed up when I was nervous.

Like when I had to address too many people at the same time. My salutatorian speech took twice its allotted time, even though it had only half as many words as it was supposed to have.

Rob tapped Charlie on the shoulder and took over at the microphone.

"Sorry to interrupt, Charlie, but I saw some nasty looks out there a minute ago when you mentioned the delay in starting." *Some?* "We're all pretty exhausted, but we need to show our late arrival a little bit of understanding."

I had to give Rob credit for trying, but as uptight as I was by then, he might as well have been a judge pronouncing sentence. "Guilty as charged. Take her to the gallows and hang her by her long wavy hair until it's permanently straight. But first brand a humongous *I* on her forehead with a red Sharpie: the personal pronoun I to signify her self-centeredness. Then make a crossbar with another I for Irresponsible. Together, those brands form a cross. After all, she claims to be a Christian. And may she spend her earthly life remembering that Jesus was on time for His crucifixion. He didn't dawdle over a chocolate milkshake in the upper room."

I glanced down at the sweatshirt I'd bought at DFW and realized I hadn't removed the price tag. Millie Q. must have meant to pay me back by overlooking it—or had I bought it yet then? After pulling the tag off, I looked at it again and snarled. That woman! She took the tag off my watch and stuck it on my sweatshirt when I wasn't paying attention. After starting to think a four-letter word, I made myself switch to something shorter and safer.

Oh, man.

I'd only cursed aloud once today—once that I knew of, anyhow. I prayed I wouldn't give in to the temptation to do it now. Getting here had taken too much effort. I wasn't going to let them send me home before the end of orientation.

But self-control was more challenging after I noticed several places on my sweatshirt that looked like humongous, ketchup-soaked sponges. Why had I insisted on buying a white shirt instead of a red one?

Wait a minute. I haven't had any ketchup today. This is pizza sauce.

I'd gobbled down two good-sized meals of pizza at DFW to store up memories of the taste for the two weeks I'd be in Mexico without it. But the sauce on my shirt served as a filthy reminder that I'd grown sick of pizza—oh, so literally sick!— for the first time in my life. Even though pizza was nature's most perfect food, enough was enough.

The stains might come out eventually, but would my face ever return to its normal color? My blush probably matched the dried stains closely, and I imagined going to the cosmetics department at Macy's and asking for lipstick in Papa John's or Pizza Hut red. Maybe they'd stock slight shade variations for other well-known pizza chains.

Charlie took the microphone again.

Huh? What, Charlie? Why are you looking at me that way?

chapter five

The room couldn't have been much quieter if everyone else had been off in la-la land, too. Charlie was looking at me expectantly. I guess he'd figured out who I was. The people sitting in the front rows turned around to face me, and I felt my blush deepening—if that was humanly possible.

But the question I couldn't answer was whether he'd asked me a question, so I didn't know whether I was supposed to be answering a question or not.

As if certain he had, I felt like shouting, "I've never flown before. I tried doing the right things, but I did them all wrong." I wanted to scream, "What kind of Christians are you to be looking at me that way?" in my most accusatory tone of voice.

Maybe there's no defense like a good offense, but I didn't dare to attempt one. I'd already been offensive enough.

I could have been a blind, crippled dog lying in the garbage heap, covered in pizza sauce and unable to resist a stranger's beatings. But human laws prohibited things like that, and any person in the room would have called the authorities if they'd seen such a thing happening.

But I didn't have anyone—not a human, anyhow—to fully intervene for me in my pizza-stained embarrassment. And to make matters worse, I still had no idea why Charlie was staring at me and saying nothing.

So instead of reacting offensively, I played dumb and closed my eyes to avoid the stares. After all, this was America, and nobody was going to make me testify against myself. It's not like I was a secret-laden terrorist.

I couldn't close my ears to the growing number of snickers from team members in my section of the ballroom, though. I half-expected them to stampede toward safer, more hallowed ground at the front near Rob and Charlie.

At first, Charlie indirectly condoned the negative buzz by failing to acknowledge or shush it. Unfortunately, I couldn't ignore it. Once the murmurs calmed a little on their own, Rob took over.

"I must not have made myself clear earlier. We claim to be Christians. Let's forgive and forget what's happened and move on."

Good words, Rob. So are you going to. . . ?

He glanced at his wristwatch and frowned. Not a casual "Whoops! Better keep this short!" frown, but a booming, "this stupid girl wasted all of our orientation time" scowl.

Although Rob had said the proper Christian thing and probably had the best intentions, I wasn't sure I trusted his ability to completely forgive me. I might have to settle for his spoken forgiveness for the time being.

If the kids believed in Rob's forgiveness, they'd probably follow his lead, too. But they'd be apt to ignore his plea for my amnesty—it's called mercy in Christian lingo—if they didn't.

Even though nobody had said anything unpleasant to me, my untimely mistake obviously hadn't endeared me to this group. I didn't expect instant forgiveness, but a drop—a single atom—of tolerance and understanding would have been so. . . reassuring.

So Christlike.

Maybe they'd let me evangelize by myself for the next one million, two hundred and nine thousand seconds (give or take a few). Unless the attitudes behind those cold, staring faces warmed up, no one would want to team up with me. I didn't want anyone to be miserable having me on his team.

Just give me a translator, and I'll be fine on my own. The spiritual needs of Silver City are too important for me to waste time taking a little rejection too seriously—not as long as I'm still free to witness for my Lord.

A gentle hand touched my shoulder, and a whisper reached my ears. "Don't worry about it, gal. Everything will be fine, you'll see." Although I didn't think the Holy Spirit had a gender, God had just spoken to me through the decidedly female voice of someone sitting immediately behind me.

I turned my head just far enough to identify my Barnabus. I smiled, and a dark, African American face smiled back. I wanted to thank her for helping calm my storm with her own "Peace! Be still!" while everyone else looked like they wanted to rock the boat and do whatever else they could to make me seasick.

Slightly reassured, I faced front again and settled back into my chair. Rob and Charlie changed topics, and Christian love reigned again—at least on the surface.

But I couldn't be sure what dangers lurked beneath.

chapter six

Rob and Charlie started giving statistics in tandem about how many states our team members represented (22); the total frequent-flier miles our flights to San Diego would add up to (I missed that number); the ratio of boys to girls (2.24:1—that threw me for a loop since it meant algebraically that the team included 44.44 girls, and I'd always believed that people existed only in integer quantities); the number of different high schools represented (121); the average GPA of the team members (3.25, although I suspected a few people had overactive imaginations); the total and average weights of the participants (some must have actually lied on that one); and the total years team members had been Christians (578). This exercise was supposed to be good, wholesome, attention-grabbing, team-building stuff.

It worked. I was more comfortable than at any time since Rob first mentioned my tardiness.

But my mind—my attention, anyhow—was already slipping backward into first gear, and I was in danger of having it land in neutral. Because Mom and Dad had economized instead of sending me to San Diego nonstop, I'd already had a super-long day. I left home at 3:00 a.m. to be at the Atlanta airport by 5:00, and my flight to Dallas/Fort Worth left at 6:45.

It was 5:38 Pacific time now. At least I was pretty sure it was.

Since I'd slept very little on my first flight and none at all on the second one, I'd be tired now, anyhow. But anxiety about reaching San Diego had gone the second and third miles in frazzling me.

Now I just wanted to reach Ciudad de Plata and settle down for a good night's sleep. Of course, no one had explained our exact sleeping arrangements, just that the cost of the trip included a place to sleep. Although I still thought we were to stay in the homes of Silver City church members, my memory of details—especially when I was this worn-out—could be as bottomless and one-directional as quicksand.

I didn't really care where I slept, though—not as long as my mattress was soft. I hated hard, lumpy mattresses. They reminded me of camping out and sleeping on the ground when I was a kid. I hated it then, and—as a persnickety teen—I refused to go camping anymore.

Any place I couldn't get a good signal on my cell phone was too far from civilization. I'd already made sure Silver City provided roaming coverage, even if international rates applied.

As exhausted as I was, Rob and Charlie's endless statistics were like counting an infinite number of sleep—uh, sheep.

I opened my eyes and perked up again when they started talking about the importance of flexibility in doing mission work, though. As great as Pastor Ron was—and as mission-minded—he'd never said anything like this.

"No matter what a person expects to do on a volunteer trip, surprises occur," Rob and Charlie pointed out. "We've experienced a few of our own today."

Like having to deal with me?

"Things change, and someone may be asked to do something she doesn't feel qualified to do."

Talking about me again? But you couldn't be. I'm well prepared for evangelism in Silver City.

"How we respond to those challenges—the extent to which we're willing to say yes to God no matter what—reveals the depth of our faith. Or the shallowness."

Not bad lay preaching, guys.

"The request to lead this new trip just ten days ago has brought both of us far out of our comfort zones."

New trip? You said you'd been pulled into this at the last minute, but this project had been planned for months. Betsy Jo and I heard about it as long ago as March or April.

"We could've given good excuses—legitimate reasons, actually—for saying no, but we realized God had uniquely qualified us for this project. Probably more than anyone else who might have been available. Well, we were partially qualified, anyhow. We'll depend on Him even more to make up for our deficiencies."

Uniquely qualified? What qualifications do you need except for being a believer who's sincere about evangelizing the people of Ciudad de Plata?

"Pulling everything together in such a short time has taken all the prayer and faith we could muster. The challenges of this project have kept us on our knees constantly. Wisdom in watching over 144 young adults and keeping them safe will require ongoing prayer."

Keeping us safe? Is Silver City less civilized than they told us? Did Betsy Jo's mom do the right thing in yanking her off this project?

"Because you're adults now—well, all but one of you—you don't need chaperoning."

I sighed. Wouldn't he ever tire of talking about me?

"Expect us to treat you like adults. But anyone failing to live up to our conservative standards will go home. This warning is your last one."

Although I was still chewing on my questions about the safety issue, I noticed Rob narrowing his eyebrows at someone in the crowd. I couldn't keep from smiling. He wasn't looking at me this time.

I forgot about my minor concerns when Rob and Charlie

continued. They couldn't have gotten my attention more completely if they'd thrown me in shark-infested water and rung a dinner bell. They answered questions I didn't know to ask. Thrust into complete wakefulness and gasping for sanity like a mountain climber sucking air at a high altitude, I knew I wouldn't sleep again.

Not until I was home.

chapter seven

A s you already know," Rob said in a "but I'm going to tell you again, anyhow" tone of voice, "your project changed significantly two weeks ago. Each of you originally signed up for evangelistic outreach under a different pair of project leaders. You were going to Ciudad de Plata, a fair-sized Mexican city just two hours south of San Diego. It has the McDonald's you heard about and plenty of places to buy souvenirs. And, yes, Silver City is a dark, sin-ridden place in bad need of God's light. You were to work with a local Protestant church, and they were looking forward to your coming to help with outreach."

Our project changed significantly? We "were going" to Ciudad de Plata? The church "was looking forward" to our coming? Why not "we are" and "they are"? What's happened, Rob? Why are you speaking in the past tense?

Everyone nodded. Everyone but me. This information wasn't news to them.

Shortly after Charlie reached for the microphone, I was glad I was sitting down. I might have collapsed.

"Then a freak windstorm—probably a twister—roared through the tiny village of Santa María de los Campos, destroying or severely damaging every tiny residence."

"Every residence, yes," Rob said. "But the village contains one small building the twister didn't touch. Because of its miraculous survival, Charlie and I have begun referring to it as the "Passover" Church, even though it doesn't resemble a church and doesn't look like it's been used in ages.

"We have no idea what it is. It's far too ancient to have been built by the current villagers. The residences were apparently left over from an earlier generation as well. That's the report we've received from the anonymous person who reported Santa María's needs."

"We don't know how many people died," Charlie said, "but the villagers lost everything except the proverbial clothes on their backs.

"You already know Santa María is smaller than Ciudad de Plata. What you probably don't realize, young people, is how tiny it is. Tiny and immeasurably less civilized than Ciudad de Plata. It has no McDonald's. No malls. It has no goods to sell, no goods to buy. Even before the storm, it didn't have electricity, plumbing, or running water.

"Santa María has no resources for housing you. The villagers themselves don't have anyplace indoors to sleep."

A number of selfish grumbles resounded throughout the room, but the quiet sounds of unselfish shushing calmed them down.

"Santa María is so far in the boonies that regional maps show it only as an unlabeled pinprick that could place it anywhere in a fifty-mile radius. After knowing about Santa María for centuries, the authorities still don't take it seriously enough to send census workers to count the decreasing population, which we believe may be down now to forty or fifty.

"Census takers couldn't find the village, anyhow, but we have what they don't—a detailed, hand-drawn map, complete with directions and GPS coordinates. Without those, we'd never find it, either.

"Nobody knows what the villagers did for a living before the storm or how or if their children received schooling. We don't know the spiritual condition of the villagers, either. The fact that someone discovered and reported Santa María's desperate situation is a miracle, and we don't have a clue about who he is or how he knew.

"Heavy rains drench the area every year, beginning around this time next month, so they need homes ASAP. The villagers are equally desperate for food and water, clothes, and bedding.

"Rob and I have collected a semi full of those supplies—donations from a number of generous and caring people, not all of them Christians. That truck has gone ahead of us today. We've also obtained a remarkable quantity of construction materials by challenging our subcontractors and even our competitors to match or exceed our contributions. Trucks bringing everything necessary for rebuilding Santa María from the ground up will follow our buses. We hope to have enough leftover material for the villagers' future use.

"But the one thing nobody donated was grunt construction workers to put everything together. Not skilled workers, you understand, but folks who'll do their best to follow simple directions. That's you.

"Each of you has come in faith, believing God wants you here—to help the people of Santa María survive. Not one of you opposed the project change. That's required quite a leap of faith and obedience—"

"What?" I hadn't exploded that loudly at Millie Q. "I sure as. . ." A curse word was headed for the tip of my tongue, but I quickly threw up a successful roadblock. "I sure as blue blazes didn't hear about any such change. You've kept saying 'you already know,' but this is all news to me."

"Young lady, calm down, please." Charlie studied the legal pad on his clipboard as if God had just jotted down detailed instructions for pacifying a crazed female. In Greek, Aramaic, or preferably the original King James English. Rob whispered something in his ear, and he looked up again.

"So you're Kimberly—Kimberly Hartlinger?"

I nodded, no longer concerned about whether every eye

in the ballroom was watching me. I was hot—too hot to worry about disfluencing. If I didn't think about it, I wouldn't do it.

"I'm Kim, please! Kimberly was my great-aunt. . . ."

I couldn't believe I'd brought that up in the midst of my turmoil, but stress reveals itself in strange ways.

"Uh, Kim, we sent e-mail to everyone scheduled for Ciudad de Plata. We explained the situation, although not in the detail we've just presented, and we asked for honest feedback. . . ."

"I. . .I never received such a message."

Maybe no one could blame me for not receiving a message, but voice after voice clobbered my ears with assurances that they had gotten it.

"I did," one girl said from the other side of the room.

"So did I."

"I got it about two weeks ago and responded immediately."

"Me, too."

"I received mine."

The last voice belonged to the African American girl sitting behind me. But unlike the other responses, hers sounded factual and straightforward. Unlike them, her tone didn't say, "I got my message, so why didn't you?"

Group consensus grew so loud and unruly that Charlie had to shout into the microphone. "Quiet, please!" I crumpled at the realization I was the only person present who didn't know about the project change before now.

And I still didn't know the details.

"Kim. . . ?"

"Uh, I'm sorry. I. . .what else did this message say? I would have read it if I'd received it. I've really been looking forward to this trip. I was ready for it—physically, emotionally, and spiritually." I paused, but not long enough for anyone to comment. "At least I was ready for evangelism in Ciudad de Plata."

Although my disillusionment bordered on bitterness, I was curious—no, more concerned than curious—about what else I didn't know about this trip to—where? Santa María?

"Maybe the e-mail was undeliverable because she lives in the wrong time zone, y'all," said a high-pitched, youthful-sounding male voice on the other side of the room.

Laughter exploded in rapid-fire bursts all over the ballroom. Like corn popping. But this popcorn threatened to leave a bitter—not a buttery—taste in my mouth.

"That's enough!" Rob shouted into the microphone with enough sternness to assure me he was on my side now.

The laughter quieted down immediately.

"Kim," Charlie said, "there's obviously been a communication glitch, and we're as sorry about that as we can be. That doesn't help, though."

Although the extent of his understanding caught me off guard at first, I shook my head in agreement.

"You know how Santa is supposed to check his list twice? Well, each of us reviewed that distribution list several times—individually and together—to verify that we hadn't left anyone off. When we sent the project change message, we didn't receive a single delivery failure notice. Not for the follow-up messages, either."

He brought his clipboard over and pointed to my name on a printed, sent message. "Is this your e-mail address, Kim?"

I sighed, barely able to say, "Yes."

The fight had gone out of me. Although I still didn't know why I'd failed to receive those messages, I couldn't blame Rob and Charlie.

"Kim, you asked what else the message said. We offered a refund to anyone who didn't feel God calling them to Santa María; no one has asked for one. We also told you—those who received the message—what to bring. That list was far different from the one you received for Ciudad de Plata."

"And what's on the new list? Please."

The first hearing of earth-shattering, ten-day-old news still had me reeling. Too overwhelmed to wonder whether I might have been the only person to stay home, I also didn't consider the possibility that—with even a hint of advance notice—I might have been enthusiastic about the project change.

Maybe this kind of project was what my work with the migrant children had prepared me for.

"Since the village is entirely outdoors now, we told you to bring a sleeping bag and a small pillow. The Passover Church is in the center of the village. You young ladies will sleep in a field about two hundred yards on one side of it and the boys equidistant on the other side. Since Santa María's rainy season isn't due for a month, you won't need tents."

Although I focused hard on absorbing this information, many of the other team members began fidgeting, apparently bored at having to listen to what they already knew. More and more of them got up and went to the side of the room to get water from a table that almost overflowed with plastic pitchers, glasses, and a bowl of cubed ice. They didn't seem to be in a rush to sit down again.

"We told you to leave your small electrical appliances at home. You couldn't use them in Santa María—no electricity, remember?—and the dust and daytime heat might ruin them. You would have little use for makeup, shampoo—all that sort of thing. We said bring strong insect repellent, even stronger sunscreen, and lots of hand sanitizer. Stuff your suitcase with all the deodorant you can find room for. Without access to anything but bottled water, well, you get the idea. . . ."

"I paid seventy-five dollars for excess, overweight baggage," I said in a purposely pathetic tone of voice. "I brought a battery-powered karaoke box to sing with in Ciudad de Plata—I bought it just for this trip—and I have a professional hair dryer. I have a full makeup kit, shampoo, conditioner, and a variety of skin care products, and you're saying I brought it all for nothing? I paid seventy-five dollars to bring what everyone else knew to leave home?"

A nasty spark had lit my fuse. It was burning down fast, and everyone knew it. Apparently reluctant to chance setting me off further, people tiptoed back to their seats. Nobody was laughing.

"I can only imagine how frustrated you are, Kim. We all feel for you, don't we, gang?"

A light breeze of nods and grunts blew in my direction from different parts of the room, but real empathy was conspicuously absent. These kids didn't care what the best of intentions had cost me.

I felt a pat on my back. At least the girl sitting behind me cared.

"Kim, we told you to bring your grungiest clothes and the most comfortable shoes you could afford to ruin. We suggested leaving your used work clothes in Santa María. The village women might be able to make something from the remnants, no matter how small."

I quieted down again, but I was nearly in tears.

"I brought my favorite American Eagle jeans—I'm wearing a pair of them now—some really nice Aéropostale skirts, my best Hollister tops, and several pairs of Gucci leather flats." I didn't care if I was whining or not. "You expect me to do dirty, sweaty work in clothes like those?"

"Long live Miss Prep!"

"Somewhere else."

"Like back home on whatever planet you came from."

Rob grabbed the microphone from Charlie. His face was two shades past livid. "That's enough!" He could barely control his voice. "You sound like the crowd at Jesus' crucifixion. Do we have to send all of you home—tonight?"

That got everybody's attention. He meant it.

"You need to work together like a little church—a beacon to Santa María's darkness. Everyone has a right to his opinion about what God has planned, but you need to minimize your differences—or you won't accomplish anything. As Christians, you should be fair, honest, and loving in dealing with differences. In this branch of the Christian family, a verbal snipe—especially sarcasm—is as serious and out of place as a physical attack."

Quite a few people began studying their shoes with new interest. This time, I didn't have to.

"Kim," Charlie said after several moments of dead silence, "I may not appreciate the way you've expressed yourself,"—did I swear without realizing it?—"but at least you've been honest. I respect that. If you didn't receive the messages about the project change—and I believe you—I'm sorry. I'm sure Rob will gladly refund your money and get you on the next flight back to Atlanta. We'll pay for your excess, overweight baggage, too."

I wondered if somebody might laugh at Charlie's last remark, but nobody did. I guess they were all still too terrified of being sent home. I had to hand it to Charlie. His offer was not only kind, but one he didn't have to make.

I noticed a strange look on Rob's face while Charlie was talking, though. I couldn't quite interpret it. But then he caught me off guard with an understanding smile.

"Absolutely, Kim," Rob said. "Just say the word if you want to go home."

I hadn't missed his use of the word *if*, even though Charlie hadn't expressed any doubts about my leaving.

I looked around the ballroom at all the kids waiting for me to "say the word" and head for the door. If Rob hadn't rebuked the crowd so severely, they might have broken out chanting, "Say the word, Kim! Say the word! Go home, Kim! Kim, go home!"

Suddenly aware of that gentle touch on my back again, I twisted around and looked at the girl behind me. She was whispering something I couldn't quite hear. But I knew it wasn't "Go home, Kim."

I might not have had the heart to stay if she'd turned against me. Despite my inability to read her lips, her eyes said, "Stay."

Although I sensed God trying to encourage me through her, my blatantly negative behavior before this group of fellow believers didn't make me feel any better. My disfluency, conspicuously absent during my selfish and thoughtless tirades, showed up now in full force. *Lord, please help me get through this.*

"Rob, uh, Rob and Charlie, thank. . .thank you. As much as I. . .as much as I want to go home now, and. . ." I started coughing before I could point at the other kids and add "as much as I think they want me to." *Okay, Lord, I'll tone it down.*

"I don't think God. . .I don't think God wants me to go home. I'm shocked to hear myself say that. As much as I might prefer evangelism to construction and Ciudad de Plata to Santa María, God has brought me here for a reason. Maybe He did it this way because He knew I wouldn't come if I had any inkling of what I was getting into."

I stood up, turned around, and faced the team members sitting behind me. Although they appeared to be listening, I wondered what they were thinking.

"I want to be part of this team. I didn't expect to do construction in Mexico, but I want to help rebuild Santa María and evangelize the villagers in the process. I don't believe in coincidences. So—if you haven't caught on yet—I'm going to

Santa María with you."

I'd become so engrossed in sharing what was on my heart that my disfluency disappeared by the time I reached the middle of the second paragraph. Maybe sooner.

"I've made mistakes, and I don't expect to become everyone's favorite girl by tomorrow, but I'll try to do better than I've done today. I hope you'll forgive me for causing so many problems. If you don't do it today or tomorrow or next week, that's okay. But sometime between now and eternity."

In a book or a play, on TV or in a movie, a suddenly humbled and forgiving group of Christian young adults would break out in enthusiastic applause—maybe give a standing ovation—at a moving speech like mine. But the only response was a silence so strong I feared it would last throughout the evening and beyond.

Only God knew how far beyond.

chapter eight

"Hello. I'm Aleesha Jefferson." She spoke with a boldness that an often-shy person like me hadn't expected. "Would you like to eat with me, Miss Kim?" Although nobody had said anything overtly negative to me after Rob's call down, no one else had expressed the least interest in my company.

Aleesha's eyes twinkled with a special kindness that made her invitation sound as sincere as her earlier encouragement. She wanted my company as I much as I wanted hers. I wasn't blind to the fact she was the only African American in the room other than a few of the servers setting up the buffet table, and I knew some Christians weren't as. . .accepting of their non-Caucasian brothers and sisters as I was.

I raised my right hand to give her a high five, but she extended hers in a handshake. In a compromise move, we knocked knuckles and giggled.

"I hope they don't feed us pizza, Aleesha. I've already had my fill of that today." I explained about getting sick at the airport.

"My word, Miss Kim! You're wearing enough pizza on that sweatshirt to have a bedtime snack every day for the next two weeks."

"Aleesha, how long are you going to keep calling me Miss Kim?"

"Only till you change your name to something else. Then I'll address you as 'Miss Something Else'. . ." She winked at me and then laughed. "I've been taught to address my elders that way."

I gave her a "you think I'm older than you?" look.

Shaking her head playfully, she added, "And people I meet for the first time."

"Well, Miss Aleesha, just don't give me any special treatment."

"You're special to God, aren't you? So you're special to me. I love to tease, though. You might as well get used to it. I'm just warming up."

"Deal," I said, extending my hand at waist level, expecting a handshake. She held her hand up in the air—palm out—ready for a high five. We knocked knuckles again.

After sitting down side by side at one of the empty dinner tables, we started giggling over the various pieces of silverware we couldn't figure out a use for. Didn't this hotel know all but two of us were just teens?

Five minutes later, we moved to opposite sides of the table. Not because the closeness was bothering us. We were both getting sore necks staying turned toward one another.

Our whole meal was fun. Although Betsy Jo had always been easy to talk with, she could be reserved at times. Aleesha wasn't like that, and she didn't act the least bit stuffy.

"What's your favorite book?" she asked.

"*Gone with the Wind,*" I said. "Book and movie." I hoped that would gain some brownie points with her.

"Hmm. Bottom of my list."

"Why's that?" I was incredulous. "After all, that lady who played Mammy—I forget her name—won an Academy Award for her part. First black woman to do that."

"Maybe you haven't noticed the demeaning way Margaret Mitchell portrayed black people."

"Uh, sorry about that. But I dream of being Scarlett O'Hara searching for my Rhett Butler."

She smiled. "No problem. You have a right to your own perspective, even if it's off-color." That set off a lengthy giggling spell.

"I have something in common with Scarlett," I told her.

"What? Chasing after married men?" Man, did she keep a straight face when she said that.

"No, ma'am. I always think in terms of tomorrow." It seemed like time for a change of topic. "Why did you come on this trip?"

"It's my graduation present." She grinned. "I already had everything else I wanted."

"Oh? You have a car?"

"Nope. You?"

"Recent model Mustang convertible. I wanted a 'Vette, though. Do you have an iPod or MP3 player of some kind?"

"Oh, you mean MVP3—the third Most Valuable Player?" She cackled. "That means no. I do all the singing I need to hear. But you have one?"

"Yes." I hesitated. I hadn't intended for this conversation to become a bragging contest that I seemed to be winning.

But if I felt uneasy about it at first, I shouldn't have. Aleesha was eating this conversation up. She'd probably never been around such a spoiled white girl before, and she was making the most of it.

"Go on, girl," she said. "What's next? A cell phone? Don't have one of them, either, although everyone else in my family does. Even the baby."

My tongue must have drooped halfway to the floor.

"Don't go getting caught up in racial stereotypes, girl. I didn't say 'my baby.' I was talking about my kid sister. I'm not getting married until I'm fifty—if then—and not having kids till I'm seventy. By then it won't matter whether I'm married yet or not."

She chuckled to herself, and I hoped she couldn't hear my sigh of relief.

"Aren't you going to ask why everyone in my family has a

cell phone but me?"

I wasn't used to conversations that moved along so quickly. Talking with Aleesha was anything but boring.

"Uh, wh—?"

"Because I'm so shy. I hate to talk. That's obvious, isn't it? The way you've had to drag every word out of me. . ."

I thought I'd fall off the chair. Instead, I knocked over both glasses of iced tea.

"Kim, you haven't asked about a computer."

We sat there mopping up the tablecloth with our fancy cloth napkins.

"That's because I don't have one. You do?"

"A laptop of my very own."

"Oh." I tried not sounding jealous, but I hated sharing the family computer with Dad.

"But, Kim, there's still one thing you haven't asked me about. . . ."

What? A boyfriend? I had too many to say I had one. I wasn't going to guess, so I just looked at her.

"Ask if I'm happy."

"Aleesha, are you. . . ?" I couldn't imagine this upbeat girl having a negative answer.

"I told you I have everything I need, but I never said I was talking about stuff. My family is pretty well-to-do, but we do our best to put God first, others second, and ourselves last. And unnecessities are at the bottom of our list of interests. Who wouldn't be happy living a life like that?"

"Amen!" But then I sighed. It sounded like my life might be missing something.

chapter nine

I can't remember what was on the buffet, but it wasn't pizza
and there was a lot of it. We felt like two deer a taxidermist
had gotten hold of by the time we finished.

Before Rob and Charlie herded us out to our buses, Rob
asked if anyone was into weightlifting. He didn't offer an
explanation, and Aleesha and I were probably the only ones
who understood the question, even though I'd confessed
publicly to the mortal sin of excess baggage.

"Don't drop any of that." I laughed at the muscular volunteer. When he began lifting the first of my suitcases, he strained
and grunted so convincingly I thought he'd hurt himself. "Those
already cost a baggage handler at Dallas/Fort Worth a couple of
his toes today," I jibed once I knew he was okay.

The stony silence made his feelings clear. He would
have preferred helping somebody else—somebody less. . .
troublesome. Somebody more normal. Someone more
deserving of help.

But I'd meant it when I said I didn't expect forgiveness
today. Good thing.

"Wha—?"

I was starting to sit down near the front of the bus when
Aleesha pulled me by the scruff of the neck down the long
aisle to the very back.

I gave her a funny look. "Why here?" I thought she'd
come up with some rollicking explanation that would leave me
coughing from laughing so hard.

"It's just, you know, quieter back here. We can talk without being self-conscious."

Huh? A serious response? Or was it? I couldn't imagine Aleesha ever feeling self-conscious.

The question mark must not have evaporated from my face yet.

"Kim, I saw Mr. Rob getting ready to sit across the aisle from you up front. I thought you'd feel more comfortable not having him close enough to eavesdrop."

I nodded without remembering to thank her for doing that. Not even Betsy Jo would have been as thoughtful.

"So, why did you come on this trip?"

"Not for my original reason." As honest as we'd been so far, I wouldn't attempt to hide my faults now.

"Oh?"

"Yeah. To make a long story only slightly shorter, my parents were pushing me to get a summer job. I just wanted to hang at the pool and the mall."

"Tough senior year?"

I would never believe Aleesha wasn't a mind reader.

"I know you're right about that, girl." Or was it "You know. . ."? I'd overheard black girls at school use the expression. If it was good enough for them. . .

"So this mission trip would be easier than working?" Her eyes laughed at me.

I shook my head and chuckled. "I didn't say that, Aleesha. But I didn't think a job and a mission trip would both fit in the same summer. That's what I tried convincing my parents of, anyhow."

"Did it work?"

I giggled. "Yes and no. I got an involuntary, seven-day gig doing volunteer work with migrant children at the House of Bread. That's an outreach ministry of my church."

"Seven days? It took you that long to finagle your way out of it? I'm gonna have to give you lessons, girl."

"Quitting was actually my parents' decision. They did it for me." I couldn't hide my resentment.

"Huh, girl? That's what you wanted, wasn't it?"

"Surprisingly enough, no. Before the first day was over, I fell in love with those migrant kids. When I went to their camp and saw how they were living, I wanted to rescue them from that lifestyle. You know?"

She nodded. "But you couldn't take them home with you like so many stray kittens and puppies, huh?"

"No. All I took home was a lot of guilt for being so much better off than they were—that and a burning desire to improve the quality of their lives."

"You a do-gooder, Kim? No offense, but I wouldn't have taken you for one."

"Nobody else would, either. I'm too self-centered. But everybody who knows me well knows I go all out if I want something enough."

I looked Aleesha in the eye. She was listening intently.

"But I couldn't accept being powerless to help the migrants. To make real changes. So I got depressed and poured myself deeper and deeper into my work with those kids. I went to the HOB earlier every day and stayed later. I stopped wearing good clothes, jewelry, and makeup to work with the kids, and I quit worrying about my appearance at all."

"That doesn't sound like you, girl."

"I almost stopped eating, too. I could barely sleep for thinking about those kids getting stuck in the same endless cycle their parents were in."

Aleesha didn't say anything. I'd already discovered that silence on her part was significant.

"So Mom and Dad met with the director of the House of Bread and decided—without talking to me about it—to retire me before my volunteer work did any permanent damage to my psyche."

"You resented that. . . ?"

"Very much so."

"You still resent it?"

I hesitated. Maybe resent wasn't the right word, even though I'd thought it was a few minutes earlier. "At least now I can accept the fact they did the only thing they could do. They couldn't have talked me into quitting, and pushing at me might have put me over an edge I was already dangerously close to. They had to do their thing as parents and make a decision, no matter how I felt about it."

"You seem okay now."

Although her statement was positive, she seemed to want confirmation of my current emotional state.

"I am, thanks. Mom and Dad sent my best friend, Betsy Jo Snelling, and me to the beach for a long weekend of R & R. They hoped that would make me forget what I'd gotten so distraught over. I didn't expect it to help. At first, the idea of sun and surf, Thrasher's french fries, and crab imperial at Phillips by the Sea seemed frivolous, but the change of scenery helped, and I finally began unwinding."

"So you went back to the way you used to be?"

Regardless of how she'd worded the question, Aleesha obviously wanted me to say no.

"I came home 'normal' again, if that's what you mean; but the House of Bread changed me. I'll never be the same carefree, uncaring person I used to be."

Aleesha nodded thoughtfully.

"You asked why I came on this trip. I hoped I could make a permanent difference in Silver City. In fact, I convinced myself that God was going to use me in a mighty way. I was starting to get bigheaded about it, too, if that makes any sense."

"And now that God has humbled you by sending you to tiny Santa María instead. . . ?"

"I'd better start putting today's lessons about faith, obedience, and flexibility into practice."

chapter ten

Santa María turned out to be at least as far from civilization as Rob and Charlie told us and infinitely harder to reach than they had imagined.

Since only one of the three buses had onboard restroom facilities, our caravan stopped frequently after our very filling dinners of whatever was on that buffet table. Aleesha couldn't recall what we'd had, either.

We rode on the interstate for several hours before turning off onto what was still a relatively decent two-lane road, but the closer we got to Santa María, the slower our progress. After exiting onto a bumpy, unpaved road—calling it a road at all was a sick joke—we slowed to a cautious crawl. Before long, the road disappeared and the buses inched their way along a path of faded tire tracks left by unknown vehicles weeks, months, perhaps even years ago.

If the lead driver hadn't been using a GPS—a global positioning system—to supplement his photocopy of the hand-drawn map and directions, we wouldn't have gotten close enough to the village to find it. And we probably wouldn't have had much greater success turning back if we'd needed to.

His opinion, which he shared loudly, vigorously, and profanely—without regard for the ears and beliefs of the Christian gentlefolk aboard—was that the map's unknown writer and direction giver knew no one would be stupid enough to undertake such a journey if he knew how abysmal the roads were. He claimed that the map provider had purposely understated the dangers.

Ruts in the earth were numerous, although not necessarily deep. They were almost impossible to spot until we got right on top of them. The drivers, each an expert on "real" roads, must have felt like ship captains struggling to maintain control of their vessels on a stormy sea whenever they had to veer suddenly around yet another rut that popped up out of nowhere.

I quit counting the team members who got so carsick they threw the bus windows open and stuck their heads outside to keep from retching all over themselves and each other. The misery of their dehumanizing condition was so overwhelming I couldn't help feeling sorry for them.

The few of us not yet afflicted felt desperate about our situation, though. So we prayed more faithfully for our drivers than for our peers.

Two tractor trailers full of building supplies followed us, although a truck crammed floor to ceiling with food, water, bedding, and clothing had taken this same route hours earlier. Even though the ruts didn't trouble the trucks with their double tires, our ride couldn't have been bumpier or jerkier without breaking an axle. Each time we rounded a curve without turning over, we shouted, "Praise the Lord!"

Navigating the ruts didn't slow us down as much as watching for them.

When I stood up to stretch, I went up front to talk to Rob. Years of roller coaster rides at Six Flags over Georgia made walking on a wildly bumping bus seem like child's play.

"For Pete's sake, Rob," I said with equal parts of helpfulness and youthful impatience, "let me off the bus and I'll walk ahead to motion where the ruts are." Walking faster than we were riding wouldn't be a challenge.

Rob looked at me funny, and I wasn't sure he'd understood me. When he didn't respond, however, I shrugged and returned to my seat.

But a moment later, the bus stopped and Rob got out. He was gone five or six minutes. When he came back with Charlie in the lead, he looked frustrated. Charlie apparently won the toss for walking bus leader. According to the GPS, we were no more than two miles from our destination.

The first truck driver and his helpers had just finished unloading the emergency provisions when we rolled into Santa María. The villagers had already helped themselves to the supplies they needed most urgently. We'd expected and wanted them to do that.

Cardboard boxes—a few partially full, but most nearly empty—lay on the ground like gift boxes a bunch of little kids has decimated on Christmas morning. Just inside the truck's open doors, a couple of boxes stood guard over the rest.

From what that driver told us, the villagers had been thrilled to receive the necessities they'd lived without since the storm destroyed their homes. Their homes, but not the small building Rob and Charlie had nicknamed the Passover Church.

Although Rob and Charlie tried talking him out of doing something so foolish, the driver—apparently the only Latino in our group—climbed back into the cab of his truck, insisting that he must leave immediately. Morning would be too late. He'd apparently left his motor running the whole time he and his two helpers—with willing help from the villagers—unloaded the truck.

"Call me superstitious if you like,"—he said through the open window in more cultivated English than I'd expected from a Latino truck driver—"but this unharmed building among the ruins of the village makes me nervous. I am unable to explain why I feel this way, but I and my helpers must not stay here any longer. We are going back now. Do not worry about us. I have a GPS, and my truck's double tires did not fit into any of those ruts. *Vámonos, chicos!*"

While his helpers jumped into the cab, we told him we would pray for their safety. He smiled and winked. I can't explain it, but I almost sensed his relief that we had reached Santa María safely and would provide the villagers with whatever else they needed.

Could he have had something to do with Rob and Charlie finding out about Santa María's recent tragedy?

chapter eleven

Aleesha and I spent our first forty minutes in Santa María sorting through my four suitcases and putting my most essential belongings inside one. I bargained with our bus driver to take the rest of my stuff back to San Diego for safekeeping. I didn't want to have it around, reminding me how I'd acted at orientation.

Since my little karaoke unit was battery powered, I kept it with me. Proud of myself for remembering the batteries, I thought somebody could probably use it. Nobody in this crowd of unforgivers would want to hear me sing, though.

But thoughtlessness was still my middle name. I forgot to keep the accompaniment disks.

Setting up a tentless camp in a field of trash—we assumed the twister left it—was tougher than we'd expected, especially with darkness closing in. The other girls didn't waste any time staking their claims to a few square yards of dry, grassless ground each. They used the last of today's energy to push litter out of the way so they could spread their sleeping bags out flat. Many of the girls were already asleep by the time Aleesha and I got there.

Although they'd chosen the prime spots, we couldn't blame them. They'd gotten there first, and we weren't fussy. Two slots near the deserted, far edge of the field were as fine as any.

A small jungle of basketball player-height cacti surrounded the field on three sides, with the bottom of the *U* facing the Passover Church. The abundance of cacti shocked me because the area didn't seem arid enough to call desert. Then again, a man in my town had replaced the dirt in his yard with rocks and sand and grown nothing but cacti, so I probably shouldn't have been surprised.

Despite the variety of other vegetation, however, I couldn't see a single tree or bush anywhere.

Although I would have considered cactus too juicy to burn, Rob and Charlie somehow fueled a long-lasting bonfire with the cacti they chopped down to make an entrance to the girls' field. It would be the nightlight in the "facilities" at the open end of the field.

Once he got the fire going, Rob gathered the girls together. He apologized for waking some of them up. "I'm almost old enough to be your grandfather, so don't ask me to explain what I mean when I say 'Use this shovel to keep your facilities clean and sanitary' unless you really want me to tell you. But I'll give you a hint. This is your litter box, and nobody's going to clean it unless you do."

Even in the moonlight, I could see the glow of blushing faces.

But when he added, "Just throw your monthly flammables in the fire," Aleesha and I almost rolled on the ground. Rob was funny as well as practical.

I might learn to like him a lot.

chapter twelve

A leesha, take a look. What's wrong with this picture?"
        I pointed first to her luxurious Tweety Bird sleeping bag, unzipped moments ago for the first time, releasing a beautiful smell that reminded me of a new-car interior. Her full-sized inflatable pillow lay on top of it.

Then I pointed to my unadorned section of dirt, painted in the dullest of authentic earth tones and overrun with a variety of little creepy-crawlers.

"Good thing your clothes are already filthy, huh, girl? If you plan to sleep on the ground right there, maybe you shouldn't bother putting on clean nighties. And I'd plan on using plenty of bug spray before you go to bed."

Then she gave a thumbs-up, as if her advice would make up for my lack of bedding.

I couldn't tell if she was trying to be funny.

We'd already done plenty of laughing, and the joy of our friendship had more than made up for having to brush my teeth in the dark; rinse my mouth with bottled water only to have trouble finding somewhere to spit it out without spraying someone; and wipe my foamy mouth on my sweatshirt sleeve like I did when I was little.

Aleesha's support today almost kept me from griping about having to go beyond the perimeter of the field carrying the shovel to "do my business." She warned me in no uncertain terms that if I wandered too far in the wrong direction, I might end up entangled in a sea of seven-foot cacti where no one would find me until morning, quivering painfully with a quiver's worth of needles stuck indelicately in my tender posterior.

Being so slight of build has its disadvantages. I lacked the protective padding Aleesha had and wore so well. Those cactus needles would have struck several vital organs without taking time to introduce themselves to my skin on the way through.

Although Rob—father and grandfather that he was—had supposedly "seen it all," I'd rely on Aleesha for medical attention on that part of my body. And how we would laugh about me getting into one more avoidable predicament.

But should I laugh now or not?

Once again, Aleesha read my mind—or my face, anyhow. "Girl, I'm just having fun with you. I'm afraid Tweety Bird wouldn't approve of us sleeping together."

"I'm glad to hear that. I wouldn't, either."

"But you don't really plan to sleep on the bare ground, do you?" She must not have caught on yet that I didn't have a choice.

"I'd rather sleep standing up." I didn't mean to sound so serious. I was just tired.

"White girls can do that?"

Aware that she was teasing me as much as I was teasing her, I gave her a "black girls can't?" look that was pretty convincing if I do say so myself. "Only when we're tired of sitting down all day. But it helps if we have something to lean against. We're not cows, sheep, or horses, you know."

I couldn't keep from giggling then, and we laughed together. Several of our nearest neighbors peeked at us from their sleeping bags with an exhausted, "can't you shut up and let us sleep in peace?" look in their half-closed eyes. But we were too tired to shut up, and they must have been too tired to verbalize their complaints.

"Girl, we gotta find you something to sleep on before you start sleepwalking and trip over somebody important—like me."

I shrugged, clueless. For warmth, we could move closer to the fire, but the temperature wasn't a problem. Softening the ground and making it clean enough to lie on? That was something else.

"Hey!" she said. "That first truck brought bedding for the villagers, right? Maybe they didn't take it all yet. We might find something lying around on the ground where they unloaded."

I had serious doubts about the villagers leaving anything usable lying around. Those folks wouldn't be fussy. After all, they were starting housekeeping from scratch—without houses at that.

"Come on." Aleesha grabbed my elbow with one hand and a small flashlight with the other.

If flashlights aren't at the top of the list I've never seen, they should be.

We picked our way carefully among sleeping bodies that sprawled out this way and that. When the girls cleared trash to lay out their sleeping bags, they filled the gaps between them like masons slathering concrete between bricks in a wall. Stepping on the girls would have been safer for us, although not for the girls.

We must have spent ten or fifteen minutes reaching the cactus-less door to the field. I wouldn't have wanted to make that trip without a flashlight.

We clasped one another's hands—black fingers intertwining with white, white with black—and giggled all the way to the tractor trailers.

"When two friends hold hands while walking together," Aleesha reworded the familiar scripture verse, sing-songing it in a little kid voice, "if one falls down and goes boom, they go boom together, and they can't help one another up again because they'll both be laughing too hard."

We spent twenty minutes checking the boxes on the ground. Nothing.

The two eighteen-wheelers that had come with us contained building supplies. Only one of them was open, but we decided to check it anyhow. The floor of the trailer looked fifteen feet high. As short as I am, climbing up would be a literal exercise in futility. But Aleesha managed it easily, and she reached down and pulled me up.

Yep, just construction materials. If worse came to worse, I could borrow a sheet of plywood to sleep on. I wouldn't have to lie directly on the ground then. But as difficult as navigating among the sleeping girls had been, I could just see the two of us carrying a heavy sheet of plywood without bashing one or more girls in the head.

Would I have to sleep in the truck? And be that far from the facilities? No way!

Then Aleesha flashed her light on a small box near the door. There we found it—one lone blanket nearly hidden in the shadows. Somebody had apparently tossed it there—a reject. What better choice for someone like me who felt like a total reject in her teammates' eyes?

Will things be any better at the end of two weeks?

"You seem down now," Aleesha said after we lowered ourselves to the ground. The blanket draped over my shoulders like a flag on the casket at a military funeral. "We'll pray."

She didn't ask if I wanted to. She took for granted that prayer was the only cure for my mood. I was going to learn a lot from this girl.

So we cleared enough litter to kneel in the dirt and started talking to God. Although I don't recall our prayer time completely, I remember begging God for peace and contentment. And thanking Him for His forgiveness.

I felt like He and I were looking at each other—eyeball to eyeball—and I imagined Him saying, *People despised and rejected My Son, too. Let Him help you with your rejection.*

We prayed for the other team members the way Jesus prayed for His enemies. "Father, forgive them, for they don't know what they're doing." But at least my enemies weren't putting me to death. Not yet, anyhow.

Amen.

Once we got back to our sleepsite, Aleesha couldn't stay awake long enough to help me unfold my blanket. I was just glad she spotted it. Watching that dark lump cuddled in a nearby Tweety-covered sleeping bag with her face turned heavenward and her mouth curled into a smile couldn't have been more reassuring.

chapter thirteen

With Aleesha asleep, I was stuck with my own company. Exhaustion tended to make me irrational and pessimistic, but I'd never experienced those problems so profoundly.

My depression came back big-time. It was like Aleesha and I hadn't prayed at all.

While flapping my borrowed blanket to unfold it, I responded to each loud report of the material with an unspoken curse. The wool felt rough and stiff after years of confinement in some long-forgotten closet or drawer—that's how I pictured it, anyhow—and the mothball stench was a noxious gas contaminating air that had been pure a moment earlier.

Why hadn't the donor used a sweet-smelling cedar chest instead?

When I was about to conclude she'd sewed the blanket shut as a cruel joke, it billowed to its fullest, and I spread it out on the ground. While waiting to see if the mothball vapors would make me barf or pass out, I wondered if I dared to sleep on it.

Although the stink would eventually dissipate in the open air, I didn't expect it to happen tonight. What could possibly make my life more unbearable on the first day of a "life-changing" mission trip? Pastor Ron hadn't warned me that "life-changing" might mean "life-giving."

Kim Hartlinger, what are you doing in Mexico? What really? Will this trip be the second ministry of your summer to go sour?

I felt sorry for myself, and I detested that, but I couldn't turn off the negative feelings. Where was that sense of peace God had given me half an hour earlier?

I dropped to my knees on top of the blanket—not to pray this time, but to lie back and try to unwind.

I landed faster and harder than I'd meant to. My right knee buckled under me, and I did a shoulder roll onto my back, jarring my head so hard on a rock hidden beneath the blanket that I thought my upper and lower teeth had jammed together permanently.

I bolted upright so fast my equilibrium went haywire. I covered my mouth with both hands to keep from saying several of my choicest swear words more than once.

Antagonizing the other girls more than I already had, especially in the middle of the night after such a long, exhausting day, wouldn't win me any points. As much at fault as I'd been, I needed to act civil—no matter what they thought of me.

Or I of them.

These eighteen-year-olds weren't like the kids back home. I'd been naive enough to expect them to be similar—despite our denominational differences. Well, so much for love and forgiveness within the Christian family.

Christian unity? What's that, Rob and Charlie?

As I sat on the blanket nursing my injuries, I breathed a quick prayer of thanks that my un-Christlike language apparently hadn't awakened anyone, and then I added three postscripts of sincerest apology, one each to God the Father, Jesus Christ the Son, and the Holy Spirit.

Although I detested my susceptibility to swearing, I was thankful God forgave that sin more easily than Mom and Dad. . . .

"Kim, what kind of example do you think you set for others—especially younger kids—when you talk like that? Do

you want them to grow up thinking that's the proper way for a Christian to speak? Yes, they're just words, but are they the right words for a Christian to use? Jesus' call to follow Him is an invitation to be your best. You never know whom you may offend or give the wrong impression to. You might even drive somebody away from Jesus with inappropriate word choices."

I wished they'd reword that sermon. I'd heard it often enough I could say it along with them.

Oh, they were right about swearing being inappropriate, of course, although I thought anyone it might deter was in worse shape than I was. But I never argued with Mom and Dad. Not about swearing, anyhow. Why should I? Even I could see that it didn't have any positive aspects.

But hearing filthy language off and on all day every day of my senior year hadn't helped. I didn't have the courage to complain to my schoolmates about the way they talked. So I let their words sink deep into my subconscious, take root there, and sprout as noxious weeds in an otherwise well-cultivated verbal garden.

Usually at the most inopportune times. Like at DFW this afternoon and just now when I bashed my head on the rock.

Worst of all, though, I wasn't always conscious of cursing. Sometimes I didn't remember doing it. At least I never took God's name in vain. I was sure of that. But I was scared I might do it yet and have lightning strike me some sunny day—like an unseen hand zapping an annoying, unsuspecting mosquito.

Figuratively, if not literally.

I needed to kick this swearing habit, and I needed to do it yesterday. I'd made a fresh start at orientation. I was proud of holding my tongue when I didn't feel like it. But. . .I'd just blown it again.

Only thirteen precious days remained for giving up

cursing. Could I do better tomorrow? I'd have to. After all, tomorrow would be another day. For both me and Scarlett O'Hara.

I reached under the blanket to examine the rock I'd hit my head on and snickered without amusement at finding myself between a rock and a hard place in more ways than one. My confidence about how much I'd accomplish on this trip had evaporated with the change of projects. Why didn't I feel more enthusiastic about Santa María when I felt so sure God wanted me here?

Why had He brought me this far and let roadblocks and detours keep popping up? The worst one was my own self-doubt. If I couldn't live up to my own expectations, how could I ever hope to live up to God's?

If God had wanted to close the door on this trip, why didn't He do it before I left home? At least I'd be lying comfortably in my own bed without a budding headache rather than tossing and turning on a stinky old blanket in a dirt field in the wilds of Mexico among a bunch of snobby Christian girls.

Not that the boys were much better. But at least they were out of sight in their own field.

Touching the back of my head as delicately as if it were made of butterfly wings, I winced in pain. But at least I couldn't find any traces of blood—wet or dried—on my scalp or in my hair.

I'd inherited some outstanding physical traits from my Vietnamese mother. Not just the glossiest head of black hair a girl could hope for, but also dark brown eyes and slightly darker-than-normal Caucasian skin that resembled a permanent low-grade tan. Each summer, I worked hard at improving on it. Since my face didn't have any Asian features, nobody knew about my mixed background unless I told them.

Because I had so much of my dad in me, I looked like an

all-American hybrid. At least I didn't get his boring, pale blue eyes. How often I wished I'd inherited a few inches of his height, though.

An all-American hybrid?

Yes, but I also looked vaguely like the natives of Santa María, who weren't nearly as dark as some of the Latinos I'd seen. The exterior similarities didn't do much to make my interior feel the least at home in my new surroundings, though.

After pushing some trash out of the way and running my hands over the adjacent ground to find a spot free from rocks, I realigned my blanket and knelt again. After a slower, more careful descent, I made a pillow-soft landing any airline pilot would have been proud of and stretched out full-length.

I nestled my head in the crook of my left arm and closed my eyes. Unused to going to bed early, I was more exhausted than sleepy. Experience had taught me that sleep was the best way to drive away negative feelings; but the harder I tried to relax, the more I woke up.

What I wouldn't have given to hear a sweet, soothing lullaby, but I was too many years and too many miles from anyone who might sing one to me. I wouldn't dare call Betsy Jo on my cell phone at this time of night and wake her for something like that.

Aleesha could have done it, but I didn't want to wake her up, either. We'd gotten off to too good a start.

I scratched my nose with fingernails that would be the uttermost of ugly nubs by this time tomorrow and sighed.

Thy will be done.

As I prepared for the sleep that had to come eventually, I rolled up in my borrowed blanket. Aware that I resembled a size-two caterpillar in a size-twelve cocoon, I imagined God and His night-duty angels chuckling at me, and I managed a slight smile. But restoring my normal sense of humor—not to mention my feeling of purpose and well-being—would take more than that.

chapter fourteen

Day 2

K im?" The female voice spoke in a mechanical tone. "Miss
Kim Hartlinger? It's dawn, and this is your wake-up call."

The female voice sounded vaguely familiar; but since I was
still 99 percent asleep, I ignored it and hoped it would quit
bothering me.

"Wake up, Kim." The voice changed to such an overly
sweet tone that I thought I was lying in my bed at home.

But my bed wasn't hard and lumpy.

"Time to rise and shine, Kim."

"Mom, I'm up." My grumble was barely audible. I thumped
a multi-legged critter off my nose where he was having way
too much fun bodysurfing on the residue of last night's insect
repellent.

After turning onto my stomach, I buried my face in my
arms to keep out the light. I wasn't alert enough to wonder
where the bug had come from or why I was lying in a field
of light.

"This isn't your mother, little one."

No, the voice definitely wasn't Mom's.

I looked into Aleesha's alert, wide-awake eyes. Her face—
mostly her smile—glowed in the early morning light.

"Do all black people wake up so alert?" I said with a whiny
moan.

"You told me you weren't prejudiced, Kim. Was that a little
white lie?"

I yawned, but not in response to the question. "No, not
even a little Caucasian or half-Asian half-truth."

We laughed together then. I'd already concluded that Aleesha was loving, lovable, and slow to take offense at anything people didn't mean offensively. She never stopped demonstrating what an original she was. Some people might have called her a show-off, as if all of us aren't original and don't show off sometimes, but Mom would have described her as a "character."

Aleesha was her own person for sure.

She attributed my occasional racial misconceptions to ignorance. The ignorance of living a segregated life in an integrated world—that's how she described it—and she was right.

I couldn't help the fact I didn't know more than a handful of African Americans by name. As the kids of university professors, they probably never drove through ghettos or modeled any of the popular racial stereotypes.

Aleesha hadn't answered my original question, though, so I tried again. "So, are you saying every African American in the world jumps out of bed fresh-eyed at dawn? Aren't any of them sleepyheads like me?"

Lord, didn't You make some of them need caffeine to wake up, too?

"I hear you thinking, girl. . . ."

"You can't do that," I said as if she'd caught me making an innocent slur. "Nobody can. Nobody but God, anyhow."

"Well, if not, how come I know what silliness you're thinking?"

"Silliness, Aleesha?" I said, trying to channel my thoughts to something so innocent my mind wouldn't be worth reading.

"What you were just thinking about. . ." she said, ending with a dramatic pause. "What you were thinking about was both silly and irrelevant, and I'd be embarrassed to say it aloud if I were you."

"Oh." What else could I say?

And what else should I have expected from a personable, extroverted theater and drama major? If Aleesha had lived in Elizabethan England, she would've managed to become the first woman to play a female role at the Globe Theatre. Now she'd undoubtedly insist on playing the Bard of Avon himself if *Shakespeare in Love* was ever remade.

I remembered that she hadn't answered my question, but she'd dodged it so long I forgot what it was. So I tried something else. "So what's this business about getting up now?" I glanced at my wristwatch. I'd carefully reset it to San Diego time before landing, unaware that I'd end up in a village time had apparently ignored and forgotten about.

"Come on, girl," she said. "Daylight has been on its way for half an hour now. We'll see the sun soon." She started humming, whistling, and thumping a rap version of the Beatles' "Here Comes the Sun." She was good, but why did that surprise me?

"My watch says 5:45 a.m.," I protested. "I have plenty of time left to sleep. The sun may be on its way, but I'll wait for a formal appearance before making my own, thank you very much."

"Kim, Kim, Kim, Kim," Aleesha said, as she wagged her head from side to side in mock disapproval.

"Aleesha, Aleesha, Alees–" Although my disfluency often involved repeating words unnecessarily, I got so tongue-tied trying to say Aleesha's name four times in a row that I gave up rather than start stuttering.

Several years earlier, a casual acquaintance with a speech impediment asked if I had one, too. I'd never thought about it before, although I knew Mom and Dad would have done something about it if they thought so.

Nonetheless, a question like that coming from someone

a horrible speech impediment had turned into an expert—someone I didn't even like that much—made me so self-conscious I had worse problems from that day forward. Especially addressing groups of one or more whenever I thought somebody was actually listening. Although I seldom had problems in relaxed conversations among good friends, I could stumble over or start repeating words anytime I started thinking too hard about what I was saying.

The power of suggestion had proven more dangerous than the actual disfluency.

Maybe that's why my oral French skills were inferior to my written ones. And why I was only class salutatorian instead of valedictorian. My teacher had to give me a B once for the way I messed up oral French.

I knew and comprehended the rules perfectly. The French in my head was flawless, and my teacher seemed to understand that; but she had to grade me on how it came out.

Some people thought I'd begun speaking disfluently just to get attention, especially since I'd never had the problem to such a, uh, pronounced degree before. Most of my friends thought it was cute, although some of my teachers thought I was showing off. The boys loved it, although they quickly learned I never had a problem saying no and proving I meant it.

I hated having a problem like that inside my head. One way or the other, that is. But the harder I tried to speak fluently, the worse things got. Stressing out over the inability to relax is tough. . . .

"I guess you didn't hear that part of orientation yesterday, huh, Kim?"

I'd wondered if I was missing anything important when my mind started wandering during orientation, but I was too exhausted to care.

"After the shock about the project changes, I'm not sure I

listened to that much of orientation." At least I could be honest with Aleesha about it.

"Kim, Kim, Kim," Aleesha said gently and sympathetically.

I didn't try saying "Aleesha, Aleesha, Aleesha" back. Aleesha was a nice enough name, but I was 100 percent sure it wouldn't roll off my tongue easily even once.

"So, what did I miss hearing?" I yawned involuntarily and lay back to unroll from my blanket. The mothball smell hadn't weakened since last night.

While waiting for Aleesha's response, I instinctively grabbed my cell phone from my purse and powered it on to check for voice mail and text messages. *Surely I'd have something from Betsy Jo by now.*

But Santa María was even further in the boonies than they'd told us. My phone couldn't find a signal. We weren't even in a roaming area.

I tossed it offhandedly on my blanket. It bounced off and hit a nearby rock. The battery cover popped off, and the battery flew out. I enjoyed a good belly laugh about that, and Aleesha looked at me like I was crazy to think breaking my cell phone was funny.

Actually, I was laughing with relief that my head hadn't popped open the same way when it hit that same rock last night. It had to be the same one. It was the only one in sight.

Aleesha smiled at me as if pretending I was normal, and her acceptance made me feel like I was watching the sunrise. . . .

I couldn't say whether guys considered Aleesha pretty, but I wouldn't have wanted to compete with her. Although she was a few sizes larger than me, she was also taller by inches. A number of them. Better proportioned than me, she even had a definable waist. I was too old to keep beating up everyone who called me "snake hips."

Although her workwear wasn't Gucci, American Eagle, Aéropostale, or Hollister ("At least I had enough sense to leave all my fancy clothes at home," she'd ragged me unmercifully), she wore her clothes well.

If Millie Q.'s teeth had looked more like Aleesha's—she'd never worn braces—I wouldn't have noticed them. Aleesha had a radiant, unblemished complexion my friends would have killed for and wore modest, understated makeup. And I would have killed for her tan. . . .

"You missed the part of orientation about aligning our work hours with local daylight hours. We'll get up at dawn and prepare for the day ahead. Although we'll dress, eat breakfast, and get organized, we won't start work until there's enough daylight to prevent accidents. Without power for lights, we won't be able to work or play after sunset.

"Even with flashlights and those cactus-fueled bonfires, walking around in the dark would be dangerous. The litter the storm brought is mostly single layered in our fields—"

"Except between the sleeping bags," I pointed out.

Aleesha nodded. "But even a single layer can hide dangers we'd easily see in daylight. So we'll go to bed with the chickens. You know what Ben Franklin said; Rob and Charlie insisted on quoting him. . . ."

"Oh, yes!" I said, hissing my s with sibilant disgust. "I hear that every morning at home. But at least I haven't heard it since yesterday." I laughed at myself, and Aleesha had the good taste not to.

Together we quoted Rob, Charlie, and my parents in a silly, singsong voice that reminded me of the mice in *Babe*: " 'Early to bed and early to rise makes a man healthy, wealthy, and wise.' "

Aleesha repeated those words but put them to a hip-hop rhythm. I enjoyed her twist on something so boringly familiar, and we did it as a duet several times. Aleesha was one clever gal. For me to appreciate hip-hop—especially this early in the morning—she had to be good.

And she obviously had good sense. She'd picked me as a friend.

"So I really need to get up, huh, Aleesha?"

"Yes, ma'am, that you do, Miss Kim."

"Well, Miss Aleesha, at least I seem to be dressed already. Yesterday's travelwear is the closest I've got to construction clothes. Refreshing my deodorant might help, though."

I hadn't expected to laugh at myself so easily today, especially since I'd never slept in dirty clothes before, much less worn them a second day. . . .

I changed clothes three or four times a day at home. That's one reason I had so many of them.

That's also why Mom made me do my own laundry. *See, Mom, I'm learning responsibility!* I threw some of her laundry in with mine from time to time, too, and the only things I ruined were her favorite white skirt and top. How was I supposed to remember not to wash whites with new, never-before-washed vividly colored brights that might run?

As daylight brightened, I noticed a hole in the pants leg where my knee had lost the battle with the rocky ground last night. If I had to ruin my favorite clothes, I'd do it one outfit at a time. Leaving any apparel here might not be a sacrifice. I probably wouldn't want to put such filthy clothing back in my suitcase. They'd leave it smelling worse than mothballs.

How much less important that seemed now than last night, though. Yesterday's stress and fatigue hadn't helped my clarity of vision.

Neither had the shock.

"I'm starving," Aleesha said. "I wonder what's for breakfast."

"I can smell the coffee from here. . . ." I licked my lips. I hoped they'd brought the kind of sugar substitute I liked; I detested the other popular kind.

"It's a mirage, Kim. There's no electricity here. No running water. Remember? Ergo and therefore, no coffee. Not hot coffee, anyhow."

"Oh."

I felt dumb for forgetting about our uncivilized circumstances. But how would we have a nice hot breakfast without electricity? After all, breakfast is the most important meal of the day.

Maybe Rob and Charlie had brought gas grills. *Yes, that must be it.* I sniffed the air for the scent of food cooking, but the breeze must have carried the aroma in a different direction.

"You're not imagining things, Kim. You're smelling some super-strong, coffee-flavored candy I brought to make up for not having the real thing. It contains mega-amounts of caffeine. You want a piece? Under these circumstances, you must pretend to enjoy the amenities you're pretending to have."

"Sounds great, although I'm not sure I'd consider coffee just an amenity. I'm glad to know I'm not going crazy, though."

"Girl, that doesn't mean you're not going crazy. It just means you're not going crazy about smelling coffee."

I started laughing so hard I couldn't respond at first.

"Can you drop a piece of that candy in my cup, please, and do you have a spoon I can stir it with? It'll help me pretend better. Then let's see what they're going to feed us."

chapter fifteen

Some of the most gorgeous yellow flowers adorned the cacti in the area. I couldn't imagine ever losing my fascination with them.

While strolling over to the mess tent, Aleesha explained that it wasn't a tent at all, nor was it any more covered than the field we slept in. It was the site—the rough equivalent of a dirt foundation—where the largest of Santa María's buildings had stood before the storm. I never found out what the lost building had been, although I wondered about it enough.

My experience on local, church mission trips had taught me that teens and young adults can be quite imaginative—even sarcastic—in perceiving and labeling their surroundings. "Mess tent" in this setting was just one example. Another was referring to the well-worn dirt path that separated the mess tent from the rubbish-covered, so-called Passover Church yard as "Broad Street."

Rob and Charlie had set up several large tables at the north end of the mess area. I may have made a few wrong turns going to church when I was a new driver, but I knew the sun still rose in the east even in the wilds of western Mexico, and it was barely visible to our right.

On closer examination, I discovered the tables were plywood sheets propped up on sawhorses. I considered asking to sleep on one. At least it would be free of rocks and pesky pebbles.

Pebbles?

When I moved my blanket away from that rock last

night, I didn't realize I was placing it on hundreds—probably thousands—of tiny pebbles. They left such an. . .impression on me that I dreaded having to sleep on them again tonight. If the nursery tale princess had that much trouble enduring a single pea, my sleeping arrangements would have driven her bonkers.

But then I thought about Jesus' whipping prior to dragging His cross to Skull Hill. If I remembered correctly, stone, metal, bone, and glass comprised the working end of that whip.

My pebbles had been uncomfortable, but not excruciating. And they hadn't torn my body to shreds and left me bleeding and unbearable to look at. I uttered a deep prayer of thanks for the torture Jesus endured on my behalf and decided to ignore the pebbles.

Every square inch of those makeshift tables in the mess tent contained food—all of it packaged or canned. Nothing was fresh. Or hot.

I wasn't sure what I'd expected, but this wasn't it. The first bag I looked at turned me off so much I opened my mouth to voice a complaint. But Aleesha already knew me too well.

"Flexibility, Kim."

"Oh."

Flexibility? Sure, I can eat whatever's here as long as it's not pizza. No tables or chairs for our dining pleasure, either? Sure, I can stand or sit on the ground to eat.

"Is this mess tent big enough to hold most of us?" Aleesha said.

"Maybe. But I don't think we'd have room to hold our food."

Aleesha couldn't argue about that, so—starting with our first breakfast—we took our food "outside," pushed a bit of rubbish out of the way with our feet, and sat down on the dry earth.

"Eating on the hard ground will be less objectionable than

sleeping on it," she assured me. I must've complained about my sleeping conditions more than I realized.

I'd eaten my fill of school cafeteria "mystery meat," but some of the stuff Rob and Charlie set out for breakfast looked more deadly than anything I ever faced in school. If God had slaughtered the Devil, boiled him in the lake of fire, and then cut him into strips, the results might have looked half this bad.

"You're sure this is food?" I said. "It looks like something that's turned to leather. After all, without electricity and refrigeration, we can't have perishable foods. Is this some kind of all-veggie 'meat' that a sadistic, vegetarian food manufacturer has squeezed every last drop of flavor out of and packaged in plastic wrap that looks tastier than the food itself?"

I was proud of my exaggerated description.

"My dear Kim," Aleesha said. If she sounded like she was addressing some dumb little kid, at least she'd done it patiently. "You may not have noticed this, but most of the food on the table is in cans. Does your mom keep cans in the refrigerator?" Before I could respond, she added, "Mine doesn't."

Duh.

"And that leathery meat you spoke so disparagingly about?" she whispered in my ear when she saw me hesitate and shudder at the sight of it. "It's beef jerky, and it's great. No refrigeration needed for that, either. They preserve it in lots and lots of nice unhealthy salt—just like country ham."

I shook my head. If I'd ever eaten country ham, I couldn't remember it. That must have been one of those things Dad didn't like.

"You know," she said, "like Smithfield ham."

"Oh." I didn't want to admit I'd never had that, either.

"Beef jerky is wonderful, but you're right about the leathery look. It'll give your teeth a healthy workout, for it's verrrrry chewy. I feel sorry for anyone here who's braces-impaired."

Although Aleesha laughed heartily, she seemed serious about people with braces staying away from beef jerky.

Then I discovered I wouldn't have to eat it myself, and neither would anyone else.

Aleesha had referred to the cans on the table, but I hadn't paid attention to the variety of individual-serving, easy-open cans of various fruits, vegetables, and processed meats Rob and Charlie had brought along.

Easy-open cans that toddlers could get into blindfolded with one hand tied behind their backs and adults couldn't fight their way into under any circumstances. Not with a hammer, a chisel, and a hacksaw.

Although eating something familiar like potted meat or pork 'n' beans might have been safer, I couldn't ignore Aleesha's salty recommendation of the jerky.

Besides, the other team members probably thought of me as "Miss Prep" now, and I needed to demonstrate my humanity—not to mention my flexibility—during the next thirteen days and show them that "Miss Prep" and "Miss Priss" are not the same.

The villagers ate with us that morning; we probably outnumbered them four to one. Arriving at dusk, we'd barely seen them last night, but I wondered if they would feel self-conscious knowing that so many American teens had given up beach time to rebuild their homes.

I hoped not. Everyone needs help sometime. I was glad we'd been available.

I wondered how much they knew about us. Probably a lot. Although generally shy, they acted friendly and grateful. That's how I read their body language, anyhow.

Regardless of my rude introduction to Santa María last night, I didn't feel the least out of place today. My new world looked much better in daylight.

But I hadn't heard one villager speak a word of English, and everyone in the civilized world spoke at least a few words of English. It was the universal language, right? Or was Santa María really that uncivilized? So uncivilized that none of its residents knew any English?

Surely not.

I thanked God for our translators, even though I hadn't figured out who they were. Maybe some of the kids. I'd thought it strange that Rob and Charlie didn't introduce them at orientation.

I could get used to this beef jerky stuff, even though I probably looked like a dog that had gotten hold of bubble gum.

But it was either just as tasty as Aleesha said or I was too famished to object to the taste and texture. I probably would have reacted just as favorably to three-day-old roadkill.

Charlie approached us while we were still sitting on the ground. He crouched and faced me. "Excuse me, but may I speak to you?"

He straightened up and I followed him several yards to an out-of-the-way spot. I didn't think much about his interruption at first, but when he didn't suggest sitting down, I almost panicked. Had Rob permitted Charlie the pleasure of raking me over the coals about yesterday?

"Kim,"—he didn't sound angry, though—"did I hear correctly that. . . ?"

I smiled when he finished. I'd made one good—perhaps I should say one sound—decision last night, anyhow.

chapter sixteen

Aleesha pulled me closer in so we could hear better. She hadn't needed to, though. That karaoke system of mine made a great PA system for use with a group this size.

"Guys and girls, girls and guys," Charlie started, "good morning to you all. I trust everyone slept beautifully under God's heavenly blanket of stars."

Almost everyone nodded or grunted their affirmation. Before I could open my mouth, though, Aleesha stuck her forefinger in front of my lips and said in a low voice, "Shush, Kim! Don't you dare complain about hitting your head on that rock or about those pebbles."

"I was only going to take another bite of food."

She gave me a strange look. Then I realized I'd already cleaned my plate and Aleesha knew it. That girl was too observant sometimes.

She was right, though. If I hoped to make up with this crowd for yesterday's mishaps, I shouldn't start today on such a negative note. I needed to renew my resolve to quit whining.

"All right, already! I'll be good. I'll keep quiet."

Aleesha smiled and patted me on the head, mouthing, "Good girl!" the way a dog owner might praise a stubborn puppy that's finally achieved housebrokenness after nine months of messes on the oriental rug.

"We're going to have a great day in the Lord today," Charlie said. "It's His work we're here to do, and we want to create a favorable and lasting impression on our new friends."

I looked around at the villagers' blank faces and realized

that none of them had a clue what he was saying. *Where are our translators, Charlie?* Every once in a while I saw their eyes brighten, maybe at hearing an English word that was similar to the Spanish, but those times were infrequent.

"Some of you may have noticed that the villagers don't speak any English," Rob said, his face scalding in a sea of red. "Are. . ." I couldn't imagine why he looked so scared of continuing. "Are any of you fluent in Spanish?"

Rob, don't tell me we don't have translators.

One hundred forty-four young adults looked at one another before shaking their collective heads no.

"I took Spanish for a couple of years, but I barely passed it," one girl said.

"Same here," a boy responded from the opposite side.

"I used to translate written Spanish fairly well, but I'm out of practice now. It's been two years since I last tried, and I never was good at English to Spanish. And to translate spoken Spanish? Forget it."

"That's my problem, too," a voice spoke from the middle of the group. "Native Spanish speakers go far too fast for me to follow, and it sounds a lot different here than in high school."

If that observation had been a locomotive, almost-audible nods of affirmation would have overloaded the cars that followed it.

"Yeah!" somebody yelled with a laugh. "Here it sounds like a foreign language and not a school subject."

A caboose reverberated with laughter and one single loud, "Amen."

"What about it, brothers and sisters?" Rob said. "Isn't anyone here better at Spanish than these poor honest souls who've admitted that only a miracle. . ."—he stopped to gasp for air—"that only a miracle could transform them into translators at any time in the near future, much less today?"

When he started gasping again, I squelched an inadvertent laugh just enough that it sounded like a loud burp. Rob's unexpected diplomacy tickled me, but better to belch than sound disrespectful.

Although everyone looked around for the source—I pretended to do that, too—no one bothered looking at me. They probably didn't think Miss Prep could be that crude.

"Are any of you Pentecostals who can speak in tongues or interpret tongues?"

I couldn't tell if he was serious or not. If the strange looks I saw on dozens of faces were any indication, neither could anyone else.

Rob searched the crowd for a more positive response. He hadn't looked this frustrated when he mentioned my lateness at orientation.

Then I made the mistake of yawning without covering my mouth.

"What's that, Kimberly, uh, Kim? Speak up."

"Me? Oh, I'm sorry. I was just yawning. I'm not bored, though—just sleepy."

Although the laughter lasted forever and I felt my face burning slightly, I didn't feel nearly as embarrassed as I had at orientation. So I decided to say something positive while I had the floor.

"I took four years of high school French, though—mostly As and one B. I don't suppose any of the villagers knows French, huh? *Parlez-vous français?*"

I addressed my question to a group of villagers standing in the back. They smiled at me as naively as if I'd said, "You're standing on a bomb, and it's about to explode."

My French would be useless in Santa María.

"Thanks anyhow, Kim," Charlie said. "At least you're

willing to use your talents. Not your fault they're the wrong ones. If anyone decides he or she can help even a tiny bit with basic translating, please see Rob or me later."

"I've got a question for you," someone yelled from the middle of the mess tent. The voice sounded like the caboose "Amen!" from several minutes before.

Rob looked around the general area the voice had come from, trying to pinpoint the questioner. "Sure," he said after giving up. "Go ahead."

The questioner gave an offhanded wave so Rob and Charlie could see who was talking to them. "Why do you need any of us to be fluent in Spanish? Good thing that wasn't a project requirement or none of us would be here."

"I wouldn't, either," Rob said as he examined his shoes for a few seconds.

Charlie responded to the questioner without hesitating. "You're right. I'm going to sound like I'm making excuses. For myself—for both of us."

Rob nodded. Then he closed his eyes. I wondered if he was praying for Charlie or hiding from the truth.

The questioner shifted his weight and folded his arms. He reminded me of a bull getting ready to charge. I may not have been an expert on body language, but I knew a take-no-prisoners attitude when I saw one.

After what seemed like an eternal pause, Charlie continued. "You know how quickly this project turned around. Even Kim understands that now."

Although I didn't think he was trying to be funny in the midst of a potential mutiny, I couldn't help laughing—first at myself and then at the amazed faces of everyone who didn't believe I could laugh at myself. I'd show them yet how different I was from the girl they'd come to hate yesterday.

"We didn't realize the original translators were members

of the church at Ciudad de Plata. So when Rob and I became last-minute team leaders, I wrongly assumed—"

"*We* wrongly assumed. . ." Rob said.

I admired Rob's insistence on sharing the heat.

"We wrongly assumed that the change of venue. . ." Charlie made the mistake of pausing to breathe.

"What's on the venue for lunch, Charlie?" a naive-sounding female voice said.

Charlie couldn't continue for the laughter—his own and everyone else's. Even the take-no-prisoners questioner was laughing. Laughter might help bond this group, but that wouldn't be enough by itself.

These Christian young adults had no respect for age or rank. They wouldn't have exempted Jesus from their teasing. He wouldn't have had any problem dealing with it, though. He probably put up with worse from His disciples every day.

But I wasn't too shy to pull a punch of my own.

"Gee! Can't somebody please translate from English into English for that little girl over there?"

Overwhelming waves of laughter surged toward the shore, but this time I wasn't the tsunami's target. I was riding the wave, and it felt great.

"Thanks, Kim!" somebody shouted.

"With your permission, I'll finish explaining," Charlie began again before anyone could chase that rabbit any further. "So we figured changing our project destination—"

"Is that simple enough for you to understand?" someone yelled to the venue heckler.

"In spite of changing projects and locations," Charlie said, "we thought we'd still have our original translators. We expected them to show up at orientation when they didn't meet us at the airport.

"During the orientation meal, Rob called the emergency

number for the mission organization we're working with. They admitted they should have let Rob know we'd need to find translators, but nobody thought of it."

"We still didn't know what a pickle we were in," Rob said. "We assumed someone in Santa María could translate. I knew in my head how small Santa María is—"

"And how uncivilized," Charlie said.

"So I should have realized I wasn't going to find a capable bilingualist on every street corner." He smiled tentatively. "But I didn't even know Santa María had no street corners—and no streets. I don't know when I was last so wrong about something so important."

Charlie took over. "You should've seen us trying to invite the villagers to breakfast this morning. We finally gathered them together, but—when we had the blessing—they didn't realize we were praying. We even tried crossing ourselves, but that didn't appear to mean anything to them. They just kept on talking amongst themselves."

Shock showed on everyone's face. Even the take-no-prisoners questioner's. He unfolded his arms, bowed his head, and closed his eyes.

chapter seventeen

It makes no sense," Charlie said, "but the villagers seem to understand why we're here. Our tools and building supplies didn't appear to surprise them. Maybe whoever reported their dire circumstances promised to send helpers and supplies. Not knowing is frustrating, but we may not get an answer this side of heaven."

Rob leaned toward the handheld microphone. "They obviously want to help."

"Their involvement is imperative," Charlie said. "Of course, after what they've been through, they may not be capable of strenuous work. So we won't expect more from them than they're able to do. Rob. . . ?"

"Charlie and I arose at dawn like we were all supposed to do, although I can't fault anyone who couldn't make it up then after such a long and trying day yesterday."

Rob, you're okay. I'm liking you more all the time.

"Tomorrow is another day, and we'll all have a fresh chance to get up on time."

If Rob proved to be another *Gone with the Wind* fan, that would be a big point in his favor.

"Come on, Rob, get to the point!" Charlie said with mock impatience.

Although most of us knew Charlie was teasing and laughed at him, several kids looked terrified. They must have thought the two men were about to argue or maybe get into a fistfight.

"Do you want to tell this?" Rob said, still laughing.

Charlie shook his head. "You tell it. You're the boss."

"The point—the bottom line, for those of you planning to be business majors—is we took a quick survey this morning. We confirmed the existence of thirty-eight villagers. Six are between the ages of five and ten. We didn't see anyone younger than that. Twelve villagers are too old to do construction. Two others appear incapable of helping, even though their ages wouldn't be prohibitive. We may be able to involve some of them in light tasks if we can find a way to explain our needs."

In early May, I'd taken a couple of better-than-average photos of some baby robins in a nest in the pyracantha bush beside our front porch. Watching Mom Robin feed her little ones mesmerized me. The babies appeared to eat with gusto, and they didn't seem to object to being dependent on their mother.

But suppose those babies had been adult birds that were unable to find food or feed themselves? How would they have felt about being dependent on stronger, healthier birds—if other birds were even willing to help care for them?

Was that how the more helpless villagers would feel about not being able to share in the rebuilding?

"In short,"—Charlie spoke without the microphone until Rob held it up in front of him—"eighteen villagers appear capable of helping. So, between you, them, and us, that makes, uh, 164 laborers."

"One hundred sixty-five! Don't forget the Holy Spirit!"

I wasn't sure who'd said that, but she sounded amazingly like the ditsy venue girl. If so, she was a lot smarter than she'd let on.

Yesses and amens filled the air, and the villagers glanced at one another with concerned faces about why we'd suddenly begun applauding, whistling, and whooping at the volume of thunder. Maybe they didn't use such forms of approval.

"You're spot-on about that. The Holy Spirit is the Big Boss here."

Rob took the microphone back.

"We count eighteen distinct family units in Santa María, but we see the remnants of many more houses than that. We assume the storm killed a number of villagers—perhaps even whole families."

We got quiet fast. The time for humor had passed.

"We have thirteen days—"

"Really just twelve, because we leave for home early that last day," Charlie clarified.

"Twelve days in which 164 people, almost entirely novices, will build eighteen brand-new residences with major and presumably miraculous assistance from the Holy Spirit."

As the realities of our assignment finally struck home, leaving us speechless, I suspected that most of us were groaning inwardly. As apprehensive as I was, I tried replacing my silent curses with a prayer for strength, patience, and—above all else—the will to obey.

God wanted me here. I believed that more today than yesterday. And yet the task looked more impossible in the morning sunlight than it had in last night's darkness.

"Of course, these houses won't be big," Rob said, "or fancy. The villagers didn't live in mansions before, and they won't now. The most important thing is getting everyone inside before the rains come. We'll use the existing dirt foundations—they don't have block foundations like ours—and place a simple one-room cottage on each one. Picture a fair-sized, single car garage if that tells you anything. Anyone who's attended summer youth camp has probably slept in similar housing and hated it."

I smiled. Other heads nodded.

Rob and Charlie went on to describe how plain these cottages would be. They would have closeable doors a generous Jewish competitor had contributed, but no windows; plywood floors, but no interior or exterior paint; and a few shingles to keep out the rain, but no insulation.

"Bringing electricity and plumbing to Santa María isn't our job," they reminded us. "The villagers will be thrilled with whatever we provide. From what little we can figure out, their former houses may not have been as nice as these new ones."

Memories of the migrant camp ran through my head. These simple cottages would have seemed palatial there.

"You've heard the term 'bare bones'? Well, that's what we're doing. If we have time for minor improvements, great. But we can't overemphasize the importance of getting everyone inside again—"

"And keeping the outdoors outdoors," a thoughtful male voice said from across the mess tent.

The team wasn't shy about saying, "Hallelujah!" and "Praise the Lord!" Skepticism and uncertainty gave way to optimism and excitement. If experienced builders like Charlie and Rob—and especially God, the Builder of the Universe—believed we could do it, our only choice was. . .do it.

The project that had sounded humanly impossible minutes earlier seemed miraculously possible now. I thanked God for the millionth time since last night that I didn't take the easy way out by going home.

When Rob and Charlie started talking again, I reached into my purse and dug around for the nail clippers. I always carried them for cutting loose threads. I was a fanatic about getting rid of those danglers, and I never took a chance by just pulling one out.

My favorite clothes might be little more than loose, dangling threads by the time I left Santa María, but that was okay. Santa María's lack of a place to shop didn't matter. I could do that at home.

Pleased and amazed that I wasn't letting my vanity interfere, I attacked my fingernails with newfound motivation. Aleesha raised her eyebrows and smiled. She was probably the only person who noticed. That's the way I wanted it. I wasn't cutting my nails for show, but for doing my fair share of work.

chapter eighteen

We're going to divide into teams, and each one will build a cottage from the ground up. Each team will have a captain, selected for his or her carpentry and woodworking experience or—in many cases—proven leadership skills. Rob and I will be floaters, keeping you team leaders on target and assuring ourselves that the captains have everyone else under control, too."

"How many of you know what a plumb line is?" Charlie asked.

Almost every hand went up. I giggled at seeing the villagers raise their hands—just as if they'd understood the question, too.

"Good. Rob and I are going to be the plumb lines that keep the team captains straight. They'll be plumb lines to keep everyone else straight. Rob and I will rely on the Holy Spirit to keep us straight."

That made sense to me, and—from the smiles I saw—to everyone but the villagers.

Rob and Charlie would directly oversee anything requiring close precision—installing the doors, for example—and double-check every stage of our work before we did something so wrong it couldn't be undone.

They promised not to micromanage, though. (I had to ask Aleesha what that meant.) Not as long as the team captains were honest enough to ask for help when they needed it.

"You're not going to do a perfect job," Rob said. "Don't expect to. You're unskilled workers God has called according to His purposes. You're answerable to Him and Him alone, and He expects your best—no more, no less."

"Building houses that will stand for years is more important than making them look good," Charlie pointed out.

The two men would leave hand tools and leftover materials for the villagers to do additional building if they wanted, but they wished they could leave detailed, written instructions as well. The materials and way of building things were probably different than what the villagers were accustomed to.

Of course, at this stage of our relationship with the villagers, we didn't know if they could read or write. And there was still that problem of the language barrier.

"After dividing into teams, we'll clear away those remains we mentioned. Then we'll start building the modules we'll make the houses out of. We have one single cottage design, drawn in detail on the back of a paper napkin."

Not everyone realized Rob was teasing. Although he was the senior builder, he didn't seem quite as outgoing as Charlie or as inclined to joke around. But he had his moments.

"I'm just teasing about the napkin, guys, but I'm dead serious about standardization. We need to cut each piece of wood precisely enough to fit any house equally well. That means taking time, being careful, and double-checking every step. If we start by constructing our building blocks, assembling the houses will be like spreading melted butter on hot bread."

I hadn't heard that expression in ages. How long ago did my grandma die? I was in elementary school.

"Guys and girls, you know how Rob is. . . ." Charlie said, barely able to fight back a laugh.

The team members who'd feared a disagreement between Rob and Charlie earlier were the first to laugh at them now. No one could resist joining them.

"In brief, you'll build eighteen back walls, eighteen front walls, and thirty-six side walls. We cut some of the bigger pieces ahead of time, but you'll still do an awful lot of measuring, sawing, sanding, and hammering the next few days. You—"

"You know Charlie," Rob said. He wore a mischievous grin. "He means the skeletons of all those walls. We couldn't lift them if we assembled them completely. Oh, and Charlie was going to let the villagers drown when it rains. He forgot about pre-building sections for eighteen roofs."

"Okay, smarty-pants!" Charlie roared with laughter at his own oversights. "Let's divide into teams now, and then we'll decide who does what."

Before he could proceed, a female voice spoke from somewhere to my left.

"So will this be like the 'barn raisings' you see in movies about rural people?"

"Very much so. Let's divide up."

I was always the last person chosen for a team in phys ed, and I'd experienced that kind of exclusion from kindergarten straight through high school. College was bound to be the same. I wasn't any more an athlete than a home repairer.

I wondered if I'd finally overcome my youthful klutziness the way I outgrew a childhood allergy to chocolate. My inability to use my hands constructively without breaking something was one of my least admired childhood traits, and Mom and Dad forbade me to use a hammer or saw for any reason.

At the time, I couldn't see why they made such a big deal about the huge holes in the wall of my room. After all, it was my room. Maybe I should have kept the holes small enough to put a 20 x 30–inch poster over—if not a framed 11 x 14 picture.

Permission to use a screwdriver was conditional on one or

preferably both parents' being present to supervise. My most skillful efforts to fix things around the house—I had the best of intentions then, just as I did now—had cost them a small fortune in real repairs.

As the team captains took turns selecting team members, they wouldn't need to know about my ineptness to realize that Miss Priss was their least desirable choice. In school, a team could only use a specified number of kids. But here, everyone would be chosen, and last place would be the ultimate humiliation.

Jesus' teaching about the first being last and the last first wasn't as encouraging as it should have been.

And having to stand here—as short as I was, they'd overlook me if I sat down—while eighteen mostly male pairs of eyes assessed the availability of more than a hundred better choices made it tough to keep from swearing silently.

But I'd been good so far today and managed to convert this yet-unspoken curse into a "Blazes!" instead. My parents disapproved of saying darn, dang, or heck because they sounded too much like the "real thing," but—under these circumstances—avoiding the real thing beat the, uh, eternal hot oven broiler out of worrying about my parents' silly rules.

I'd be the last one chosen. I had no doubt of that. I was the smallest, and everyone but Aleesha would still be angry with me today. I wasn't naive enough to believe that laughing with me earlier signified forgiveness or acceptance.

Not only would I be last, I'd end up with the biggest, burliest, most brutish boy as my team captain, and he'd pay me back for yesterday by sticking me with the dirtiest and most deplorable tasks.

Then the happiest of realities set in. Charlie told us to number off from one to eighteen.

The team captains wouldn't do the choosing. In fact, they

had to number off, too.

I ended up on team #8. My captain was an ugly guy named Frank. I could tell from the expression on the back of his head that he'd love assigning the most awful jobs to me. When he turned to face me, he looked angry—almost rabid—about being stuck with me. That's when I recognized him as Mr. Take-No-Prisoners.

I wasn't sure if Frank disliked me because he was unforgiving, because of my recently acquired "Miss Prep" reputation, or because he didn't like people and it wasn't me at all; but I was dying to hold my fingertips in his face and shout, "See, Frank? I've already cut off my fingernails so I can do my best. Have you filed down your fangs?"

But I was satisfied that God, Aleesha, and I were the only ones who knew about my nails. Both personal prayer and sacrificial nail clipping should be done in a closet.

I was okay about Frank, though. I could put up with anything now. God had calmed me down enough since last night to assure me I could meet today's challenges gracefully.

We'd gotten up early enough and formed teams so quickly that Charlie and Rob started leading the teams to their building sites at 9:15. I couldn't understand why boy genius Neil accompanied them as they went from villager to villager, but they managed to communicate sufficiently well to place the intended owner of a specific house on each team.

We posted the team numbers on homemade signs at the front left corner of each tiny lot. Since they were sequential, I thought of them as house numbers. The houses would be on both sides of Santa María's single street—just as they'd originally been—with the so-called Passover Church and the mess tent dividing the residential area into two sections.

Thinking about the decreased number of cottages needed almost made me cry. How many people did that twister kill?

I'd never witnessed the aftermath of a natural disaster before, and dwelling on this one would nauseate me if I didn't start thinking about something else.

Charlie and Rob came back around to give each team its assignment. Although they assigned most of the teams to the "glamour jobs"—measuring and cutting boards to the right length for the infrastructure—they asked the remaining five teams, including team #8, to clear off the foundations. Frank looked like they'd asked him to chew nails.

More accurately, he looked like he wanted to spit nails.

I was tempted to offer him a good swear word but decided against it. If he had a sense of humor, I hadn't seen any sign of it yet. Maybe he belonged to one of those always-serious denominations that never dances, goes to movies, or smiles. I giggled to myself wondering how he would react to somebody speaking in tongues. Maybe I could get Aleesha to pretend to do that sometime.

Regardless of Frank's dour attitude, I was elated. I was ready to be faithful and flexible and do whatever he asked me to do. Since I'd gotten pretty good at bulldozing my room at home whenever the floor got too buried in stuff to walk on, today's assignment would be a badly clichéd piece of cake.

Clearing rubble would be much the same, I thought, except we wouldn't have to watch out for valuables.

Before we could cart away the debris, we had to dismantle the smaller pieces of the three houses the twister hadn't carried elsewhere. Some of them weren't that small, and we would have to break them down more. We could probably do our part in a couple of hours.

Crowbars, axes, and sledgehammers, here I come. Mom and Dad, you can't speak one word of protest. Destruction is the rule today, and I'm in hog heaven.

I looked closely at one of those sledgehammers. I was

impressed. Although it was bigger than me, at least my figure was slightly more feminine than its handle.

Frank handed me a short ladder and told me to whack away at something that was about to fall anyhow. But before I could put my fear of heights beneath me and start climbing, I heard loud voices.

"We have to take all three buses back," someone said. Who. . . ? Oh, maybe the lead driver, the one whose language was worse than mine had ever been.

Rob didn't give an inch. "No one in this village owns a car, and there aren't any telephones out here. We're not going to be left without something to use in case of an emergency. We paid for these buses to remain here. . .we could make all three of you stay."

I couldn't see the lead driver, but I could picture his face glowing a fiery red. "You're not keeping us here for two weeks in this godforsaken place."

"You go. You take two buses and only two buses. You hear me?"

The driver let loose with a long string of expletives, and several minutes later I heard the sound of two bus doors hissing shut like a pair of angry turtles.

I waited for my heart rate to go down a bit and started up the ladder, crowbar in hand. But God must not have intended for me to get very far.

Or was the Devil interfering?

chapter nineteen

Although I still felt a little spacey when Rob guided me to the front row opposite the driver's seat, I wasn't nearly as dizzy as I'd been the previous night after hitting my head. At least I didn't land on my noggin this time.

"Your arm is broken," Rob said quietly. "It looks like a clean break, if years of parenting and grandparenting have taught me anything about fractures."

The pain throbbed and radiated throughout my entire upper body far too much for my tastes. In a wilder-than-Wild West setting like Santa María, I wondered if anyone had a bullet I could bite.

I settled myself as comfortably in my seat as I could and pressed my head against the window. I thought about something Rob told me a few minutes earlier.

"I woke up during the night," he said, "aware that you were out there without a sleeping bag. I got up and brought my spare blanket to the edge of the field, but I couldn't spot you and couldn't chance terrifying the other girls by tiptoeing around and shining a flashlight in their faces. Tiptoeing?" He laughed. "Trying to walk through the trash between the sleeping bags, I would probably have fallen on someone. What would my family and my church think if Charlie had to send me home early for such misbehavior?"

After a good giggling spell, I told him Aleesha had helped me find a blanket.

"Thank You, Lord," he whispered. How many times now had Rob proven himself the opposite of who I thought he was at orientation?

He apologized for needing to have a quick powwow with Charlie before we left, but Charlie needed instructions on handling things while Rob and I were gone. Before going off to find his partner, he handed me a bottle of water and several acetaminophen.

"I hope this helps."

I closed my eyes and tried to keep from thinking. Although I refused to dwell on this morning's incident, I realized that—just like hitting my head on the rock last night—it shouldn't have happened. I never used the word accident to describe anything that greater care would have prevented.

I sighed loudly. No one heard it but God, though.

Unable to silence my thoughts completely, I tried thinking about something else.

From where I was sitting, I could see the tiny building we kept referring to as a church. It fascinated me. Despite Santa María's near annihilation, the building not only looked intact but showed no visible signs of damage. Only the immense buildup of debris in the yard, several feet deep in places and pressing firmly against the door and base of the building, gave any indication that the storm had come anywhere close.

God alone knew where all the rubbish had originated. Surely this storm really had been a twister. But since we rarely felt the effects of hurricanes in my part of Georgia and the only tornadoes I'd seen were on TV and in movies, I didn't have much to base my opinion on.

Some people might attribute the building's survival to the tornado's spasmodic, unpredictable nature; others might call it coincidence—pure luck. But the only explanation that worked for me was God's intervention.

The building didn't seem to fascinate the villagers the same way it did me. If anything, it appeared to terrify them, and that fascinated me even more. Even during the short time

I'd been sitting on the bus, I'd seen them walk across Broad Street rather than walk near the building. If a child wandered too close, a parent snatched her back just as if a moving car had been approaching.

I couldn't help thinking that the structure could have been anything—a school, a storehouse, a hospital. Even a church that looked nothing at all like a church. But it obviously hadn't been used for anything in many years. Why had they let a perfectly good building go unused? And why hadn't they housed the elders and the children there after the storm?

I could guess at an answer to my last question: Their ordeal had probably left them too weak to clear a path to the door. They couldn't have gotten anyone inside. Not without concerted, energy-draining effort.

I wondered when the villagers had last been inside.

I wanted to know so many things about Santa María and her people that I caught myself wishing I could speak even a little Spanish.

chapter twenty

I'd overheard Rob and Charlie talking earlier about clearing the litter from the doorway and using the Passover Church as a break room—a refuge from the sun. They'd keep bottled water inside, along with a number of snacks.

Charlie and Rob had called for volunteers to clear a narrow pathway to the door, and the four willing workers seemed cheerful about their filthy task. They probably just wanted to be the first team members inside. But despite their motives—good, bad, or indifferent—they were typical, dumb males.

They shoveled the litter with rectangular scraps of wood and dumped it just out of the pathway instead of carrying it somewhere else to dispose of. They might as well have been kids shoveling snow from one side of the sidewalk and dumping it on the other side. Whenever the villagers got around to cleaning the churchyard, they would have just as much to cart off as if these guys hadn't done anything.

I closed my eyes. I couldn't stand watching those four boys any longer. Sure, we'd be able to reach the door when they finished, but the churchyard would resemble a junkyard more than it did now. Even though the building probably wasn't a church, the appearance of the yard offended me.

If by any chance the building had ever been a church, the condition of the yard was a sacrilege. God had to feel the same way I did.

Opening my eyes, I watched the volunteers making what they undoubtedly considered good progress. But as far as I was concerned, they hadn't even started. I wished I could make the churchyard look decent.

Fat chance of that with a broken arm.

chapter twenty-one

W ell, Kim," Rob said when he got back on the bus, "I'd call this a tough break, but I don't want to make light of today's misfortune. Especially after yesterday."

I smiled.

"That's okay. I should have stood my ground—"

"Stood on the ground, you mean?"

I giggled.

"I should have stood my ground and stood only on the ground and refused to go up that ladder. I'm terrified of heights."

"You were less than fifteen inches off the ground when you fell. That's what I don't understand. Does your acrophobia normally kick in at such a low altitude? You were barely airborne yet."

Although Rob smiled after making a Pastor Ron–type joke, I could tell from the way he wrinkled his face that he was trying to help me relax.

"Sometimes." *Do I dare to be honest?* "But this time I was so focused on my task I wasn't conscious of being in the air. I'd die before I told anyone else this, but I fell when I caught my heel in my cuff and didn't realize it. The manufacturer didn't design these slacks as work clothes. The shoes, either."

I hoped the truth wouldn't turn him against me again, but I needn't have worried.

"Kim, I promise not to tell anyone."

No matter how much I'd questioned his sincerity yesterday, my doubts were gone now. Rob was real, and my secret wouldn't make me more of a prep clown than I already was.

When he continued, though, he had a new twinkle in his eye.

"Yes, Kim, better to let the rest of the team keep thinking you're simply inept."

"I thought you weren't going to tell them the truth, Rob." Laughing made me twist my arm so awkwardly it started throbbing again.

"Okay, Kim, you've got me on that one. I'll lie like a rug if you prefer."

We both laughed, although I couldn't help noting Rob's shameless use of one of the corniest, most unappealing clichés around. Oh, well. At his age, he's entitled. . . .

"I need to tell you something, Kim—now that it's true confessions time."

Rob, why is your face so pale? You look scared to death. Is it that bad?

"Kim's Confessional is now open and ready for business," I said playfully, hoping I could help him relax. "Drop your money in the box, and don't let me hear the sound of coins clanking unless they're twenty-four-karat gold."

After a moment of silence, his face returned to its natural color. Although he smiled before starting his story, his eyes no longer twinkled with merriment. Instead, they hinted of a sadness I hadn't seen there before.

"Kim, I misjudged you yesterday when I shouldn't have judged you at all, and I'm sorry. I thought you were just a whiny little preppy girl, afraid she'd break a fingernail doing manual labor—"

"Look." I showed him both hands. "I cut my nails off this morning. It was like Abraham sacrificing Isaac except God didn't intervene and stop me!" I laughed. "Oh, I'm sorry. I interrupted. . . ."

"Now I'm more impressed and feel worse still. I thought you were just making up as many excuses as you could after finding yourself in a situation you couldn't handle. You were honest just now. . . ."

"Yes?" I spoke as gently as I could. I'd never had an older adult—especially a man—share his feelings with me this way. I wished my dad could be like that.

"I hoped you would go home. I wanted you to, but I couldn't tell or ask you to. God made me give you the choice."

"I heard you say *if* instead of *when*."

He paused. "When you chose to stay, I had to reassess my feelings about you. I couldn't have been more wrong. Please forgive me."

Although the ruts in the road were barely noticeable now, I thought it might be dangerous to hug Rob while he was driving. But I gave him a one-armed hug, anyhow.

"I could tell everybody else wanted me to leave, too—they probably still do. I don't know how I'll make things right with them."

My left arm—the unbroken one—lay draped across the back of his neck. I sniffed once. Old Spice. My dad's aftershave.

"I'm so sorry about my behavior," I said. "I started out a mess, and now I'm a broken mess—in more ways than one."

chapter twenty-two

Neither of us had spoken for a number of miles.

"Wasn't someone else from your church supposed to come on this trip?"

"Good memory, Rob." I almost called him Pastor Rob. "Yes, my best friend, Betsy Jo Snelling. We heard about the Ciudad de Plata project at the same time and talked our parents into it later the same day. We've done everything together as long as I can remember. . . ."

"Why must women go to the bathroom in pairs?" He chuckled. "Are they afraid they can't find their way back singly?"

"Betsy Jo and I don't take togetherness quite that far," I barely finished saying before breaking into a giggle. "But we do act like twins sometimes. . . ."

"You dress identically?" Now he was laughing, too.

"Oh, be good, Rob."

I couldn't guess which emotion predominated—Rob's relief at having his confession over with or his gratitude for being forgiven of his "sin." But together they seemed to free the little boy in him. I wished I could see that side of my dad more often.

"I'm good for nothing, Kim. At least I'm as imperfect as any other average Christian. You'll discover that soon enough—even if I've fooled you till now."

I loved laughing with Rob, but I wanted to finish telling him about Betsy Jo. I was still peeved at her parents— especially her mom—for making her cancel out. I probably wouldn't have had any problems on this trip if she'd been along. She was my number-one guardian angel, and I was the first to admit how much I needed one.

I wanted to say, "That's hard to believe. You seem like a great Christian." Instead, I changed subjects. "Not to tamper with your imperfections, but I'd like to get back to Betsy Jo. . . ."

If he'd objected, I wouldn't have protested. He nodded, though.

"We submitted our applications at the same time. We applied for passports at the same time, too. The church blessed our going at the same business meeting."

Rob's eyes twinkled, and he had a mischievous look on his face.

"No." I shook my head. "I didn't say they blessed us out."

"Huh?" He looked flabbergasted. "Blessed out?"

"Where I come from, that means 'cussed out,'" I said. "Anyhow, we became pin cushions together, getting our shots at the same time. Not just the required shots, but everything the Center for Disease Control recommended. Mr. and Mrs. Snelling insisted on that for Betsy Jo, and—"

"You really do everything together, don't you?"

I loved listening to him laugh at a higher pitch than the bass voice he spoke in.

"We shopped together for trip supplies, including matching Bibles with Spanish on one side and English on the facing page. Oh, and wouldn't you know it? Betsy Jo speaks great Spanish. In fact, her Spanish is better than my French, but don't tell her I said so."

I expected him to express frustration at almost having a translator along, but he remained silent. Unable to read his expression, I continued.

"We made a list of big things only one or the other of us needed to bring—things we could share."

"Like that hair dryer?"

"Exactly. We were so excited about this trip and thankful it would keep us from working this—"

"What. . . ?"

"Never mind," I said in a more guarded tone. "I'm not up to being that honest today. I outgrew that, anyhow. Praise the Lord!"

"So why didn't Betsy Jo come? She cancelled just before we sent out the infamous change-of-plans message. I removed her from the mailing list myself. I'm surprised her parents let her cancel after investing so much money."

"That's what's so frustrating. She didn't cancel. Her parents made her drop out. They're so protective, especially her mom. I'm not sure Mr. Snelling agreed with his wife, but once she makes up her mind, well, that's it."

"Ugh! I know that type—full of well-intended 'smother love.' "

Smother love? I'd never heard that expression before, and it took me a minute to catch on.

"Exactly. Anyhow, Pastor Ron convinced the Snellings initially that the trip would be safe, and that was quite an achievement. Betsy Jo's parents are really big on missions, thank goodness, and this project enchanted them so much they didn't consider possible dangers the way they usually did."

"And it would have been safe," Rob said without the slightest hint of uncertainty. Then he glanced at me and hesitated, his voice growing almost defensive. "It is safe! It will be. . ."

His voice died out for a moment. I wondered if he was praying. When he resumed, his tone was confident again.

"It will continue being safe."

At first I thought he was trying to convince himself and not me. He struck me as the kind of leader—and the rare kind of man—who insists on taking full responsibility for everyone under his care. He probably blamed himself for my accident, and what could be sillier than that?

Why should any adult have to accept responsibility for a klutz like me?

Maybe that's why "responsible adults" seem overly serious at times. The buck stops at their door. I wondered if that was my dad's problem. Or part of it, anyhow.

"Safe in spite of my accident this morning, you mean? I agree. But that was before Betsy Jo's parents got on the Internet and started reading about drug wars in several Mexican border towns."

"I've been following those stories, too, but that's nowhere close to Santa María. No closer to Ciudad de Plata, either."

"I know, and that's what my parents pointed out. Pastor Ron, too. But the Snellings weren't willing to take any chances. They—Mrs. Snelling, anyhow—never gave Betsy Jo's non-refundable plane tickets a second thought, and they didn't act like they cared about the money for the project, either. Their daughter's health and safety was worth more than all the money in the world. They're not wonderfully well-off, though, so getting that money back would have helped. They're not poor or anything like that, but they didn't have an inheritance like we did to pay for this trip."

"I didn't know any of this."

I waited a minute or two to see if he would say more, but he didn't. Apparently lost in thought, he looked lonely sitting in the driver's seat. I almost felt guilty about breaking the silence, but I needed to finish.

"I wanted to cancel then, too. You can understand. I'm not a very experienced traveler. . . ."

"That part of the story sounds familiar and very, very believable."

He didn't sound like he was trying to be funny, although his tone was pleasant enough.

I rejoiced once more over his forgiveness of my past blunders. I felt as squeaky clean and sweet smelling as if I'd just emerged from a long soak in a spiritual bathtub.

"I was going crazy at the prospect of handling a cross-country flight by myself, and my stomach knotted like a tightening noose as departure time came nearer. Betsy Jo and I had planned on being the same great team in Mexico we'd always been at home. How could I function without her?"

"Do you think that might have kept you from integrating into this group—if she'd come, I mean?"

Rob, you are one honest and insightful fellow.

"I've wondered about that. I honestly don't know. But it's like you said last night about flexibility in doing mission work. Now is the time to depend on God. I wasn't ready to do that when I left home yesterday morning. I thought I'd have to do everything on my own despite my fears. If Betsy Jo had come, chances are I would have depended on her more than on God."

"And now?"

"Now that God has grounded me—in more ways than one—my only choice is to trust and obey Him."

chapter twenty-three

We finally reached an intermediate-quality road.

"Rob, how am I gonna do construction with a broken arm?"

"Don't worry about that. You still have one good arm, don't you? We'll find something you can do. I don't mean busy work, either. Maybe you can hold nails for hammering. You know, try for a broken hand next."

Rob's laughter was infectious, but I didn't get any warm fuzzies envisioning myself in a complete body cast by the time I got home.

"Seriously, though, you can carry small supplies to the teams or entertain the children while their parents build."

"I'd like working with the children. Carrying small supplies would be fine, though. But they'd have to be small. I'm not that strong. Don't tell anyone, but I'm not very coordinated, either." We roared together at my understatement. "Or maybe you've figured that out."

Rob nodded. "I've had my suspicions." I wished my dad and I could have this much fun together.

"Entertaining the children would be fun, though. Although I haven't been around kids much, I worked with some migrant children for a while this summer. I loved it."

I decided against telling Rob the whole story.

"What, Kim? I thought you loved little kids because you're so much like one."

"Sometimes," I said. I didn't use that pensive tone of voice very often. "Not always, though. Peter Pan didn't want to grow up, but I do—most of the time. Then I get into an adult situation and I'm petrified. Given the opportunity, I'd stick one foot in adulthood and keep the other in the territory I'm comfortable in."

"The best of both worlds. . . ?"

I nodded.

I started thinking about Dad. I'd probably spent too much time lamenting his resemblance to a charred steak to try finding out how tender he was inside. Maybe he'd grown up too much. I'd never considered the possibility before.

"I didn't want to grow up," Rob said. "I had more fun being a kid, but circumstances deflated my little-kid spirit. When I graduated from college, married my childhood sweetheart, and started a career, I became an adult against my will. I kicked and screamed the whole way, but there was no turning back."

"Oh, my." *Are you trying to predict my future by describing your past? Please, no. I can't take it.* "Anyhow, count me in on babysitting or material handling or anything else you need me to do. I can be as flexible as God wants when I have a mind to be, and He's been doing some mind surgery on me the past twenty-four hours."

"Glad to hear that. Speaking of minds—or should I say 'If you don't mind. . .'?—may I talk with you about something else I've been thinking about since yesterday?"

"I'm listening."

I wished talking with my parents was this easy—especially Dad—but maybe that would come when they grew more mature. I giggled to myself.

Mom was great most of the time. Dad was probably an okay guy, but—as much as I loved him—I couldn't imagine talking like this with him. If I didn't understand him—if I couldn't see past the overdone exterior—he must have felt the same about me. How could he possibly understand someone who seemed so underdone?

Then again, I was still a teenager, and nobody understands teens. Not even other teens.

I guess nobody understands parents, either. Not until becoming one, that is.

"I notice you have a cell phone with you. Most teens have them now. . . ?"

"Many. Maybe not quite most. When I got up today, I discovered that mine doesn't work in Santa María." I twisted my mouth in a make-believe pout.

"Ah? But it'll work in San Diego, won't it?"

"It should. It had a fresh charge when I left home, and I haven't used it since then."

"So it would've worked yesterday at DFW or in San Diego—if you'd tried using it?"

"Yes, it. . .Rob, no! I haven't called my parents to give them an update. They don't have any idea where I am. They get upset whenever I change plans without letting them know. They'll have a cow over this. I'll call from San Diego. I promise."

"Good idea. But let me update you. Charlie called your folks when you didn't show up in San Diego at the expected time. They were worried, of course, but they assured him you'd left Atlanta on schedule. They tried calling you but couldn't get any answer. . . ."

"I didn't have it on me at DFW, and I didn't think you'd appreciate my digging through my luggage to get it out in San Diego."

Rob shook his head and grinned.

"Okay, smarty-pants!" I said with a single giggle. "I admit it. I forgot to get it out."

"Your dad called to verify that you made it to DFW,

though. He sounded frantic about what might have happened after that."

Dad was frantic enough to check on me? He always has Mom make his calls when he can get away with it.

"Once your folks discovered you were booked on a later flight, they tried calling Charlie back. They got me instead. I told your dad about the change in plans. That's when Charlie and I decided we'd better wait for you. Especially since we'd planned to emphasize flexibility at orientation. We couldn't let you come this far without having a welcoming committee—or maybe a lynch mob."

He looked like a big kid when he grinned like that.

"No, Rob! That's why you waited? I should've called my parents collect from Texas and had them call you. What else could I have done wrong yesterday?"

I was so animated I bashed my arm against the window and started whimpering and crying again. The first eighteen years of my life hadn't seen me cry as much as the past twenty-four hours.

"Be careful, little gal," Rob responded. The kindness in his voice made me stop sniffling. "You're my new daughter now, and I don't want you suffering needlessly—not physically, emotionally, or spiritually. Yesterday is over. It won't haunt you any longer than it takes to forgive yourself."

I wriggled out of my seat again and threw my good arm around Rob's neck in a tight hug, making him swerve slightly. I cried from joy, relief, and gratitude this time. Not pain and regret. This mission trip would be a success—at least in God's eyes.

We didn't talk much for the rest of the drive to San Diego. We didn't need to.

I thought a lot about the remarkable relationship we'd established. My rapport with Rob was as unique and wonderful as my friendship with Aleesha. What a super Christian this man was.

I wanted to be more like him.

Yesterday's four-plus-hour trip took only two-and-three-quarters hours today. The tractor trailers had smoothed out the ruts so much we seemed to be on a different road from last evening. Now that we were on blacktop, we felt like we were flying.

The border guards glanced at my swollen arm, the empty bus and luggage compartment, and our passports, and flagged us through.

"Take care of yourself, young lady."

Even these men, who had no reason to care about me, expressed more sympathy than the kids on the team.

Oh, no! Team 8 will be one member short. Frank was angry enough about being stuck with me before. But how will he feel about me being so useless?

Although my arm bothered me, the acetaminophen helped.

I suffered more from worrying about my incident's effect on today's work. Charlie would keep things moving the best he could, but he'd admitted he didn't have Rob's experience. I dreaded becoming an object of greater contempt once we got back to Santa María.

By then everyone would be raging fiercely about how much my accident messed up today's work by taking Rob off the job. No one would care that Charlie offered to drive me so Rob wouldn't have to.

Or that Rob had insisted on doing it himself.

So one frazzled project leader and a hundred forty-two frustrated team members—Aleesha would be the one exception—were probably already blasting me behind my back. Plus the eighteen villagers who were helping and the twenty who couldn't.

Forgiveness wasn't likely to be the word of the day in anyone's vocabulary, English or Spanish.

chapter twenty-four

After getting me checked in at the emergency room, Rob said he had some errands to run.

"I've always wanted a satellite phone. They're usable anywhere in the world, even where regular cell phones don't work. I can rationalize that purchase now because of your accident and my responsibility for the whole group. Same for a quality GPS. I might need it to find my way back to the hospital." He laughed.

I didn't realize how clever he'd been finding his way back to San Diego without a GPS. Although the price of electronic devices tends to go down, those two items could still be pretty pricey. I'd often admired them when I was techno-window-shopping. Maturing sporadically into young womanhood hadn't lessened a lifelong fascination with electronic gadgetry.

The doctor, nurses, and x-ray technicians at the emergency room were as sympathetic and pleasant as the ones back home. The break—as Rob had said initially—was clean, and I chose an eerie shade of purple for the cast. I wondered if it glowed in the dark but didn't ask for fear of sounding too childish.

Since the emergency room team took me almost upon arrival, I had to postpone making the call to my parents. Once they finished, that call became my top priority.

Although I didn't think about the time difference between San Diego and Georgia, that worked to my advantage. Mom and Dad were eating supper when I called, and they offered to poke a broiled lamb chop through the phone. They were thrilled to hear my voice. Especially my dad. He asked several times if I was "really okay" and offered to fly out and help me if I wasn't up to traveling home by myself.

I must have shocked the daylights out of him when I said I wasn't coming home and didn't need pampering.

"In that case," he said, "give us your address, and we'll overnight some proper work clothes to you."

"That's really sweet of you, but I don't think FedEx, UPS, DHL, or any of those other companies with familiar initials make deliveries to tiny Santa María. Our bus driver had to use a GPS to locate the village. Even that wouldn't have worked if he hadn't had the coordinates. That's how far off the beaten track it is. Now, you might be able to get something to me by carrier buzzard, but I'm not sure which companies use them. Thanks again, but I'll make do with what I have. All you have to do is replace what I ruin in Santa María."

"We'll gladly do that, Kim," Dad said.

I could tell he was smiling. Not laughing at me, but smiling—like he'd actually been glad to talk with me. He barely let me talk to Mom at all. I couldn't believe how nice talking with him had been.

Then Mom and Dad gave me a simple message from Betsy Jo, one that made less than no sense. "I hope you're not too disappointed with your Bible."

How could a person be disappointed with a Bible? A Bible is a Bible.

Although I felt greatly relieved having my parents' amazing forgiveness for failing to call the day before, they told me something so revolting that even the thought of returning to Santa María nauseated me.

chapter twenty-five

Rob's willingness to forgive me had helped to establish our great new relationship, but this news would turn him against me forever. Would he put me off the bus and make me walk—not to Santa María, but back to Georgia? If our roles had been reversed, I'd insist on it.

I'd rather sleep blanketless on a billion pebbles for the rest of my earthly life than confess a sin of such indescribably gross omission to Rob.

"Kim, girl, you okay now? You look a little spacey."

"Sure enough, Rob. I have enough codeine in me to kill the pain for hours. It hasn't dimmed my appetite, though."

I hoped he'd take the hint. Although I was starving by then, I was more concerned about making him pull off somewhere than about eating. I didn't want to make my confession while he was driving. He might throw me off the bus. Without stopping. Then again, maybe I deserved to break all my bones this time.

"Taco Bell okay?" he asked, laughing.

"Uh, how about something non-Mexican while we're on this side of the border?"

"Sure. Not that you're going to get anything Mexican in Santa María."

Without seeking further input from me, Rob pulled into a Pizza Hut parking lot. I dared not tell him I'd eaten pizza twice at DFW yesterday and my anxiety had churned it up so grotesquely that I literally grew sick of pizza for the first time in my life.

At least waiting for a pizza to bake would give me enough time to spill my guts before Rob did.

But as circumstances would have it—maybe Satan planned it this way—this Pizza Hut had a buffet that was still open. Nothing would keep us from getting our food immediately. I quickly did some mulling over the upcoming conversation as we sat down with our plates fully loaded. Never before had I piled a plate higher with salad than with pizza. I didn't even use a tomato-based dressing.

"You want to say the blessing, Kim?"

"Next time, if you don't mind."

I was fighting to keep the codeine from knocking me out completely before I ate and made my ultimate confession—my final words. I might have fallen asleep during my own blessing.

Better to doze during Rob's. I'd discovered during the past twenty-four hours that his prayers weren't always the shortest.

"Rob (yawn), I called my parents like I promised," I said four minutes later at the conclusion of his blessing. He apparently had to say amen more than once to wake me up.

"Good, Kim. They glad to hear from you?"

"Yes, and they were (yawn) amazingly understanding (yawn)." I started perking up a little after that. "You didn't tell me you called them when I reached San Diego. You assumed I was too scatterbrained to?"

Rob gave me the strangest look.

"No, Mom and Dad didn't say that. But were you expecting me to be blond or something?"

"Or something, yes. Go on, please." He was staring at me.

The harder he stared, the more terrified I felt. "I. . ."

How could I tell him? I was a deer on the highway, blinded by the lights of oncoming traffic. No matter what I did, no matter which way I moved, a car was going to smush me.

"Kim?"

"Rob,"—I breathed a quick prayer before spitting out my confession—"my parents looked on the computer after talking with Charlie yesterday and found the missing messages. They were sitting there healthy and unread. All seven of them. They must have been in my inbox all along. I'm awful about checking e-mail, but I didn't expect to get any messages about the mission trip. Honestly, I thought I checked my e-mail several days before leaving. Obviously I didn't."

Rob didn't say a word. He stared at his plate now and not at me.

I learned then what watching a dangerous storm brew felt like—and knowing I had no chance of moving out of its path.

"Betsy Jo kept me informed about the trip. But she was no longer on the mailing list, so she didn't receive the message. You've forgiven me for how I acted yesterday, but can you ever forgive me for being so careless and stupid?"

His look softened. "Forgive you, Kim?"

Are you surprised that I'd dare to ask your forgiveness? "Yes, I want you to. I desperately need you to."

"But forgive you for what, Kim?"

Huh? "For what. . . ?" *Is that a yes or a no, Rob?*

"God has been teaching me a little trick, Kim. Old dog, old trick. But even after years of practicing, I don't always do a great job of it. Yesterday at orientation is proof of that."

"Ah?"

I didn't realize I'd begun holding my breath expectantly until I suddenly gasped for air.

"Once we seek God's forgiveness," Rob said, "He puts our sins out of His mind as far as the east is from the west. He wants His children to do the same thing. But we can't forgive someone seventy-times-seven times unless we forget each instance once it's over with. Make sense? So, what did you say you needed forgiveness for?"

I scooted my chair out so fast I almost knocked it over. I threw my arms around Rob—I think I hit him with my cast—and wept aloud for what seemed like hours.

I didn't know exactly how the woman caught in adultery felt after Jesus forgave her, but at least I had an inkling. Rob would never cast the first stone except on rare occasions like orientation.

I didn't care what anyone else in that Pizza Hut thought of my behavior. The joy of forgiveness had exhilarated me just as much the second time around.

We turned out to be the only ones in the dining room. The other diners had left before we started talking, and none of the employees were in sight. So our entire "public conversation," complete with mutual tears, remained private.

Rob sent me to the bus while he waited for the cashier to return, and I must've fallen asleep before he got there, for the next thing I remember was the sound of Aleesha's voice at dawn the next day.

chapter twenty-six

Day 3

"Wake up, princess. No peas for you last night."

Huh? What are you talking about? Would you quit shaking me? I might wake up, and I don't want to.

"Oh, no you don't. . .no more sleep for you. And no more codeine for a while, either."

I don't know how she did it, but Aleesha got me up and dressed and kept me upright while I stumbled my way to the mess tent for breakfast.

My parents were my age or younger when *The Twilight Zone* was a popular TV program, but they told me all about it. Although cable networks still showed reruns and stores carried each year's episodes on DVD, I'd never seen one.

But when Aleesha and I entered the mess tent for breakfast a few minutes later, I felt like I'd either fallen down the rabbit hole with Alice or wandered into *The Twilight Zone*. Maybe both.

"How are you today, Kim?"

"I'm so sorry about your arm! Does it hurt much?"

"Can I do anything to help you, Kim?"

"Oh, wow! What a horrible thing to happen on your first day here, Kim."

"May I sign your cast? Please? I want to put an encouraging scripture verse on it."

"I'm so glad you stayed, Kim."

"I'm looking forward to getting to know you better these two weeks. Let's eat together sometime, okay?"

"I've got some extra work clothes. They might be a little

baggy on you, but they'll be clean—at least starting out—and you're welcome to them if you like. I have some safety pins if you need 'em."

"Was it scary missing your flight day before yesterday? I wouldn't have had the presence of mind to figure out what to do next. But I'm blond, in case you haven't noticed."

"So what's it like living in Georgia?"

"Your dad is really a college English professor?"

"How do you get your hair so shiny?"

"What a fabulous tan! You aren't really Hispanic, are you? That's what some of the girls have been saying. We all think you look so terrific. Especially the boys."

"You're so petite! I'll never lose enough weight to wear clothes like yours and look good in them."

"Do you have a boyfriend?"

"What are the kids like in your church?"

"Have you ever been on a mission trip before?"

"I love your Southern accent. I hate those fake ones you hear in movies and on TV, but yours is real, and it sounds neat!"

"I thought people down South always said 'y'all.' But you speak English good."

"You have a cell phone with all the minutes you want, un-limited texting, and a car? Wow! Has God ever blessed you!"

"Is it true you've done volunteer work with migrants? Cool!"

"I'd have run home as fast as I could if I'd broken my arm yesterday. You have a lot of spunk!"

"Some of us are already talking about having a team reunion. You'll come, won't you?"

"Do you enjoy music, Kim? Are you a good singer? You must be since you brought that karaoke thing."

"Do you know what you want to major in, Kim? If you do,

you're so lucky. I haven't got a clue what I want to do."

"Your mom and dad are still married after all those years? How wonderful! Mine have been divorced since I was ten. Yours must really love each other."

"It's an honor and a privilege to have you on my team, Kim. Welcome back, and let me know what I can do to help you."

An honor and a privilege? Frank? Was that really Frank who just said that? Frank who hated my guts yesterday and seemed almost gleeful about my accident? He'd just smiled at me, too.

I'd never seen him smile before.

If this wasn't *The Twilight Zone*, it must be heaven—or at least a convincing preview. Never had I witnessed such a complete reversal of attitude. It was more than I could have dreamed of, much less hoped for.

But I noticed something curious about the way the team members welcomed me back. Several things, actually. Although the team members didn't line up as such, they kept appearing at regular intervals. Like someone had assigned each person a fifteen-second time slot, and as soon as one person approached the end of his allotted time, another one showed up.

But stranger than that was the way each of them looked at Aleesha before addressing me. I could best describe the looks in their eyes as a cross between fear and hesitation. They looked at her again afterward as if asking whether they'd done a satisfactory job.

When Aleesha gave a nod—apparently one of approval—their look of relief reminded me of Rob after I forgave him yesterday.

Aleesha never smiled once until the last person finished greeting me.

Just before graduation, one of my favorite teachers

confessed that she never let her students see her smile until after Thanksgiving. Feigning an almost frightening authority in the classroom before letting her hair down and revealing her humanity helped establish a standard of discipline that lasted throughout the school year.

But why did I remember that story now, and how did it relate to Aleesha and the other team members?

I didn't keep count, but it seemed like every single team member spoke to me that morning. Although their well wishes sounded 100 percent sincere, they came across as premeditated; I felt as though I'd just watched an entire graduating class try to write meaningful yearbook inscriptions for someone they knew about but didn't know.

The fact that no one had given me a chance to respond made me feel like I was the yearbook. Strange. Very strange indeed.

Aleesha grinned from ear to ear.

"Sometimes stereotypes work to a person's advantage," she said, "especially in the hands of a budding drama major."

She laughed, and I stared at her as if she had three heads. Still under the influence of codeine, I might not have found two heads to be particularly unusual.

"Call it a little old-fashioned fire-and-brimstone preaching, if you like," she said as we headed away from the mess tent.

I shook my head vigorously—as if that might make things clearer. It didn't do anything but make me dizzy.

We settled down on the ground near the churchyard. Aleesha opened a small can of meat for me, and I said grace. When I looked at it more closely, lying motionless in the can like a body in an aluminum coffin, I almost retracted my blessing. I liked potted meats fine, but not served that way.

"Let me know if you need help getting up, Kim," one of the guys said as he passed by.

"I will, uh. . ."

"My name is Geoph. That's with a *G-e-o* and a *p-h.*"

"With what. . . ?" I responded more loudly than I meant to.

"Geoff with a *G-e-o* and two *f*'s. I was just teasing about the p-h. I wouldn't want you to think I was 'p-h unbalanced.' "

I smiled back. I couldn't imagine anything unbalanced about him. He was gorgeous, and he looked so English. Of course, since I'd never met anyone from England, I was just imagining that part. Although *G-e-o-f-f* was a British spelling, his accent didn't sound any more English than Aleesha's or mine.

"Thanks, Geoff with a *G-e-o* and two *f*'s. I'll let you know if I need help. I just might. You never know."

I never had any problem attracting guys. I didn't even have to try most of the time. Unfortunately, I was just as good at making girls jealous, and I never meant to do that.

But Aleesha was the only person I wanted to talk to now. Giving up this chance to let gorgeous, humorous Geoff practice his charms on me meant I was serious about finding out what Aleesha had done.

chapter twenty-seven

I sighed as I watched Geoff walk away, but I felt confident I'd get to talk to him again.

"So what's up, Aleesha?" I tried keeping my tone casual. Although I would've preferred hearing a voluntary confession to having to badger her about the team's strange behavior in the mess tent, I'd bug the daylights out of her if I had to.

"Whatever do you mean, Kim?" she said, her arms folded and her eyes upturned in feigned innocence.

"I know you've seen *The Twilight Zone*. You told me you have."

"Yes, yes, great show—filmed in living color like every other show back then: black and white."

"Who but you!"

We giggled together.

"Now, what were you saying a few minutes ago about stereotypes, budding drama majors, and fire-and-brimstone preaching? Come on. 'Fess up."

"You really expect a full confession, girl?"

"Yes, and the sooner the better." Concerned that I might have sounded too impatient, I toned down. "I'm not upset with you, Aleesha. But I need to understand what happened in the mess tent a few minutes ago. You obviously had something to do with it. That's all."

Then I punctuated my words with a patient smile.

"That's okay, then. Your teammates—all one hundred and however many of them there are—were sincere in what they said to you."

"Yes, they sounded like it. But wh—?"

"They knew they'd better be."

"You didn't threaten to beat them up, did you? They looked half-scared." I smiled once more to show I was teasing. Mostly so, anyhow.

"No, girl. And don't go suggesting any more ideas like that. You're trying to give up swearing. I'm trying to give up violence."

"Aleesha? You? Violence?"

"Yes, Aleesha. Yes, me. Yes, violence. If there's any violence around, I want to be as far from it as I can."

"Oh." I must have sounded disappointed.

"Gal, I'm a pacifist for sure. You know that now, but they don't. So I preached a little sermon to them while you and Mr. Rob were in San Diego. Let's just say I emphasized a few points from the Bible the way only a very talented but extremely modest freshman drama and theater major of the dark-skinned persuasion can do."

Aleesha started laughing then, and she laughed until the tears streamed down her face. Although I tried to resist laughing—her confession sounded too serious to take lightly—her laughter was contagious. One of us would look at the other and start to say something, and then we'd break out laughing all over again. We must have gone on that way for five minutes, although it seemed more like twenty.

People have a hard enough time ignoring female teenagers in the midst of a giggling jag, but it's worse when the observers are teens, too. After several minutes, we'd attracted quite a crowd.

Eighty or ninety of our group gathered around, plus some of the villagers. The girls started laughing first, but the boys soon became innocent and unwilling participants, too.

We'd momentarily become one in common laughter.

As soon as the laughter died down, everyone looked around as if to say, "That was fun. What shall we do next?"

Aleesha wasn't one to ignore a crowd, or so I was about to discover. I didn't know if the actress in her was coming out or if she was just a purebred country ham seeking an appreciative audience to try her saltiness on. Either way, she took advantage of the opportunity to address the group. "Ladies, gentlemen, and, uh, respected elders. . ."

Rob and Charlie performed awkward bows of acknowledgment. Their faces were still red from laughing so hard.

"Miss Kim and I have been discussing how nice you were before breakfast, and that surprised her in light of certain recent, unfortunate events that shall be spoken of no more. Nonetheless, she's grateful for your interest and well wishes. She'd better be. Right?"

Cautious laughter rippled through the crowd.

"But her curiosity has put me in a bind. Not only has she insisted that I explain, she's also questioned whether I've threatened you with violence. Would anyone speak to that, please? Totally voluntarily, of course."

"No, Kim," Geoff said. "Aleesha didn't even hint at violence. All she did—do I have to call her 'Miss Aleesha'?"

"Call me whatever you want to as long as you do it with a modicum of respect, boy. Even if you call me 'that fool black girl' just do it with respect and we'll be fine."

She giggled. Several other people in the crowd did, too, but not as many as I'd expected. People didn't seem to know how to take Aleesha. I wasn't so sure myself now.

Was this the same girl who'd befriended me at orientation and become my second best friend after Betsy Jo, or had that girl disappeared in *The Twilight Zone*, leaving this new Aleesha in her place?

On the other hand, Geoff couldn't have looked more

shocked if Aleesha had told him she was a cannibal and he was to be her next meal.

She must have felt sorry for him, though. "I'm just teasing, Geoff. Just apply the Golden Rule. Now, what were you starting to say?"

"Uh, right, Aleesha," Geoff said. Although he sounded a tad hesitant, he continued. "Kim, Aleesha preached us a little sermon. That's all."

"A little sermon? Aleesha? This Aleesha? The one standing right beside me? Her?" I started to point at her, but pointed at the ground instead as if I'd just discovered I was holding a smoking gun. Or at least a loaded one.

Disbelief overwhelmed me. So Aleesha had been serious when she told me she'd preached a sermon.

Once more, she stood with her eyes upturned in mock innocence. She could have modeled for a cherub statue.

"That's right, Kim," a blond said from the edge of the mess tent. I recognized her as the girl who'd admired my presence of mind dealing with the missed flight. "She reminded us of some things we Christians had forgotten about."

Another voice chimed in. "She brought up what Jesus said about being known by our fruit. . .and she pointed out how rotten our fruit had been yesterday and the day before."

And another. "Aleesha mentioned what Jesus said about cutting back unproductive vines to produce more and better fruit."

"Judge not, that ye be not judged." The voice spoke in what I took to be a foreign accent.

"New York City," Aleesha whispered when she saw the questioning look on my face. I just knew he was foreign. "Foreign" is anywhere not in the South.

She beamed as one person after another brought out different sermon points.

"Jesus only had one opportunity to forgive the people who crucified Him, so He didn't put it off. He did it from the cross despite the fact His enemies weren't sorry for what they were doing. Then Aleesha reminded us how sorry you were."

The blond spoke again. "Jesus said if we loved one another, it would show—and if we didn't, it would show even more. What influence would we have on these villagers if we failed to love one of our own team?"

One very shy-looking boy—he didn't look old enough to be part of our group—appeared to be struggling to make himself say something. That had to be Neil, the boy genius who'd graduated from high school at sixteen. I felt sorry for him. I used to be that bashful myself. He must feel pretty out of place with this group. I made a mental note to befriend him and show my acceptance.

I understood firsthand how rejection felt.

"Kim. . .Miss Kim," he said as if he'd never addressed a slightly older girl before, "Aleesha was your Good Samaritan when the rest of us walked on by, ignoring your needs. We knew you were hurting; but instead of tending to your wounds, we pressed a figurative crown of thorns down on your head."

"Aleesha said that?" I said, gasping.

"No, ma'am," the man-boy said, apparently too modest to admit that those comparisons were original, "but we could see what we'd done. Passing by on the other side of the road and leaving you lying there was horrible, but we came by and beat you up even more."

That was one smart kid all right.

The momentary quiet exploded into spontaneous applause—the kind that would have felt great after my "I'm staying" speech at orientation. Shy, young Neil had forced himself to speak, and he'd said eloquently what was in everyone's heart that day.

One by one, others shared bits and pieces from Aleesha's impromptu sermon. Her powerfully inspired sermon had me in tears. I started to appreciate the diversity of our group and to imagine how each of our individual gifts might prove useful.

Whoops. My turn. "I can't thank you enough for your support."

I felt a blush bathing my face at the clichéd way I started. Before it could turn into a flood, I struggled to find something more precise—more meaningful—to say. I wanted to speak fluently, but my nerves took control of my tongue, and I stumbled through my speech the best I could.

"The—the truth is I. . .the truth is I don't know how to express my grati—to express my appreciation any better than that. I'm embarrassed to admit how disillusioned I—I felt during orientation, and it didn't get any better at breakfast yesterday or right after my accident. But you've given me a much-needed lesson in forgiveness, too. I hope we can work together as a. . .as a team now. I'll do my best to help any way I can—even with—with my broken arm."

"Amen!" Aleesha said.

From somewhere—perhaps an angel started it—"When God's People Come Together" filled the mess tent with ever-increasing volume as one person after another joined in singing. Enough kids knew the parts to give the sound an unbelievable a cappella richness. Singing in an angel choir couldn't have been a more glorious experience.

> *"When God's people come together,*
> *His Spirit makes them one.*
> *When God's people feed on His Word,*
> *Their hearts beat to His truth.*
> *When God's people pray together,*

He gives them hope and strength.
When God's people sing together,
His joy flows from their lips."

After a number of repetitions, someone changed songs. The new selection couldn't have been a more perfect follow-up.

"Wherever there is need, that's where I must go
With feet that move in Jesus' name so the love of
God will show.
Wherever there are problems, that's where I
must be
With hands that work in Jesus' name so God's love
will show through me.
Wherever there are problems, wherever
there is need,
As the hands and feet of Jesus Christ,
Let me go as God's love leads.
Let me do as God's love leads.
Let me serve as God's love leads."

Hands reached out to hands, and nobody wanted to quit singing. Aleesha's voice—rich, clear, and beautiful—rose above the rest.

The villagers held hands with us, too, even though they didn't understand what we were talking about or why and what we were singing. But the Spirit had obviously moved them. Whatever they witnessed that morning was good.

Just as suddenly and unexpectedly as the singing began, we reached a stopping point. I didn't realize until several minutes later that I was still holding hands with the person on my left. The one on my right was gently touching my shoulder.

Part of me was dying to say, "I've got to ask one last

question." Not wanting to break the mood, however, I remained silent. I couldn't be the one to poke a hole in this reverent balloon of fellowship.

"Kim, you look like you want to say something," Geoff said more loudly than he needed to. Although I might feel guilty about it later, I resented his doing that.

I shook my head. I frowned. I glared. But he was unstoppable. He couldn't have shattered the worshipful atmosphere more completely if he'd meant to.

"This feeling of love and unity is overwhelming," I began. I could barely speak for sobbing. As tears of joy kept running down my face, I forgot about my anger at Geoff. I'd never experienced God's presence in such a real way before.

I still didn't want to talk, but I had to. "Maybe Geoff did us a favor by bringing us back down to earth. We can't build houses in the valley if we stay on the mountaintop all day."

I saw smiles and nods of agreement. "But I do have one more question, and it's bugging the daylights out of me. You all looked like you were scared to death of Aleesha when you spoke to me earlier. Yet you've insisted she didn't threaten you—"

"Oh, we didn't exactly say that, Kim," Geoff said.

"She threatened to preach the sermon all over again if we didn't show we'd learned our lesson the first time around," the blond explained. "She told us she'd keep repreaching it until it took, and she'd make it longer every time."

"But it took the first time, didn't it?" Aleesha said, grinning.

Throughout the rest of that day and well into the evening, I heard bits and snatches of team members humming, whistling, and singing "When God's People Come Together" and "Wherever There Is Need" while going about their construction chores.

Tears filled my eyes every time I heard it.

chapter twenty-eight

I was on my way to worksite #2 with some requested bottles of lukewarm water—I was at full capacity with three under my good arm and one in my hand—when one of the girls stopped to talk to me.

"Hi, Kim. How's the arm? You don't know me, but I'm Judith and I'm so sorry about how I've acted the past few days."

She was right. Not only did I not know her, I couldn't remember her from the endless procession of make-righters who had greeted me before breakfast.

"Don't worry about it, Judith. All is forgiven." For the life of me, I couldn't remember the motion the pope makes when blessing people. I tried to sound convincing, but that was especially tough when I didn't know what I was forgiving her for. What specifically, that is.

Maybe I should have asked, but dredging up details about something I thought was completely behind me didn't seem right.

"Just don't let it happen again," I said with what I meant as a mischievous grin, never suspecting that anyone could be sensitive enough to take an obvious, smart-aleck joke like mine as a serious reprimand.

I didn't notice my blunder until I saw her face turning beet red. She barely managed to squeak out, "Oh, I won't," and then her tears started flowing.

Had I just shot Bambi's mother? Or maybe Bambi. I felt awful. Maybe worse than Judith, if that was possible.

Some people sob. Others weep. And some. . .

A product slogan says, "When it rains, it pours." Well, Judith's tears were in danger of putting even the highest sections of Santa María—they didn't appear to be more than a foot higher than the lower sections—under salt water. She just kept on raining and pouring, pouring and raining.

I felt horrible about my insensitivity and wondered whether offering to amputate my tongue might make things right again. No, she might take that literally, too, and I wasn't ready to sacrifice the most important organ in my body. *She'll get over it*, I told myself. *She's too sensitive. It's her fault for over-apologizing*.

But no matter how I tried rationalizing my thoughtlessness, I couldn't escape the fact I'd hurt the poor girl's feelings and needed to make things right.

I wanted to form a time-out sign, but I didn't have enough hands and arms to do it. I probably wouldn't have done it right, anyhow. I've never been fond of sports.

"Joke, Judith," I said. "Horrible, tasteless joke. I can be so thoughtless. Can you ever forgive me?" As far as I was concerned, I was prone on the dry, hot ground kissing her dirty, stinky shoes. I couldn't get more humble than that.

Although the tears stopped and a slight smile came to her lips, her blush didn't fade. I'd never seen one last so long. The longer her face stayed red, the worse I felt. I've seen permanent markers come clean faster. Had tears affected her makeup in some weird way that altered her skin color?

"Oh, Kim, how wonderfully Christian you are to forgive me so easily that you can joke about it." Her sincerity was as scary as her awkward-sounding sentence.

How could I free myself from this girl's naive adulation? I didn't want to be overtly offensive, and I didn't want to make her cry anymore. I just wanted to climb off the pedestal before I fell off.

It was taller and scarier than any ladder I'd ever attempted climbing.

I decided to try something extreme. I looked around to make sure nobody would overhear me. I purposely let a mild vulgarism escape. Surely hearing me talk that way would deflate her opinion like dropping a basketball on the point of a nail.

"Kim? You have problems with your language, too? You are so human."

Her over-the-top sincerity made me want to say a much worse word, but I couldn't. Maybe this habit-changing thing was working better than I'd realized.

Lord, what. . . ? Huh? Okay, thanks.

"Judith, you give me too much credit. I'm not mostly saint and slightly human. I'm all human and a weak one most of the time at that. If I were as wonderful as you think, I wouldn't have acted the way I did at orientation, and I would have forgiven everybody on the team without waiting for apologies. Jesus did that when His enemies weren't sorry for their actions. Don't expect me to do that. I can't keep from being hurt and angry when people wrong me.

"Speaking of 'hurt and angry,' Bamb—uh, Judith—I need to beg your forgiveness now. I shouldn't have embarrassed you so thoughtlessly."

She might have been sipping drops of water from the crevices of a wet sponge with a straw the way she appeared to take in the nuances of everything I said. When I finished, she threw her arms around me.

"I don't care what you say, Kim. I still think you're the finest Christian here."

I turned red then. *Lord, please don't let anyone else be under the delusion Judith is under.*

Judith was just one of dozens of team members who, freed now from Aleesha's threat of sermon reruns, stopped to say hi whenever they saw me. Some of them hugged me, and a few apologized again, but most of them said how great it was that we could put our mutual sins behind us.

And nobody else—*thank You, Lord*—tried putting me on a pedestal.

We worked hard that morning, but we spent much of the time building good relationships.

I kept my permanent marker with me at all times. Everybody wanted to sign my cast, and nobody else in Santa María had a marker for that shade of purple.

Thank goodness for my thoughtful emergency room nurse, who'd even given me a spare. She must have had a teenage daughter.

Geoff stopped to hug me, but his embrace wasn't the gentle, innocent, sideways kind Christian males are known for using on their Christian sisters. He clasped both arms around me as if trying to keep me from escaping and squeezed tight, holding his hands flat against my back for a moment.

I was afraid he was going to kiss me. I honestly believe I would have bit him as hard as I could if he had. I had nothing against kissing boys, but. . .

He seemed to enjoy taking advantage of my temporary incapacitation. Although his overly friendly embrace had made my skin crawl, I was too busy with construction activities to dwell on it once I wiggled out of his grasp and giggled as if that's what he'd expected me to do.

I spent most of the morning dividing a barrel of nails into eighteen equal portions—Rob finally came along and told me I didn't actually have to count them. Then I started carting bottled water and small supplies as needed. If I couldn't lug more than five pounds of anything one-armed (three pounds if the load was breakable), at least I was doing something useful.

The other team members agreed.

"Good show, Kim. You're right on time."

"How'd you know we needed that right now?"

"I'm glad we have somebody like you we can count on."

"I can't believe how efficient and responsible you are."

I jotted that last comment down word for word and asked Martha—the girl who'd said it—to sign it.

"Martha, I want to show this to Mom and Dad. They've never said such a thing about me. Not once in their lives. They probably won't believe it."

"Here's my phone number, too," she said with a smile. "If they question you, have them call me."

I wouldn't get a reputation for dependability by accident. I'd have to work hard to earn it. But this was a start.

"As far as the east is from the west. . ."

That's how different today felt from the preceding couple of days. I felt good about being in Santa María. Great, in fact. I hoped the villagers could see the improvement in my attitude— and in everyone else's.

Yet I seemed to wrestle with God every time I prayed, and I prayed a lot while carrying out duties that required no thinking. I humbled myself at the beginning of my prayers only to start complaining about the things God wouldn't let me do.

I wasn't talking about construction, either.

How was I ever going to plant the first gospel seed in Santa María? The communication gap was impossible to bridge. No matter how I might try narrowing the breach, it wasn't going to happen. That realization was an acid eating away at the joy I should have been experiencing.

I'd learned the importance of evangelism earlier in the summer. That was an integral part of every House of Bread ministry.

Although relief work in Santa María was crucial, what would we accomplish of an eternal nature unless we could explain why we, the affluent, cared enough about the welfare of impoverished strangers to give up part of our summer to help them?

Trust and obey. Wasn't that what the old hymn said? I knew all about flexibility, trust, and obedience now.

So when would God give me an assignment to obey? He wouldn't have brought me to Santa María just to sort nails and carry water, no matter how necessary those tasks were.

Or would He?

chapter twenty-nine

On our San Diego "ambulance" ride, Rob made things so right that he became my dad away from home. Much to my amazement, amusement, and mild irritation, he started calling me Kimmy shortly after our return to Santa María. I wouldn't have tolerated such a nickname from anyone else.

Dad would've had a bigger cow about it than me, though. And if he'd named that cow Elizabeth, he wouldn't have let anyone get away with calling her Lizzie, Libby, Bessie, or Beth. If he named his cow Elizabeth, that's what he'd expect people to call her.

I giggled at the thought of my dad and a cow coming within fifty yards of one another.

Rob was thoughtful about Kimmy, though.

"Do you mind if I call you Kimmy, Kimmy?" he asked several hours after he started doing it. His tone of voice told me the question was a mere formality. He'd assumed agreement.

I didn't answer his question. Not directly, that is. "Call me anything you like," I said. Of course, if I'd guessed that the whole team might call me Kimmy, too, I might have expressed my objections.

Might have. But probably not. This seemed important to Rob.

I was probably more gracious about Rob's nickname because Dad didn't have a pet name for me. Although Mom frequently called me wiggleworm, Dad never addressed me once as baby girl or sweetie, much less princess, munchkin, or kitten.

Betsy Jo's dad still called her doodlebug, although it embarrassed the daylights out of her. She didn't understand why I'd envied that when we were younger, and I didn't tell her I still did.

Of course, when Dad was angry about my carelessness, he didn't hesitate to address me as Kimberly Leigh. Ugh. Why had he insisted on an "l-y Leigh" name? That sometimes made me feel redundant.

I still remembered conversations from my youth when Mom and I attempted a verbal Mission Impossible.

"Dad, would you please call me Kim instead of Kimberly? My friends do. My teachers do. Everybody at church does, including the preacher, the choir director, and Pastor Ron. I don't know if you've noticed this or not, but Mom has called me Kim since I was little."

"You can't fight a tidal wave." Mom smiled at Dad.

That's what Barbra Streisand said to Ryan O'Neal in that great old movie *What's Up, Doc?* Mom may not have been an actress, but she could come up with a movie line for almost any occasion. She was even better quoting relevant scripture verses.

"But Kimberly is your name," Dad said, as if those five words settled everything.

His response had to start with *but*. That's how he was. I wasn't sure he'd even listened to Mom.

"We named you after your great-aunt Kimberly," he said, as if he hadn't belabored the point a million times already. "She didn't go by Kim. She insisted on Kimberly, and you should, too."

An old-fashioned response like that from an intelligent, well-educated, forty-four-year-old didn't fit.

Or maybe it did. Dad acted older than his years, especially

regarding life in general—that meant most of the time.

Maybe rearing me had aged him faster than it did Mom.

"Dad, I understand about Great-Aunt Kimberly, and it's wonderful you named me after her. What a tribute to her long years of missionary service in South America. But it's such a, uh, formal-sounding name for a teen today. I'll bet even Aunt Kimberly would prefer Kim if she were part of today's generation. Things are so much faster paced now. People don't have time to say Kimberly anymore."

"She's got a point, Scott," Mom chimed in.

I admired her fearless, straightforward yet nonaggressive approach. Mine was generally full speed ahead through the china shop.

"Several points, in fact," Mom added. "Times change."

Then she dropped the subject. Although she was still on my side, she knew when to stop. She would back off and try again—often successfully—at a more appropriate time. If I ignored the danger signs and forged ahead—as I tended to do—I was apt to lose both the battle and the war.

But teens are supposed to be impatient. When we're patient, grown-ups think we're either sick or trying to pull something over on them. And if we're patient several times in a row, we risk having them think we've matured so much they can expect us to act like that all the time.

I've learned over the years that people aren't apt to respond the way we want when we badger them. Not oldsters or midlifers. Not teenagers. So maybe Mom's tidal wave quotation was a warning for me to back off and not just a hint to Dad that continued resistance would be useless.

Changing my dad into a periodic Kim-ist took a number of years. And a number of additional tidal waves.

When Dad said Kim, he sounded like someone butchering an unknown word in an unfamiliar language. Although he'd made progress, Kim didn't roll off his tongue as naturally as Kimmy from Rob's. Maybe I was making too much out of it, but I'd prayed about it more than once in Santa María.

At least Dad had called me Kim when I phoned him and Mom from San Diego, and he'd sounded comfortable doing it.

chapter thirty

Oh, no! Here he comes again.

"Geoff, how do you always manage to be where I am?"

I smiled and tried to be pleasant, but I knew that mathematical probability wouldn't explain his constant appearances. That kind of maneuvering required premeditation and plenty of advance planning.

"You're just lucky, I guess."

Not "I'm just lucky," but "You're just lucky." He didn't sound like he was trying to be cute. Oh, well, a little conceit didn't make him a terrible person.

Although his frequent appearances flattered me at first, they soon grew unsettling. I'm a hugger by nature; but after that earlier incident, I got in the habit of rebalancing my load so he couldn't hug me every time he saw me—not without my bashing, mashing, or puncturing him.

"Fancy running into you here," I said with a giggle after knocking him breathless with the plank I held precariously under my good arm. My left one. I'm right-handed. "Oh, I'm sorry!" I said as insincerely as I could.

"Here, let me help you," he said, reaching out to take the board from me. "Your hands are too soft to carry something like that."

"No, Geoff, but thanks for offering," I said with polite determination as I swung the board out of his grasp and hit him in the arm with the other end. "If you do my job for me, I won't accomplish anything in Santa María. I'm Scarlett O'Hara after the Civil War, not before."

My allusion went right over his head. Maybe he was a Yankee.

"I'd feel pampered and useless if I weren't doing something worthwhile, and I didn't pay all this money and fly three thousand miles from home to sit around and be lazy."

He didn't say anything, but his face had one of those "then why didn't you say so in plain English?" looks that are so cute on some guys. But his wasn't cute.

Only guys who accepted *Gone with the Wind* as the best portrait of human nature—after the Bible, of course—fit my mold. Maybe I'd accept a GWTW nonbeliever some day if he was at least a Christian Rhett Butler, although I doubted it.

But he wouldn't be Geoff.

He didn't catch on quickly about my not wanting help. He made a similar offer every time he saw me, which continued throughout that morning. He always coupled it with a compliment about one or more of my body parts.

Although he never said anything overtly improper, I couldn't miss where his thoughts were. Pretending to be tolerant about that was hard enough, but I was also concerned about the amount of work Geoff was shirking by spending the lion's share of his time prowling for me.

Surely that disgusted and perhaps angered his teammates, too.

The only positive thing I could still say about Geoff was his great looks hadn't changed. Even in my less mature years, though, I cared as much about the internal as I did the external. The revelation of Geoff's true colors had spun my opinion in a one-eighty away from him.

He wasn't a rainbow, but an ugly shade of gray. If I'd ever considered him quite a catch, I now wanted to scramble out of the water before he had any more illusions about catching me. He was too small-minded to be a catcher or a keeper.

I noticed the other girls eyeing him with interest, but he appeared to ignore them. Under other circumstances, I might have felt flattered that he wanted me and not them.

But I could live without any more of Geoff's attention.

I'd learned some tough lessons during my tenderer years. One of the most important was that mission-trip romances distract the guy and the girl and interfere with their involvement in the mission activities. They spend as much free time together as they can and fail to bond with the rest of the team.

Although mission trips should be a time of spiritual and emotional growth, hormones—even properly disciplined hormones—can block the way to more eternal goals. To poorly paraphrase a famous evangelist: On a mission trip, kids are apt to fall in lust, not in love.

And that's not counting the impracticality of maintaining a long-distance relationship afterward. How many mission-trip romances have died from the truth of the song that says something about loving whoever a person's with when he's not with the person he loves?

If Geoff understood the dangers of mission-trip romances, he ignored them. Nothing kept him from using a contemporary version of the caveman-with-a-club method to attract my attention. If I'd met Geoff closer to home; if he'd been slower, subtler, and more subdued in his approach; if he'd shown some genuine interest in me as a person, he would have been irresistible.

Regardless of his low GWTW quotient.

If I had one reason to believe I meant more to him than fresh meat, I might have ignored my observations about mission-trip romances and fallen hard.

But he didn't meet any of my most essential criteria, and I needed to make him understand I wasn't the least interested in him. Until he accepted that, he'd keep misunderstanding me—just as Millie Q. had. He would never believe I wasn't just playing hard to get.

I was impossible to get. For him, anyway.

I might just have to use that caveman club to make him accept my lack of interest. As troublesome as this issue had become, I needed to say something sooner than later, and I already dreaded it.

Boys, especially boys who are as outwardly sure of themselves as Geoff, are still sensitive about their feelings—even if they keep them hidden most of the time—and my Southern belle friendliness had probably encouraged him at first. I hated to admit it even to God, but I'd probably wanted it to.

But that was then. At our initial meeting. Not now, just hours into my first real workday in Santa María.

I hadn't done anything else to encourage him. And now I needed to discourage him without rejecting him as a person. I was probably hoping for too much.

A club blow to the skull would make any guy feel rejected.

chapter thirty-one

W hen's lunch?" I asked Aleesha later that morning in passing.

"You missed hearing that? We don't have set mealtimes around here. When we get hungry, we stop and eat. There's plenty of food. Just not plenty of variety. Same menu morning, noon, and night. Probably the same every day, too."

"And nobody complains?"

"Everybody's too tired to."

"Even—?"

"Well, no, not Geoff." She chortled. "At lunch yesterday while you were in San Diego enjoying pizza,"—I smirked—"I heard him say, 'Not this stuff again. We just had this for breakfast.' Of course, he doesn't seem to get worn out like everyone else."

We giggled.

The snacks inside the so-called church apparently never changed, either. I'd never thought of flexibility as a willingness to endure the unchanging. Not until now.

By midmorning, I discovered how hot the mess tent tables got. I wouldn't have to do without hot food altogether. Just at breakfast when I most wanted and needed it.

I ate beef jerky like it was going out of style. I couldn't get enough of it. Why didn't Mom ever buy any? Then I remembered Dad's often strange attitudes and dismissed my question as both irrelevant and unanswerable.

After all, if Dad didn't like a food—or if he merely disliked the smell of it, the name of it, or even one of its least important ingredients—Mom never bought or served it.

He applied the same irrationality to movies, TV programs, concerts, restaurants, cars, vacation destinations, clothing styles, Bible translations—the list would reach the moon.

Maybe Mars.

I often wondered how Mom could be so patient with Dad's prejudices, but the apostle Paul answered that question two thousand years ago. Love overlooks a multitude of quirks—that's how I always read it—and Dad's quirks were probably minor compared to some men's.

Dad had an OCD—obsessive-compulsive disorder—uncle. Now he had quirks galore. No amount of love would have enabled Mom to put up with them. Come to think of it, maybe that's why Uncle Isaac remained a bachelor for life.

When Aleesha and I crossed paths again an hour or so after our previous meeting, we made a date to get together for lunch at noon.

One of the girls on team 3 had thoughtfully offered me a super-faded denim tote bag so I could manage everything single-handedly. I hugged her when she told me to keep it. I had an idea about using the bag to carry some pebbles home for an object lesson at church. In the meantime, it would be a big help in toting small items to the worksites. Things like snacks and water bottles.

The blond part of my brain hadn't caught on at first why we kept water inside the church building. The temp there was almost as hot as outside. And because the water came in sealed, individual-serving-sized bottles—I snobbishly avoided that particular brand at home, but learned to relish it here—it wasn't going to evaporate.

Then it struck me—duh!—that this building was the only shaded area in the whole village. Hence it was the only place where the intense sunlight wouldn't superheat the drinking water to temperatures we could make tolerable coffee with.

Rob and Charlie wanted everyone out of the sun during their water breaks. At first the villagers had balked at the idea of going inside the ancient building. Just as I'd noticed from the bus the day before, they acted like they were terrified of it. Terrified and maybe even superstitious. But when they saw us keep going in and out without suffering any ill effects, their faces lit up in amazement and they followed our lead, though quite cautiously at first.

Being out of the sun for even a few minutes at a time was necessary. After a single morning outside, I could already see my skin darkening. Olivia, the blond who'd spoken out several times recently, had started out morbidly pale and burned horribly the first day. Although I sympathized with her, I couldn't avoid smiling at the thought of her returning home with a universe of freckles dotting her face, arms, and shoulders like a galaxy of stars.

She thanked me repeatedly for the use of lotion from my mostly useless cosmetics collection. Such sharing was a small act of kindness, but I enjoyed helping my fellow team members any way I could.

I cared about them. And not just about my fellow team members, but about the villagers, too. Especially the villagers.

If I'd cared about the migrant children I worked with to an unrealistic extent, I thought—at least I hoped—I had a healthier approach for helping the villagers of Santa María. If not a healthier approach, at least a more realistic attitude.

My cheapie watch read 11:57 by the time I reached the mess tent. Aleesha hadn't arrived yet. Rather than wait, I threw some beef jerky, canned peaches, green beans, and an almost-liquid chocolate bar into my denim bag and headed into the church for a couple of bottles of warm-but-wet water.

I picked my way among a few badly broken, handmade-looking wooden chairs; a small, rectangular, mahogany-finished table about the size of a communion table; and what looked like an eighty- or ninety-year accumulation of dust—breathing it was probably unhealthier than breathing the hot air outside—to reach the open boxes of water bottles. Whatever this building had been, it didn't resemble a church inside, and the villagers apparently hadn't used it in ages for anything.

Aleesha was approaching the church as I came out. Several lunch items nearly slipped from her hands, but she managed to hold up a forefinger. . .be back in a minute. When she came outside again, she had a full water bottle under one arm and another she'd already drained two-thirds dry.

I had two bottles, too. One was never enough in this heat. I hadn't opened them yet, though, but I was tempted to pour some on my head when I did. I didn't know if that would damage my cast, though.

"Wha's up, girl?" Aleesha greeted me, water dribbling down her chin.

"Up? I'm up, girl. I've been up ever since you got me up at dawn today."

"Ha. You should've heard yourself snoring this morning."

"I slept much better last night than the night before. But where'd that sleeping bag, pillow, and air mattress come from? I was too out of it to ask earlier. I hope nobody gave those things up for me." I would have felt horrible if someone had voluntarily made herself miserable to make me involuntarily comfortable.

"Kim, my sermon should've made everyone offer you a little of what they had. But Mr. Rob played Santa this time. He bought you a real sleeping bag."

"It smelled wonderfully fresh and new." No mothball scent, either.

"He also bought you an inflatable pillow similar to mine. And you must have complained a lot yesterday; he got an air mattress to keep his 'princess' from feeling any more 'peas' on this pebbly ground."

"He didn't have to do that. Any of that."

"Don't tell him that. He went to a lot of trouble finding an army surplus store. Just say thanks. He also bought you a small flashlight, extra batteries, and—would you believe?—a number of packages of plastic litter box liners. He cracked me up by pointing out they'd accomplish the same thing as using the shovel, but would be easier to use single-handed."

So that's what I'd found beside my sleeping bag. I'd put a couple of them in my pocket without knowing what they were for.

"You've got to be kidding me. He really loosened up some yesterday, but that. . . ?"

"You two didn't get back until well after dark last night, and—man!—did you both have pizza on your breath. Anyhow, you fell asleep on the bus coming back—"

"No wonder! Between being worn out the night before, full from an early supper, and knocked out by the codeine I took shortly after leaving the ER, I couldn't have stayed awake coming back if I'd tried."

"That's what Mr. Rob said. He was so cute sneaking into the girls' field and making sure he didn't see anything he shouldn't and finding me and asking me to help get you situated. He showed me the stuff he'd bought for you. He purposely kept it a secret. He wanted to surprise you. We left you on the bus while we set up the air mattress and put the sleeping bag on top. You should have seen us trying to tote those things to our sleepsite without tripping."

I couldn't keep from laughing.

"Then I borrowed your borrowed blanket to smooth out a small hole under my sleeping bag. Girl, did you ever notice the smell of mothballs in that thing? The stink kept me awake forever till I finally pulled the blanket out and threw it downwind."

I treated Aleesha's mothball question as rhetorical, although I had trouble keeping from giggling at her. Implying that the smell hadn't bothered me was delicious fun.

"We brought you to your renovated sleepsite—you never woke up the whole time—dumped you into your new bedding, and zipped you in. Mr. Rob checked the directions on the prescription and woke you just enough to give you more."

"Is that why I've felt so dopey this morning?"

Aleesha cackled. "Haven't you ever been drunk, girl?"

I wasn't sure if she was serious or not. But in my innocence—or was it my lack of opportunity?—I could've been mildly offended if I'd let myself be.

"No," I retorted gently. Then I added in a robotic voice that emphasized each syllable equally, "People in my church do not drink. Not in front of other church members, that is." I wanted to throw in, "Christians shouldn't need alcohol to have a good time," but decided that kind of self-righteousness was uncalled for, even though I thought it was true.

"Uh-huh," she said with obvious disbelief after laughing at my antics. "And I believe in Santa Bunny and the Easter Claus." She looked at me and narrowed her eyes. "But that's okay. Really okay."

Those last five words expressed an amazing acceptance of a naiveté that must have seemed foreign to her. Or maybe she'd stereotyped me because of other white girls she knew, only to land in a quandary when she discovered how different I was.

"Kim," she whispered confidentially, "I've never tasted liquor myself—I can't stand the smell—but don't tell anybody. That would ruin my rough 'n' tough reputation."

I smiled as I made a lip-zipping motion with my left thumb and forefinger.

"Anyhow, we had a whale of a time waking you enough to swallow those pills, but they got you through the night."

"Did they ever! And halfway through this morning, too. I thought I was hallucinating when the kids started showing me they'd learned something from your sermon. You're a miracle worker, gal!"

Aleesha sat there grinning from ear to ear.

"Oh, man!" I snapped my fingers.

"What, girl?"

"We spent hours in San Diego yesterday. Rob did all that shopping and didn't once suggest buying work clothes."

She shook her head. "Men."

I couldn't complain, though. I hadn't thought to ask him.

chapter thirty-two

Aleesha and I weren't intentionally sitting by ourselves, but nobody else had passed by yet. We'd done a good job so far of avoiding cliquishness.

I was barely conscious of the young village girl who'd maneuvered discreetly into a spot three or four yards away, and I doubt that the sudden appearance of a space alien would have startled me any more than the discovery that she was staring at me intently. Her laughter at seeing me jump sounded weak. Perhaps shy.

She was probably eight or nine, although I wasn't experienced at guessing children's ages. I was more interested in her long black hair, smooth light brown skin, and dark brown eyes that didn't seem to miss anything that was going on.

I motioned slightly to Aleesha and pointed to the girl while she was looking away. When the youngster turned toward us again, Aleesha and I waved our hands and smiled. Whether she was scared or still embarrassed, I couldn't tell, but she didn't wave back. She looked down at the ground for a minute before raising her head again to see if we were watching.

We were.

I scrunched my nose, crossed my eyes, and gave her a goofy-looking grin. This time she giggled the way only children can. Those giggles broke the ice—or cracked it slightly, anyhow.

I waved again. Although she barely moved her hand, she waved back. Aleesha and I motioned for her to come closer and join us. She looked around as if seeking approval from an absent parent, but her curiosity must have been stronger than any instructions her mother might have given her. She rose to her feet in a single flowing motion.

That's when I noticed her arm.

Before I could point it out, though, Aleesha excused herself to visit the facilities and return to work.

"You want a litter box liner?" I said, and she cracked up. But when I pulled one from my shirt pocket like a magician pulling an endless kerchief from his hat and held it out, she took it.

"Rrrowww! Rrrowww!"

Sounding more like a tomcat at midnight than a lady cat at noon, she meowed all the way across the field.

I shouldn't have stared, but I couldn't take my eyes off that little girl's right arm, which stopped just shy of where an elbow should have been. If someone amputated her forearm, the skin had recovered remarkably well. But it looked too smooth—too perfect—to result from amputation. As if I had any medical knowledge to base my opinion on.

She'd probably been born that way.

Either she hadn't caught me glancing at her arm or she'd gotten so used to thoughtless staring that she no longer cared. If I saw my team members gazing at my cast, I knew their sympathetic stares were as temporary as my incapacity.

But this little girl's condition wasn't going to change. Whether a doctor in San Diego could fit her with a prosthetic arm, I didn't know, but Santa María seemed to be on the opposite side of the world from San Diego.

Or maybe on a different planet.

How I longed to talk with this youngster, but our separate languages made that impossible. How could I even learn her name?

I pointed at the ground to my left, the spot Aleesha had

deserted a moment earlier. The little girl sat down with a remarkably graceful motion.

"*Buenos días.*" Her voice was so quiet I almost missed hearing her.

"Hi!" I answered cheerfully, uncertain how she'd respond to my English.

"Hi!" she responded clearly enough, although with some uncertainty.

Could this young girl possibly know a little English? With a false sense of hope, I continued.

"My name is Kim. What's yours?"

Her face went blank, and it struck me that hi was a simple word—obviously a greeting—to parrot back. Her English was as limited as my Spanish.

I repeated my question in French. I hoped my frustration hadn't shown.

Her light brown face wrinkled and her eyes narrowed in confusion.

Definitely no French spoken in Santa María. But I already knew that. Why did I keep trying?

I pointed to myself. "Kim," I said. "My name is Kim." It was tough not saying extra words as if she might magically comprehend them.

"Kim," I said as I pointed to myself again. Then I pointed to her and said, "You. Who are you?"

I might as well have been quoting Shakespeare in Sanskrit. I lost heart quickly. After all, my generation expected instant gratification, and my inability to communicate with this little girl was anything but instantly gratifying.

"Kim," I pointed to myself once more. I unconsciously wrote my name in the dirt with a stick as I repeated it. I didn't expect a response, but I couldn't give up. Not yet.

"Keem," she said clearly but hesitantly after looking at

my name on the ground. She pointed at me. "Keem," she said once again.

"Yes, yes! That's it! You have it! I'm Kim."

Once more, she couldn't understand the rest of my words, but she understood my praise perfectly, and her smile grew bolder.

"Keem," she repeated. "*Señorita* Keem."

Señorita? I knew that meant "Miss." Everyone knows that. Even people who study French for four years in high school and don't have one Hispanic friend know that. Using it with my name showed that she'd made a logical connection.

I was so excited I could barely sit still. I pointed at myself once more and said, "Señorita Kim." Then I pointed at her and said, "And you are. . . ?"

She looked unsure of herself at first, but then her eyes brightened.

"Mey YAH-mah Ahn-heh-LEE-tah."

She pointed to herself before gently pulling the stick from my hand and writing Anjelita in the dirt beneath Kim. Then she pointed to me again and said, "Señorita Keem."

Ah! So J *in Spanish is pronounced like* H *in English. What other differences are there? Good thing I'll never need to pronounce any Spanish. I'd never catch on.*

Anxious to keep this learning activity going, I went through the same routine myself. "Anjelita." I pointed to her. "Señorita Kim." I pointed to myself.

We took turns doing that for several minutes. I'd never experienced such a joyous learning breakthrough before, no matter how minor it might have seemed to someone else.

I decided to try something more daring. Anjelita seemed bright enough. Maybe I could make one more connection in this language lesson before returning to work.

"*Amigo*," I said, unaware that I was using the masculine

word form. I pointed in the direction Aleesha had gone. Anjelita looked like she might be catching on, but I must've confused her when I said, "Aleesha. My amigo."

Although she looked unsure of herself for a moment, Anjelita didn't strike me as a child who'd let a puzzle stump her long. "Oh! *Amiga*. . .Aleesha."

Was this pretty, young lady correcting me—me her elder, me the high school graduate, me the American who looked slightly Latina—on one of those Spanish words everyone knows? I would hope so. She was the Spanish speaker here, not me. At least I knew now that the word pronounced *oh* means the same thing in both languages.

"Uh, *sí*, amiga. Aleesha."

"Aleesha *es tu* amiga." Her smile was radiant.

I wasn't sure what she'd said, but I felt terrific that we'd connected again.

I looked at my wristwatch for the first time in quite a while—that same cheapie watch that had caused such problems at DFW. An hour and a half had passed since I stopped for lunch. The time had passed too quickly, especially since meeting Anjelita.

Although I didn't want to stop talking—"wording"—with Anjelita, I needed to return to work. Learning as much as I could from Anjelita would be great fun, but I couldn't master enough Spanish between now and the end of next week to share the gospel with the villagers, and that was bugging the. . . blazes out of me.

Once I'd taken the orientation lesson about faith, obedience, and flexibility to heart, I accepted construction as my official role in Santa María. We had to provide for the villagers' physical needs first.

But evangelism was still my passion. God had to want these villagers in His family, and I couldn't believe He'd bring a team like ours to Santa María without providing some way to share His Good News. But how?

I sat with my legs stretched out in front of me. To get up, I would have to lean on my good arm and maneuver onto my knees, being careful not to land on a rock. Although I didn't see her that time, Anjelita was so nimble she made it to her feet before I could roll to my knees.

Ah, sweet youth.

"*Adiós,* Anjelita," I said with a smile, assuming she'd go off somewhere to play. Adult company had to be boring by now.

Although I'd seen other children playing together that morning, I couldn't remember seeing Anjelita with them. Had she been doing something else at the time or was she avoiding them?

Would they have been avoiding her? Surely not.

Anjelita didn't run off. She followed me to the area where the materials stood in neat, efficient stacks. I started grabbing an eight-foot 2 x 2, one I should have known better than to try lifting by myself. Before I knew what was happening, Anjelita took the other end and somehow tucked it beneath her good arm. Grateful for her help, I motioned with my head in the direction we needed to go, and together we bore our burden toward its destination.

We'd gone only a few yards when Geoff appeared out of nowhere.

"You've already got a kid here, Kim? You need to be more careful about who you have fun with." Although he smiled and spoke in a pleasant enough tone, I didn't care for the implications. The more I saw of Geoff and the more he said to me, the less certain I was about his goals or his motivation. He didn't scare me, but I wouldn't be surprised if such a time eventually came.

I found it curious that he didn't offer to help this time. It was the first time he didn't.

chapter thirty-three

After delivering the 2 x 2 to the team that requested it, I motioned to Anjelita to follow me to the girls' field. She hadn't been to our campsite before. I changed into the work clothes I'd received that morning. I meant to do it during lunchtime, but forgot in the excitement of meeting Anjelita.

Because the guys were supposed to stay far from the girls' field and no one—no one but Rob, that is—had dared to break the rule, I didn't feel self-conscious about changing clothes in an open field in broad daylight. Who could see through the ring of tall cacti, anyhow?

Nonetheless, I kept an almost-constant eye on the "doorway" that led back toward the church.

I must have turned beet red when I noticed Anjelita watching me. Watching? She was staring. Intently. I don't know what kind of underwear the women of Santa María wore, but Anjelita had apparently never seen any like mine. I finished dressing as fast as I could.

Because of my petiteness, the offer of safety pins had proven fortunate. Those jeans wouldn't have stayed up without help—lots of it. I could've worn the shirt by itself as a modest dress. Someone had loaned me a pair of cheapie sneakers. They were several sizes too big, but I cut some cloth off the pants I'd ruined the first night and padded the inside of the shoes. Not regulation preppy footwear.

And not adequate, either.

I finally tried wearing three pairs of heavy socks at the same time. My feet stayed sweaty—in Santa María, all of everybody stayed sweaty—but between the socks and the super-efficient Velcro fasteners on the sneakers, I managed to keep them on my feet.

I stuck an ink pen and small notepad in the shirt pocket so I could jot down my assignments rather than risk trusting anything—no matter how small—to my too-often leaky memory.

Even though I felt more strongly than ever that I should evangelize the villagers in some way only God knew about, I took my minor role in construction seriously. I would be faithful and do whatever my teammates needed me to do. Dependability was the best way to thank them for accepting me now.

Anjelita and I wound our way through the girls' field. Although pieces of loose trash had begun blowing away from the lanes between the sleeping bags, we still had to be careful making our way toward the door for fear of tripping. At least we wouldn't fall on anyone in broad daylight. Everyone was busy at work, and no one would have attempted to siesta in the afternoon sun.

I could hardly wait to see the look on my parents' faces when I arrived home and began demonstrating my dependability. Maybe that would be just one part of a brand-new me. I smiled, knowing how much this trip had already changed me. And this was still just the third day.

I fell into silent prayer as we walked.

Lord, You've blessed me in so many ways. Thank You for Mom and Dad and the way they've kept after me to grow up and especially for letting me come on this trip. Help Dad to quit being so uptight, and help me to understand him better. Thank You for Betsy Jo and Aleesha, the two best friends a girl could ever hope for. Thank You for Rob and Charlie and their lessons about faith, obedience, and flexibility. Thank You for making Rob my substitute father and for his wonderful examples of forgiveness. Thank You for all of the other team members, and please forgive me for judging them so harshly.

Also, forgive me for my unloving attitude toward Millie Q. and for this horrid cursing habit. Keep me aware that others may judge You by how I act and what I say. Thank You especially for bringing Anjelita into my life. Help me to be the best example I can be. Lord, You know how impatient I am about doing evangelism. I want all of the villagers to become Your children, yet I can't see any way that's going to happen. Help me to wait patiently. Help me to be more faithful, flexible, and obedient. In Your most loving name, I pray. Amen.

I didn't realize I'd said amen aloud until I saw Anjelita's eyes scrunch up in a puzzled look. But then she said it, too. I couldn't tell whether she was mimicking me to learn another English word or if amen was the same in both languages and she said it because it was familiar.

Then again, Rob and Charlie had said they didn't think the villagers knew anything about prayer. They'd even crossed themselves before praying only to see blank looks on the villagers' faces. I had no reason to think them wrong.

I sighed and took out my pad and ink pen. I scribbled some of the Spanish words Anjelita had taught me. Especially the names of the villagers she'd begun pointing out to me.

I didn't spell anything correctly. I didn't try to. Using a well-practiced system of phonetic spelling I'd developed in high school, I could write down any word the way I heard it and practice saying it until I had it down cold. Even if I'd had access to a Spanish dictionary, I never would have found the words on my list, for I had no idea how Spanish spelling and pronunciation worked. Except for the letter *J*, that is.

Even though French and Spanish are vaguely similar— they're both Romance languages—their differences frustrated me as much as their similarities fascinated me.

Anjelita and I formed a unique team that afternoon, each of us doing half a person's work to accomplish a whole person's task. If I carried the bucket of nails, she brought the hammer. If I brought extra water for a team, she carried some snacks. If a board or tool was too heavy for one of us, we picked it up together.

She was a high-output dynamo—I could barely keep up with her at times—and as cheerful and cooperative as any child could have been. Although she couldn't complain in words I understood, I would've recognized whining.

She didn't whine, though, and I didn't expect her to. After all, she was more of a volunteer than I was. She could stop working anytime she wanted, say adiós, and go play or take a siesta. She had to know of a shady spot somewhere.

But she didn't stop. She offered help freely and never attempted to withhold it.

"Anjelita, where have you been all my life? I've always wanted a kid sister. Now I have one. You're sweet and adorable—not spoiled rotten like me—and I thank God for bringing you into my life."

She looked up at me and smiled as if she understood every word. Her unconditional love melted me. She probably wasn't a Christian, yet she acted more like one than a couple of the kids in the youth group back home.

God couldn't have matched the two of us any better. Anjelita was quiet when I was quiet. She chattered away when I was more talkative, even though our conversations were exchanges of nonsense. She laughed when I laughed, and she whistled, hummed, or sang whenever I did. If one of us wiped the sweat from the other's face, the recipient returned the favor.

She would be my shadow as long and as often as her

parents permitted her to be. That thought thrilled me. *Would God somehow use her in witnessing to the other villagers?*

As much as I hoped so, I couldn't imagine it.

chapter thirty-four

During midafternoon, the other five children of Santa María approached us. They scooted in where we could almost touch them and scampered away again as if making a game of escaping before we could catch them. Although they looked apprehensive when they came near, they giggled loudly once they got safely out of reach.

Their game didn't puzzle me as much as their apparent lack of interest in joining us.

While regrouping for another "attack," they stared at us. Although I couldn't interpret their looks, I wondered if the sisterly relationship between Anjelita and me had somehow elevated their opinion of her.

But no, that interpretation didn't fit the uneasiness in their glances.

Something had heightened their interest in Anjelita, though. Perhaps the fact she had gained the affection of this American stranger and not them. Although they continued their mock raids, curious looks came to replace apprehensive ones.

Anjelita set her load down, and her eyes urged me to do the same. After I complied, she patted my cast lovingly with her only hand. Then she touched the stub of her missing arm. She seemed to want the five "normal" kids to notice what the two of us had in common. And maybe recognize that physical problems didn't limit our need for acceptance.

None of the villagers—children or adults—could have missed seeing the team's acceptance of me. My broken arm didn't bother them. If anything, it had become a symbol of faithful determination.

I thought we were making some progress with the kids. But then Anjelita and I caught the oldest girl—she looked like she might have been eleven or twelve—staring at her while we took a water break at the church later that afternoon. Like a child with a dare she couldn't refuse, the youngster came closer and shouted, "*Maldita!*" at Anjelita. She tripped over her own feet trying to back away to safety and fell to the ground.

She trembled from head to toe. Although I wondered at first if she was having a seizure, I concluded that terror had overwhelmed her and left her powerless to escape.

Anjelita approached her. I thought she was going to help the fallen child up.

But she snapped at the older girl with such rage that the other children ran off, leaving their friend behind. "Crista, *no soy* maldita!" Anjelita screamed those words repeatedly as if she couldn't get them out of her system: "No soy maldita!"

The strength and depth of her venom shocked and terrified me. When she quieted down again, I held her close and wiped the tears away with my shirtsleeve. She'd never seemed quite as small and vulnerable before.

I remembered that she'd preceded her first "No soy maldita!" with another word, one that sounded like KREES-tuh. I was afraid she'd used Jesus' name in vain until I remembered my lesson about amigo and amiga. KREES-tuh had a feminine ending, so she wasn't saying Christ.

Maybe KREES-tuh was the name of the girl who'd angered Anjelita and still lay cowering on the ground.

Mahl-DEE-tuh. What is mahl-DEE-tuh? That word—or was it several short words grouped together?—sounded vaguely familiar, yet I couldn't place it. Not unless. . .wait. It sounded ever so vaguely like *maudite*, which was French for. . .

for what? I'd learned hundreds, maybe thousands of French words in high school. How could I make myself remember this one?

Instead of frustrating myself further, I let my mind go blank for a moment, and the answer came almost immediately.

Cursed! Maudite meant "cursed"! Maybe mahl-DEE-tuh did, too. That made sense. If that bratty Crista had accused Anjelita of being cursed, then. . .of course. "No soy maldita"— Anjelita must have told her, "No, I'm not cursed!"

Where would a child get the idea that someone as precious as Anjelita was cursed, anyhow? That question required amazingly little thought.

As limited as my past contact with kids was, I knew American children tend to repeat what they hear at home. Whether that was also true in Santa María's culture, I didn't know, but where would a child acquire such cruel attitudes except from the most important adults in her life?

Or from other children who're quoting their most important adults.

If I was right about parental prejudices infecting their children's attitudes toward Anjelita, why did they feel that way?

She was just a child—a normal child, as far as I could tell, in every way but one. Surely the villagers didn't think her missing arm was a sign of being cursed. Such a barbaric idea belonged in biblical times, not now.

And yet—as Pastor Ron had pointed out on numerous occasions—the world was probably no less barbaric now than in Jesus' day.

So why should I be shocked to discover that people still equated misfortune with punishment? Punishment can affect the innocent as much as it does the guilty. Sometimes more. What sin did the villagers think little Anjelita was being punished for? Who had committed it, and when?

And if they didn't believe in the God I knew, loved, and served, who did they think was doing the punishing?

Once more, I fretted about the villagers' spiritual needs. My heart ached for them to know and love my God. But without any knowledge of Spanish, reaching them would require a miracle equivalent to the parting of the Red Sea. God hadn't provided a Spanish-speaking Aaron to translate for me, and I didn't think He would.

Although I would keep looking for a way to witness to the villagers, the immediate need was changing the children's attitude toward Anjelita. If I could reach them, they might reach their parents. If my theories were correct, that is.

I reached into my jeans pocket for a small container of acetaminophen. I'd browbeaten myself into a medium-sized headache dwelling on deeper issues than I normally think about. I looked at the ground where Crista was still cowering. She hadn't moved. Petrified by fear, she hadn't attempted to escape. My angry glare bound her as securely as a ship's rope.

Crista couldn't take her eyes off my cast. Maybe she thought I was permanently disabled, too. She probably had vivid images of horrendous injuries beneath my cast, or maybe she thought the cast itself was the injury. Covered with vivid purple and written all over, it must have looked horrible to someone who didn't know what it was.

Despite my anger—or perhaps because of it—God began nudging me. *Lord, no! You don't expect me to be this flexible, do You?*

I knew the answer before I asked, though.

Although I was still hugging Anjelita, I freed my good arm and beckoned Crista to join us. She didn't respond. Her face was dripping with sweat—and probably not just from the heat.

Anjelita must have thought I was crazy to act friendly toward Crista, but we looked into one another's eyes as we'd done so often that day, and I want to believe she saw God's love there, even though she didn't understand it.

I said in a near whisper, "It's all right now, Anjelita."

And it was. Anjelita smiled at me and then turned to Crista and motioned for her to come join us. She didn't hesitate this time.

During a prolonged three-way hug, I let Crista—I encouraged her to—examine my cast. She'd apparently never seen one before.

Then came the moment of truth. Anjelita extended her stub to Crista and, after what sounded like a bit of gentle coaxing, Crista touched it so lightly with one finger that she probably didn't ruffle a single feathery hair on Anjelita's arm. She ran her hand over the smooth skin on the stub and then examined Anjelita's upper arm.

She held her own arm up for a closer look, apparently comparing it with Anjelita's, and her eyes opened wide with fascination. I could almost read her mind. "Duh! Is this all we've been afraid of?"

After hugging Anjelita with both arms, Crista kissed her cheek and started to leave. But then she came back and kissed me, too. When she scampered off, her step was light.

Moments later, all of the children returned. Whether they would accept Anjelita now, I couldn't say, but at least the fear had disappeared.

With the confidence of an experienced teacher, Anjelita carefully taught me each child's name. After pronouncing a name slowly and distinctly, she made me repeat it until I got it right.

Of course, with my Georgia drawl, a mind soaked to capacity in the rules of high school French, and a little stumbling over my own words, I couldn't say how right "right" was. Maybe that's why my efforts to master the kids' names tickled them so much.

Even Anjelita laughed with them.

Although she seemed willing to share me with these would-be friends, she was determined to control our interaction. When Estéban and Felicita tried to get my attention and tell me something without going through Anjelita, she shook her head, her long dark hair blowing this way and that in the breeze, and said no along with other words she spoke too quickly for me to jot down.

I understood *mi amiga*, though—*my friend*. Anjelita wanted to be the children's only means of access to me. If I'd been God, she would have insisted on being the high priest. That didn't surprise me as much as it disturbed me.

These children may have given up believing Anjelita was cursed, but they didn't argue when she said no. They jumped back as if being near her was like sitting on a treetop during a thunderstorm.

But she always smiled again. Soon. The danger was past. The children resumed whatever they'd been doing, their apprehensions forgotten. I hoped these incidents would soon lessen in frequency and severity.

Close to suppertime, Anjelita ran to greet a village woman I hadn't noticed before. They smiled, kissed, hugged, and giggled. The "and what have you been doing with my daughter?" look she gave me wasn't exactly a stare, but it didn't contain a single detectable hint of warmth.

I recognized my name in the conversation between Anjelita and her mother. I didn't see anyone around who might be her father, though; I wondered if he'd died in the tornado. She dragged her mom over to where I was waiting, pointed to her, and announced, "Señora Rosa."

Wanting to show Rosa how pleased I was to meet her, even if she didn't feel the same way, I walked forward to hug her. But she backed up as if trying to avoid physical contact. I stopped as if I'd encountered a police roadblock.

Her reaction didn't bother me at first. I knew other people who didn't hug strangers. Nonetheless, I came from a family, a church, a whole town full of huggers; and no one remained a stranger long. The women hugged one another. The children not only hugged but pecked one another on the cheeks, grown woman style. Even the men were as apt to hug one another with a masculine clasp as they were to shake hands. They often did both.

The more I thought about it, the more Rosa's reaction drained the joy from my heart like water dripping from a soggy paper cup. In my head, I knew better than to take it personally, even though my heart didn't always listen to my head.

But more than rejecting a harmless hug, Rosa seemed indifferent about—perhaps *resistant to* was more accurate— meeting me and learning my name. Had I unwittingly gotten into the middle of a family squabble?

Maybe Anjelita had disobeyed her mother by being gone all afternoon and Rosa was blaming me. Yet the way mother and daughter had greeted one another was not the way parents and children act when they're upset.

Despite her dark cloud-covered reaction, Rosa was a beautiful woman in her late twenties or early thirties, and Anjelita looked very much like her—the same perfect skin, dark eyes, and long, shiny hair.

Anjelita rarely stopped smiling, but Rosa hadn't smiled once. Strange.

As friendly as the other villagers had been, my presence apparently pleased them. They acted like I was one of them, and I felt at home. Rosa couldn't have been more the complete opposite.

I wanted to reach out to her—to get closer. Her life story

would be fascinating, especially regarding Anjelita's handicap. But even if by some miracle—and that's what it would take—she grew to accept me, how would I be able to hear it?

My linguistic limitations had become a double curse. I couldn't witness to the villagers, and that was a huge issue. But I couldn't communicate with Anjelita's mom and establish a favorable relationship with her, either.

Despite my best efforts to be warm and pleasant, Rosa was the only unfriendly villager I'd encountered. At least she wasn't openly hostile. And she didn't turn her back on me.

But neither did she show the first small sign of interest.

Maybe she's just cautious around strangers, I tried convincing myself. *Cautious and perhaps scared. I can understand that. I can relate to that. As far off the beaten track as Santa María is, she's probably never seen very many unfamiliar people. Perhaps none before this North American invasion.*

But my ragged feelings rejected the idea. *In that case, why hasn't everyone in Santa María reacted the same way?*

I wondered if Rosa knew Jesus as her personal Savior. While I'd known some truly grumpy Christians—many of them became youth workers—I believed Christians who tried to live in the center of God's will were apt to have a discernable spirit of love, hope, and patience that even the severest hardships—and the most incorrigible of teens—can't destroy.

But I couldn't detect that kind of spirit in Rosa.

Or in Geoff, for that matter.

chapter thirty-five

Charlie approached me after supper when no one else was around. Even though he looked more serious than usual, I was no longer apprehensive about anything he or Rob might say. That was a major improvement over orientation.

"Kimmy. . ." He hesitated, apparently unsure what to say. I stayed quiet and let him think. Only Rob had addressed me by that nickname until now. I hoped the whole team wouldn't start using it.

Lord, I told poor Millie Q. that nobody would ever call me Kimmy. Please give her the grace to forget she ever met me. Boy, would Dad have had a fit if he'd heard Great-Aunt Kimberly's name desecrated that way.

"Kimmy," Charlie said, "we need your advice. There's a small problem."

Oh, fiddle-dee-dee! What's up, Charlie? When I instinctively drew back, I probably looked like one of the children retreating from Anjelita when she said no. That story had made the rounds at supper.

"Don't worry. You haven't done anything wrong. You've been terrific, and everybody has praised your positive spirit and willingness to do the most menial of tasks without fussing. . . ."

Although I should have just said thanks and waited for him to continue, I didn't. Fatigue from my first day's efforts had increased my impatience. I wanted to make him talk faster. But God had some things to say during Charlie's pause.

Be patient, Kim, or I'll start calling you Kimmy. That really got me. *Just listen to the man and wait for him to finish. I didn't give you one mouth and two ears for nothing, you know.*

But I couldn't wait.

Kimmy! God said before I deliberately disobeyed Him.

"I'm happy to do whatever I can," I said. "So what's the 'small problem,' and how can I help?"

"It's that little girl, the one with the missing forearm."

"Anjelita? My little friend?"

"Yes, her. Anjelita."

Charlie pronounced her name accurately. Maybe he'd studied a little Spanish when he was in school.

"What about her? There's nothing wrong with her, is there?"

He shook his head and smiled with unquestionable reassurance.

"She hasn't done anything wrong, has she?"

"Not *wrong* wrong," He sounded like he didn't want to tell the whole truth. "But. . .she's too young to work in the construction area. She's a child, and even the finest children are sometimes, uh, heedless. You couldn't see this, but she caused several nasty near misses this afternoon."

I gasped audibly.

"The team members hesitated to say anything. They know how fond you are of—what'd you say her name is again?— Anjelita and how much fun you have working together. Everybody got a charge out of watching the two of you, but team members had to react quickly several times to protect Anjelita from danger."

"Oh, man! I had no idea. . . ."

"I know. That's why several of the team leads talked to Rob and me. Please understand: They weren't complaining behind your back. They wanted to find a solution without involving you. Their only concern is everyone's safety. Especially Anjelita's."

"I couldn't stand it if something bad happened to that little girl." I wiped my eyes with my sleeve. "I'll be responsible for her safety."

Later that evening I'd remember using the word *responsible* and wonder what my parents would think.

"We knew you'd feel that way. How about stopping her from helping you?"

"Oh, Charlie. . ." I didn't know what to say, but this wasn't the time to quote Barbra Streisand's "You can't stop a tidal wave."

"The question isn't really 'Can you stop her?' It's 'How will you do it?' "

Oh, man! A real tidal wave.

"I don't know much about children, Charlie. I hope she'll prefer playing tomorrow. Maybe her mom won't let her work. That's not good enough, huh?"

"Afraid not."

I knew that as soon as I asked.

Neither of us spoke for a while. The sunset across the fields captivated us. I doubt that I was the only one praying silently with open eyes, mind, and heart. We'd soon need to retire for the night, but we had to solve this problem first. Or have a substantial reason to believe the problem would disappear on its own.

Our silent amens didn't lead to a solution.

"Charlie, I need to sleep on this one. But tell me: What if Anjelita and I worked on something useful outside the construction area, something that has nothing to do with construction?"

"No problem. Construction's going great. Rob is a whiz of an organizer, and most of the team is learning quickly. Some people have more potential than others, but almost everyone is motivated."

I wondered if he was thinking of Geoff when he said "almost everyone."

"At this rate," he said, "the villagers would just have a few minor tasks to finish on their own if things bogged down unexpectedly. And that's a worst-case scenario. We plan to finish their houses before we leave. Everything's under control. In case you got lost in my verbiage, everyone will bless anything you do to keep Anjelita safe."

"Thanks, Charlie. I have an idea, but I need to pray about it. But it's okay to keep Anjelita working as long as it's outside the construction area?"

"Absolutely, Kimmy." He gave me a brotherly Christian hug that made me wonder even more about Geoff. "You have your flashlight with you?" I nodded. "Have a great prayer time and a good night's sleep."

Rather than chance being drawn into conversation in the girls' field, I sat down where I was and began praying. But I must have fallen asleep, because all I remembered when I came to was a strange encounter I'd had with an angel. I didn't think it was a dream, but. . .

"Good evening, Kim. I bring you peace."

"Hello, Angel." I hoped that was an acceptable way to address a heavenly being. It's not like she had wings, a harp, or glowing clothes, though. If anything, she looked like one of the villagers. But she was speaking—or should I say thinking—English to me, and that was supernatural enough.

"God knows your idea for protecting Anjelita," she said.

"Good. Will it work? Is that what He wants me to do?"

"It will keep Anjelita safe."

"Good. But is this what God wants me to do?"

"Kim, do you want me to be honest?"

"As a messenger from God, you can't lie, can you?"

"Touché. I'll tell you the truth. God agrees that your project is important. It will benefit the villagers, but not as much as the task He has in mind for you."

"Oh, I'll gladly set this one aside and do what He wants." My plan was going to take a lot of work. "You know I'm trying to be faithful, flexible, and obedient."

"Kim, you've got a good heart, and you've made a good start, and I like making rhymes when I have the time, but God knows you better than you know yourself."

Was it okay to laugh at an angel? I'd never met one before, and this one was a hoot.

"When you receive your other assignment, you'll think it's impossible. But that's okay. God knows you're not ready for it yet."

I was drenched in sweat now, even though the temperature had already dropped into the sixties. Not ready for my other assignment yet?

"Kim, this has nothing to do with willingness. It has everything to do with relying on God rather than on yourself. You may not realize it, but you're planning to do the first project on your own, and God's going to let you. But you'll have to depend on Him for the big one."

"His project is bigger than mine? I'm not even sure we can finish mine in the time we have."

"You can, Kim, and you will. I won't tell you more about the other one until you're ready. But I promise you'll laugh at the idea."

"Me laugh? I'll never do that."

"That's what Simon Peter said about betraying Jesus."

chapter thirty-six

Day 4

I was glad Aleesha was more awake than I was.

"Are you sure this is the best thing to do with my hair?" I asked. I'd gotten up promptly at dawn, determined to keep my hair from getting grubbier than it already was. I would never get used to stirring up dirt whenever I moved or to sweating constantly.

At home I washed my hair twice a week—occasionally three times—and kept it looking perfect. Referring to the large binder of hair care tricks I'd collected over the years, I never had a bad hair day I couldn't do something about. If one-armedness could be mistaken as God's curse, hair like mine must signify His great favor.

But in Santa María I would go without washing it for two full weeks, and brushing one-handed was nearly impossible. Braiding would help tremendously, but that was a definite two-handed task.

"Yes, ma'am, Miss Kim," Aleesha responded playfully. "I just can't do french braids like you asked me about. You may have noticed I'm not French?"

"You're not from Haiti, Côte d'Ivoire, or Rwanda?"

We both giggled.

"I suppose one of the other girls could help you do a french braid if you want to ask. I won't hold it against you longer than the next fifty years—or until death, whichever comes first."

I ignored her offer to back out. Whatever she did to make my hair easier to deal with would be fine.

"Maybe you should've broken a leg instead of an arm.

Then you could braid it yourself."

Even at dawn when my mind and body resisted wakefulness, Aleesha could make me laugh. "I wouldn't move around or get so hot and sweaty with a broken leg. My hair would still get filthy enough, though. You're sure you can finish before breakfast? I thought something like this took hours, even for more darkly complected, less French-looking girls with shorter hair than mine."

"I never said we'd be the first ones at breakfast today, girl. But this will be the perfect solution. I can work fast when I have to. Besides, I have special shortcuts. They don't always work on our hair, but they'll be fine for yours. I just wish your hair was clean right now."

"You and me both." My sigh probably woke up our nearest neighbors.

"And eighteen inches shorter."

"No way."

"Don't get me talking so much or we'll never get done."

I snorted involuntarily. Aleesha couldn't not talk much.

"Cornrows. Who would ever have thought it?"

"Modified cornrows, mind you. These won't be the real thing, but they'll be the best ones you can get at a beauty shop in the middle of nowhere."

"Be good, Aleesha, and be quiet."

We both giggled. I couldn't tell what she was doing, but Aleesha had proven so multi-talented, I assumed she was equally good at anything she put her mind to. The results would be delightful, not just satisfactory.

Aleesha worked for an amazing ten or fifteen minutes without saying a word. I was quiet, too, except for yelping when she pulled my hair too tight. I felt my confidence level slipping.

"Can I see the mirror? Please?"

"Not yet, girl, but it's lookin' good. You won't get the full effect with a mirror. I'll take several shots with my digital camera when I'm done."

I could kick myself for forgetting to bring my new camera. My parents had given it to me for this trip.

"You'll wish God had made you black for sure then." She winked. "But you still wouldn't be as beautiful as me. Hold your head still."

I shook my head in amazement. Aleesha could morph from serious to silly and back again faster than anyone I've ever known.

"How am I going to live without you when we go home again?" I asked her. "My life is going to be so dull."

"You've got that right," she said. "You remember I have a laptop? I'm big on instant messaging but not so good about answering e-mail."

That admission freed me to admit my irresponsibility about failing to read the project-change messages. She cackled.

"That's about what I would've expected from a black-headed blondie like you. Now hush. You're slowing me down." She jerked my hair again.

After a lengthy period of silence punctuated only by a few yelps on my part and an occasional "whoops!" on hers, she said, "It's coming along just fine, but don't touch it." She was just teasing. And I'd made sure she didn't have scissors before she started.

Patience was tough, though. Prolonged silence made Aleesha seem like a stranger, if not an alien from another universe.

If this hairdo made us look more like sistuhs—or was it sistahs?—that would be fine with me. It would certainly draw some interesting stares, though.

I spotted a pair of small eyes peering at me. Anjelita must

have come to see if we were up. That shouldn't have surprised me; but after the way Rosa reacted to me, I wasn't sure she'd let Anjelita hang around me anymore. That would've settled the safety issue, but the loss of her company would have been devastating.

I would have been out of luck about my pet project, too. Keeping Anjelita away from the construction zone was the only way I could justify it. And doing it without her would be impossible.

Anjelita's arrival—hopefully with her mom's approval—settled the issue of an alternate activity. Good thing I couldn't explain the problem to Anjelita, though. She'd never have to know that her childish heedlessness had caused our change of activities.

Or that it had given me an excuse to do what I wanted to do.

"Hi, Anjelita," I smiled as I greeted her. "How long have you been watching us this morning?"

I'd probably never break myself of saying things she couldn't understand. Not really a bad thing, though. My parents never talked down to me, and I eventually learned most of the words they used and ended up with a better than average vocabulary. Maybe Anjelita would benefit from having me treat her the same way.

"Buenos días, Señorita Kim."

I'd forgotten how soft and tiny her voice was.

"Buenos días, Señorita Aleesha."

Although Aleesha seemed so intent on what she was doing that she could only say hi, she smiled.

"Buenos días" was another of those Spanish phrases familiar to most Americans who're otherwise ignorant of Spanish. As I repeated it back to her, I got out my pad and pen. I would record every Spanish word I heard in Santa María, even the few I already knew.

Although Anjelita yawned periodically, her eyes twinkled with fascination at watching Aleesha.

"You want to take a closer look, Anjelita?" Aleesha spoke slowly as if that might make her English more understandable.

Anjelita wrinkled her forehead in puzzlement.

Aleesha motioned for her to come closer. I felt a small hand examine my modified cornrows from my scalp all the way to the ends. Even in Spanish, the sounds of childish delight were unmistakable.

"You finished and let her see it first? That's not fair!" I said in mock protest.

Anjelita giggled at the pouty face I made.

"You'll live, missy," Aleesha said. "And get those hands down."

After hearing a click, I considered grabbing Aleesha's camera so I could view her handiwork, but before I could turn around, she'd begun piling my cornrows on top of my head and using something—hairpins, I assumed—to hold everything in place.

The camera clicked again.

I wasn't sure if Anjelita had ever seen a camera or a photograph, but she peeked over my shoulder as Aleesha handed me the camera with the original picture in the window.

I gasped. *Aleesha, you're a genius. . . .*

"Well, girl, what do you think?" she said, laughing.

"The other one. I want to see the other picture, please."

Aleesha pushed a button on her camera. If I'd been a puppy, my tail would've been wagging a mile a minute.

"You're a miracle worker. And you said you couldn't do a french braid. But this is perfect—better than I've ever done. And the way you looped it around on top. You're sure you don't want to become a beautician?"

Aleesha's face broke into a huge smile before she

responded in her usual modest way. "Well, what did you expect me to do, girl? I'm good, but I can't put hair that long into any kind of cornrows in forty-five minutes. I took my sweet time just to fool you."

"I don't mind when the results are this great, but why did you keep pulling my hair?"

"I didn't even start braiding your hair till five minutes ago; I just played with it to make you think I was doing something special, and I grabbed and yanked a handful of hair every once in a while to keep you guessing."

I shook my head. *Maybe I'm more naive than I thought.*

Anjelita peered into Aleesha's face with a look no normal mortal could resist and held out several strands of her own hair—hair twelve to fifteen inches longer than mine. She wanted a french braid, too.

Little Miss Copycat. I smiled at her.

"No, not today. . .not now," Aleesha said.

Anjelita understood the word *no*—it meant the same in both languages—and Aleesha's unsmiling headshake meant no as well. But she couldn't have understood that "Not today. . .not now" only meant "wait until later." Aleesha looked and sounded like she meant "Leave me alone; I don't want to do your hair."

Anjelita's face flamed into a brilliant red. At first, I thought she was angry, but I'd witnessed her anger the day before, and her reaction to Aleesha was quite different. More likely, Aleesha's apparent rejection caught her so off guard it embarrassed her.

Before things could get further out of hand, I made signs of eating. That distracted Anjelita enough to clear some of the hurt from her face. But not all of it.

Aleesha's face revealed every bit of the anguish she felt over her harsh-sounding miscommunication. She could be blustery on the outside, but she was as warm and gooey inside as a campfire-roasted marshmallow. She'd undoubtedly threaten to preach a never-ending sermon to the first person who accused her of that, though.

Aleesha led the way to the mess tent, and Anjelita walked with me several steps behind. She looked like she might start crying any second. When Aleesha stopped abruptly, Anjelita and I came within two millimeters of rear-ending her.

"Your taillights aren't working," I teased.

But Aleesha solemnly ignored my quip. Turning around and looking into Anjelita's eyes, she pulled the hair away from both sides of the little girl's head and smiled.

"*Mañana*—tomorrow," she said.

Everyone knows mañana, but Aleesha had been trying so hard to say "not today" that she'd overlooked the obvious. And so had I.

Anjelita wrapped her arm-and-a-half around Aleesha, and the events of the past ten minutes became history.

chapter thirty-seven

Aleesha must have thought my addiction to beef jerky was crazy. I ate more of it than she did. If I had some other meat for my entree, I gnawed on jerky for dessert.

I may have been crazy, but I wasn't stupid. I knew I'd be as sick of jerky by the time I got home as I was of pizza now.

I caught Rosa's eye across the mess tent, smiled at her, and waved. This time she smiled back, though ever so slightly and still with a bit of hesitation. Although the bunch of loud extroverts from North of the Border may have overwhelmed her, she looked lonelier than shy—like she needed someone to talk with. I wished like crazy I could have been that someone.

She sauntered across the mess tent and smiled at me again as she got closer. She spoke a few words to Anjelita, who followed her without arguing, perhaps to their sleepsite. The location was one of my many unanswered questions.

Anjelita didn't say anything before leaving. I hoped her absence would be brief. And temporary.

After brushing my teeth, I checked the mess tent and returned to the construction area. Nobody had seen Anjelita. I approached the leader of the first team and offered my help. I explained that when and if Anjelita came back, I would need to leave my task incomplete.

She understood. But she couldn't see how I was fretting inside.

Lord, if Anjelita doesn't help me today, I can't begin my cleanup project. Angel said You'd permit me to do it. But how can I prepare for the more difficult task if I don't get to do the less important one?

Praying didn't help. I'd just resumed my fretting when I heard a voice. . . .

"Peace to you, Kim."

Was that Angel's voice? I looked around, but no one was close by. Had I fallen asleep standing up? I instinctively sat down and closed my eyes.

"Angel? I just finished praying, and then you spoke. Does God let you eavesdrop on my private times with Him?"

I was curious, not upset.

"No, but He passed this along to me as a follow-up to last night's discussion."

"So you're God's ambassador to me the way the team members try to be His ambassadors to Santa María?"

So help me, I heard Angel smiling at my question. That made me smile, too.

"Kim, the problem isn't just your lack of preparedness for the big project. You aren't even properly prepared for the litter-cleanup campaign."

I opened my mouth to protest—mentally at least—but Angel kept going.

"Kim, did you listen to yourself when you were praying?"

I nodded.

"God doesn't think so."

Huh?

"You referred to this project as yours. Yes, you came up with the litter cleanup and you want to do it for the best of reasons. You don't know if the Passover Church was ever a church, but you want to teach the villagers to respect it in the hopes they will become Christians and use it as a church someday. But you won't succeed unless you view this as God's project."

I couldn't speak.

"You also said you can't do the cleanup campaign without Anjelita. You think the Creator of the Universe is incapable of helping you do this project without Anjelita? Don't forget He can also do it without you."

Oh, man. Was I about to start this project on the wrong foot or what?

"Kim, God's not upset with you. But you reminded Him of Moses asking for Aaron's help. Moses didn't need Aaron, but God agreed to the request as a personal favor."

I nodded.

"Get to work, girl."

When I opened my eyes, Anjelita was looking down at me. She wore clothes that were more appropriate for work than the flimsy attire she'd had on earlier. Elated at being able to start my pet project—no, God's project—I gave Anjelita such a tight hug that she had to push me away to loosen my hold.

"Jayne," I said to the leader of team 1. "I'm sorry, but I won't be able to get those boards for you."

"No problem, Kimmy. Keeping that kid safe is more important."

I nodded.

"So what's your plan?"

After explaining that it was God's plan and not mine, I told her about the litter cleanup. She responded with a hug, a smile, and an enthusiastic, "Go for it!"

Then I went looking for Rob and Charlie. Anjelita tagged along behind me, her posture straight and tall—as if yesterday's improved relations with the other children had infused her with all the confidence in the world. *Thank You, Lord.*

I found Rob and Charlie together—a rare circumstance.

"Great idea, Kimmy!" They said almost in unison after I outlined my plan. *Grrr.* When would I quit thinking of it as mine?

"Although the villagers don't seem to have any notion what a church is, clearing the yard may touch them in some unexpected way."

When I expressed concern about the time and energy we'd waste carting away rubbish, Charlie offered to build a bonfire adjacent to the churchyard. He noted that the area contained enough cacti to fuel fires for a thousand years without affecting the local ecology.

Once the three of us finished talking—Anjelita looked like she understood and approved of everything—she scampered off toward the construction area.

I called her name and followed it up with a soft-spoken no, hoping it wouldn't resemble the harsh no she'd used on the other children or the one Aleesha had said to her earlier. Then I took the stub of her right arm and led her toward the tiny Passover Church.

"Anjelita," I said as if she could understand me, "all this debris in the churchyard looks pathetic. I can't believe it doesn't bother the villagers, but they're too busy rebuilding their homes to do anything about it. But you and I, Anjelita, you and I have the time and the freedom to do what they can't do. I don't care if it takes every bit of the time I have left here. . . ."

I hesitated. How long would God's more important project take?

"We're going to make the yard of this so-called church look respectable."

She smiled as if every word was intelligible.

As often as I'd looked at the building, I'd never realized how tiny it was. The wooden shed in my backyard was 10 x 15—a meager but sufficient one hundred fifty square feet. The church was probably somewhere between twenty-five and forty feet wide and fifteen to thirty-five feet deep. I've never been good at estimating distances.

The area of the churchyard was more important than the size of the church, though. Tracking our progress would be easy if we could figure out the square footage.

Anjelita never ceased to amaze me. She seemed to understand what I was doing. My bottom lip almost hit the trashy ground when she took measured steps across the front of the yard and wrote "26" in the dirt.

I nodded. That sounded reasonable.

After pacing the pathway to the church door, she scribbled "17" below the 26. Seconds later, she wrote "442"—the approximate number of square feet we needed to clear. I couldn't have done that math in my head; yet she'd done it faster than somebody using a calculator. An unusually good school must have once occupied the area of the mess tent.

Where to start, where to start. . .

When I did a once-over of the yard, I didn't spot a thing worth salvaging. I might have been looking at the bottom layer of a sewer that had dried out before it finished draining—but this was a million times worse. The storm had carried off most of the big pieces of trash, and I didn't see any sign of waste products—for that I was grateful!—but the sheer quantity of solid trash was overwhelming. Not to mention the stench.

If a major blizzard's worth of snow had fallen in the churchyard, digging out would have seemed less daunting. In a few spots, the pile was just a foot high, while others were closer to three. I used two feet as an average to calculate that we faced 884 cubic feet of—I couldn't let myself think the vulgarity that would have best described it—snow drifts. Rubbish drifts.

Both were products of the wind. Snow would have melted, but the rubbish was here to stay unless we disposed of it. Moderate breezes were slowly clearing our campground and other parts of the landscape—even the sides of the church—a little more each night, leaving the ground increasingly visible.

The churchyard stayed the same, though.

Not a square millimeter of churchyard had been visible the evening we arrived. Not a square millimeter was visible now. Although the yard contained thousands of pieces of loose trash, I had a feeling time and climate would solidify them like concrete, making future removal impossible.

I used to resist thinking about the Devil as a literal being. I thought of "him" as a concept—a symbol God placed in the Bible to help us better understand the nature of sin and evil. Considering the task before us, however, I wondered if the Devil himself hadn't dumped this trash in the churchyard in anger over God's protection of the building.

I muttered an obscenity under my breath. I hadn't cursed aloud since that first night in Santa María, and I was proud of my progress. I didn't realize what I'd said, though. Neither did I realize a pair of small ears had heard me all too clearly.

I heard Anjelita repeat that word back to me a few minutes later. At first, I didn't realize what she said. I was too preoccupied. I looked gratefully at Rob's bonfire and finished my assessment of the rubbish. If I was right, most of it was flammable.

Then I did a double take. "What did you just say, Anjelita?"

It had just dawned on me that not only had she said the same word I'd used, she'd said it with my tone of voice. She couldn't have picked that up anywhere else. I must have said it without realizing it.

Of course, she had no idea what she was saying. Even though the word I'd used was probably an appropriate description of the mess we were getting ready to dispose of, Mom's sermon about my language was more relevant now than ever.

Mom and Dad often described me as irresponsible. I had to agree this time. My face felt hotter than the bonfire. *Lord, please forgive me.* I knew He would before I asked—I knew He had afterward—but I needed to undo the damage before it got worse.

I kept my cool. Getting upset with Anjelita would be counterproductive. The fault was mine, but I had to keep her from using that word again. If this incident didn't make me clean up my language for good, nothing would.

I tried saying the vulgar word we'd both said and then crossing my index fingers in front of my mouth, but I guess Anjelita had never seen a "no smoking" or "no swearing" sign.

Then I shook my head from side to side and said, "Kim, no"; but because I forgot to say the word first, she didn't know what I was referring to. Next I said it as clinically as I could, added, "No," and forced my lips together with my thumb, forefinger, and middle finger.

Anjelita was cracking up.

So was I. My teaching methods were not only ineffective, but silly.

So I tried a different tack. I spoke the offending word and then slapped myself lightly on the mouth and cheek. Although the sound was barely audible, Anjelita caught on immediately. Her mouth drooped, and she closed her eyes for a few seconds. I guess she didn't want to see me watching her.

I was ready to move past my own faux pas and its temporary effect on Anjelita. I hugged her and smiled, and she smiled back, secure in the assurance that all was well.

chapter thirty-eight

The walkway to the church door was only wide enough for putting one foot in front of the other, so I decided to begin by widening it. But unlike those guys who'd created the path by piling rubbish on each side as they went along, Anjelita and I would have to pick it up handful by handful and tote it to the fire.

Only after Rob brought Anjelita and me work gloves did I realize what a health hazard the debris would have become. I was thankful to eliminate—or at least minimize—the risks the villagers would have to endure. This project was truly God's, for He'd known all along how important it was.

Although Anjelita's glove—she only needed one—was way too big for her, I used my remaining safety pins to resize it so it wouldn't fall off. Her little fingers probably felt lost inside, but at least she wouldn't have to thread a needle, play the piano, or perform surgery while wearing it. I couldn't see any point in fastening its mate to the stump of her arm, although it might have fit.

Despite my inability to use the hand of my broken arm, I put a glove on it. There was no telling what it might come in contact with.

Now that we were ready to begin, Anjelita looked at me curiously. Leaving her at the outer perimeter of the churchyard for a moment, I tightrope-walked my way to the doorway and picked up as much as I could in my usable hand, cradling it against my shirt to try carrying more than one handful. When I came back, I carried my load to the fire—

perhaps a twenty-foot trek.

Anjelita stared at me the whole time.

But before I could get back from dumping my armload, she went to the door, picked up her own armload, and headed toward the bonfire. I watched closely to make sure she didn't get too close, but I shouldn't have worried. Rosa must have taught her to be careful of flames.

We returned to the churchyard, taking turns going up the path for a new load and standing aside frequently so others could go inside for water, snacks, and shade. I didn't think about it much at first, but we wasted a lot of time waiting.

Looking at the churchyard after what seemed like hundreds of trips to the fire, I was sick about the lack of visible results. Even though we'd only begun, I couldn't help fretting about whether we'd be able to finish before heading home.

And Angel had called this the less important task. Would I still have time for the more important one?

This twister must have had almost supernatural power. Not all of the litter was paper, nor was all of it lightweight or flammable. I could see an old rubber tire protruding ever so slightly from its cover under other pieces of junk.

Did the storm really bring all this stuff here? Had any of it been here before? I felt sick to my stomach at the thought of the villagers using what I considered almost-sacred property as a junkyard. I couldn't be sure either way, though, so I tried putting it out of my mind.

I wondered how many usable items—perhaps some that were brand-new—the storm had brutally kidnapped in another town or village and savagely dismembered before dumping them in this churchyard grave. Did any of Santa María's possessions lie buried here, too, or had the twister carried all of them to the next village?

If an actual Devil did this, the next village churchyard—if

it had one—would probably be the most severely littered place, too. I considered the so-called butterfly effect: Something as insignificant as the fluttering of a butterfly's wings can have unforeseen results elsewhere. Even on the other side of the world.

Can that happen with people's thoughts and feelings, too? Maybe Betsy Jo is praying for me at this very moment, and I'm experiencing its touch. Not necessarily because God has answered her prayer yet, but just because she's praying.

I've heard Christians—especially missionaries serving all over the world—say they sometimes know they're the object of a current prayer. That idea used to strike me as eerie. But not anymore.

Anjelita was a wonderful little worker. Although she couldn't carry as much as I could, she moved faster. I envied her boundless energy. Even at eighteen, I didn't have the pep I'd taken for granted when I was younger.

Whenever we tossed rubbish into the fire, a puff of smoke rose to the sky—a mystical tribute to God, who'd brought me to Santa María instead of Ciudad de Plata.

During our lunch break, Charlie stopped to talk. "Great job, you two. You may think this will take forever, but you'll see a difference soon. You won't finish today or tomorrow; but the time will come, and you'll feel good about it."

I already felt good about it—good and frustrated—but I didn't interrupt or argue.

"Kimmy," he continued, "would you mind changing your mode of operation just a bit?"

Hmm. What can we do differently? I twisted my eyebrows to express my curiosity and waited for him to explain.

"That path to the church door is quite narrow," he began. I nodded. "There's no place to step aside and let someone else by. People frequently have to wait for you or Anjelita—

sometimes both of you—to finish gathering your load and head for the fire before they can head for the door. They have similar problems when they come out. We're wasting precious time."

I wanted to interrupt and complain about the haphazard way those guys had created the path in the first place. Then I wanted to say something about the time we wasted waiting for everybody else to get by. But something deep inside reminded me of my two ears and one mouth, and I remained quiet. Maybe those original path clearers had rushed so they could get to the more important task of building.

That insight erased the resentment I'd been harboring—not that I could even remember which guys had cleared the path.

"I appreciate your wanting to start by widening the pathway. We need that. What I was wondering, though, couldn't you work just as effectively from the end of the path furthest from the building and move diagonally toward the sides? That way you'll clear the walkway by working from where you've finished without standing on the path itself."

I must have looked dazed.

"Here's what I mean, Kimmy."

He drew a rough illustration in the dirt and labeled it in a typical male's almost-illegible handwriting.

"Great idea!" I surprised myself by saying. "Why didn't I think of that?" God was making major changes in me, and those lessons about flexibility and faithful obedience had begun sinking in and taking root. I spent a lot of my work time pondering how God might try changing me next. I hoped He wouldn't ask me not to major in music.

I didn't need to explain to Anjelita that we would work at an angle from the outer end of the pathway toward the sides of the building. Charlie had gestured quite a bit while drawing the diagram, and she appeared to take in his meaning without having to comprehend any of the explanation.

People quickly noticed that Anjelita and I had changed our angle of attack.

"Great job, girls!"

"We won't be in one another's way all the time now."

"It'll be so much easier to reach the church when we don't have to tiptoe."

Anjelita may not have understood the words, but she beamed from ear to ear at hearing other people acknowledge her beneficial efforts. Our efforts.

I imagined I'd feel the same way when I heard the Lord say "well done" at the end of my earthly life. But I hadn't come close to earning that kind of praise yet. I felt certain of that.

But praise was different from salvation, and my salvation didn't depend on good works. I would never stop thanking God for that.

The afternoon would have seemed long and tedious except for one small, joyous thing. Anjelita was an excellent whistler. I'd never heard the songs before, though. So much for thinking all Mexican songs sounded like "La Cucaracha" and "Cielito Lindo."

Her favorite songs—at least the ones she repeated most frequently—had subtle, haunting, beautiful tunes. I couldn't imagine a mariachi band playing songs like those in the Casa Grande restaurant back home. But I could hear them on a traditional Mexican flute, if such a thing existed.

I went off in space for a while in spite of Anjelita's music— or perhaps because of it—and worked on autopilot. This cleanup wasn't the most mentally challenging task we could have taken on, and the less I thought about what my hands were doing, the better.

Anjelita touched my shoulder at one point during mid-afternoon, and I stopped and smiled at her. I resumed my work. But then she shook my arm, obviously excited about something, and pointed toward the opposite side of the yard.

I couldn't believe what I saw.

chapter thirty-nine

I thought at first we'd gained spectators. But, no. They were helpers.

Back from space now with eyes wide open, I saw a number of people toting armfuls of litter to the bonfire before returning to their construction sites. Although they couldn't carry two armfuls at a time—they usually had several water bottles under one arm—they often made a second or third trip, and I could already see a tiny bit of progress on that side.

As much as the physically capable villagers surprised me by helping, too, I couldn't hide my excitement when I saw the senior adults—too old to assist with construction, but still young enough to care—take to the project with enthusiastic smiles. To be sure, they were turtles compared to Anjelita and me and great at getting in one other's way; but I recognized that their help would play a major part in finishing this project.

I wouldn't have time to do the task God was preparing me for unless we finished the first one early. But I grew more convinced than ever that the timing was beyond my control. I wasn't responsible for the results. If I'd tried holding on to the ownership of the litter cleanup, we wouldn't be nearly as far along.

Why should I be surprised that God could accomplish what I couldn't?

By the time we stopped for supper, I could see a small but very real dent in each side of the churchyard. The bonfire burned brightly from the various materials we fed it. Although we purposely avoided burning the tire when we got to it, a piece of rubber must have fallen into the fire. It took forever to burn. The column of thick black smoke and the noxious stink made me long for the pleasant smell of mothballs. Momentarily, anyhow. But who could complain about the stink of burning rubber in the midst of such progress?

Anjelita and I were so tired and sore after supper we could barely get up off the ground. If we'd attempted to work another minute or two, our bodies would have rebelled. We compromised by dragging ourselves back to the churchyard to survey the progress.

Ten or twelve team members had jumped in to take our places while we were eating, and others were coming from the mess tent now, apparently intending to help. I didn't know where they got the strength to do one more lick of physical labor, but they seemed to sense that cleaning the churchyard was as important in its own way as building houses.

The litter cleanup seemed like a good way to witness to the villagers, even if we couldn't explain why we were doing it. Perhaps God's big project would allow me to explain, but that would be up to Him.

Finding an out-of-the-way spot fairly close to the bonfire, Anjelita and I crumbled to the ground to watch. I was too tired to notice for several minutes that I'd sat on a pile of small pebbles. But it didn't matter. I didn't have the energy to move.

Anjelita leaned against me, and I draped my left arm over her shoulders. I was barely conscious of her slipping silently from my grasp, laying her head on my lap, and falling asleep. I was too busy dreaming about crawling into my own sleeping bag and dying.

I expected to sleep more soundly tonight than any time since our arrival. Well, not counting the night the codeine put me out.

After twenty minutes of wondering how much longer

I could stay awake, I saw Rosa coming. From the way she smiled when she spotted Anjelita, she must have been looking for us. I waved her over.

Careful not to awaken Anjelita, Rosa stooped down and gathered her up awkwardly. I was afraid she might drop her daughter, but she didn't.

Rosa's smile expressed the approval and appreciation she couldn't verbalize, and I smiled back before kissing Anjelita on the forehead. Rosa's ability to get to her feet carrying a dead weight shocked me. Maybe she'd done that often over the years.

Then something touched my heart and said, "Now is the time."

I didn't resist or make excuses but scrambled to my feet—I'd never do it as gracefully as Anjelita, even when my arm mended—and hugged Rosa as she turned to carry Anjelita to their sleepsite. Although she couldn't hug me without dropping Anjelita, she smiled.

Thank You, Lord, for this small sign of progress in becoming Rosa's friend.

As she walked away with Anjelita draped over her shoulder, I wondered about the fact I'd never seen her with a man. But I didn't have any way to inquire.

chapter forty

Against my better judgment, I sat down again after Rosa took Anjelita. Team members carrying rubbish to the bonfire had drifted away by twos and threes to prepare for bed. The sunset was no longer visible, but darkness hadn't fallen.

After praying awhile, I felt emotionally refreshed. I almost fell asleep, though. Had my eyes been open to see darkness approaching, I would have been on the way to my sleepsite.

I yawned a couple of times. Was I dreaming, or had someone just said, "Nice hair"?

"Nice hair, I said," Geoff said loudly and with unmistakable irritation.

That brought me out of my half-prayerful, half-sleepy trance, and I opened my eyes. I didn't feel like having him or anyone else intrude into my private devotional time, but since I'd picked a public place to pray, I couldn't blame him for interrupting. I'd do my best to be pleasant.

But Geoff's attitude had already begun showing, and I wasn't sure I was up to the challenge—not even with God's help. My loss of respect for Geoff didn't make it any easier, either. His Prince Charming allure had evaporated—poof. If anything, he'd changed from a prince back into a frog. He might not have been Rhett Butler at his worst, but I couldn't imagine his ever becoming Rhett at his best, either.

I started gushing as nervously as if Rhett were listening rather than Geoff. "My hair? Thanks, Geoff. Aleesha did it this morning. She really tricked me, though. It was so funny.

She made me think she was putting it in cornrows, if you can imagine that. I didn't find out until she finished that she'd done a regular french braid like I'd wanted in the first place." My nervousness started disappearing. Slowly.

Geoff looked at me with a "what a dumb girl" expression. "Oh."

Not exactly every girl's idea of the perfect compliment. He hadn't shown the tiniest tidbit of interest in what I'd said. He looked thoroughly disgusted. Maybe even angry. But why?

I hadn't seen Geoff all day. I hadn't missed him, either. Yet now he stood looking down at me—staring, actually; and his gaping made me so self-conscious, I buttoned the top button of my modest work shirt.

"Geoff, if you don't sit down soon, you're going to make my neck stiff from looking up. You can sit here on the ground if you like or if you don't like. It's all equally hard and all equally dry, drier, and driest, not to mention being very dirty." I made myself giggle once in a nervous effort to sound cute and nonchalant; but my cheerlessness, awkwardness, and insincerity must have been as obvious as his attitude toward me.

I pointed to a spot several very-safe feet away. He sat down. Much closer than I wanted. Although he didn't scare me, I had serious concerns about his intentions. I still remembered those unbrotherly hugs.

Of all things, a thought about poisonous snakes flashed through my mind. They were okay in their proper place, but— if one came anywhere close—one or the other of us would have to scoot pronto.

"I'm pretty sweaty and stinky this evening, Geoff. You need to back off before the fumes knock you out."

Whether or not he saw through my suggestion, he still didn't move. So I backed off several feet. He didn't attempt to follow me.

"So where's your. . .little friend this evening?"

You haven't even asked about my arm! Everyone else does. "Hi, Kimmy! How's the arm?" has become the standard greeting from the team members. The villagers approach me off and on all day, touching my cast lightly, and speaking gentle words of consolation and encouragement. But not you, Geoff. You don't even care about my arm, do you?

His inquiry about Anjelita had consisted of polite words, but the way he said them was rude. Harsh. Disapproving.

I shivered involuntarily at the realization that only Anjelita's company had kept Geoff from approaching me until now. "Anjelita was so tired she fell asleep on my lap. Her—"

"Lucky girl."

I didn't bother to finish my sentence about Rosa taking Anjelita home. Geoff's tone of voice had gotten to me, and what he said didn't bother me as much as what he didn't say. . . and what he seemed to be thinking.

"Kimmy, aren't you uncomfortable in short sleeves now the temp is dropping?" He must have noticed I was shivering. The temperature was only partially responsible.

I didn't want to lie, but I couldn't admit the whole truth. "I suppose I am. I'm heading to bed in a minute, though. I'll be warm then. Thanks for asking."

"Kimmy, I can warm you up all over. . . ." Geoff had never said anything overtly improper, yet innuendos were always close to the surface, ready to pop out unexpectedly like a jack-in-the-box. This Geoff was a one-eighty from the one I'd met at the beginning of the week. And he couldn't have been more different from the other boys on the team.

Since the team members were supposed to be Christians and most of them demonstrated their faith through both words and actions, I decided to check Geoff's relationship with God. After all, that's what we should've had most in common.

"I'm never that cold. Geoff, I don't know how to. . . well, you seem so different from the other Christian boys I know—especially the ones on this trip."

He laughed—it was more of a smirk—yet he didn't seem amused. He clearly considered himself to be in control of this conversation. "Tell me about it."

His sarcasm made me more conscious of my challenged speaking than at any time since orientation. I knew what I wanted to say and how to say it, but the relevant body parts balked at having to work together to verbalize distinctly.

But garbled speech would make me sound weak, and I couldn't let Geoff detect anything that might signify vulnerability. I already felt like a field mouse facing an owl that's missed his last several meals. "Geoff. . .Geoff, you. . ." *come on, Kim. . .*"you want, uh, seem to. . ." *calm down, girl. . .* "have your head. . .your mind. . ." *Lord, help me. . .*"in less spiritual places than they do."

Thank You, Jesus.

"Maybe it's because I know how to have fun, Kimmy." Coming from Geoff, Kimmy sounded like a dirty word—one so crass I wouldn't have used it myself. No degree of fever could have made my face as hot as hearing him say it. I was thankful the darkening evening would cover my embarrassment.

What made him enjoy intimidating me? A feeling of superiority?

Maybe. But there had to be more to it than that. "I've known many Christian boys who know how to have the kind of fun I enjoy."

Reacting as if drooling at the thought of something evil he'd found out about me, he turned my innocent statement against me. "I'll bet."

My concerns sped past irritation. I barely kept from lashing out in anger. *Lord?* "Geoff, this may sound judgmental, but I'm only asking out of concern. Are you a Christian? A true believer, that is?" I've always avoided saying "born-again Christian" because it's redundant. Someone who's not born again isn't a Christian. It's as simple as that. I wouldn't have said "true believer" if I hadn't had such doubts about him. I needed to make myself as clear as possible.

"I'm a Christian only when it's convenient and gets me what I want."

Although his confession shocked me, it was probably the most honest thing he'd said. I hoped it wasn't true. I suspected that some of the people in my hometown were hypocrites—even a few of the active members of my church—but I'd never heard one of them admit it. Shaken by Geoff's response, my mind spun in confusion about what to say next.

Instead of responding directly to his confession of conditional Christianity, which seemed to signify he wasn't a Christian at all, I blurted out the first thing that came to mind. It was the worst thing I could have said. "And what do you want, Geoff?"

"You," he said quietly and confidently. Geoff wasn't making any effort to be diplomatic, much less romantic. He hadn't done a thing to win my favor. His dating game—he'd barely made it past caveman-style—wasn't acceptable. And what girl wouldn't resent his possessiveness about something that wasn't his and never would be?

Something? That was how he saw me—as a something and not a someone. He might as well have been an impatient diner drooling over a tender cut of beef. No, considering my personal standards of conduct, lamb would be a better comparison. Maybe he suspected that and found me more appealing because of it.

The Holy Spirit must have been working overtime that evening, for I soon forgot my apprehension. "You don't waste any time, do you, Geoff?"

No more walking on eggshells. I sensed God's approval—perhaps even His encouragement—to act stern and direct in opposing Geoff's bluntness. I wasn't Jesus clearing the temple of money changers, but I felt some of that same fire burning inside. Christian love tempered my words, though. How little I knew about Geoff. How could I help him unless I got to know him better, and how could I do that without listening more than I talked?

That's it, Kim. Two ears. One mouth.

I wished someone else had been close by, though. Not a defender—I didn't need one—but a witness. But no one was in sight.

If I knew anything about boys, Geoff was the kind who'd talk about a girl behind her back, saying things that were neither flattering nor true. Or was I stereotyping and condemning him on meager and questionable evidence? His attitude might have been a false front, but how could I be sure?

"I've finished playing," Geoff said. "You've been interested in me since we first met. Sweet talk isn't necessary now. We both want the same thing."

"If you were as smart as you think you are, you'd know talking like that won't win me. You've been so clever—never saying anything improper. . .always implying it. It's turned me off, Geoff. And, for your information, I don't believe in mission-trip romances. They detract from the work."

He snorted. Maybe he didn't believe anyone would come to Santa María for selfless reasons. I wondered why he'd come.

"So who said anything about romance?"

I shivered at being so close to someone who made no effort to hide his motives. "So why did you come here, Geoff? From what you're saying, you don't have much of a relationship with God through faith in Jesus Christ. Do you think God wants you to behave this way?"

"Kimmy, Kimmy, I have faith. Faith in myself. I don't need to have faith in Jesus or a relationship with God. So don't bother asking if Jesus is Lord of my life. I'm lord of my own life. The only lord I need. And I'm doing just fine this way."

I sighed aloud as I prayed silently about where to go from here. I couldn't have felt more ill at ease if I'd been talking with the Devil himself. I couldn't tell Geoff to get lost. If he'd told me the truth, he already was. I wondered whether anything could halt or even slow his pursuit of me.

I hoped Geoff would apply his brakes voluntarily. Christian boys could make mistakes. Christian girls, too. But at least I could trust their good intentions. I didn't trust Geoff, though. Knowing enough self-defense basics to get by didn't make me feel any better about being alone with him in the dark.

Just as I opened my mouth to respond, I remembered what I'd come to Mexico to do: evangelism. But God had placed me in relief work and home construction instead. Now I'd come full circle back to evangelism.

Other evangelism in Santa María seemed impossible. Somewhere—perhaps just a few hundred yards away—slept the villagers of Santa María. If they weren't Christians, they weren't religious hypocrites, either.

The villagers had what we called a church, but that didn't mean they'd heard of Jesus, much less believed in Him. The building looked unused when we first opened it up for breaks. It didn't look any churchier inside than outside, and the villagers undoubtedly viewed it as just another building. One with supernatural longevity.

This blasted language barrier. . .

Yet two feet away sat Geoff, a boy who'd almost bragged about not being a Christian. If he hadn't known enough about Christianity to sound convincing, the mission agency wouldn't have let him come.

But he didn't know Jesus. Not personally.

Although he and I didn't have a language barrier, we were opposite sides of the same coin. I didn't know how to bore a hole to the other side to reach him, and I wasn't sure I wanted to. Could I possibly learn to love and accept someone I loathed and distrusted as much as I did Geoff? I wondered if even Rob had the spiritual maturity to do that.

How could I reach out to a guy who'd purposely mistaken my friendliness for a sign that I wanted what he wanted?

Who are you, Geoff? The real you. And how can I stand being around you enough to find out?

If God brought me here to plant gospel seeds in Geoff's heart and maybe even convert him, I'd have to rely on the heavenly Father more than ever and be flexible and obedient beyond the call of duty.

Duty to God has no limits, though. If it did, the sky wouldn't be the limit; heaven would.

So my mind flashed from Geoff to God, from God to Santa María, and from Santa María back to Geoff again during the briefest of moments following his claim to be lord of his own life. Although a smattering of seconds can seem like an eternity, these few hadn't lasted long enough. I was no closer to an appropriate response than before. I wasn't apprehensive about Geoff's intentions now, but I was desperate to pray and to think.

And to talk with. . .

"Kim? Kim!" the familiar voice broke through the darkness.

chapter forty-one

A flashlight beam moved in my direction. "What you doing out here in the dark, gal? It's time to be home in bed."

I'd never been so keenly aware of God's perfect timing. He answered a prayer I hadn't prayed in a way I wouldn't have thought of suggesting. *Thank You, Lord.*

"Coming, Aleesha!" I shouted. I wondered if I sounded as relieved as I felt. "We'll talk again tomorrow, Geoff," I whispered to keep Aleesha from hearing. She probably didn't realize anyone was with me. "I promise."

Although I could barely see Geoff in the darkness, I sensed how much Aleesha's intrusion irritated him. Without so much as a good-bye, he stomped off toward the boys' field like a petulant star athlete the coach has benched mere seconds before he can break the tie in the championship game and lead his team to victory.

I heard him mumble something about "that. . . " The last word wasn't clear, but what I think he said made me sick. If he was an expert at anything, it was in making himself unlikable.

Aleesha and I talked in whispered tones as we made our nightly visit to the edge of the field and came back to change into nightclothes. No one slept as close to the bonfire as we did. Our relative isolation proved to be a blessing that night. Although the other girls sometimes stopped by for a late-night chat, I couldn't talk about the evening's events with anyone but Aleesha.

No matter how much I needed to pray, I needed to unburden to human ears first and receive human feedback.

Even if it made me feel like a gossip.

Aleesha knew so much about so many things. She could read people. All kinds of people. Maybe that's why she accepted me before anybody else did. I could count on her to react with both her head and her heart.

If anyone could say whether my concerns about Geoff were legitimate, she could. She could also help me figure out whether my compulsion to reach out to him was my idea or God's. Had God brought me to Santa María to bear witness to Geoff? Was he the major challenge God needed to prepare me for?

But Angel said I'd laugh at the ultimate project, and I wasn't laughing about Geoff.

Aleesha spent several minutes digesting everything I told her. "Girl, you've got a sure 'nough mess on your hands."

"Aleesha, no." I'd almost convinced myself things weren't as bad as I'd thought.

"I've been studying Geoff; I've been studying everybody here. When you're a minority of any kind—even among a Christian majority—you can't help paying attention to your environment. Experience helps you interpret what you see and hear. So I can tell that most of the people on this project—definitely Charlie and Rob—care about these villagers as much as you and me."

I nodded, although I doubted whether Aleesha saw it in the darkness.

"But Geoff stays as far from these villagers as he can. If he has to interact with one of them, he does it grudgingly and doesn't try masking his feelings. The villagers would have to be deaf, dumb, blind, and dead to miss that bad attitude of his. Geoff is only one person, but one seriously bad apple can do a lot of damage. I guess you know what that means."

"Mmm."

"Geoff resents the time you and Anjelita spend together, but that's another issue. I don't think he cares the least little bit about the villagers' needs. I don't know why he came here unless someone made him."

"Like his parents? I asked him about that. Why he came, I mean. He never answered. You think someone pressured him into coming?"

"Why would he act so resentful about being here if he had a choice?"

"But I was resentful at first, too." I marveled that the memory of orientation didn't redden my face in the darkness.

"Yes, but you still came as a volunteer."

I grunted.

"Something else to keep in mind. My observations aren't the most objective."

"Meaning. . . ?"

"Meaning Mr. Geoff doesn't have any more use for us. . . thick black-skinned folks than he does for those light brown-skinned Mexicans."

"You're kidding."

"Girl, you're a sweet young lady, a fine and gentle young lady—when you aren't cussing, that is. . . ."

We both cackled. I looked around at the girls camped closest to us. They were still sound asleep.

"I've been good for at least a couple of hours." I'd have to tell her about teaching Anjelita not to curse, but not now.

"I'm sure you have, Kim, honey. But my point is this. You aren't a woman of the world like I am. I've seen things you haven't seen. Things you don't know enough about to recognize if they up and bit you. I'm not gonna tell you more 'cause I don't want to discourage you."

I almost laughed at Aleesha for calling herself a woman of the world, but I managed not to. She was already more of one than I'd ever be. "Am I that naive, Aleesha?"

"You know that's right, girl, but don't change. That's one of your most charming and endearing qualities. If you were like me, we'd lock horns all the time. I don't take well to competition."

"I can't imagine us ever tangling."

She didn't let my comment distract her. "Kim, you're always looking for the best in people. I guess Jesus was 'guilty' of that 'bad habit,' too, and look where it got Him. But He saw inside people's hearts. He knew who was sincere and who wasn't. And He knew who would betray Him."

"Can you do that, Aleesha? See inside people's hearts, I mean?"

"Almost. Sometimes, anyhow."

I was so tired I started losing my focus of the conversation. I hoped she wouldn't notice. "So you. . .read minds?"

"No, Kim. I'm not clairvoyant, and I'm not Claire any-body-else, and you know it." Aleesha had the most amazing ability to be outspoken without being offensive. With me, anyhow. "That was your fatigue mouthing off. But God often shows me if someone is who he claims to be. Not who so much as what. Whether that person is real or not. So I'm apt to be cautious when somebody would jump in noncautiously. . . ."

"Incautiously," I said without meaning to. I hated having other people correct my English, but my dad was an English professor.

"Incautiously, whatever. It helps keep me out of trouble. I thank God every day for that gift."

"So is that the same as 'streetwise' or 'street-smart'?"

"You're catching on, girl. But those concepts are more complicated than I've been describing, and most streetwise people don't see their ability as a gift from God."

I groaned inaudibly as Aleesha continued.

"Then there are people who think they—"

"Who think they're streetwise, but aren't?" I asked. "I thought you either are or you aren't. Like being a Christian."

"You've got it, honey. But I'm talking about people like Geoff. He acts like he's street-smart, but he hasn't got a clue. He thinks his bad-boy attitude is all there is to it. So he puts that attitude on before he gets up in the morning and doesn't take it off again until he crawls back in the sack at night." She paused for a few seconds. "They say you can't really speak a language till you start dreaming in it. . . ."

I nodded invisibly in the dark. "Uh-huh," I said, yawning once before each syllable.

"Well, he only daydreams this role he wants to play. His act isn't very convincing—not to someone who knows what it's really like. I can't see inside Geoff, but I can tell you he's a fake on the outside. He's not nearly as bad as he wants people to think."

"I. . .Aleesha, I'm almost dizzy from trying to take this in."

"At least it ain't 'cause you're blond, girl." On those rare occasions Aleesha said "ain't," I knew she was teasing.

Although I needed to hear more, I could barely keep my eyes open. Or my mind. "You've. . .given me a lot to think about. I'm not sure which thread of this conversation to ask more about." I thought for a minute. "You said Geoff has no use for black people. How can you tell? Has he said or done something specific?" I was thinking about what I thought he'd said when he heard Aleesha coming earlier.

"He doesn't have to. You know that attitude of his? It has a slight 'odor' that's immediately recognizable to somebody who's smelled it before, even though it's not something anyone else would notice. I'm familiar with it, so I recognize it now."

"So Geoff 'stinks'?" I wasn't trying to be funny, and neither of us laughed. Geoff's situation was pathetic, not amusing, and I felt the blood flood my face in embarrassment at the way I'd misstated my reaction.

"Yes. If I sound judgmental, that's why you should form your own opinion. Don't believe what I'm saying just because I believe it. Don't chance accepting my prejudices." She added in such a quiet whisper I could barely hear her, "Yes, I have them." Then she spoke a little louder. "At the very least, Geoff seems seriously lacking in that 'rare and sweet perfume' the apostle Paul referred to."

"I wouldn't expect to smell that 'perfume' on Geoff. Not anymore. He's pretty much admitted he doesn't care about not being a Christian."

Once I got my second wind, Aleesha and I whispered long into the night. We'd likely suffer from the loss of sleep, but Geoff's situation seemed more important. We agreed that he'd maintained a good front the first couple of days in Santa María, but we couldn't imagine what made him take down his mask.

Or trade masks.

We tried assessing his spiritual condition, but we could only guess at it. I was more concerned about his attitude toward Aleesha than about the way he'd treated me, but she disagreed. We discussed his motives and ways I might respond.

After hours of batting ideas around, nothing was more conclusive than when we started. We didn't have a God's-eye view of the facts, and neither of us could see inside Geoff's heart.

"I think you should talk to Mr. Rob," Aleesha said when we started yawning and digressing. We got giggly, too, and we were in danger of falling asleep with mouths still moving.

"I don't want to rat on Geoff."

"Somebody besides you and me needs to know what's

going on—especially now that it's reached this point."

"I suppose I could tell Rob I'm concerned about a team member who isn't a Christian."

"That's good, Kim. It's true, and if God leads you to share more, you'll do it out of genuine Christian concern."

It was beyond me how she could think—much less express herself clearly—when she sounded as tired and sleepy as me. I barely took in her last comment, but I managed to mumble "Amen."

At least I think I did.

chapter forty-two

Day 5

I got up extra early the next morning, but not because I felt like it. Aleesha was still asleep, and I didn't wake her. Would I ever rub it in that I'd gotten up first for once.

My mind was still on overload, and some of the specifics were foggier now than last night. I wanted to catch Rob before anyone else could. He was always the first person up, or so he claimed.

But despite my intentions to find him quickly, I wasn't moving very fast. I giggled at myself for yawning in rhythm to my dragging footsteps—or perhaps plodding along to the beat of my yawns.

Each of the other early risers I ran into told me I'd just missed Rob—sometimes by mere seconds. I'd already spent five or ten minutes looking—there weren't many places for him to be—when Anjelita appeared out of nowhere. We hugged.

On impulse, I grasped her shoulder firmly with my left arm. As if she understood what I wanted to do, she took hold of mine, and I started swinging her around and around in a circle. That probably wasn't the safest thing to do, but we had so much fun I never considered the dangers.

Anjelita couldn't keep from laughing when I set her on her feet and promptly fell down. Although she staggered the first couple of steps, she remained upright. Her sense of balance never failed to amaze me.

I tried to imagine her reaction to the rides at Six Flags. Although we still had well over a week to spend together, my eyes welled with tears at the thought of going home without her.

Looking at her from the ground, I noticed that her hair now had a braid like mine. She must have gotten Aleesha up as soon as I left our sleepsite. I jumped up awkwardly, brushed myself off, and wiped my left hand on my work pants. I didn't want to touch Anjelita's hair with filthy hands. I hadn't thought about it before, but her hair was always clean at the beginning of the day. I wish I could have asked her how she did it.

"So pretty!"

She hugged me as if those words had made sense.

"*Belle...*" I slipped into French for a moment.

Anjelita looked at me curiously. "*Bella?*" she asked.

I was about to learn that the two words for "pretty" were similar. But because they didn't sound that much alike, I didn't catch on at first.

"Belle," I repeated. I got out my notepad, turned to a clean page, and wrote it down for her.

"Bella!" She grabbed the pen and pad from my hand and wrote down "bella" for me to see. Although the similarity between the Spanish and French words was more visual than auditory, the discovery was fun.

Rob joined us. "Buenos días, Anjelita," he said. "And to Miss Kimmy as well."

I smiled.

Rob's greeting had probably exhausted all the Spanish he knew, but it made me wish I could pick the brains of every team member who knew any Spanish. I could build up quite a vocabulary that way—more than I could possibly master in the limited time available.

I still wouldn't know how to string the words together sensibly, though, and I couldn't justify distracting the builders with a personal project, especially one so unlikely to prove beneficial.

I was only vaguely aware of Anjelita's convincing, "Hi,

Rob!" response. She'd picked up a number of English words, and she'd learned almost all the team members' names. The guys' names, anyhow. Smart girl! Rob's voice brought me back to the real world.

"Kimmy, I understand you've been looking for me all over the vast acreage of Santa María."

"Everywhere except where you were at the time," I said. I didn't try fighting back a giggle.

"No wonder. I was out looking for you."

"You expected me to be up this early?" I grinned.

"Divine revelation."

"Ah."

"So here we are. Ladies first."

"Can we move to a more out-of-the-way spot, please?"

He led the way with Anjelita and me trailing behind. Anjelita was so good at amusing herself while others conversed in English that her presence—even during the most serious of discussions—never created problems.

Rob picked a spot well out of the flow of normal foot traffic, but I still looked around to make sure no one was nearby. Paranoia about Geoff, I suppose.

I took advantage of the short delay to find a starting point. I'm not great at thinking on my feet, so deciding what to say before I start not only prevents me from blurting out words like machine gun rounds but also minimizes my self-consciousness about speaking.

"Rob, everyone on this project is supposedly a Christian—it was the first requirement on a list of many. For the evangelistic project, anyhow. But I'm concerned about one team member. He hasn't done anything 'wrong' yet"—I used my fingers to put quotation marks around wrong—"but the way he talks and acts around me makes me nervous. He's as much as admitted not being a true believer, and—"

"I know," Rob said. Heavy sadness wiped the twinkle from his eyes. I hadn't seen him look this serious since he picked me up at the airport. "Geoff."

The amazement on my face apparently gave Rob all the confirmation he needed. I'd wanted to avoid telling on Geoff or identifying him specifically, but Rob had just taken that option away.

"Don't worry, Kimmy. You didn't tell me anything new. I've known about Geoff's problems long before this morning. Long before this trip, in fact."

His words shocked me into speechlessness. He'd dumped a puzzle in my lap, one I couldn't possibly solve on my own. I looked at him, desperate for clarification.

"Geoff is my nephew—my only sister's only child. They live in San Francisco, too."

"You're kidding! I've never seen the two of you together. You don't even act like members of the same family."

"That was part of the deal."

"The deal?"

I wished Rob would move his story a little faster before I died of both curiosity and concern; but he, too, probably needed a good starting place.

"Here's the scoop. Geoff's mom, Jill, has been divorced for five years. Almost six. Geoff never got over it, and he's made her life miserable. He wore her down by constantly harping at her and accusing her of being responsible for the breakup. The opposite was true—and she has irrefutable proof of that—but she loves Geoff too much to tarnish her ex-husband's image by revealing his unfaithfulness.

"Jill and I held a number of brother-sister coping, crying, and praying sessions about Geoff, believing he'd eventually come around."

I gave Rob a sympathetic "but he didn't?" look. He shook his head.

"We took him to several sessions with a Christian counselor, but changes didn't come fast enough, and Jill couldn't afford to continue. I offered to pay for them, but she wouldn't let me. I should have insisted."

I nodded. Rob's generosity didn't surprise me. I'd benefited from it myself.

"Geoff became a loner after the divorce. He spent practically all of his time in his room with the door shut. I told Jill I didn't think that was healthy, but she didn't want to disturb the status quo. I couldn't blame her. The only hours of peace she enjoyed were the ones she and Geoff spent apart.

"Then he became friends with some boys at church. We hoped his new friends would set a good example. They were the same age and attended the same school. We'd known their parents for ages—fine, respectable Christians. Hanging around kids like theirs could only help. And so it seemed.

"We didn't know Geoff's friends were teaching him an act for home that would free him to do whatever they wanted him to outside. His relationship with Jill moved from a zero on the scale to a nine. Maybe a ten. Jill didn't have to ask him to do chores around the house, and he started earning the best grades ever. He must've been starving for his friends' approval, though, for he began making a series of foolish decisions."

I couldn't imagine what Rob would say next, but I dabbed my eyes once with my shirtsleeve. Anjelita snuggled up in my arms.

"He'd probably fooled us about some lesser things, but he really pulled the wool over our eyes when he pretended to become a Christian. Not every seventeen-year-old boy has the courage to come forward at the end of a worship service and request baptism at the earliest possible opportunity. His friends sat together at his baptismal service several weeks later. Several of them took some great photographs.

"Geoff's hair was still wet from his immersion when he went joyriding with his friends, drinking beer one of the boys got somewhere. The police stopped them, and the driver lost his license. Underage DUI. We thank God daily they didn't have an accident. The scales dropped from the parents' eyes that day, and we saw things clearly for the first time.

"The other boys blamed Geoff for getting the beer. He didn't deny it, but neither did he admit it. Although Jill and I still don't know the truth, we suspect he meant to ingratiate himself with his friends by keeping them out of additional trouble. We don't know where he would have gotten beer, anyhow. Jill and I don't drink, and neither of us keeps anything like that at home. I don't know about the other boys' parents."

"Rob! How awful! But he made a profession of faith and was baptized." I couldn't imagine that he'd only pretended to become a believer. "As for his actions, well, he was still a baby Christian. He still is. . . ."

Rob's news, no matter how upsetting, boosted my spirits. My greatest concern for Geoff was spiritual, although the trouble he'd gotten into was too serious to gloss over. But this was the information I'd been dying for.

I needed to learn everything I could about Geoff if I had any hope of helping him. "Maybe so, Kimmy. But Jill and I are skeptical. Although he told us he and the boys were just drinking to 'celebrate' his baptism, Jill and I are scared that his profession of faith was a sham—a mockery. Something the other boys put him up to."

Maybe I didn't know boys as well as I thought, but I couldn't picture a seventeen-year-old faking conversion to Christianity to please a bunch of other guys. Yet his conversion could have served as an initiation rite. Pretending to become God's while intentionally denying God control of his life was horrible enough.

"Kimmy, the long and the short of it is the parents grounded the boys for the duration of their senior year. They permitted the guys to get together once a month—always strictly supervised—at one of their homes.

"Several of them—not Geoff, though—were star athletes. Their parents yanked them out of all sports activities. Popular athletes are apt to face temptations these boys had already proved incapable of resisting. They resented the curtailment of their activities more than anything else, but we didn't know how much.

"Each boy reached his eighteenth birthday during the school year. They didn't rebel openly toward their folks or assert their adult status. If anything, they acted calmer and more mature than ever. Geoff and Jill got along great. We were thankful for that.

"The boys attended church with their folks and became what everyone else considered model Christians. Jill and I were more skeptical than the other parents. But we gave them the benefit of the dou—"

I raised an eyebrow at Rob. He stopped in mid-word. Then I winked. "Other parents. . . ?"

He thought for a second, laughed at the implication that he was one of Geoff's parents, and then continued.

"And so the parents—along with one uncle—met one evening to evaluate the boys' attitudes and behavior. Concluding that our punishment had been effective, we agreed to set them free on senior prom afternoon. That was around the beginning of May.

"When they voluntarily offered full details of their plans for the evening, we pronounced them successfully rehabilitated. Parents prayed with their sons before they left for the prom. They all looked clean and glowing in their suits.

Poor guys probably thought we'd never finish taking pictures.

"None of them had dates. That seemed strange since Geoff had been dating a girl from church for about a year; but he didn't offer any explanation, and we didn't think we should ask.

"The parents—and uncle—met again sooner than expected, though. Late that night, several hours after the prom, we had to go to the police station. The boys were not only completely sober, they hadn't been drinking. But had they evermore outdone themselves otherwise."

I had the hardest time keeping from interrupting, but I needed to hear the whole story first. Rob would answer my questions after he finished.

"Months before getting out of their home-prisons, they'd decided to deface some tombstones with black spray paint. They searched online for local cemeteries and identified tombstones that looked so age weathered no one would care about them anymore.

"Each boy painted his parents' names on different stones and entered the date of the prom as their date of death. If the results were any indication, they worked with a flourish, competing to see who could do the most professional-looking job. Just as they were finishing, the police showed up. The boys insisted they didn't hate us. They just wanted to express their indignation over a wasted senior year. They thought this would be a fun way to do it, and no one would be hurt."

My eyes began misting, and I opened my mouth to say something, but I couldn't.

"Yes, Kimmy," Rob said, anticipating my unasked question, "Geoff planned to deface a stone for me, too. . . ."

"Planned to?"

"Yes. Turns out he was the only boy with the gumption to scrap the plan. That's what we want to believe, but maybe he was too scared to do it. He still got in trouble, but not as much as the other boys. Unfortunately, he'd purchased spray paint, cans of paint, and brushes, so the judge couldn't pretend Geoff had simply been in the wrong place at the wrong time. I have to give the other boys credit, though. They voluntarily told the police Geoff hadn't done anything.

"But he'd been there supporting the other boys, and—after the trouble they'd gotten in before—the judge sentenced him to seventy-five hours of community service and scheduled it to begin during the summer after graduation. The other parents refused to bail their sons out, so their boys spent a few days in the pokey and faced stiff fines when they got out. The judge took a special interest in Geoff's case, though. Said he'd wipe Geoff's record clean—upon the completion of his public service."

"How did all of this affect him?" I asked while Rob took a breath.

"I think it scared the daylights out of him. He acted embarrassed at first. But then he copped the attitude that's bothering you now. It's been a constant mask—his only companion—and rarely does he let it down. He can't seem to face himself—or anyone else—without it. Worse still, he doesn't think God wants to forgive him."

"Rob, no. That is so sad. . . ." Tears streamed down my face, and Anjelita wiped my eyes with the sleeve of her whole arm. Although she didn't understand what was wrong, she was crying, too.

"A public mask of respectability had been important before— when he was with his friends—but he won't let anyone get close now. Various people have tried, but nobody can reach him."

"What about Geoff's girlfriend? Surely she—"

"Jane refused to go to the prom with him after he told her what the boys were planning to do. Although she wasn't sure he'd go through with it, she was the one who called the cops.

She broke up with him right after that and quit speaking to him at church. You can imagine how devastated he was."

"Oh, man. I'll bet he resents girls now. You don't suppose he'd, uh. . . ?"

"I could be wrong, Kimmy, but I don't see Geoff as a potential rapist. I'm no psychologist, but I think Geoff is confused and angry about the way those guys misled him and messed up his relationship with Jane. He needs someone his own age to talk with, but he's probably scared that any girl he's attracted to will reject him once she discovers the truth.

"So no, I don't think he's dangerous—not to anyone else, anyhow. His anger is self-directed. It's part of the mask. From what the pastor told us, Geoff probably believes no girl will accept the real him unless she first accepts the angry, obnoxious Geoff."

I looked at Rob with tears in my eyes. I couldn't speak. I suddenly realized I was clinging to Anjelita like a life preserver. I changed the subject to keep from bawling aloud. And because I had one more question. "Rob, you mentioned a 'deal' several minutes ago. . . ?"

"Yes. Jill was beside herself after the arrest, and Geoff kept procrastinating about his community service. He didn't want anyone to see him in public. So—"

"So you offered to bring him on this trip?"

"Yes. I didn't know anything about the original project, but Geoff wouldn't have done evangelism, and it wouldn't have counted as community service. The new project sounded perfect, though. I talked to the judge, and he agreed that this trip would surround Geoff with wholesome companions and inspire him to make a turnaround. It didn't matter to him that the community service wasn't local, since Geoff would be under my supervision.

"He lowered his mask an inch or so by jumping at the

chance to come to Mexico. But he pushed it back up when I pointed out I'd be responsible for his actions—good or bad—and I'd send him home and back to court at the first infraction of the rules. He still agreed to the deal, though—community service in Santa María with perfect behavior or home again, back to the judge, and probably off to jail for a few weeks with a prison record that wouldn't go away.

"I promised not to tell anyone on the team about him or our relationship. He'd sink or swim on his own. Not even Charlie knows."

"You're breaking a confidence telling me." *Rob, I've been counting on you to keep mum about my secrets. Have I made a mistake trusting you?*

"Kimmy, you aren't just anyone. You're my daughter away from home, and that makes you part of Geoff's family. He just doesn't know it yet. Besides, I think you might be just the young lady Geoff needs to talk with."

I nodded. Rob made perfect sense. Now that I understood Geoff's situation, it was time to change subjects. "Rob, you said you were looking for me earlier. What did you need?"

"Oh, that?" He chuckled as if our conversation had been hilarious instead of tragic. "I wanted to caution you about Geoff."

So much for changing subjects. "Why?"

"Everyone has noticed the way he looks at you. His team captain has complained about Geoff not getting much work done. He spends too much time maneuvering to be where you are."

"That's for sure. . .the day before yesterday, anyhow. Then Anjelita and I started working together, and he's been conspicuously absent ever since. Aleesha and I concluded he didn't like having a little chaperone."

"I don't have to remind you that what I'm telling you is confidential. . . ."

"What about Al—?"

"Confidential between you, me, and Aleesha, that is. Her perspective will be helpful."

"I wouldn't want to tell anyone but Aleesha."

"Geoff stayed away from you yesterday because I had a talk with him. I didn't mention you specifically, but I reminded him of his responsibilities and told him he was either going to do his share of the work or go home. That didn't go over very well."

"Going home would be disastrous, wouldn't it? He might keep his mask on forever."

He nodded. "By the way, if Geoff is jealous of anything, it's Anjelita's freedom to spend all day with you. Finding the two of you together when he's not working probably rubs him the wrong way."

"I'd never thought about that."

Rob cleared his throat. Twice. "It's confession time again, Kimmy. Last night, I saw Geoff approach you after Anjelita's mom took her. I was curious."

"Oh?" I thought I knew what he was going to say.

"I found an out-of-sight spot where you wouldn't see me."

"You were spying." Pretending to sound stern and disapproving took all my effort. I was about to crack up laughing. For an upper-middle-aged guy who made such an effort to live by his convictions, Rob could act pretty adolescent at times.

"Yes, spying, and I'm sorry. It was wrong. I asked God's forgiveness last night, but He told me in no uncertain terms to ask yours first thing this morning."

I just shook my head, avoiding eye contact. I didn't want him to see how tickled I was. "Spying," I repeated, leaving the word hanging like a drenched beach towel drying on a clothesline when rain is expected any minute.

"And not just spying," Rob continued. Never had I seen

a grown man look so conscience stricken over such a tiny offense. "Eavesdropping. I listened to the whole conversation. I'm sorry, Kimmy. I wasn't a very responsible Christian adult last night."

I put my hand over my mouth to suppress the laughter and hoped that the merriment in my eyes wouldn't give me away.

"Again, I'm just as sorry as I can be. Will you forgive me, Kimmy?"

Here the poor guy was pleading his heart out for forgiveness, and I was doing my best not to laugh. I finally gave up, took my hand down, and let the laughter erupt like a carbonated drink someone shook before opening.

Rob couldn't resist. As confused as he looked, he soon started laughing with me. One of us would point to the other, and we'd start all over again. The tears poured down our cheeks.

We didn't realize that Anjelita had slipped away until we saw her coming back. She'd been to the mess tent, and her arm-and-a-half carried enough food for the three of us. That little girl always amazed me. She brought Rob and me the same foods she'd seen us eating all week.

But when she saw us wiping our eyes, she dropped her load—she didn't take time to set it down—and ran to console us. Then she discovered we were laughing, not crying.

Infectious laughter has no language barriers.

When the three of us stooped to pick up the food, Rob's small can of baked beans started rolling away, and he and I both dove in the dirt after it. After amusing a cheering crowd of onlookers with our lack of dignity, we whooped and clapped as the can disappeared into a small animal burrow.

"I'll report you to the SPCA if that can hurt any animals," I said. The tears from my laughter were making mud out of the dirt on my face.

"Good shot!" Charlie said, barely able to speak for laughing.

"First hole-in-one I've ever made," Rob said. "I've been trying for years."

"No wonder you succeeded now." Charlie's face was red from laughing so hard. "Look at the size of that hole. You couldn't have missed it with your eyes closed."

Then I saw Geoff. He looked at the three of us on the ground, filthier than we would've been at the end of the day. He stared at his uncle as if he didn't recognize him—or didn't want to. Then he looked at me.

I couldn't guess what he was thinking. His mask was too effective.

"Geoff?" I wanted him to join us. "I promised to talk with you today. I've got time now if you do."

He looked the other direction and then went out of his way to walk around us like a biblical Jew avoiding Samaria.

chapter forty-three

Day 6

One of the most precious things Anjelita did for her "big sister" that week was to play matchmaker. No matter what we were doing, she kept her eyes on every guy around, trying—as it turned out—to find one for me.

She didn't know how I felt about mission-trip romances. I doubt she would have understood even if I'd had the words to explain it to her. Bless her little heart, though. She just saw me as a woman in need of a man.

A number of team members had started dating, and Anjelita pointed them out to me. She looked in my face, possibly checking for signs of jealousy, frustration, or loneliness. Smiling her most encouraging smile, she extended her hand—palm up—toward the crowd of guys in the mess tent as if to say, "This field of fellows is white unto harvest. Do your job as a woman and pick one."

She pointed to this boy or that one and watched my reaction. Her taste was good, her recommendations excellent. Too bad I wasn't interested. She suggested only the picks of the litter.

I wondered if Anjelita had a little of Aleesha's street savvy. She not only failed to recommend Geoff but frowned whenever she saw him. Did she sense his disinterest in her and her people? Was her nose sensitive to his "bad smell," too?

Each time Anjelita pointed to another guy, I shook my head and said, "No, thank you." The way she pursed her lips and looked at me suggested that her failure to find her sister a man made her feel miserable. Perhaps like a failure at an important task.

I hated that.

At first, her matchmaking was interesting. She forced me to put each guy in turn under my microscope of personal standards and examine his qualifications in detail. I didn't have nearly enough information to go on, though. I didn't know much more than the first names of many of the guys.

Perhaps matchmaking was a standard practice in Anjelita's culture, but I couldn't imagine picking out a fellow the way I'd shop for, say, a new hair dryer. For that, I'd look online and compare features. The reputation of the brand, wattage, weight, available colors, and price would all play a part in my decision. Then I'd check out my favored choices in a brick-and-mortar store and see how they compared to the online advertising.

But selecting a guy was more like shopping for a car. Although I'd done that with Mom and Dad several times before, I really began paying attention to details when we went shopping for my sixteenth birthday present. Boy! Did I learn to be picky then.

I'd want one of the manufacturer's finest, a one-of-a-kind model that didn't require a lengthy breaking-in period. Although the body style wasn't overly important, he'd need a certain sparkle—a special flair—before I'd bother checking the mileage rating and opening the doors to inspect the interior for quality of mind and spirit.

I placed a great emphasis on retention of value. I'd invest more of my time and attention in keeping a guy like that on the road than if I settled for the first one who caught my attention. Although some body parts might prove defective over time and others would wear out, my fella would have greater value in old age than in youth.

Price rarely mattered. Like Scarlett O'Hara, I could get almost any man I wanted—and some I didn't want. I'd refused to go out with several of my male teachers after I turned eighteen. But at least I never coveted somebody else's man the way Scarlett obsessed over married Ashley Wilkes.

Long before the end of the day, I tired of Anjelita's matchmaking and wanted her to give up. She might stop when she ran out of boys, but I was scared she'd cycle through them again in the hopes I might change my mind. I had no idea how she planned to get the guy interested in me if I didn't cooperate.

I sat on the ground eating supper. Anjelita had wandered off, as she sometimes did. She was never gone long.

"Hi, Kim. . .uh, Miss Kimmy." The greeting was enthusiastic, but then he quieted down like someone who's just discovered how high the high diving board is—á la Mr. Bean. "Do you mind if I join you?"

Unable to recognize the voice, I looked up. It belonged to Neil, the boy genius, whose grin was growing shier by the second.

"Sure, Neil, I'd love to have the company. Anjelita seems to have deserted me for the moment."

"She seems like a sweet little girl. If I ever have a daughter—"

"Or if your future wife does. . ."

He started turning red, and I felt horrible. Maybe Neil wasn't robust enough to survive my company. He looked pretty scrawny.

"Neil, I'm sorry. You were serious, and I was trying to be cute. Please continue. If you ever have a daughter. . ."

Although the red had faded from his face, his ears still had a cute glow. I'd had a lot of firsthand experience with embarrassment this summer. I felt for Neil.

"I'd be exhilarated. . .ecstatic. . .tickled pink if she turned out like Anjelita." He sounded like he was trying to talk like a regular guy, but—well—he wasn't one. Despite his questionable maturity level, no one would have mistaken an eagle like Neil for a pigeon. I had to keep from giggling, though. He said "tickled pink" at the exact moment his ears lost their last tinge of excessive pinkness.

"I wish I could take Anjelita and not bother having kids of my own," I said.

After chatting pleasantly for several minutes, I spotted Anjelita. She appeared to be watching from a partially hidden position. I motioned for her to join us, but she grinned and shook her head so vigorously that only her French braid kept her hair from flying in a million directions.

"That Anjelita," I said with a laugh. "She's trying to play matchmaker today. She's worried because I don't have a boyfriend. I appreciate her concern, but her efforts are getting to me. I hope she doesn't do it again tomorrow."

Neil remained silent for a moment. Then the words burst forth like the rush of air from a punctured balloon. "Do you know why I came over here?"

"Because you knew I've been wanting to get to know you better and hadn't gotten around to it yet?"

"Uh, before you say any more, I've got a girlfriend back home. She's my age. Young men and older women sometimes make suitable couples, but only when they're substantially older than you and me. . .I."

"And you think I. . .we. . .Anjelita and I. . . ?"

Neil's face reddened more severely than before. He resembled someone whose necktie had been jerked ten degrees too tight. "Not anymore. She pointed over here as if indicating that you were alone and might want company. Although that surprised me, I was more gullible than I might have been if she hadn't caught me staring at you."

"Staring? At me?"

Neil's attention was flattering, but he must not have realized what he said.

My mistake.

"My girlfriend, Anne, has hair the same length and thickness as yours, but she never braids it. So I often look at you—at the back of your head, that is—and try to imagine Anne's hair that way."

"That's really sweet, Neil." I wasn't about to admit my relief at discovering that our disinterest in one another was mutual. Embarrassing him a third time would have been unforgivable.

"When Anjelita caught me peeking, she must have thought I was interested in you."

"Oh, wow. How much more mixed-up could things get?"

He looked a little sheepish at first but quickly regained enough composure to begin smiling. "Tell me. Would it help any if we pretend. . . ?"

"Pretend?"

"That we've become sweethearts."

"You're the genius here, not me. If you think that'll work, I'm all for it." Wait! Didn't I have a similar idea earlier? Maybe I'm smarter than I give myself credit for. I'm no Neil, though. "I promise not to come between you and Anne."

Neil smiled and slipped his hand over mine. As we intertwined fingers, I leaned my head against his shoulder. At least I tried to, but his shoulder was too scrawny to bear the weight, and we both fell over, domino-style.

After straightening up again, we looked at Anjelita—she came out of hiding when she saw that her plan had worked—and smiled like newlyweds with cake still on their faces. We raised our joined hands in the air and waved to show how happy we were.

I'd never seen her more pleased with herself. Apparently

satisfied that she'd brought her self-appointed task to its ultimate and successful conclusion—oh, man! I was starting to think in Neil-words—she left the mess tent. Returning with Rosa several minutes later, she pointed at Neil and me and said something to her mom.

Rosa looked at Anjelita with mom-pride and lit up the fast-fading day with her smile. The last time I saw them that evening, they were skipping like two little kids, hand in hand, with Anjelita whistling one of those haunting Mexican melodies I'd fallen in love with.

As soon as mother and daughter were out of sight, Neil released my hand. Why didn't it surprise me that our hands were sweaty?

We got up to head for our respective fields, but he surprised me by taking my hand again—this time in a firm, gentlemanly handshake—and thanked me for a wonderful evening. Although I wanted to peck him on the cheek, I didn't. He'd still be blushing when he got home to Anne if I anointed him with that kind of innocent display of appreciation.

We agreed to perform the romantic drama again only if Anjelita resumed matchmaking. She didn't.

chapter forty-four

Day 8

The days were running together. I couldn't remember the day of the week anymore, much less the date. The construction crews enjoyed some variety. Building a modest, one-room shack from scratch involved a variety of tasks. They didn't do the exact same things day in and day out. Besides, they were adding to something, not taking away from it.

But every day was too much like the day before for Anjelita and me. We continued our daily grind, and almost everyone helped when they had time, opportunity, and inclination. Some people did more than others.

Progress was remarkable, and I quit fretting about whether we could finish. The Passover Church would have a spotless yard days before time to leave.

That didn't brighten the dullness of the routine, though. I wouldn't have admitted this even to Aleesha, but I was sick of debris and dying for God to start me on the more important project.

But He wasn't ready to do that yet, and I had to remind myself every day that He was the boss, not me. "God is God, and I am not." How often had I heard Pastor Ron say those words?

I couldn't say if this was true of Anjelita, but the work was wearing me down physically, even though each armful weighed very little. Not even work gloves prevented us from getting blisters on our hands. Even on our arms. I thought I'd keel over laughing at a dollar coin–sized blister on the stub of Anjelita's arm. It didn't seem to bother her, though.

Although she sometimes looked like she'd prefer doing something else, she never lagged. Whether her commitment was to me or to the project itself, I couldn't tell. But I knew— and I think she did, too—we needed to keep up a good front for the sake of the senior citizens who helped us almost all the time now.

And—bless Anjelita's heart!—she'd become the acknowledged team leader of the children, who spent hours of their daily playtime helping.

She may have lacked Charlie and Rob's finesse in guiding rather than bossing her team, but she could bark orders as deftly and relentlessly as any drill sergeant I'd ever seen on TV. She kept her troops alert, on the move, and on target. She even made them march like soldiers. I couldn't imagine where she learned anything like that.

Her constant watch care over her volunteers moved me. If she noticed someone lagging from thirst or fatigue, she made the child sit down and rest while she went to get him water or food. Then she made her soldier rest a few more minutes before allowing him to return to the battle. She sent more than one child home on R & R for the remainder of the day when she saw it was in the child's best interest. She seemed to realize instinctively that what was best for each child was also best for the team and for the project.

She would make a fine mother someday, if she could find someone among this handful of children to marry when the time came. She was one of four village girls. Only the two youngest children were boys.

I discovered a new aspect of Anjelita's ingenuity that morning.

She'd been to my campsite so often she knew nobody used the mothball blanket. It lay where Aleesha threw it. She hadn't bothered folding it.

But upon arriving at the churchyard, I saw the blanket spread out on the ground. A moment passed before I realized Anjelita had brought it from my sleepsite.

When she saw my eyes open wide in surprise, her mouth curved into a mischievous smile. I'd never seen her look so impish.

"*Transportación*," she said in her simple, childish manner.

"Transportación?" That word was too close to its English equivalent to mistake for anything else. "Are we pretending this blanket is an automobile? And where will we drive it?"

If God wasn't in charge of my word choices at that moment, I don't know who was. *Automobile* always seemed like an old-fashioned word. I never used it. Why say four syllables when the one-syllable *car* worked?

But car wouldn't have done the trick with Anjelita. If I'd said "car," our communication would have died like a car running out of gas. But—I'll always believe it was divine intervention—automobile had come out of my mouth instead of car.

"*Automóvil?*" she said.

"Sí, automóvil."

I was almost delirious at hearing another Spanish word that was enough like English to recognize. I jotted transportación and automóvil on my memo pad as Anjelita talked.

"No, no! No es un automóvil!" She pointed to the blanket and laughed, and I couldn't help but laugh, too.

Okay, so she didn't think of the blanket as a car. Not even a make-believe one.

"Transportación," she repeated. In some other part of the world, she might have pretended that the blanket was a flying carpet. But what kind of transportation did she intend to use it for here and why was it so important?

Anjelita wrinkled her eyebrows at my inability to follow

her. But she soon made herself clear. She picked up a handful of rubbish and dropped it on the blanket. She kept throwing on more. She didn't seem to expect my help. I wasn't sure she wanted it. She must have hoped this demonstration would break through my denseness.

When the blanket was perhaps three-fifths covered with rubbish—that didn't take long to do—she picked up one corner and dragged it toward the bonfire.

Then I caught on. The blanket was a litter for litter.

I ran to catch up with her and helped pull her load to the fire. Although we had to throw a few larger items into the fire by hand, we were soon able to flap the blanket and empty the remaining contents into the flames. I couldn't imagine how many trips carrying that much at one time might save us.

We jumped back from the fire when larger-than-usual flames shot up from burning a larger-than-usual load. While I stood there admiring the blaze, Anjelita dragged the blanket back to the churchyard and started loading it again. I ran back and helped this time. Amazingly soon, we were on our way to the fire again.

At first I was concerned about wearing holes in the blanket until it became unusable. But Anjelita had apparently instructed her troops to clear the sharpest rocks from the pathway.

God knew what He was doing when He sent this blanket to Santa María. The mothballs had done their job, and the material was remarkably intact in spite of the shabbiness of age.

I thanked God for this special gift and its unknown donor—someone I'd recently blasted for using mothballs rather than aromatic cedar. But the scent of her gift was a sweet perfume of love. One that was more powerful than mothballs.

Geoff was watching. He was alone, and I'd never seen him look lonelier. I caught his eye and waved. He looked like he wanted to wave back but couldn't allow himself to. He hadn't spoken to me since the conversation Rob overheard. I didn't know how to make Geoff speak to me, but—now that I knew about his background—I was more anxious than ever to have a good talk with him.

Or for me just to listen. Two ears, Kim. One mouth. "Geoff? Geoff!" I waved again and motioned him over. He turned his back but remained where he was.

"Geoff! I promised to talk with you several days ago. Is this a good time for you?"

He turned toward me. Anjelita paused for a moment. The blanket was full, but she started dragging it by herself when she saw I was too preoccupied with Geoff to do my part.

He opened his mouth as if he might respond but closed it again. He rushed away, presumably to his worksite. I tried not thinking about him. His problems were beyond my ability to do anything about, or so it seemed.

Or was Geoff my next project—the one I couldn't possibly handle on my own?

chapter forty-five

Anjelita and I made phenomenal progress that afternoon, and I thought we would complete our cleanup by the end of the next day. She must have been extra tired, though. No sooner did we finish our supper than Rosa came to get her. Anjelita was already asleep on the ground.

I marveled that Rosa could do construction all day and still have enough energy to pick Anjelita up and hoist her over one shoulder. Maybe motherhood supplied that kind of strength.

But before Rosa stooped to pick her daughter up, she and I smiled at one another, and she hugged me first. I was elated at this sign of progress in our developing friendship. Maybe affection and not friendship, for we barely knew one another.

We had nothing in common but Anjelita, who undoubtedly shared details about my day-to-day life with her mom. I could imagine the two of them chattering and laughing together as they tried to figure out what made this petite, black-haired eighteen-year-old tick.

Yet Rosa wasn't just an acquaintance, either. We were some-how part of the same family—relatives who've recently met and become fond of one another despite their inability to com-municate verbally. She had progressed from uncertainty about me to a willing acceptance to a feeling of genuine affection.

I couldn't have accomplished that on my own. And I couldn't share God's Good News with Rosa without God's help, either. Not any more than I could get Geoff to remove his mask.

⌒

Night hadn't fallen yet. Although I probably had an hour of

daylight left, I felt like I was walking down a dark road on a moonless night. I'd had it—physically, mentally, and emotionally.

I was also spiritually dry. I'd gotten so caught up in my concerns about Geoff and the villagers that I'd lost the vision. That's the only way I could describe it. I couldn't tell whether I was on the roadway or on the shoulder, perhaps ready to tumble down a steep hillside.

That wasn't the only problem, though. Visions of the migrant children I couldn't help this summer still haunted me. I was experiencing a similar hopelessness about everything I wanted to accomplish in Santa María.

Lord, are You sure You can use me? I'm no good for anything.

In need of refreshing. I closed my eyes to pray. Before I completed the first sentence, I realized what was wrong. I'd been in Santa María for a week now without even opening my Bible. Praying more faithfully than I'd ever done before was important, but it didn't take the place of Bible study. I opened my eyes and got to my feet.

I picked my way through the campsite maze to my sleeping bag. I seldom opened my suitcase, but I'd left my dual-language Bible inside where it would be safe.

I got it out, laid it on my sleeping bag, and closed and latched the suitcase. Most of the other things in the suitcase didn't look familiar. They'd belonged to a different Kim Hartlinger in a different world, and I didn't know if the new Kim would ever need them again.

I carried the Bible to the area near the mess tent where I'd tried praying a few minutes earlier. I wasn't alone, but people rarely interrupted one another while enjoying their private times with God.

I hunkered down against my favorite rock. The position may have been miserable, but it was better than sitting upright without any support.

I opened the Bible—Santa Biblia, it said on the outside cover—and asked God to lead me to the passage He wanted me to focus on.

But something wasn't right.

The middle-aged salesclerk who'd sold Betsy Jo and me our Bibles at the religious bookstore back home had trouble understanding what we wanted. But we thought she'd finally gotten it straight.

Now the message Betsy Jo sent care of my parents made sense: "I hope you won't be too disappointed with your Bible."

Disappointment was a mild word to describe what I felt upon discovering that my side-by-side Spanish-English Bible was in Spanish. Only in Spanish.

I didn't know if unilingual was a word or not, but this revelation of our clerk's stupid mistake led to a loud drat and two doggones. A mistake that serious deserved stronger language, but I'd been super-conscientious about what I said since breaking Anjelita of her innocent cursing.

How dumb had that salesclerk been? We told her we were coming on an evangelistic mission trip to Mexico and needed a single Bible that was printed side by side in both languages.

Yes, ma'am, both languages—Spanish and English.

What part of that hadn't she understood? She might as well not have been listening. I thought adults her age were required to listen more carefully to teens than teens listen to adults of any age.

Kim, do you always listen to Me? a small voice asked gently and patiently.

Lord, I responded, *don't expect patience now. Please.*

Oh, but I do. I've been processing your prayer requests, Kim. You have the answer to Santa María's needs right there in your hands.

I'd been a professing Christian for several years. Because

my conversion took place over a period of months, I couldn't be sure of the exact date. But no matter when it took place, I'd never had such a personal experience with God before.

Yet this encounter was as mysterious and undecipherable as God Himself. Although He'd preached a personal sermon during my intended Bible reading time, He might as well have been speaking in tongues. I could relate better than usual to Jesus' disciples, who usually followed up His parables by pleading, "So what's that really mean?"

I've been processing your prayer requests, Kim. You have the answer to Santa María's needs right there in your hands. He'd spoken those exact words. Nice simple words. Although I understood the meaning of each one, I didn't understand His answer one bit better.

Use your head, I thought. *This is like doing a math problem, except the rules for solving it are in my Spanish Bible.* But this problem had too many unknowns, and the answer wasn't in the back of the book. The book was the answer.

Godly insight struck like a powerful summer thunderstorm that drenches the thirsty fields after a devastating drought. He understood the process. I didn't need to. God's Holy Spirit could use this Bible—so useless looking in my hands—to sow and reap a bountiful harvest.

Here I am, Lord. Send me. As I echoed Isaiah's words, they swirled around in my head to the tune of the MercyMe song. But I'd already responded to the call. I'd come to Mexico. I was in Santa María instead of Ciudad de Plata. God led me here—where He apparently planned to use me.

Thinking of flexibility, faithfulness, and obedience, I should have responded, "Lord, You've sent me. I've come. I'm here. Now use me, and don't let me get in Your way."

But why was I so hesitant to say that? My mind quit whirring for the briefest of moments. Then I exploded in laughter—pure, honest, mirthful laughter.

Lord, this is silliness. Pure craziness. Everyone will know I've lost my mind. They'll think I'm Noah building the ark when nobody knows what rain is, much less a flood. Isn't there some better way? Some more. . .conventional way?

Just do it, a little voice answered back. *Do it if you meant what you said.*

Just do it and they will come? I couldn't believe He was serious about this.

Godly silence.

I must have fallen asleep then. I dreamed I was sitting on the home bench during the final part of *Field of Dreams*. Daylight couldn't have been brighter than the lighted ball field and the miles and miles of approaching car headlights. A baseball game was in progress, but God alone was seated in the stands. Seated in? His omnipresence supported, surrounded, and hovered over the stands and the playing field.

But God wasn't just the sole spectator. He was also the coach for the home team, which consisted of Charlie, Rob, Neil, Aleesha, and several other team members I couldn't identify because of the light in my eyes. They were short several players, though, and I kept whining from the bench, "Let me play. I want to play. I'm on this team. Don't keep me out of the game."

God's voice answered, "Kim, don't you think you'd look silly trying to play baseball with a broken arm? What could you do? You're not that good a player using both arms."

"Lord, I looked silly clearing rubbish off the playing field, too, but I got it done, didn't I?"

"You, Kim?"

"Anjelita and me, I mean." I didn't mean to sound like I'd done it single-handedly. "And all the others who helped."

"And what had to happen before I gave you enough helpers

to get the job done?"

"I had to acknowledge that the project was Yours." I thought for a moment. "I had to be obedient. I had to depend on You."

"You're ready, Kim. Head out to the mound."

I felt like hugging God but fell to the ground instead. He raised me to my feet.

"By the way, Kim, you'll only need one hand and one arm out there."

I started to protest. "But, Lord, sometimes the ball is hit to the pitcher. . . ."

"Do you trust Me, Kim?"

"Of course I do. But don't you want Anjelita to stand beside me and help?"

"You'll need helpers, and Anjelita will be one of them. But she won't play such an important role this time."

"Any way You want to do it, Lord. Just let us win this game. . .for Your glory."

The dream ended, and I realized I was still praying. *Lord, I'll do what You want, but You're the only One who can make it work.* I mouthed those words silently as I accepted God's challenge to do the impossible and depend on His promise of help.

I felt peaceful and yet excited at receiving my real assignment. God had commissioned me to do what I was dying to do from the beginning. But He wanted me to do it in a way I wouldn't have thought of or attempted on my own. I couldn't back out if I'd wanted to. I'd made the commitment.

I couldn't keep from adding a postscript to my prayer, though. "Please don't expect me not to laugh about this."

chapter forty-six

Day 9

We had more helpers than usual, and we could see additional ground with each passing hour. We would complete the litter cleanup today. Competition for the honor of removing the final handful of trash was ferocious—in a good-natured way.

The composition of each snow-trash drift had been a mystery when we started. But unlike snowdrifts, made of flakes that bond together as a mass, small bits of visible space separated the objects in the churchyard.

Anjelita and I had made a game of looking for items of interest as we worked. Whenever one of us discovered a cup handle or half an ink pen or the bill of a baseball cap, the finder held it high and paraded back and forth in front of the church to the cheers of the current helpers.

If the finder could make the object wearable, she ended the parade by putting it on and returning to work. It was a finders, keepers game, and I wasn't too old to enjoy anticipating the reaction at church when I came home with some trinket of unknown origin.

But a toothbrush stamped Made in USA on the handle had been my best find so far. The storm had battered it so badly I couldn't guess at its original color. I was thinking about taking it home as a joke.

Anjelita had been slightly more successful than I. But only another child would consider a ragged shirtsleeve a treasure.

At least our little game kept both of us alert as we searched in vain for a treasure of immense value. We hadn't found one yet, and I couldn't imagine succeeding on the final day of our cleanup.

I wondered if everything in the yard had come from elsewhere. Or did the tornado bury some of the villagers' possessions here, too? It didn't matter. Nothing was intact. Even the dilapidated toothbrush was bald. The twister made sure of that.

We spotted another rotting tire but couldn't reach it yet. Hiding unsuccessfully behind it was a glittery object I assumed to be just another piece of broken glass. Those fragments required the most time and care in disposing of safely. I wouldn't let Anjelita handle them, and I was super-careful. I didn't particularly relish the thought of slicing and dicing any of my body parts.

I was slight enough already.

This piece of glass glittered so brightly I thought it might be a mirror fragment. After working my way to a spot near the front wall of the church, I leaned against the rotten tire and pulled out my treasure.

The old necklace was remarkably intact. It was in far better shape than anything else we'd come across. I thought it was toy jewelry at first, but the chain was too long. On closer examination, I recognized that it was too precious to be a child's, anyhow. It looked like an antique.

An unusual gold setting held a colorless jewel firmly in its claw. The stone itself perplexed me.

I'm unusually good at recognizing gems—I'd spent months of my life window-shopping in jewelry stores—but I was clueless about this one. It wasn't a diamond, although the cut looked similar. The small stone's reflective power astounded me. No wonder I mistook it for mirror glass. As I turned the necklace this way and that, a rainbow appeared on the ground in front of me. Ah. So some unknown jeweler had fashioned the stone into a prism.

I wasn't sure at first whether the chain and setting were real gold, but a few drops from my water bottle and a little buffing against my pants leg made the necklace shine like my fourteen-karat class ring. If I was right, its worth was beyond my ability to estimate.

The necklace must have been strong to survive its frenetic trip to the churchyard without major damage. The chain and setting contained only a few tiny nicks that gave them character. Although one facet of the prism had a slight scratch, the stone didn't appear to be in danger of cracking or falling out.

Any fashionable woman would wear magnificent jewelry like that with pride. How the owner must have grieved her loss. A necklace like that was probably a family heirloom—priceless and irreplaceable. No matter how much I wanted to find its rightful owner and return it, I had little hope of doing so.

I wondered if the owner had survived the tornado. I wiped my eyes with my sleeve as I considered the irony of an inanimate piece of jewelry outliving its owner.

Lord, please bless the owner if she's still alive.

Anjelita had gone for water a few minutes earlier. I was dying to show her my find. She'd be thrilled that one of us had finally found a real treasure.

When I put the necklace on, I felt regal. Had it ever belonged to royalty? Perhaps this wasn't just a family heirloom, but one small part of a larger treasure. No matter how wild my imagination ran, I'd never learn the real story.

My necklace—yes, it was mine now—was heavier than I'd expected. It was. . .substantial in its feel, although exquisitely feminine in appearance. I wondered if its previous owner had been as petite as me.

A smiling Anjelita appeared a few yards away. She had an

open, half-empty bottle of water in her hand and an unopened bottle under her half arm for me. She'd spilled water on her pale blue dress running to see what I had. I stood up just as she reached me, the necklace dangling handsomely against my filthy T-shirt. I might have been royalty out slumming.

I'd seen Anjelita happy many times that week, but her smile and eyes brightened more than ever now, and she squealed a number of times with delight.

But then she started crying so suddenly I thought she'd either cut herself or one of Santa María's abundant creepy-crawly critters had bit her. I checked her legs and bare feet for cuts and bites but didn't see any blood or signs of injury.

Sometimes even another woman can't interpret the mood of a female who's in the midst of a crying jag. I looked into Anjelita's face but saw no trace of pain or sorrow. Neither did I see anger or frustration.

She simply looked—how should I say it?—less happy than when she first saw the necklace. Her reaction was illogical. Why would a necklace make her cry? Did it remind her of some trinket she'd lost in the storm?

Her tears insisted that there was more to it than that.

Just as suddenly as she'd begun crying, she quieted down again. I could hear an occasional sniffle, but her initial joy at seeing the necklace had vanished. She looked baffled. Uncertain.

Beyond that, I couldn't read her. Her battle appeared to be personal.

"Anjelita, isn't it beautiful—uh, es bella?"

What a pathetic use I'd made of the few Spanish words I'd mastered. I heard too many to write down more than a few of them. Would a more committed effort—or at least a more disciplined one—have helped now? And would it have made my God-assigned task any easier?

Then again, if God expected me to do more than make a fool of myself, I'd need all the faith I could muster and let Him do the real work. I would just be His mouthpiece.

But I wasn't going to be Aaron speaking for Moses. God would do the speaking as if He were a ventriloquist and I His dummy. I'd feel like one, anyhow, and I still chuckled at His plan.

But that didn't solve this problem with Anjelita.

"Es bella?" I asked her once more.

She didn't seem to be listening. The necklace held her complete attention. She extended her hand toward it but withdrew it again as if the necklace was too hot to touch. After she did that several times, I took her small, soft hand in mine and—with the gold chain still hanging from my neck—I let the pendant touch her fingertips.

Her eyes sparkled. "*Una collar,*" Anjelita whispered in a tone I can only describe as awestruck.

"Ko-YAR?"

"Sí, *mi* collar, mi *prisma.*"

She bent down and wrote collar in the dirt. That must have meant "necklace." Prisma sounded like "prism." She must have assumed I understood mi. Unfortunately, I ignored that most important word.

My little sister's fingers explored the necklace as if caressing the face of someone her family has just found after giving up hope. But heartbreak tainted her smile.

Since every discovery belonged to the finder, the necklace was clearly mine, and I looked forward to taking it home as a souvenir. Whether I would wear it, time would tell. I questioned whether its elegant beauty would look appropriate on a frame as petite as mine, though.

Then I realized how badly Anjelita wanted the necklace. She didn't care that I'd found it, not her. The selfishness in me wanted to scream, "This isn't yours. Don't you dare ask for it." The self-righteousness wanted to preach, "Don't covet someone else's belongings. I'll keep this trinket to teach you to be satisfied with what you have."

With what you have?

I lived in a spacious house with a garage that was roomier than Rosa's new cottage. Even my bedroom was bigger. I owned so many unneeded clothes I didn't have room for more. A number of trinkets—some fairly valuable and most of them unused—crowded three jewelry chests on my dresser. How many purchases had I never even removed the price tag from?

I had abundance—overabundance.

And standing before me was a pretty, young child with nothing to call her own but the clothes on her back. She fondly handled a pendant I had no earthly use for. She acted like it was important to her. Immensely more important than it was to me.

Melting in shame at my selfishness, I bent my head forward so I could slip the chain off and let it fall around Anjelita's neck. Bowing before Jesus couldn't have been more humbling.

Anjelita's mouth dropped open in shock.

She threw her arms around me, said, "*Muchas gracias!*" over and over again, and took off at full speed. She ran only a couple of yards before coming back and giving me the tightest hug imaginable.

"*Mamá!* Mamá! Mi collar! Señorita Keem. . .mi collar!" she cried out as she started searching for Rosa.

Less than two minutes later, Rosa arrived at the church-yard with Anjelita's hand in hers. Her smile was radiant, and she threw her arms around me and started talking in the most excited Spanish I'd heard since coming to Santa María.

I wondered if she was praising—or at least thanking—me

for giving Anjelita the necklace. She may have been trying to explain something. Unable to listen fast enough to catch any of the familiar words she used, I had no idea what was going on.

But I'd definitely done the right thing.

chapter forty-seven

We completed the churchyard cleanup around two o'clock that afternoon. I was especially indebted to the senior adults and the children. Both groups put in nearly full-time hours after becoming involved. I went to each individual and expressed my thanks the best I could.

Even though everyone else had only helped part-time, we wouldn't have finished without them. I thanked each team member personally. I didn't know who'd helped and who hadn't, but that didn't matter. Any victory in Santa María was a team victory.

"I understand a little how Jesus may have felt when He wept over Jerusalem," Neil said as only he could. "I've shed the tears of a lifetime in Santa María, but I've smiled the smiles of a lifetime, too."

It was almost time to begin my special assignment, and I still giggled at the thought of it. I didn't have the confidence or imagination to come up with an idea like that, and the Devil—whether personal or conceptual—wouldn't have suggested it.

But I needed to do one small thing first. I hoped God wouldn't mind.

Acres of wildflowers grew on and around the girls' field. After borrowing a hand tool from Rob—I don't know what it was, but it had a pointed tip—I led Anjelita to a lush concentration of flowers. I knelt on the ground and maneuvered the tool blade gently to free the root ball as well as the flower. I dug up several more while Anjelita supervised with a look of curiosity.

Although she looked glamorous in her necklace, the chain was so long the prism nearly reached her waist. After motioning for her to bend down, I doubled it for her. I didn't want her to lose it now.

I just needed a flower or two to demonstrate what we were going to do. Then we'd dig up as many as we needed.

Anjelita's face lit up when she saw that the hole I was digging in the churchyard was big enough to plant the dirtball in. I should've known how quickly she'd catch on. Against my better judgment, I let her use the pointed hand tool to dig spots for additional flowers. My hand hovered just inches from hers as if I could move fast enough to prevent accidental injury.

I shouldn't have bothered, though. She'd been careful picking up litter, and she'd been careful near the flames. She treated the sharp digging tool with similar respect. Together we pressed the ball of roots firmly into place and covered them with dirt.

The wildflowers seemed hardy enough to survive in their new home if we could just help them recover from being transplanted. Because the rubbish had helped prevent moisture from evaporating, the churchyard wasn't as dry as the ground surrounding it. The flowers still needed water, though. At home, I would have unreeled the green garden hose or filled a plastic watering can, but I didn't have those options in Santa María.

"Rob, may we pour some bottles of drinking water on these flowers? They may not survive if we don't."

His apologetic look tore me up. "I'm sorry, Kimmy, but we need to leave as much water for the villagers as possible. I don't know where they got water before the storm or whether that source will become available again. They may have to survive on this bottled water for a while."

So many questions. So few answers.

Once people saw what we were doing, though, water for the flowers flowed in a steady trickle of abundance. Whenever someone drank a bottle of water, he left an inch or two and poured it on the thirstiest-looking flower he saw. With help like that, the wildflowers would soon look as vigorous as they had in the field. I sang praises to God at the top of my lungs for the way He clothed and cared for the least of His creations.

We lined flowers along the front wall of the church and defined a wide pathway to the door with others.

Then Anjelita got my curiosity up. She somehow slid her hand beneath a flat, five-inch rock that would have been too heavy to grasp from the top even if her hand had been big enough. She managed to lift it to her chest. She let it drop on the pathway side of the flowers, but I still couldn't figure out what she was doing.

But when she picked up another rock—there must have been mega-tons of them in the area—and dropped it a foot or so from the first one, I understood. She was making a rock border to separate the walkway from the surrounding churchyard. Her sense of aesthetics fascinated me, for she was purposely zigzagging rocks and flowers in parallel rows, creating a closer—yet still an uncrowded—look.

Although my hand was slightly larger than Anjelita's, she must have been stronger than me after years of doing everything single-handedly. My eyes burned from sweat by the time I wrestled another rock up, and I thought my hand and arm would fall off by the time I dropped it in place.

We completed the bordering in less than an hour and collapsed in the churchyard with several bottles of water each.

Before I finished my first bottle, I jumped up again—if anyone could describe such an exhausted motion as jumping. But no amount of fatigue would keep me from testing an idea.

I maneuvered a rock into place on the yard side of the

flowers, including those that fronted the building. Anjelita squealed. She must have loved the idea, even though it meant moving more rocks.

But she and I barely had the energy to force ourselves to move. I considered using the blanket, but by the time we could roll a rock onto the blanket, drag it where we needed it, and kick it into place, we would die of premature old age.

Only God's strength enabled us to finish. After admiring our handiwork, we dragged ourselves to the mess tent, got supper, and collapsed. Almost too exhausted to eat, we stared at our food for a number of minutes.

Various guys and gals congratulated us on our churchyard beautification, and we were elated over our accomplishments. God's accomplishments. Those flowers were His, and so were the rocks. The whole idea was probably His, too. His idea, His materials, and His strengthening of our weak, worn-out muscles had created something gorgeous and glorious. More important, though, the ancient, unused building now looked worthy of being used as a church. If my new assignment accomplished its goals, maybe it would be.

Although I hadn't seen anything of Geoff the past several days, he stopped to comment. I wondered if his heart had softened any.

His first words answered my question. "Why the blue blazes did you waste time building a rock garden? The litter cleanup was dumb enough."

After everyone else's compliments, he might as well have slapped me in the face. "Why do you say 'waste,' Geoff? Beauty is never a waste." I hadn't intended to sound defensive; but Geoff was treading on holy ground, and I was too exhausted to put up with any of his mess.

"Those flowers won't survive," he whined. "They may last until we leave for home, although I doubt it, but what'll happen after that? The villagers won't water them. It's not like that building you foolishly refer to as a church means anything to them, anyhow. They used the yard as a junk heap before the storm. You may have gotten rid of the debris, but the yard will be overgrown with weeds and more rubbish soon enough. It's going to go back to looking like, uh. . ."

I knew what four-letter word he wanted to use. I'd used it often enough in the past. Maybe he would've said it if he hadn't been so afraid of Rob sending him home. No matter how much the thought of bad language offended me now, I wouldn't have told on him. I hadn't given up on him yet, although this conversation wasn't raising my hopes.

I'd never noticed how opinionated Geoff was. And every opinion came across as if it were a well-known and indisputable fact.

But I knew—or at least I had my own opinions—that he was wrong about everything. "Yeah, Geoff, I know. Anjelita and I took a chance. I don't know about the water, but I'll bet Anjelita tends the flowers as much as she can. She's quite proud of the churchyard, and I think the other villagers are, too."

"Anjelita!" he said under his breath.

"Don't pick on her, Geoff." I couldn't have gotten much angrier if he'd slapped Anjelita. Although I was proud of myself for not cussing him out, I yielded to a stronger temptation.

I punched him in the arm as hard as I could. I didn't hit him nearly as hard as I'd meant to. But I did the best I could left-handed. My assault didn't even leave a red mark.

I was ashamed of myself, but Geoff did his best to humiliate me more. "Woo, baby!" he said in an exaggerated tone. "You'd better watch that temper. It's not very becoming to the Christian Judith thinks is the finest one she's ever known."

Has Judith bragged on me to everyone who'll listen? And

did she have to say something to Geoff of all people?

He was laughing. Laughing hard. He'd won a strategic victory, and he was awarding himself an imaginary trophy.

Somewhere Satan was rejoicing, too. A more personal Satan than I'd believed in before.

I couldn't respond at first. I could justify my anger, but I couldn't rationalize hitting Geoff, no matter how puny my punch. What had Pastor Ron told us repeatedly? Anger isn't sinful, but acting out inappropriately is.

Geoff's attitude made me sick. I wanted him to go away and leave me alone. That little voice inside disagreed, though. God wasn't finished with me for the evening.

But what could I do when Geoff was so good at battering my most sensitive spots and bringing out my worst? Jonah tried running away from God because he didn't want to obey Him. It didn't work. And I didn't even have the option of trying to run.

If I avoided witnessing to Geoff—or failed to be nice to him—God would get my attention some other way and turn it in Geoff's direction again. As impossible as it sounded, doing the right thing willingly would be more comfortable than provoking God into making me do it.

"Geoff, you're right." I was trying to work my way to a painful apology. "As perturbed as I was—"

"And you still are, aren't you, Kimmy?" He trampled on my words as if they'd been flowers.

I trembled at the sound of his snort. It wasn't a laugh, but the sound a large animal might make when preparing to attack and devour a defenseless, smaller one.

"Yes, I am. Geoff. Do you know how hard it is to be nice to you?" I breathed a deep prayer for guidance in the upcoming discussion, aware that I couldn't have gotten off to a worse start.

"I'm glad to hear it, Kimmy. I don't want you to be nice to me."

I thought about what Rob said about Geoff wanting acceptance on his own terms. "So you say, Geoff. But— doggone it—I'm going to be nice to you, anyhow. If Jesus could love and forgive the people who put Him to death on the cross, I should be able to love and accept you the way you are."

"Now you're talking, Kimmy. Admit that I'm the enemy."

I'd never met anyone so expert at taking words out of context. "Jesus spent His time on earth turning enemies into friends. I think He did a pretty good job of it. Don't you?"

His silence stunned me.

"Geoff, I don't know all of your background—"

"But you know a lot of it, don't you? Uncle Rob told you, even though he promised not to tell anyone; and you feel sorry for me. You've made me your pet mission project. Save the planet! Save the whales! Save Geoff! Isn't that what you want to do?"

Lord. . . ? "Geoff, you've given me every reason to think you're not a Christian. Knowing and following Jesus is the most important thing you can do with your life. I'm not sure I've ever met a boy as unhappy as you, but I know one thing. You'll never be happy without Jesus in your life."

Geoff might take my words as clichés—or perhaps as the beginning of a mini-sermon—but I couldn't worry about that. They came straight from my heart. I'd told Geoff what I believed, not what Pastor Ron taught me to say or what I thought I should say.

I was no longer an eighteen-year-old girl talking to an obnoxious male peer, but more of an adult than I ever thought I could be, trying to talk patiently and lovingly with an obstinate, disobedient child—one whose misbehavior cried out for attention.

I was so concerned about Geoff now I didn't care what he said. *Jonah, I think you've arrived in Nineveh. But will the crowd listen?*

Without waiting for Geoff to respond, I threw my arms around him in a sisterly hug, being careful not to hit him with my cast. He wept as he hugged me back. I was in tears, too, confident that we'd finally connected.

But the Devil—how personal he was—wasn't about to give Geoff up without a fight. Geoff broke away from my grasp and stalked away into the dusk, cursing me at every step while trying to stop crying.

With each step he took and every swear word he thrust in my direction, I cried harder—for him.

chapter forty-eight

Day 10

Dawn had broken moments earlier, and Anjelita appeared out of nowhere. Tears flooded her face, and she hugged me so tightly I was afraid something terrible had happened to Rosa. Before I did anything else, though, I checked her neck for the prism necklace. It was there.

Regardless of the urgency of her tugging, I couldn't go anywhere without throwing on my clothes. Although I got dressed in less than two minutes, Anjelita paced as impatiently as if I were taking hours.

Wait. If something's happened to Rosa, Anjelita would still be at her mother's side. It must be something else.

But even as she led me in a half walk, half run toward the churchyard, I had a nasty premonition about what I'd find. I hoped I was wrong. . . .

Yes, someone had leveled our flower garden. The culprit tore all the wildflowers up by the roots, threw them in a pile, and trampled them so viciously not one was intact. The perpetrator also picked up the rocks and scattered them throughout the churchyard.

Anjelita and I clung together and wept aloud—she, because our touch of beauty had been made desolate and ugly; and me, because of my certainty that Geoff was the culprit. Reminding myself that Jesus had prayed for His enemies under worse circumstances, I tried to focus my thoughts and prayers on the boy who kept doing his best to become my enemy.

I was determined to do the humanly impossible: to keep praying rather than giving in and hating him.

We remained in the churchyard for a number of minutes. Although Anjelita couldn't understand my promise, I told her we'd remake the flower garden today. The calm in my voice seemed to help.

She couldn't see the knot in my stomach, though.

As daylight brightened, I made eating motions. Anjelita smiled weakly and took my hand. We'd gone just a few yards toward the mess tent when I saw Geoff coming our way.

Lord, help us both. . . .

"You snitched on me, didn't you?" An accusation more than a question, his words were the snarl of a wild beast straining every muscle to the max to break free from a trap.

"What are you talking about, Geoff? I haven't—"

"You told Uncle Rob. He's sending me home."

Defensiveness grabbed me with such force I failed to take in what he'd said about being sent home. "I haven't seen Rob today, and we haven't talked about anything important in several days. Not even about you."

"But somebody has. Who would do that but you?"

I shook my head in innocence. I said, "I didn't" with such calm he couldn't ignore it.

His venom weakened. "Kim, you're. . .serious?"

"I am. I last saw Rob yesterday before supper. That was at least an hour before you and I talked. I wouldn't have told him about our discussion, anyhow. That was between you and me."

And God.

"But you must've told him about the flower garden this morning. . . ."

"That was you? You did that?" I hated pretending to be surprised, but I wanted him to admit what he'd done and apologize. Not so much for my sake, but for his. Most of all, I wanted him to turn to Jesus and seek His forgiveness.

"You knew it was me. Who else would. . . ?"

"I wondered. . . ." I spoke as quietly as I could. He wasn't going to goad me into anger or rash behavior today.

"Kimmy, I believed you were different when we first met. I still think so. I've listened to you—even when you thought I wasn't. I was plenty angry last night, true, but I wasn't angry at you. . . ."

"No?" I spoke as meekly as I could. The ungodly side of me was dying to retort, "You could've fooled me."

"I was angry at myself. You were right—about everything—but it was easier to feel sorry for myself than to repent again."

Repent again? What a strange statement. "It's not too late, Geoff." Not too late to repent of your sins, but perhaps too late to avoid the consequences.

"Yes, it is. I messed up here just like I did back home. I can't imagine the trouble I'll be in when I go back to court. I brought it all on myself. I'm a loser."

What should I say? I had no idea I'd come this close to reaching him. Yet now that he'd barricaded himself behind this mask of negativity, I wouldn't have any more chances.

Not if he went home today.

I was about to take Geoff's hand and pray aloud where we stood, but Rob appeared from the direction of the mess tent and addressed Geoff more sternly than I'd heard him speak to anyone.

"Geoff, go on. Get your things ready. Pick up something to eat from the mess tent. We're leaving in fifteen minutes. We'll call Jill on the satellite phone and tell her to expect you. I hope you'll feel good explaining why you're coming home."

After wincing at Rob's reference to his mom and drying his eyes on his shirtsleeve, Geoff dragged his feet in the direction of the boys' field. He trudged along as if he couldn't bear the weight of his own world. He made me think of Jesus dragging His cross to Golgotha. Had He sensed a similar feeling of dread and defeat?

"Rob. . . ?"

"Hmm?" He looked at me through misty eyes.

Although I had his attention, I couldn't verbalize my request. My heart and mind were colliding like bumper cars at an amusement park.

Geoff hadn't reached the boys' field yet. I could still see him, but I'd been wrong comparing him with Jesus and His cross. Geoff looked like a whipped dog with his tail between his legs.

Jesus never had a reason to look like that. Geoff did.

Throughout my encounter with Geoff and now again with Rob, Anjelita remained silent. She seemed to realize that Geoff was the culprit, although she couldn't possibly know how Rob was punishing him. She squeezed my hand. I think she knew I was more concerned about Geoff than about the garden.

Should I? I had to. I'd ask. I'd beg if I had to. But what if Rob refused?

I summoned all of my courage and prayed for more. Under circumstances like these when my disfluency was apt to be at its worst, I found myself speaking clearly, simply, and sincerely. "Rob, please don't send Geoff home."

Chances were Rob would refuse, yet my heart told me I'd done the right thing—the godly thing—by interceding for Geoff.

I should've had more faith in Rob, though. He didn't argue. Tears overflowed his eyes. Perhaps he knew Geoff's spiritual and emotional well-being rested in my hands more now than ever.

"You're sure?" he said.

I nodded. *Lord, please keep me sure.*

chapter forty-nine

Although Rob didn't send Geoff home, he didn't get off scot-free. I saw him after breakfast, setting out rocks at the borders Anjelita and I had defined yesterday. If using more rocks than Anjelita and I had and placing them closer together was any indication, he took this one last chance seriously.

I smiled when I saw him using a tape measure to place the rocks equidistant from one another. Duh. How come I hadn't thought of that?

At the rate he was going, he would soon be replacing the wildflowers. Boys must prefer building flower gardens from the outside in. I giggled to myself as I wondered whether Geoff had ever painted himself into a corner, but I got serious again on realizing he'd done a good job of that the past week. And probably the last year or two as well.

I was in a corner of my own, but at least I'd come willingly. Although the rock garden had caused a slight delay, I couldn't postpone the more important project any longer. I didn't want to test God's patience.

I started laughing on the way to retrieve the Bible from my sleeping bag, where I'd looked it over with renewed confusion earlier this morning. Anjelita walked beside me. Each time I laughed, her high-pitched giggle echoed back. Laughter would never be the same again without her.

In four days, I'd have to say good-bye. Although I tried to keep from thinking about it, the prospect of leaving was already tearing me up. Shakespeare had been wrong; Parting wouldn't be the least sweet. Only sorrowful. After two weeks of relating and functioning like conjoined twins, we'd suffer the painful operation that separated us for good. Cut off from one another's day-to-day realities by lack of e-mail, telephone, and regular postal mail, only fond memories would keep our kinship intact.

Although Aleesha—many other team members, too—had taken dozens of pictures of Anjelita and me and would e-mail them to everyone who wanted them, Anjelita would never see them or receive a copy. That tore me up.

Unless I returned to Santa María someday, we'd never see one another again in this life, and unless Anjelita became a believer, our separation would be eternal. At first, I'd fretted about that for hours at a time; but then I realized God's strange-yet-amusing plan was truly worthwhile.

The only hope for Anjelita and Rosa—for the whole village—required me to sit in the hot sunshine outside the building I prayed might someday be used as a church and read aloud from the Bible in Spanish, a language I had no idea how to pronounce. I might as well be speaking with a pig's oink.

Logically, I had a zero percent chance of success. But God was in complete charge of this plan, not me. So chance and human logic didn't apply. *Lord, when the time comes, won't You give me a little encouragement? Just a small sign that I'm accomplishing. . .that You're using me to accomplish something.*

If I was going to be God's "Evangelizer Bunny," He'd have to be my never-failing battery. I'd need His power just to keep going and going and going.

I put the Bible under my arm when Anjelita and I started back toward the church. I tripped and almost fell once. I was apt to do that several times daily—graceless creature that I was—but Anjelita had grown expert at watching out for me. Although she couldn't grab me this time, she managed to catch the Bible while I steadied myself.

I marveled at her agility. Although she had a permanent disability, she barely seemed aware of having limitations. She could do almost everything other people did. She just did them differently.

After Anjelita caught the Bible, I let her carry it. I had no idea what translation it was, but I would croak if it turned out to be a Spanish rendering of the original King James Version. I'd prefer using the most modern version possible. Then I noticed Version Reina-Valera 1909 in small letters at the bottom of the front cover.

No matter what Reina-Valera meant, this translation apparently dated back to 1909. One hundred years old. I sighed before comforting myself with the thought that at least it was still three hundred years newer than the King James Version.

Even if I couldn't guess what *Antiguo y Nuevo Testamento* meant, a Bible this thick and using such tiny print had to include both the Old and New Testaments. My eyes weren't comfortable with anything smaller than a nine-point font, and CD liners often required the use of a magnifying glass.

This Bible appeared to be in six- or seven-point print, and I dreaded the headache I'd get trying to read it. I made a mental note to figure out the exact font size when I got home. Just out of curiosity. But by then, it would be a moot point.

Actually, the print size was already a moot point. I'd committed to reading it—bleary eyes and headache or not.

Anjelita looked at the front cover of the Bible. She read the words Santa Biblia aloud, but they didn't seem to hold any special meaning for her. I assumed someone her age would have a limited reading vocabulary. Not knowing how she'd learned to read or write, I couldn't appreciate how advanced Anjelita's education was.

The back cover was plain.

Anjelita looked like she was dying to open the Bible and start reading, but she couldn't carry it in her hand and flip pages with the stub of her other arm. Not while walking. She tried balancing the Bible on her half arm, but she couldn't hold it open that way. That angle would've made reading almost impossible, anyhow.

She looked like she wanted to stop where we were and sit down with the Bible to discover what it was. Even though I loved seeing her excitement over the Biblia, I had to motion for her to keep moving.

The sun shone brightly now, and I touched her necklace without removing it. I turned the prism one way and then another until it projected the colors of the rainbow on the cover of the Bible.

Did she have any idea how special this book was? If so, would she come to accept it as the love letter God sent to shine His light on lives lost in darkness? Would she ever see this book as the prism that scattered God's perfect white light and created the rainbow colors of a believer's life?

chapter fifty

G eoff was still at work on the flower garden.

Anjelita pointed at him with the stub of her arm, and we both smiled. I didn't know if we were thinking the same thing, but when she winked at me, I set the Bible down in a safe place. Making sure Geoff wasn't looking, I cunningly picked up the tool we'd used the previous afternoon and hid it behind my back. I'd never stolen anything before, and I was surprised at how well my first heist had gone. Speeding toward the girls' field with my loot and my little accomplice, I felt like a thief making her getaway.

But this was just a game. We'd been the victims of the real "crime," not the perpetrators.

Geoff wouldn't miss the digging tool for a while. If he needed it before we brought it back, let him think he'd misplaced it. I giggled as I imagined him looking everywhere for it, perhaps fearful he'd set a rock on top of it. Anjelita giggled with me.

I was just as glad she couldn't ask why I was so happy. Explaining would have been a challenge. My mind was so set on "heaping hot coals" on Geoff's head that the pure joy of repaying evil with good made me giddy.

When we reached the near side of the girls' field, we saw that more wildflowers had sprung up overnight, many of them colored more brilliantly than the ones we'd transplanted the day before. I'd never seen such vivid reds, blues, purples, oranges, and yellows. Even the white flowers looked like God had just given them the freshest of new paint jobs.

I knelt carefully—I'd learned my lesson well that first night in Santa María—and started digging. I sensed Anjelita's approval. But how I longed to explain we weren't helping Geoff because we were nice people, but because I thought Jesus would have done it and we ought to do it in His place.

I'd heard many sermons and Sunday school lessons about turning the other cheek and going the second mile, but those concepts would be unfamiliar to Anjelita with her apparent lack of familiarity with the Bible.

But what about me? Although those concepts are familiar, they've only been theory until now. I've never tried putting them into practice before.

Anjelita disappeared for a moment, returned with the old woolen blanket, and stretched out beside me. As I lifted each flower and root ball from the ground, I passed it to her, and she set it on the blanket as if handling a newborn baby. The blanket's mothball stink had finally dissipated, and the sweet perfume of wildflowers had started taking its place.

I marveled at God's ability to grow such a profusion of wildflowers in such unlikely-looking ground. Had the storm that leveled Santa María also brought flower seeds? *Lord, these signs of new life are exciting. Thanks for involving me— no matter how slightly—in Your rejuvenation process.*

As we dragged the blanket toward the churchyard, I glanced at Anjelita and quoted the scripture about continuing to forgive the people who've wronged us. That's seventy times seven, four hundred and ninety forgivenesses per person on a purely mathematical basis—if I could still multiply correctly without a calculator.

I giggled to myself. What kind of counter did God intend for us to use on those four hundred and ninety offenses? Probably just something that registered zero or one. One meant "not forgiven." Zero was "forgiven." Did the human side of Jesus have to struggle with forgiveness? I had to believe He did, and I worshiped as I considered that mystery.

Whether I'd helped anyone in Santa María or not, this trip had done more for me than I could comprehend. I'd heard other people—kids and adults—talk about mission trips they'd gone on. Almost invariably they'd said, "I went to be a blessing, but I came away blessed. I'm different now. I'll never be the same again."

How true that had been for me—infinitely more than any other mission trip I'd ever been on.

I didn't realize I'd gotten lost in thought until Anjelita stopped and I kept going. The blanket pulled so taut that two-thirds of the flowers spilled, and I plowed straight into Geoff.

I'd never noticed how tall he was. Of course, everyone was taller than me, but he was a skyscraper now compared to single-story me. I thought guys his age weren't supposed to grow more, especially in the short time we'd been in Santa María.

I looked into his eyes, and they looked clearer and more carefree than I'd ever seen. Maybe not carefree, but. . . forgiven.

On his way to pack, he'd looked so burdened down. Maybe I'd never seen him look any other way. I'd never seen him stand up so straight before. As if he no longer bore the weight of his mask.

No wonder he looked taller.

chapter fifty-one

I sat down on the hard ground in front of the church with the Santa Biblia on my lap, braced my back against the hot building, and prayed my body wouldn't start aching hours before I finished for the day.

Geoff had graciously left that spot bare for me. He smiled and gave a thumbs-up when he saw my Bible. I couldn't believe it. He wasn't just different from yesterday; he was night-and-day different from earlier this morning. Maybe Rob had explained his change of mind about sending Geoff home.

My reading spot was several feet from the doorway a steady stream of laborers would soon pass through for water, snacks, and shade. Because they often stayed inside during their breaks, I'd have to project my voice through the open door.

Only Anjelita would hear every word. If she could stand listening to me butcher her precious heart language for hours at a time, that is.

Everyone else would hear my reading piecemeal—with a number of pieces missing. I couldn't imagine what good that would do, but this was God's project, and my assignment was to obey and leave the results to Him.

The other team members might think I was crazy, but that didn't faze me. If they didn't already know the truth, maybe it's high time they learned it.

Although Aleesha knew me better than any other living person but Betsy Jo—parents don't count because they think they understand more than they do—I didn't tell her my plans ahead of time. God's plans, that is. I'd get her reaction later.

Anjelita plopped down awkwardly at a spot where she could see people coming and going. My back was to the door. I wasn't sure our positions were the best.

Where should I begin? Genesis? No. Revelations?
Absolutely not, and you know better than to put an s at the end of that name.

Flipping through the pages, I wondered if I should focus on familiar passages or read a Gospel straight through. Like other Christians who're willing to admit it, I couldn't remember the location of most of the passages I loved. Scriptures like John 3:16, the Twenty-third Psalm, and Matthew 28:19-20 were exceptions.

I felt so dumb, though. I could quote a number of scriptures with some degree of accuracy, but I'd never find them in a Spanish Bible. That would require a major miracle, one I didn't sense coming.

Lord? I asked silently.

You decide, Kim. My Word won't return to Me void.

A Gospel, then?

No response.

A Gospel seemed a better choice than something I might pick randomly. With my luck—I've always hated that word because Christians aren't dependent on luck—I'd end up spending days reading all the "begats" of the Bible. Even in Spanish, they'd put me to sleep.

Important stuff, I assumed. Else it wouldn't be there. But for evangelizing the villagers of Santa María? No way.

Okay, Kimmy, which Gospel?

Keeping Anjelita's attention was so important I rejected the book of John. The "Word" references in that first chapter require care, and I didn't think she'd find that as appealing as another Gospel.

On mission trips to the beach, we'd passed out portions of

Luke. Someone told me Luke's Gospel was a great beginning-to-end narrative of Jesus' life and ministry.

Besides, Luke included the familiar account of Jesus' birth, and Anjelita would enjoy that. If my memory served me right, kids loved hearing about babies and other kids. And if I found myself reading "begats," I'd skip them.

Looking for the Table of Contents—I wasn't sure I'd recognize Luke when I saw him—I came across the *Introducción*. Had to mean "introduction." Although the page was incomprehensible, it probably explained the Bible's purpose. That seemed like an appropriate place to start.

Luke—San Lucas—was easier to identify and locate than I'd expected. It was right between San Marcos and San Juan. I tore a page from my memo book to use as a bookmark.

Anjelita had started wiggling restlessly as soon as we sat down. I gathered she was impatient for me to start, even though I'd spent only a couple of minutes thumbing through the Bible and making decisions. *Calm down, girl. I'll start now.*

I was nervous—terrified. My tumbling, twisting tongue was almost sure to add to my difficulties. My Georgia drawl might complicate things more by converting single syllables into multiple ones, and I'd probably butcher my efforts further by unintentionally applying my knowledge of French.

Lord, will anyone understand a word I read?

Kim, you do your part and I'll do Mine.

I was about to begin the introduction when I heard foot-steps enter the church. I was set. My first audience was nearby.

But I couldn't start. I had to know who was going to hear me. That was the problem with our positions. I scrambled up and motioned for Anjelita to switch places with me. Now I could see who was coming and going and project my reading into the building.

Without waiting for the first listeners to come out, I started reading aloud.

"La historia de la Biblia es la historia de Dios creando el mundo y luego haciéndose a sí mismo disponible para la gente de ese mundo. Es una simple línea recta desde el corazón de Dios hacia el nuestro."

Oh, man. That didn't sound the first thing like the Spanish I'd heard the villagers speak daily, and Anjelita's quizzical expression told me I'd already lost her. But she was quick to make things right—at least for her. She scooted so close to me we shared the same sweat for hours to come.

Instead of reading to Anjelita, I would read to whoever entered the church, and she would read along silently. Surely some of the words were too big or the ideas too complex for someone Anjelita's age to comprehend, but I couldn't help that.

They were all too complex for me.

I'd spent four or five excruciating minutes doing my ignorant best to read those first two sentences from the introduction. At that rate, I'd never make it to Lucas.

What slowed me down more than the page full of unfamiliar words was noting the similarity of certain Spanish and English words. *Historia* and *history*, for example.

But I also found similarities between Spanish and the French I knew so well. *Mundo* was close enough to *monde* that it probably meant "world." I was less certain about *gente*, which reminded me of *gens*—people. The capitalization of *Dios* made it God, especially since the first paragraph of an Introducción to the Santa Biblia would most likely refer to God.

Okay, Kim, quit wasting time trying to understand what you're reading. Just read it and pray that somebody can make sense out of it.

But what chance was there of that? Not even Anjelita could understand my oral Spanish without sitting beside me and reading along.

I started again, though, and was well into the second

sentence of the second paragraph when two team members came out, water still dripping down their chins. They looked like they'd poured some over their heads. I hoped they hadn't done it inside. Encouraging the villagers to think of the old building as a sacred place was enough of a challenge. Modeling secular behavior inside would confuse the issue.

Kim, quit searching for distractions.

We made eye contact. I hoped they wouldn't think I was ignoring them, but I didn't have time to socialize. So when they said, "Hi, Kimmy! How's the arm?" I smiled and wiggled the fingers of my broken arm.

Losing my place would have been bad news. Everything on the page looked equally alien, especially while resisting the temptation to translate a word here or there. I made a mental note to bring a pencil next time, though, so I could checkmark my current position if someone interrupted me.

Maybe my viewpoint is a bit extreme, but I've never been willing to write in a Bible with a pen, much less a marker appropriate for writing on a purple cast.

Anjelita must have been an exceptional reader, for her finger reached the end of the introduction minutes before I got there. If Jesus didn't rapture His Church before I finished the introduction, He would surely do it before I finished San Lucas.

To keep from boring Anjelita with the introduction she'd already read and appeared to be rereading, I gave up and turned to Lucas. Almost immediately, several villagers came for water.

"Hi, Delmar. Hi, Basilio," I said cheerfully, placing my left forefinger at the beginning of the second verse of Luke, chapter 1.

Anjelita had taught me the names of all the villagers, and she made sure I could pronounce each one correctly. I was the only team member with enough time and inclination to do that. The ability to identify those men, women, boys, and girls individually was important, especially during my evening prayer time. Addressing them by name helped build rapport—even though I couldn't converse with them.

Upon hearing their names, Delmar and Basilio stopped in the doorway, turned around, and smiled. "Buenos días, Señorita Kim," they said almost in unison. Delmar held up one finger to indicate they'd be right back.

The day was so hot the insects were creeping along like cars in a funeral procession rather than lifting their wings to fly. I wouldn't have wanted to keep the two men from getting the water and shade they needed.

I wondered if they would be as receptive to the message of Luke as they were to hearing God's petite, sometimes willing—yet often wavering—servant speak their names.

Starting Luke before Delmar and Basilio returned would be counterproductive. For practice, I'd worked my way painfully through a single verse, and I needed a second chance. In the meantime, Anjelita snuggled close, reading silently. When she reached the end of the right-hand page, she reread both pages. I wondered if she might be memorizing some of it.

I motioned for the two men to sit down when they came out carrying two bottles of water each. Delmar, the more outgoing of the two, sat down facing me with Anjelita to his right, forming a triangle. Basilio remained standing. He wasn't aloof. Just shy.

"I'm going to read to you for a while." I glanced down at my Bible, moved my left index finger back to verse 1, and prayed that my terror wouldn't show. But the Bible slid from my lap before I could start. Once more, Anjelita's quick reflexes kept it from landing in the dirt.

The Bible shook in my hands after I took it from her.

Desperate to get the nervousness out of my system, I started acting silly.

"I'm going to read San Lucas to you—all seventeen pages of him. It'll take two or three minutes, and every word will be clear to you. That's a promise."

They looked at me with blank faces that grew in wonder when I started giggling at myself. Anjelita stared at me as if to say, "What you're reading is serious. Why are you laughing about it?"

Basilio surprised me by smiling first. "San Lucas?"

At least I'd pronounced those two words correctly. But how could I explain that Lucas was one of the authors of the big book I held firmly on my lap—more firmly now than before? I couldn't.

Okay. Enough delays. I had an audience—a real one. I began reading.

"Habiendo muchos tentado á poner en orden la historia de las cosas que entre nosotros han sido ciertísimas."

I stopped reading long enough to see what kind of impression my reading made on the two men. To say they looked horribly puzzled would be a grave understatement.

Lord, what are You doing? I don't mind making a fool of myself. But if this doesn't make sense to them, what's the point? You can help them understand, can't You? Of course You can. This will be just like Pentecost. I'll keep reading aloud in mangled Spanish, and You can enable them to hear it correctly. Is that the plan?

I hadn't meant to close my eyes, but I'd done it anyhow. And Anjelita—bless her heart—said amen when I opened them.

Basilio and Delmar still looked lost—more so, if that was possible. Anjelita had intensified their confusion by making them say amen, too, despite their cluelessness about what they were doing. At least Anjelita associated amen with praying.

Sometimes I thought she understood what prayer was.

Lord, can't You use Anjelita as Your mouthpiece? Please? You've had Your fun. I've tried. I really have. So how about letting Anjelita read Lucas aloud for me? I can sit here and nod authoritatively while Aaron takes over for Moses.

God answered my prayer with complete silence. I guess that meant no way.

The two men began asking Anjelita questions, and she must have explained—to the best of her limited understanding—what I was doing. Uh, trying to do.

How I wished she understood the real purpose of my Bible reading so she could explain it to them. I hoped she was at least telling them what the introduction said.

Whatever she said must have piqued their interest big-time. Basilio walked around to my right side and got on his knees so he could look at the Bible right side up.

"*Español! Es español!*"

I'd never heard shy Basilio sound so excited.

"*Es verdad?*" Delmar said with a look of amazement.

Although I didn't know what they'd said to one another, I took it as a breakthrough. Without knowing if it was appropriate, I instinctively responded with a simple, "Sí."

Delmar's excitement grew as he and Basilio chatted together for a few more minutes and occasionally with Anjelita. They must have figured out what I was trying so hard and yet unsuccessfully to do.

"Thank You, Lord!" I said aloud.

Delmar drew a question mark in the air above the open Bible with his forefinger. His fingers were slightly darker than mine, but far lighter than Aleesha's.

What different worlds we'd grown up in. If God had wanted, I could've been a native of Santa María listening to Delmar the foreigner butcher my language in a desperate effort to share the gospel with me.

It was a humbling realization.

I responded to Delmar's question mark by moving my forefinger to the first verse of chapter 1 again. He said something I couldn't understand, but I began rereading that verse as if certain he wanted me to.

"H-habiendo much-muchos tentado á pon-poner en orden la historia de las cosas que entre nosotros han sido ciertísimas."

I didn't look up until I'd finished. Both men were struggling to keep from laughing. They undoubtedly didn't want to offend me, but when they realized I'd caught them snickering at my pronunciation, they loosened their restraint and laughed long and hard.

God performed a miracle then. Not only did I lose my self-consciousness, I began laughing with them.

Anjelita's frown could have flavored a two-quart pitcher of lemonade. I applied enough gentle pressure to the corners of her mouth to turn her sour expression into a smile, and when I removed my hand, she laughed, too.

When the laughter settled down, Basilio pulled something small out of his shirt pocket, tore the paper cover off to reveal a toothpick, and pointed to chapter 1, verse 1. What did he want? I could read it again, but I wouldn't do any better now than the time before.

But God was in control, and I obeyed.

"Habiendo muchos tentado—"

"No, Señorita Kim," he said. He sounded self-conscious about interrupting.

Then he read the whole verse correctly. How beautiful the Bible sounded in Spanish. Although the words were even more foreign to me than the original King James Version, they had a similar majesty. Majesty and power. I'd never thought about how the Bible would sound in another language.

"Señorita Kim. . ." he pointed to the first word with his toothpick and then pronounced it for me. "Ah-bee-ƐN-doh. . ."

Oh. I hadn't come close.

"Señorita Kim. . . ?" he said, this time more insistently.

I did my best to imitate him, but I failed to make the *H* silent. There was so much to remember—including the need to forget how it would sound in French—and this was just the first word.

He corrected me, though, and I got it right the next time. His smile of approval made me feel great, though slightly embarrassed. My accomplishment had been so minor.

This kind of help was great, but Basilio and Delmar couldn't keep coaching me all day. They would need to return to their worksites shortly.

Kim, don't be concerned about that. It's beyond your control. Just make the best possible use of their time. Forget that you're reading aloud for their benefit and concentrate on what they're teaching you.

Delmar took over.

I pronounced the second word as much like Delmar as I could. Although muchos was a familiar word, I'd always said it with an a: muchas. Did the variation have something to do with the word that followed it?

Delmar stressed the syllable I'd gotten wrong and made me repeat it several times.

"Bueno!" His praise made me eager to proceed. But before I could attempt tentado, he moved the toothpick to the beginning of the verse. I was glad he hadn't broken it in frustration.

I wished I could jot down the pronunciations.

My teachers insisted that I get both words right before letting me move to the third one. Although my brain had spent too much of the summer in neutral, it roared into gear as I said, "Habiendo muchos" to their satisfaction and together they said, "Bueno!"

Basilio glanced at the sky. None of the villagers had watches. But he could apparently tell from the sun's position that he and Delmar had spent too much time with me.

They didn't seem to want to stop, though. And I didn't want them to, either.

Another villager, Ernesto, came along, and the three men held a hurried conversation. He got water, came back out, and sat down on the ground beside me while Basilio and Delmar returned to work.

"Muchos gracias!" I yelled as they left, proud to have corrected my former mispronunciation.

"Muchas," one of them corrected me with a smile as he turned briefly and then kept on going.

"Muchos? Muchas? I'll never get this. Gracious me!" I muttered.

"No, Señorita Kim," Ernesto said quite seriously. "Gracias, no gracious."

I could barely keep a straight face. Ernesto was so cute the way he lived up to his name.

He seemed as interested in helping as Delmar and Basilio had been. They apparently suggested that he keep using the same teaching method they used. He permitted me to attempt another word only after I correctly read all the words that preceded it. Thank goodness, that technique applied only to one verse at a time. Once I got it right, I could move on.

How dreary if I would have to go through all of Luke that way, though. I'd never finish before leaving Santa María. Not that I expected to, anyhow.

This challenge was in God's hands.

chapter fifty-two

"What an amazing day," I said to Aleesha as I sat down on my sleeping bag. "Ouch!"

I was so hoarse I could barely talk and so sunburned I couldn't lie back without moaning. Boy, did God allow me to suffer the consequences of failing to use sunscreen. I'd always used it to get darker, not to protect myself. With my light brownish complexion, I thought I was immune to sunburn.

That's what I pretended, but the truth was I'd forgotten to put sunscreen on that morning.

I could only blame myself for that part of my misery. But sitting on the hard ground without moving anything but my forefinger and mouth for hours at a time had left the rest of my body stiff and sore. That way of sitting hadn't been so bad at first, but once word got around about my Bible reading, the villagers began showing up to listen, not just to get snacks and water. I couldn't take a chance of losing their interest by getting up to stretch.

They listened intently and were generous in offering help. Maybe they kept me tied down to the hard ground, but they kept me hopping mentally—hopping, tripping, and trying to get moving again.

Now that my body was overbaked from five-plus hours in the sun and my mind equally charred by the rigors of my lessons, I caught myself wondering how to pronounce English in Spanish. But that exercise was so far beyond me, and I forced it out of my mind.

"Amazing isn't the word for today, girl!" Aleesha's voice

brought me back to the present. I was still so out of it I didn't remember I'd said something to her. "That sunburn. . .you trying to pull a John Howard Griffin on me?"

"John Howard Griffin?" The name sounded familiar, but I couldn't place it.

Aleesha changed from a sassy, amusing tone to an educational one. I should've seen it coming, but I didn't, and I wasn't up to learning anything else today. My protests wouldn't have stopped her, though. Neither would a planeload of nuclear bombs.

"Girl, John Howard Griffin was that white dude who pigmented his skin to look like a. . .Negro during the mid-twentieth century so he could travel around the Deep South and experience being black. That's why he called his book—"

"*Black Like Me!*" I shot back as thoughts of a ninth grade book report flashed in my brain. "You saying the sun's turning me black?"

"Sun isn't that powerful," she said with a smirk. "I think your book title's gonna be *Red Like Lobster.*"

She cackled. I just shook my head.

"Guess I'll have the same guy who took pictures of Griffin's journey take pictures of me. I met him once, you know. . . ."

Silence. That didn't surprise me.

"He used to work for a Christian missionary organization in Richmond."

"You serious, gal?" Her wide-open eyes reflected the light from the bonfire. Getting Aleesha's attention like that was a major accomplishment. She knew so much about so many subjects she usually made me feel dumb.

"I'm serious, gal," I said, grinning. "I met him on a building tour when I was visiting my aunt. She worked there." Better not admit I don't even remember if he was black or white and hope she doesn't ask.

This *Twilight Zone* was unbearable. Aleesha got quiet and stayed quiet. She'd never taken so long to respond, and she'd already set a new record. Fifteen seconds, still speechless, and counting.

Another fifteen seconds later, she said, "Guess I'll have to forgive you for liking *Gone with the Wind,* huh?"

I'd hoped to earn a few points with my vague and convoluted relationship to *Black Like Me,* but I hadn't expected Aleesha to express that much approval. If I knew her, she'd change the subject now.

"Just how amazing was today, Kim? Us mission team members noticed the villagers going for water more often than usual. Now, the day was unusually hot, but something special must have happened. Did God turn the water into wine or what?"

I took a long swig from a nearly bottle. "Nope. Still water." I snapped my fingers in mock disappointment.

Then I explained the whole Lucas thing to her in a hundred thousand words or less, every single one of them in a properly enunciated Georgia drawl.

My throat had never been this dry, though, and talking in detail about my Bible reading adventures was such torture that I wondered if my mouth was sunburned on the inside. If my tongue peeled—ugh!—that secret would go to the grave with me.

I couldn't imagine that a good night's sleep—if my sunburn permitted me to sleep at all—would restore me to normal, but Scarlett and I would wait and worry about it tomorrow, and that settled it for me. That and my confidence that God would get me through this experience.

"That's good about reading Lucas," Aleesha said.

I waited. Would she say anything else?

"That's real good."

She didn't say any more.

I reentered *The Twilight Zone*—or had I ever left it? Despite Aleesha's brief, positive statements about Luke and me, two prolonged periods of silence in the same evening were enough to scare the daylights out of me. When I'm scared, I keep talking. "Who would've thought bringing a Spanish Bible to a place like Santa María could result in an outreach effort like this?"

"No surprise to me, girl. God speaks Spanish, too. Him and old Luke there. In fact, I'll bet God taught him. Subliminally. . ." Now that Aleesha was talking again, she didn't stop. But that's the last thing I heard. By then I'd relaxed, rolled over on my less-fried side, and shut my eyes.

chapter fifty-three

Day 11

I woke up rested and refreshed. My throat felt fine, my voice sounded normal, and my tongue didn't appear to be peeling. But after a day of start-and-stop reading, evening found me exhausted and nearly voiceless again. The day had gone well, yet my progress seemed so. . .slow.

I hadn't had much free time, but I made a point of spending time with Rosa that evening.

Her house wasn't officially complete, much less ready to move into, but I understood her insistence on sleeping there. My parents had taken pictures of our house when it was under construction. I'd seen a photo of them camping out on the living room carpet one evening when they needed a reminder that the house would soon be their home.

Most of the villagers—probably all of them—slept in their unfinished houses, too.

Rosa's place consisted of interior walls of unpainted sheetrock, plywood floors, and an amateurishly constructed roof that would have flunked the seasonal rains test in its present condition. But it would be fine by the end of the next day.

Hanging from nails on opposite sides of Rosa's doorway were two treasures that grabbed my attention.

One was a good-sized golden crucifix, perhaps fifteen inches high. Far more ornate and intricately fashioned than anything I'd ever seen back home, it looked like it belonged in a cathedral. I could only guess at its age—twenty-five, fifty, maybe a hundred years old. Thousands of adoring hands and perhaps as many prayerful pairs of lips had worn parts of it thin.

Have Rosa and Anjelita ever touched this crucifix in worship? Although it's obviously important to them, I've never seen them do it. Does she know what it is? Or is it just a fancy decoration she found somewhere after the storm?

Rosa's other treasure was a photograph, weatherworn around the edges and a bit wrinkled, but otherwise intact. She took it down and placed it in my hands. The picture showed Anjelita with a girl who looked four or five years older. The back bore a time stamp—thirteen months earlier.

"Ah-LAHZ-nay," Rosa said as she pointed to the older girl.

"Ah-LAHZ-nay," I said back to her. "Ah-LAHZ-nay," I said once more to make sure I had the pronunciation correct.

Rosa smiled, but her eyes glistened with moisture. I jotted the phonetic spelling in my little notebook, handed it to Rosa, and indicated that she should write down the spelling. That was one name I wanted to be sure I could spell correctly.

Although Rosa couldn't explain that Alazne was her other daughter, the girls were too similar—eyes, nose, hair, chin, complexion, facial shape—not to be sisters. Even their ears looked alike. Had they been the same age, I would have taken them for twins. Their matching outfits would have eliminated any doubts.

I examined the photograph again. Although Alazne appeared to have two normal arms, she was leaning on crutches. If she was handicapped and not just recovering from an injury—I couldn't see the crutches in detail, but they showed signs of wear and tear—I could better understand why the villagers associated maldita with Rosa's family.

I hadn't seen any other photographs in Santa María, and I wondered how Rosa had kept the storm from destroying this one. More than that, I wondered what had become of her older daughter. I'd met all of the villagers, but not her. Rosa would have introduced us if Anjelita didn't.

Although Rosa didn't break out crying when I handed the picture back, her eyes welled up with the most immense tears I'd ever seen. My grandmom's death was the only one I'd ever experienced, and she'd been terminally ill so long, I never thought of her as alive. I didn't shed a single tear at her funeral.

But Rosa was obviously grieving. Whatever had become of Alazne, she hadn't simply run away from home.

As I looked at the photo in Rosa's hand, I recalled the double take I'd done when I first saw it. No matter how much Anjelita and Alazne resembled one another, they weren't the only two look-alikes.

I bore a close enough resemblance to both of Rosa's daughters to make me wonder for a moment whether I might somehow be hers, too. Stranger things have happened. But then I laughed at myself. Rosa would have been no more than eight or nine at the time of my birth!

No wonder Anjelita had chosen me for an older sister. I looked like hers.

⁓

Some of the people I'd known from other denominations didn't seem to be Christians. The evidence just wasn't there. They were more gossipy, more selfish, more unloving, and less forgiving than many people who don't even profess Jesus as Lord.

That seemed to be true of some of the teens in my youth group, too—including kids who'd made public professions of faith and been baptized. I planned to give them some personal attention when I got home.

What a gap between churchgoers and real Christians.

Rosa was a great mom, a hard worker, and as good a friend as she could be, considering our inability to communicate verbally. But those things didn't make her a Christian. I'd grown increasingly concerned about her probable need for salvation and prayed for her many times daily. Although this reading of Lucas would surely touch her in some way, would it be enough?

I was less concerned about Anjelita—at least for now. I'd always been taught that children under a certain age would go to heaven if they died. If that was true and she died tonight, she would awaken in Jesus' arms. After the first ten million years of warming in His love and acceptance, she might take her eyes off His face long enough to glance down and find her arm whole—perhaps for the first time ever.

But I had another reason for being less concerned about Anjelita.

Rosa was a super mom. Anjelita adored her and tried to be just like her. If Rosa became a believer, she would undoubtedly try to win Anjelita, too. Anjelita's decision would be her own, though. She was too independent to do something that important just to please Rosa.

That didn't answer the main question, though. If Rosa was not a Christian already, would she become one? Although she'd heard parts of Lucas and served as the best of my tutors, I was skeptical about finishing in the time I had left.

Even if I completed Lucas, Anjelita would be the only villager who'd heard it all the way through. No matter how intelligent she was, I couldn't imagine her being able to fill the villagers in on everything they'd missed.

If I didn't finish—if the villagers didn't get to hear about the joyous Easter resurrection and the ascension—what would Luke's Gospel accomplish?

Lord, please help me finish.

I would go as fast as my tutors allowed, of course, but I had to cover more material than I had during the first day and a half. The solution was simple. I'd started earlier and stayed later at the House of Bread to get more done.

I would do the same thing here.

chapter fifty-four

Day 12

God solved that problem in an even better way than I'd hoped. After another good night of sleep, I experienced a major breakthrough. Although my tutors couldn't teach me the rules of pronunciation, my God-given flair for languages helped me discern, formulate, and apply my own rules, and they turned out to be remarkably accurate. My weak flicker raged almost instantly into an unstoppable fire.

The villagers corrected me only when they couldn't understand me. That didn't happen often now.

Now that my reading wasn't constant stop-and-start, the villagers—entranced by Luke's story of Jesus—seemed reluctant to return to work. Judging by the timing of their coming and going, they purposely waited for logical breaks in the narrative before leaving. Even then, they tended to back away as if trying to catch a few words of the next section before they got out of earshot.

At lunchtime that day, Aleesha pointed out something I hadn't noticed. An ever-widening circle of villagers had been gathering just outside my peripheral vision and listening intently for longer and longer periods. That news perked me up.

Some of my little congregation remained outside for hours at a time, either forgetting to go inside the Passover Church for water or perhaps fearing they'd miss hearing something important in the few seconds they would need to get snacks and water. So I asked Rob and Charlie to set some water outside. It wouldn't sit in the sun long enough to superheat.

Whenever new listeners showed up, I heard whispering,

but it was very quiet. They apparently wanted to learn what I was reading about at the moment. I never heard talking at any other time.

Their level of interest remained amazingly high, yet I fought a constant battle against frustration. God's Word wouldn't return to Him void. I believed that. My reading—no, not that, but the Word itself—would have a positive effect. But would I ever know the outcome?

If I was honest with myself, I didn't want God's Word to return to me void, either. Even though I couldn't imagine Him working any miracles through me, I daydreamed about every villager becoming a Christian. And then I fretted about who would disciple them.

"Guys and girls," Charlie said to the team during supper that night, "God is doing something special through Kim's Bible reading. Be patient about the length and frequency of the villagers' breaks."

"No problem about that, Charlie." Judging by the nods of affirmation, Geoff spoke for everyone. "Listening to God's Word is the most important thing the villagers can do now. We need to keep Kimmy's project in our constant prayers." He concluded by setting a powerful example, and a fervent group prayer time followed.

The old "Hi, Kimmy. How's the arm?" greeting went into immediate disuse. Team members now asked, "What specific things should we pray about tonight?"

So I wasn't surprised to see dozens of teens sitting outside the mess tent or in the churchyard that night. Some were reading their Bibles in preparation for prayer, while others already had their eyes closed. They were serious about their commitment to pray.

Although each team member had a slightly different take on my reading, they agreed that God had brought me to Santa

María as a seed sower. A number of them pointed out that the planter doesn't always participate in the harvest. How often had I heard that in sermons and Bible studies without appreciating its significance?

A seed sower? I know that's important, Lord. Someone must do it. Otherwise, there'll be no harvest. But can't I at least see Rosa come to You?

chapter fifty-five

Day 13

Now that the litter cleanup was days in the past and progress in the reading of Lucas was good—I would easily finish today and perhaps read some other scripture after that—I began thinking about the changes I'd witnessed. Especially in myself.

I was no longer the spoiled young lady who'd left her safe, comfortable home in Georgia with a bunch of good intentions and too much luggage and ended up in the wilds of Santa María. I had discovered the hard way that I needed to align my plans with God's rather than expect Him to rubber-stamp mine.

I wasn't my usual carefree self anymore, either. No, not my "usual carefree self," but my "usual care-only-for-myself self." The lessons I'd begun learning at the House of Bread about caring for others had been a mere drizzle, a trickle, a baby beginning that ran amuck because I'd relied on myself and not God. Now God-engineered, major-flood lessons in agape love had washed over me daily and started to overflow to the other people my life touched.

Although most of the team members had matured some, Geoff's transformation was probably even more dramatic than mine. He may have started out a useless lump of fool's gold, but God remade him into the real thing—twenty-four sparkling karats' worth.

He'd taken some seriously bad risks trying to get my attention. If I hadn't loved and accepted him, his guilt would probably have crippled him beyond repair. But God didn't want Geoff to live that way, and He wouldn't let me ignore or reject him.

Not only did he become one of the hardest workers, he also did a one-eighty in his attitude toward Aleesha and the villagers. In turn, he began earning their love and respect.

He and I talked frequently and more freely than before, and our conversations were pleasant and positive. Although his high school conversion had been genuine, his emotional and spiritual immaturity had prevented him from saying no to the friends he'd trusted.

Geoff had already sought and accepted God's forgiveness, but I wasn't sure he'd forgiven himself. He hadn't surrendered his guilt.

I hoped he'd do that soon, and I'd help anyway I could.

I still believed in avoiding mission-trip romances, but—now that I knew Geoff was a Christian with much to offer in the building of God's kingdom—I had to fight off the temptation to ignore my own rule. He didn't pressure me about my stubborn refusal to get romantic.

Doggone it, though! That just made him all the more desirable.

⁓

Anjelita must have sensed that we were leaving the next morning, even before she noticed team members gathering their belongings. She clung to me as if that might keep me in Santa María and walked so close I almost tripped over her on our way to the mess tent for supper. I wished my suitcase were big enough to carry her and Rosa home in. *How much would that kind of overweight baggage cost?* I giggled at the thought.

We enjoyed our last supper together. Anjelita ate a small can of meat for a change, but I had beef jerky again. Plus a can of pork 'n' beans. Breakfast tomorrow would probably be the last jerky I'd eat in a long time if my father had anything to say about it. I'd eaten it three times daily for twelve days and enjoyed every chewy, challenging bite. Only a dog's rawhide chew would have made my jaws, teeth, and gums stronger and healthier.

Although I was actually looking forward to pizza again—perhaps at the airport—I wished I could share the experience with Rosa and Anjelita. Does Mexican cuisine have anything comparable to pizza? Although the villagers would have hosted us royally if they'd been in a position to, I couldn't believe we'd spent two weeks in Mexico without a single bite of authentic Mexican food.

But we hadn't come to Mexico to eat. We'd come to work, and—to the best of my knowledge—we'd fulfilled our assignment. We did what God asked. We reached out to the residents of this tiny community in every way we could. We shared their joys and learned to understand some of their hardships.

Although Santa María might remain unknown to census takers and tax collectors—they would never find it without knowing its GPS coordinates—it would remain in our hearts forever. The villagers had become almost as important to us as our own families—and in some ways, more important.

We couldn't stay in Santa María, though. Despite a job well done, we probably couldn't accomplish anything else. Besides, we were tired and ready to go home.

"It'll be great to get back to civilization."

"I want to see my family again, even my bratty little sister."

"I'm going to take a hot bath and soak in the tub all day."

"I can hardly wait to wash my hair."

"I want to eat hot, freshly prepared meals. And coffee. . . give me coffee. I'll bathe in it."

"Forget coffee. I want an ice cold soda—with lots of crushed ice."

"I want to wear clean clothes, ones I haven't done sweaty work in, and go hang out with my friends."

"Give me my bed again. I'll sleep for a week."

But each desire to go home had a matching lament.

"These villagers are some of the finest people I've ever known."

"I wish they lived where I could see them every day."

"No matter how hard we've worked, this has been a mountaintop experience. I dread coming back down."

"How can I just leave the villagers behind? They're my second family now."

But more than anything else, team members shared my concerns over the villagers' spiritual needs.

"We've helped meet their physical needs, but what about the spiritual ones?"

"We couldn't give our testimonies, yet I believe they would've been receptive if we'd been able to talk with them."

"I sure hope Kimmy's reading of Luke got through to them. At least to one person, anyhow."

"I'll keep praying for the villagers, but that doesn't seem like enough."

"If only we knew we could come back sometime. . ."

"Or some other Christian group. . ."

"Lord, let there be a translator next time. . .and let there be a next time. Please."

Just as I'd become part of Rosa's family, every team member had adopted one or more villagers. Although nobody set out to befriend anyone in particular, God brought us together in a mutually comfortable and comforting way. Every villager had a close friendship with one or more team members.

Despite the language barrier, we'd somehow communicated our love, concern, and acceptance to these needy people. But we weren't missionaries "up here" working with our target group "down there." We were peers—equals in our humanity—and the villagers' pained expressions indicated the depth of their grief over our leaving.

But if we'd completed our assignment, why did we feel like we were walking out on an unfinished task? Did seed planters always pay that kind of price? If God hadn't assigned me to read the Gospel of Luke to the villagers, I would have been only a groundbreaker—a tiller of unfamiliar soil—not a sower of the world's most important seeds.

At least we'd finished building the cottages, though. Knowing the villagers would be snug and dry during the upcoming rains was good.

After we finished eating, Anjelita crawled onto my lap and wrapped herself around me in a grip an octopus would have envied.

A few minutes later, Rob used my karaoke system to address the group. "I've arranged for a semi and a smaller truck to come with the buses tomorrow. Among other necessities, they'll bring small livestock."

"Livestock, as in chickens and goats," Charlie chimed in. "And in case you're not country folk, those animals give eggs and milk."

I couldn't resist. "Goats that lay eggs? Chickens that give milk? Where'd you get such special animals, anyhow?"

Everyone—Charlie included—cracked up. "I'm like a reporter, Kimmy. I don't reveal my sources. If the villagers don't know how to raise livestock, at least they'll enjoy some tasty eating till the animals are all gone."

Somebody gave a loud cackle that sounded amazingly like a hen fighting to prevent her imminent beheading. Someone else bleated like a goat running for its life, and the rest of us started making one sound or the other.

I'd never heard the villagers laugh so hard.

"The semi is also bringing seeds and garden tools. Plus young vegetable plants that can provide food within a matter of weeks. We haven't seen any evidence that these folks are gardeners or small farmers, but we'll take a chance they can figure out what to do. Churches and individuals throughout southern and middle California are also donating additional food, staples, water, clothes, and household items. Maybe enough to require a second semi."

We cheered enthusiastically.

"But there won't be any beef jerky this time," Rob said as he winked at me.

I was the only person who didn't cheer. I played the good sport and smiled, though.

The semis would bring paint, brushes, and rollers. Charlie couldn't stand the incomplete look of the unpainted houses, and he'd used his own contacts north of the border to get generous donations. I suspected that Rob and Charlie contributed heavily from their own personal resources.

I'd been listening to Rob so intently that I didn't notice Anjelita loosen her grip and lay her head against my shoulder. Her fatigue and full tummy overcame her stress sooner than I'd expected.

About twenty minutes later, Rosa came to take her home. The linens and blankets we'd brought would probably be their only beds for quite some time. I doubted that any of the villagers had ever slept in an American-style bed. I got teary-eyed about how little I knew about Rosa, Anjelita, and the other villagers. Would I ever have my questions answered?

I'd never seen Anjelita openly defy her mother, but when Rosa started to pick her up, she woke up just enough to wrap herself around me once again and start bawling. I didn't have to be an expert on children to know she was too tired and sleepy to know what she was doing.

Witnessing the struggle between Anjelita and her mom didn't make things any easier for me, though. After several unsuccessful efforts, I hand-motioned to Rosa that I'd bring Anjelita home once she was sound asleep.

I was desperate to pray, and no one was close enough to distract me. I had so many things I needed to talk to God about, and I didn't want to leave any of them out. I started by praying for each villager by name.

But like Jesus' disciples when He asked them to pray for Him in the garden of Gethsemane, I fell asleep. I probably didn't finish praying for ten villagers first.

I didn't stay asleep long. Fortunately, Anjelita did.

"Kimmy, are you awake?" I heard the sounds of whispering as a hand gently nudged my uninjured arm.

Being roused from my prayerful nap disoriented me so much I thought the whisperer was Aleesha. Aleesha with a guy's voice. She was a more convincing actress than I'd realized.

"Kimmy, I'm sorry. I hate to bother you, but I thought this might be my last chance to catch you."

"Aleesha? How do you get your voice so low?"

"Kim, it's Geoff, not Aleesha. Can. . .may I talk to you just a few minutes, please?"

Yawning and stretching with Anjelita's head on my lap wasn't simple.

"Sure, Geoff. I was praying. Trying to, anyhow. Please be super-careful not to wake Anjelita up. Okay? I thought she'd never loosen her grip long enough to go to sleep."

"I'll be careful, Kimmy. She looks so sweet. I grew up an only kid, so I wasn't around younger children at home. I wish I had a kid sister like Anjelita, though."

"Me, too, Geoff. So, what's up?" I hated rushing him to the

point, but I was so out of it I could barely focus.

"I couldn't leave tomorrow without telling you—without trying to explain—what you've meant to me. Whenever I think about how I acted last week, I get embarrassed all over again."

"No need for that. Everything's fine between us now. That's all that matters." What I'd said was true. Almost. But would he apologize?

"I'm glad. God has forgiven me many times over for my sins of the past few years, but it's hard to forgive myself and put them out of my mind."

"I understand." I was more awake now. . .more alert.

"I thought you might. There's one thing I haven't done yet, though. I need to do it, and I hope it'll make me feel better."

And was he going to. . . ? "What's that, Geoff?"

"Just saying how guilty I've felt isn't enough. I know you've forgiven me, but I've never actually apologized. . . ."

My heart beat a mile a minute at this final step in making things right. "Geoff, that's really nice of you, but what do you need to apologize for?" I hoped the slight bit of playfulness in my voice wouldn't sound like I took his apology lightly.

"What do I need. . . ? You—" He stopped abruptly, hesitated for a moment, and then started grinning. Tentatively at first, but then it grew and grew and grew. Like Pinocchio's nose. Not because of lies, though. But because of truth. "Have you ever talked with Uncle Rob about forgiveness, Kimmy?"

"Sure enough. As far as the east is from the west. . ."

"Thanks, Kimmy."

"I need your forgiveness, too."

"Huh?"

"I should've reset my counter to zero without waiting for an apology."

He couldn't have looked more confused.

"Never mind, Geoff. Things are great now."

"That's all I needed. You two sleep tight."

He gave me a brotherly peck on the cheek, clicked his flashlight on, and held his head high as he headed toward the boys' campsite. I must have fallen asleep again almost instantly. About forty-five minutes later, I woke up to a flashlight shining in my face.

"Why is the sunrise so bright today?" That's how dazed I was.

"Come on, sleepyheads. . . ." The familiar voice was unusually quiet. Although Aleesha had addressed her words to both of us, she intended to awaken only me.

She'd come to check on me because I wasn't "home" at dark. She lifted Anjelita's head without waking her, picked her up, and slung her over her left shoulder. How would I have kept my promise to Rosa without Aleesha's help? I giggled quietly at seeing Aleesha carry Anjelita like a sack of potatoes.

I couldn't see Aleesha's face, but she was undoubtedly shaking her head at this silly girl and her ability to laugh without apparent motivation. At least growing in my concern about others hadn't required me to give up my sense of humor. Or anything else that was worthwhile, for that matter.

Rosa must have been listening for us. She opened the door before we could knock. She lifted Anjelita from Aleesha's shoulder and put her down on a blanket in the right rear corner of the room. Rosa's blanket was so close to Anjelita's that the sides touched. In the beam of Aleesha's flashlight, I saw a pile of paper and an ink pen on top. Hmm. . .

Aleesha and I dropped to our knees at the foot of Anjelita's blanket—I didn't need to guard against rocks indoors—and watched Rosa wrap her daughter snugly. I planned to leave the air mattress and sleeping bag for Anjelita and Rosa if Rob didn't mind.

Maybe I wouldn't even ask. As I'd heard my mom say a

million times, it's easier to ask forgiveness than permission. How many times had I stretched the limit doing that? If I knew Rob half as well as I thought I did, though, I wouldn't need his forgiveness for this.

Aleesha's tiny LED flashlight was the only light source in the room, although I saw the reflection of a hurricane lamp and smelled a bit of lamp oil. Were those part of the emergency supplies we'd brought?

Carefully avoiding Anjelita's eyes, Aleesha shone her beam on the youngster's lower face. A pretty youngster now, she'd grow up to be as stunning and beautiful as Rosa.

Aleesha and I scooted on our knees toward the head of Anjelita's blanket, and each of us kissed her.

She smiled in her sleep.

chapter fifty-six

Day 14

"Up and at 'em, girlfriend!"

I moaned in fatigue. Last night's sleep, although solid and unbroken, hadn't left me feeling rested.

"Go away."

Although Aleesha could hide her emotions better than anyone I'd ever met, she didn't try this time. Hurt feelings hardened her normally relaxed look. She should have realized I would never speak to her that way intentionally, but she made me feel as awful as if I'd meant to.

"Aleesha, I'm so sorry. You know I wouldn't yell at you if I was awake enough to know what I was saying."

Her face brightened with the same smile of forgiveness I'd seen on many faces the past two weeks. *Thank You, Jesus, for modeling perfect forgiveness.*

"I know, Kim. . .Kimmy. . .Kim. I just can't call you Kimmy—makes you sound like a little kid or something."

"Or something? Like a little puppy? Or a little kitten? Or maybe a tiny baby bird?"

"Or something," she repeated as her mouth curled into a new smile.

"Does that mean you've forgiven me?"

"Forgiven you for what?"

"I. . .you've been talking to Rob?"

"As a matter of fact, I have. He's been giving me lessons in forgiveness, and I just used one of the tricks he taught me. He's pretty okay for some old dude."

We laughed together as we'd done so often. Although

Scarlett was right about tomorrow being another day, my tomorrow would dawn without Aleesha's encouragement. I'd wake up at home in my own bed, and I'd shoot my parents if they got me up at dawn the way Aleesha had done every day.

Or maybe I'd reach out and hug them the way Anjelita had clung to me last night. Even though I'd never been a bad girl, Mom and Dad had put up with a lot from me over the years.

I felt like I'd aged during the past two weeks. I'd started avoiding mirrors for fear I looked older, too. I'd have to start from scratch on my beautification practices.

If they seemed important enough to spend time, effort, and money on, that is.

I'd gained a new perspective on this humongous world I was part of by spending fourteen days on this grain of sand that fewer than two hundred people knew the existence of—two hundred people plus one huge, awesome God.

I felt like I'd put 3-D glasses on at the most exciting part of a movie, even though I hadn't even left North America. If Santa María was this needy—physically and spiritually—what were the furthest reaches of the earth like? Were the needs there just as great?

I had to accept the fact I was just one person and my sphere of influence would probably remain small. I couldn't imagine God calling me to be a Beth Moore or a female Billy Graham and lead thousands—perhaps millions—to Christ.

I learned something else, though, and I believed it with all my heart and soul. If God asked me to do something extraordinary, I'd jump right in—with faith that He'd enable me to succeed. If He could take a spoiled eighteen-year-old and enable her to carry out a meaningful ministry with a broken arm that limited her activities, I wouldn't worry about the educational, vocational, and marital decisions I would face someday.

I wouldn't waste time gazing into the heavens waiting for Jesus to rapture His church, either. I'd be too busy helping as many people as I could to find the new life God wanted them to have.

"Earth to Kim. Earth to Kim. Come in, please."

"I'm sorry, Aleesha. I was. . .thinking." I appreciated her respect for my privacy. I couldn't have shared those thoughts if I'd wanted to. They would have run together in an unspeakable jumble.

I needed a jumble of joy on a day of great sadness.

chapter fifty-seven

As Aleesha and I walked wordlessly toward the mess tent, the sunrise in the eastern sky electrified me. It was by far the most gorgeous one I'd seen in Santa María, and I couldn't keep from smiling. Dawn was similar to New Year's, the arrival of spring, even the first day of school. It was also a little bit like baptism. Those were all signs of a new beginning.

But everything was upside-down today. This sunrise signaled an ending. I still wasn't optimistic about the villagers' being closer to Christ than before, and I hated leaving the results in God's hands and going home knowing only that I'd been obedient.

Nonetheless, I'd keep up a good front for Anjelita's sake. Saying good-bye would be hard enough.

Anjelita! Where are you, girl?

For well over a week, she'd woken Aleesha and me without missing a single day. Yet today—the most important day—she wasn't in sight. Recalling my previous thoughts about where Anjelita would be if she died, I nearly panicked.

Maybe Aleesha couldn't read my mind, but we were both on the same page. Wordlessly, we turned away from the mess tent and headed for Rosa's house, almost at the far end of the single, so-called street. Although we didn't have a logical reason to run, we couldn't help it. We didn't slow down until we were ten feet from the front door.

The house was deathly still, and the door was closed. Rosa kept it open except at night.

Aleesha and I eyed one another as if to say, "Should we go inside?"

I twisted the knob and opened the door as quietly as I could. It squeaked ominously. We bolted toward the opening at the same time, but Aleesha got inside first. She glanced at the two blankets lying edge to edge, one enveloping Rosa, the other enshrouding Anjelita.

Aleesha turned to me and whispered, "Let's see if they're breathing."

I didn't know how to check a pulse. But Aleesha did.

"They're fine," she said in a softer whisper than I was used to hearing her use. She touched Rosa's forehead with the back of her hand and then Anjelita's. Neither of them stirred.

"Not even a fever."

She motioned for me to follow her outside. She probably couldn't stand the quiet any longer.

We were still panting hard. Probably more from anxiety than exertion, though.

"So, they're—"

"Asleep. Sound asleep."

"You're sure, Aleesha?"

"Are you doubting my medical judgment?" she said, laughing.

"I guess not." I felt drained of what little rest last night's sleep had provided.

"You know what I think, Miss Kim?"

"Not until you tell me, Miss Aleesha."

"You've talked me into it. I think Rosa kept Anjelita from waking up early today. Don't ask me how, 'cause I don't know. Maybe she wanted to keep Anjelita from seeing you leave."

"No. She wouldn't do that. . . ." I paused. "Would she?"

"My psychobabbological savvy isn't as good as my medical knowledge, even if my dad is a shrink. I still think everybody but me is nuts."

I giggled.

"But, seriously, I think Rosa wanted you to have time

to get ready before Anjelita found you. Keeping her asleep probably seemed the best way to do that. I'd have had to pack for you this morning otherwise 'cause Anjelita would've had you in her grasp like a fly in a spider web—"

I double-gulped, "Ugh! Yuck!" at her simile.

"And I might've accidentally moved that nice, new, barely used karaoke box from your suitcase to mine. Along with the extra batteries, of course."

"You may be right about Rosa. About the karaoke system: Would you by any chance just possibly happen to need it?"

"Now that I've seen what it'll do, I just might. You sure?"

I nodded.

If God used that karaoke box as effectively in Aleesha's hands as He'd used it in the village as a PA system, I'd be more than satisfied. Maybe He'd had me bring the thing mostly to give to someone who could use it more.

chapter fifty-eight

The mess tent was crowded by the time Aleesha and I got back from Rosa's. Only a few team members bothered sitting down, and they sat at the outer edge or out in the street where nobody would step on them. Facing a four-plus-hour bus ride, I couldn't imagine why anyone would choose to sit now.

Team members normally ravenous at this time of day poked at their food as if it had lost all of its appeal. Hushed conversations added to the funereal "if we've got to leave, let's get it over with" atmosphere.

Funereal? Yes, I felt that way, too.

I managed to reach the food table in spite of the milling crowd. The thought of eating nauseated me, but I needed to get something into my system while I could.

We'd leave the ton of leftovers for the villagers. I chortled loudly at the sudden realization that the so-called church wasn't the only shady spot in Santa María. The tabletop—the plywood across two sawhorses—provided shade much of the day, too.

In a rare but quickly passing moment of homesickness, I selected a small can of potted meat for breakfast. My last breakfast—the last one in Santa María, that is.

What if Christ had used potted meat or beef jerky instead of bread for that last meal with His disciples? Or warm bottled water instead of wine?

I burst out laughing. I wouldn't have been my new normal self if I hadn't.

My food tasted as good as possible under the circumstances;

that meant it was awful. I didn't crave it, and I didn't enjoy it, either—not even the jerky I had for dessert.

I slipped an unopened package into my purse, though, and worked my way through the crowd to rejoin Aleesha. She was saving a standing-room-only spot for me.

Rob and Charlie addressed the group. Using my karaoke system for the last time—Aleesha had to get it out of her suitcase for them—they got our attention with feedback.

"Guys and girls, please return to your sleepsites and bring your belongings back here," Rob said. "You might also make a final visit to the facilities."

"We're not sure how our buses will be equipped." Charlie's exaggerated cheerfulness diminished with each word as he continued. "Requesting restrooms on each bus doesn't mean getting them. We learned that lesson last time."

I turned my head to look at the countryside I'd become so accustomed to seeing and at the faces I'd grown to love. I stared at the Passover Church. Whether it would ever serve as a church or not, at least it now had a beautiful yard. What small miracles a God-led team could accomplish. . . .

Conflicting thoughts duked it out in my head. Although I'd been looking forward to the amenities of home, I'd adjusted amazingly well to Santa María's simple way of life. Life among people who spoke my language would be a relief, but I would miss hearing the beautiful sound of Spanish in my everyday life and trying to figure out its meaning.

Just as Aleesha and I started our last walk to the field, Neil tapped me on the shoulder. I barely felt it. He still looked younger than sixteen. I fought the urge to rub my hands on his face to see if he had any fuzz growing there.

"Miss, uh, Kimmy. . ." He stopped. Even after being quasi-sweethearts for part of one evening, he would probably never overlook our "major" two-year age difference.

That fast-faded, make-believe romance seemed years ago, not just days. Neil and I had been able to talk with one another periodically after that. We may not have become fast friends—we didn't have time to—but we were closer than mere acquaintances.

"Just plain Kimmy, please. I know your parents would be proud of you for respecting your elders, even if this elder is barely elder than you."

The three of us laughed, and some of the tension on Neil's face dissolved. "Kimmy, could I have the honor of sitting by you on the bus for a while? Please?"

Looking as guilty as if someone had caught him smoking behind the garage, he continued before I could respond. "Miss, uh, Aleesha, I know you and Kimmy are best friends, and I don't want to intrude on your last few hours together, but I need to talk to Kimmy about something important. I don't need to sit with her the whole time, though. Just long enough to, uh, make a major confession. . ."

His ellipsis timed out and became a period.

To make a major confession? To me? What could this cute little mouse of a boy possibly need to confess to me? We didn't know each other well enough for him to be guilty of anything important. Especially not that important. My curiosity soared sky-high.

If he needed to get something off his chest, his concerns took priority over Aleesha's exclusive company. I didn't get to tell him that, though.

"Neil," Aleesha said with unusual warmth, "as skinny as you and Kim are, the three of us should fit in one row just fine. But, boy, don't think about getting fresh with us two fine gentlewomen. We know how to behave ourselves, and we know how to defend ourselves, too."

After two weeks of having a few rough edges sanded

down, she must've felt the need to practice being her old self again.

And so much for thinking of myself as petite. I could tolerate thin. But skinny? Ugh!

Neil smiled at Aleesha before excusing himself and heading for the boys' field.

"Thanks for being my mouthpiece, girl," I said, my laughter flooding the air like water spraying from a burst pipe.

Aleesha looked at me as if she hadn't caught on at first, but then she started giggling, too.

"That's right," I said. "You never let me respond to Neil's question."

"It's that drawl of yours," she said. "You talk too slow. Neil didn't have all day to wait for an answer. Besides, he asked me."

"He asked you second. No, wait. He didn't ask you anything. He was just explaining to you while I thought about the question." I pretended to frown. "Tell me: Am I really skinny?" I didn't care if I was. I'd simply said the first thing that popped into my head.

When we got back with our suitcases, we left them in the middle of Broad Street.

"If you plan to give away leftover clothes or anything else you can spare," Rob said, "do that as soon as we break."

That sounded more personal now than it had at orientation. We'd be sharing with family and friends, not strangers, and we understood their needs from being around them. I'd already set all of my good clothes and a few trinkets inside Rosa's house, along with Rob's air mattress, sleeping bag, and pillow.

Whoops! I should give Rosa the flashlight, too. I don't think Rob wants it back, and we have enough of them at home.

I was wearing my original travel clothes—the ones I'd torn a hole in when I landed on the rock, the ones I'd slept in the first night, the ones I'd broken my arm in. The white sweatshirt wouldn't make a decent dust rag now. I couldn't see the original pizza stain anymore because I'd spilled something on the same spot at the Pizza Hut Rob and I ate in.

But I didn't care. Why wear good clothes when I could do some good by leaving them behind? Not that I planned to arrive home looking as grubby as I did now. I'd have time to buy new clothes at the airport.

But first, I'd make sure my watch was set to San Diego time. Not that I'd need to use it. I'd get the time from my cell phone except while I was in the air.

Rob and Charlie took turns conducting a project wrap-up, but nobody was very talkative. Although I felt sorry for the two men, they didn't act overly upset. They seemed to understand that we were just beginning to digest the significance of our time in Santa María; our thoughts were too intimate to share with anyone else yet.

Not even our closest teammates.

I wondered if Rob and Charlie felt that way, too. I'd observed them closely enough to conclude that even adults are capable of change. It just requires the proper stimulus.

I thought of my parents. Especially my dad.

After eight fruitless minutes of trying to get us to talk, Rob suggested we do some thinking and praying and e-mail the group once we felt more like sharing.

"Kimmy, you will read those e-mails, won't you?" Rob winked at me. "Sometime this year or next year and certainly no later than the year after that."

Everyone hooted and howled, and I laughed as hard as anyone. Although I'd trusted Rob not to reveal my failure to read the change-of-project-plans messages, someone had. Rob wouldn't have referred to unread e-mail unless the story had become common knowledge.

I glanced at Aleesha. She wore that familiar, innocent-as-an-angel look with the upturned eyes. She always tickled me when she did that. How could I finish growing into adulthood without having her around to relieve the boredom? Although Betsy Jo would remain a good friend, I didn't know if I'd feel as close to her now—or as close as I felt to Aleesha. Not having the Santa María experience in common might make a difference.

Although nobody had spoken to me about bringing my problems on myself, I'd overheard snatches of conversation the past several days—conversation that suggested my secret was out. The weird thing was I no longer felt self-conscious about it.

Team members had forgiven me for everything else. I didn't think they'd hold this against me. As far as I could tell, they'd set their forgiveness counters to zero. Not just for me, but for one other.

Now. . .what about this major confession Neil wanted to make? Surely, he wasn't the one who—

The sudden quiet interrupted my reflections. Charlie's and Rob's eyes were closed. Everyone else's, too. Why had I let my thoughts drift when I should have been paying attention? Two weeks hadn't been long enough to outgrow my irresponsibility and carelessness entirely.

But before I could think more about my immaturity, one lone voice broke into song. Then a second voice and a third. Soon we were all singing "Wherever There Is Need." We joined hands and formed a circle that would have appeared hilariously ragged if seen from above.

But Someone was watching from above, and I couldn't picture God laughing at its convoluted shape. He was more apt to be smiling at its unbrokenness.

Tears streamed down my face, burning my eyes, but I

refused to break the circle to blot them. I wanted this bond to last until our buses arrived at the airport and we departed for our individual destinations. Every mountaintop high was different, and we'd probably never experience anything identical to this until heaven—not even if we held the reunion someone had suggested two weeks earlier.

Noticing the interspersion—now there was a Neil word—of the villagers among the team members, I fretted about the spiritual gap that still separated us. Although this physical chain of hands and emotional chain of hearts included theirs, each villager was—at the same time—a missing spiritual link.

Lord, I know You've blessed my scripture reading.
But how?

If I hadn't been so caught up in this time of close communion with my new brothers and sisters, I might have resented God's refusal to answer my question. How many more times would I have to ask before it would be too late to find out?

My concerns disappeared for the moment after several repetitions of "Wherever There Is Need." I thought I was in heaven when someone started "Joyful, Joyful" and I visualized this whole group surrounding the throne of God and singing His praises in person.

I glanced to my left when Neil—I hadn't noticed him—lifted my arm parallel to the ground and draped it over Anjelita's shoulder. She folded her arm and took my hand in hers.

Her hand and fingers felt tougher, stronger than they had two weeks ago. I wondered if they'd ever be soft again. Perhaps that kind of hardening symbolized growth into adulthood. Very much like the solidifying of my commitment to God and my determination to be His servant anyway He chose.

Neil moved to Rosa's left. She took his hand and put her

right hand on Anjelita's shoulder, clasping our hands tightly. The circle had been broken for mere seconds.

Yet it still felt incomplete.

Kim, don't fret. You did what I asked you to do. You planted seeds. Don't you trust Me to harvest My fields the way I deem best?

I nodded as if responding to an audible voice. *I trust You, Lord, but I still want to see the results. . . .*

If the villagers ever "made a joyful noise," they did it that day. Each one seemed to apply his own words to Beethoven's triumphant tune from the Ninth Symphony. I doubted that the villagers were expressing love and appreciation to God, though. They were more apt to be singing praises to us.

I hoped we'd been good—no, not just good, but effective—ambassadors for God.

Anjelita sang, too. I didn't pay attention to her singing at first, but she got louder on every repetition. Then I recognized her words.

I'd read her some additional Bible verses the previous afternoon after finishing Luke. While I continued reading for practice, she must have memorized them.

I couldn't have fit John 3:16 to "Joyful, Joyful" without making it sound awkward and contrived, but she could and she had. She sang as if she thought those words were the most important ones in the world. How I hoped and prayed. . .

"Porque de tal manera amó Dios al mundo, que ha dado á su Hijo unigénito, para que todo aquel que en él cree, no se pierda, mas tenga vida eterna."

Yes, she sang as if that verse meant the world to her. Was this God's way of answering my faithless concerns?

chapter fifty-nine

The next hour was a blur.

Although the buses were forty-five minutes late, the drivers started loading our suitcases within minutes of their arrival. Cheers arose from the first team members who ran from bus to bus to bus to confirm that each one contained the tiny facilities we longed for after two weeks without. But a number of us chose to return to the far side of the fields one last time rather than compete for the bus facilities.

Walking through the deserted campsite gave me a feeling of empty finality nothing had prepared me for. I'd be gone—we'd all be gone—in a few minutes, and that was it.

What had taken Rob two and three-quarter hours to drive after I broke my arm might take these professional drivers a full four hours or more. But at least the semi that led the parade of buses into the village and the smaller truck that contained fresh-off-the-farm-smelling livestock had probably smoothed the ruts even more.

The villagers would have to spend much of the day helping unload and store or distribute the supplies the semi brought. Maybe a day of physical activity would keep them from dwelling on our absence. I hoped they'd let Anjelita and the other kids help, too. They were hard workers.

I giggled at the thought of the children's reaction to the goats and chickens. If these children were typical, they'd soon make pets of them while the adults viewed them as either a long-lasting source of milk and eggs or a short-lived source of meat and poultry. I wouldn't want to be around when the adults had to calm their children after butchering and eating one of their pets.

Then again, maybe the animals just needed the friendship of a miraculous, web-weaving Mexican spider—what would her name be? Carlotta?—that would save their lives by weaving a message in the web above their pen: STUPENDOUS ANIMALS. DO NOT EAT.

I'd overheard someone say that the villagers were going to store seeds, tools, and other supplies in the church building. They may not have thought of the old building as a church, but I still hoped it wasn't true.

Please, Lord, don't let them use Passover Church as a barn for the animals.

Then I sensed that still, small voice saying, *Mary gave birth to My baby boy in a stable. If the villagers want to use My future house as a stable or a storage shed, I don't have any problems with it.*

He was right, of course. The church hadn't become a place of worship. I'd expected miracles—I'd hoped and prayed for them—but Jesus didn't do miracles on demand, not even during His so-called trial when a miracle might have saved His earthly life. I reluctantly admitted I wouldn't want one unless it was God's will.

I'd been prayerfully considering what one last thing I could do for Rosa and Anjelita—for the whole village, really. The answer was obvious. Taking my Spanish-only Bible home again wouldn't benefit anyone, but leaving it in Santa María might have eternal significance.

Rosa, Anjelita, and I sat on the plywood floor inside their cottage while the drivers, Rob, and Charlie finished loading the buses. When I asked Rob and Charlie to be patient if I boarded last, they stared at me, struggling to keep a straight face. They couldn't keep their eyes from twinkling, though.

They gave up trying to contain their laughter when I promised not to be more than three hours late getting on the bus, and they cracked up big-time when I told them what to do if they got tired of waiting.

"Guys, you have my permission to pick me up bodily and shove me headfirst into my seat without any pretense of patience or dignity. As long as you promise not to fight over the privilege, that is."

If Anjelita had still been acting the way she did last night, they might have needed to do that. Fortunately, her extra-long night's sleep seemed to restore her sense of reason. Or maybe it just helped her to accept the inevitable without freaking out.

Rosa stared at the Santa Biblia on my lap. If the look of reverence and longing on her face was any indication, she didn't have any idea why I'd brought it with me. I'd planned to wait until the last minute to present it to her. Maybe it would help distract Anjelita when I made my getaway.

Sunlight coming through the open door made Anjelita's necklace shine more brilliantly than ever. I wondered if she'd polished it with some type of plant juice. She held the prism up to the sun every couple of minutes and projected a rainbow on my cast. We smiled at one another as if we weren't both bawling our eyes out on the inside.

She started fidgeting like someone who's struggling over a decision. I'd forgotten that even little kids sometimes face adult-sized issues. I couldn't imagine what was on her mind, though.

But she'd already made her decision, and I never would have dreamed how important it was. She, too, had a gift. She took off the necklace and kissed it as if saying good-bye to it. She looked at it and put it to her mouth again. Her lips moved slightly. She appeared to be whispering a secret to her most prized possession.

Then she put it over my head and let it fall around my neck.

She smiled the sweetest smile while waiting for my reaction, but I was too shocked to respond appropriately. Misreading my look—it must have been one of muddled confusion—Anjelita's smile faded and her mood darkened visibly.

Could Anjelita be having second thoughts about giving her precious necklace to a big sister she's known only a couple of weeks? Or changing her mind about doing it without her mother's permission?

With the best of intentions, I took it off and put it back on Anjelita. She buried her face in her mom's shoulder and sobbed as pathetically as if she were in intense pain. Apparently I'd done the wrong thing, but what would make things right again?

Voices outside called my name. Time was up. The bus was waiting, and I had to do something—the right something—within the next few seconds.

Afraid I'd forget to present my gift to Rosa when I rushed out, I placed the Bible on her lap. It seemed to shock her as much as Anjelita's present had shocked me. She picked the Santa Biblia up, looked at it adoringly, and caressed it as if it were covered with fine leather and not paper.

But then she put it back on my lap. The tears in her eyes told me how much that Bible meant to her and how much she wanted to accept it, but that didn't calm the sinking feeling in my stomach.

That's when I understood how I'd made Anjelita feel and how to correct my mistake.

I touched Anjelita's shoulder to get her attention—she'd quit crying when she saw me present the Bible to Rosa—and I motioned for her to hand me the necklace. She placed it around my neck, and this time I said, "Muchas gracias" and kissed her face several times.

"Kimmy Hartlinger, we're coming in to get you. . . ."

I looked at Rosa. I knew what would happen. What had to happen. She motioned for me to hand her the Bible.

I did so with tears of joy.

This time she kissed it and clung to it like a drowning woman hanging on to a piece of boat wreckage. I jumped up from the floor—I'd improved at doing that—and boarded the bus before Anjelita noticed me walk out. Her eyes were on her mother's slightly used Santa Biblia.

I looked back from the door of the bus and heard her voice, weakened by so much early morning singing, "Señorita Kim, *te amo*." She repeated it many times. I was almost positive it meant "Miss Kim, I love you." What else would it have meant?

I responded only once. "Te amo, Anjelita. Te amo, Rosa." Then I broke down completely.

chapter sixty

I was silent as the journey began. Everyone was. Although fatigue and soft, comfortable seats had already put many of the team to sleep, I was lost in my own little world, barely conscious of my surroundings.

With Aleesha in the aisle seat and Neil beside the window, I felt like a thin-cut slice of deli turkey between two mismatched pieces of bread—one wheat, one white. The three of us fit comfortably in the two-seat row.

Maybe Aleesha was right about Neil and me being skinny.

Although the temperature inside the bus was already comfortable, our driver cranked the AC down past frigid. Maybe he was trying to punish us for making him drive through the darkest part of the night to reach the ends of the earth. But at least he wasn't the lead driver we'd had on the drive to Santa María.

My ears and nose got cold first. Although the grungy travel slacks covered my legs, the hole in the knee allowed a cold draft to streak all the way to my feet. I had more goose bumps on my arms than other people had freckles. Neil, Aleesha, and I scooted close enough together to warm our arms some. I was thankful to be the meat in the middle.

Neil still hadn't invaded my mental space with his confession. I was glad. I couldn't deal with it yet. Too many other things were on my mind.

Not even my vivid memories of the recent gift exchange could keep me awake long, though. The last thing I remembered before dropping off was Aleesha examining my new jewelry and saying "Cool!" Not once, but twice. I didn't realize she'd never seen it up close.

Although I slept less than an hour, my nap was refreshing. Other team members were waking up, too, and I heard the slight buzz of conversations here and there.

I turned to my left. Neil was looking at me. At least he didn't have that sick puppy dog look of a guy who's falling for a girl. I would have hated deflating such a sweet sixteen-year-old boy's ego, especially since age and social immaturity were his only real shortcomings. Plus his small frame.

He'd outgrow the first two. Only time would tell if he could outgrow his scrawniness.

Ah, but he already had a girlfriend back home. And I'd worked so hard to assure him our age difference wasn't important.

The dizzy, whirling effect of those thoughts made me giggle once. Socially immature? As punchy as I was at the moment, maybe I was describing myself. I giggled again.

"If you're sufficiently awake, Kimmy, may we converse now?"

After the day's emotional free fall, our talk could only lighten the journey. Neil seemed a bit braver about addressing me now.

"Sure, Neil. You start."

His bravery suddenly turned to sloppy, melting gelatinness that looked like it might run over and under the seats and made me instinctively lean toward Aleesha. I waited for him to throw up, but he didn't. I turned to face him again.

"Go on, Neil. I'm not going to bite."

He brightened a little and opened his mouth. He remained silent for a moment and then closed his mouth again. He must have been searching for the proper starting point.

But bigmouth me had to say something cute. I must be

a direct descendant of Simon Peter, even without being any percent Jewish. "I bite very seldom, anyhow."

He turned pale. I had him pinned against the window. He couldn't escape, and he knew it. He swallowed hard and opened his mouth again, but nothing came out.

"Neil, I'm sorry. I was just teasing. . . ."

He smiled. But ever so slightly. "Oh, I know that," he managed to say. But he said it in that defensive male tone of voice that means "Really? You could've fooled me, you witch."

I'd made things bad enough for the poor kid, so I shut up and waited for him to say something. I'd keep waiting, too, whether it took five seconds, five minutes, or five hours for him to regain the courage to talk to me.

"Kimmy," he said about twenty minutes later, "have you ever done something you felt God really wanted you to do?"

You were terrified to ask that, Neil? And what does it have to do with a confession, anyhow? I resisted the temptation to say that to him, though. I was nice. "I just spent a week of my life reading the Gospel of Luke aloud in a language I can't speak. I wouldn't have done it if God hadn't convinced me to."

He was quiet for a moment. "Okay. Kimmy, have you ever abstained from doing something—something really good— because God didn't want you to?"

Huh? "Abstained from. . . ? I don't think so."

If God had closed the door on this mission trip, I could have answered yes. But He'd left it open. I started to ask Neil why, but voiced a gentler, "Have you?" instead.

"That's what I need to confess. I've been terrified to tell you how much I could have assisted you this past week. I wanted to help, but God wouldn't let me. I prayed about it. Hard. I wrestled with God nightly, but He kept saying no." Neil looked so sincere. So intent on saying things correctly—the best way possible.

"I wasn't afraid to help you," he added as if I might misunderstand his motivation, "and I wasn't lazy or unconcerned."

"First, I can't think of any way you could have helped me this week. Second, why should I get upset about God telling you no?"

He began explaining. The further he went, the more I ground my teeth and regretted assuring him I didn't bite. Every word he said made me angrier. Poor Neil must've felt more defenseless than ever in that position by the window with no means of escape. In fact, he looked so terrified I thought he might prefer to jump through the window of a moving bus rather than remain where I could reach over and wring his scrawny neck.

I'd successfully curbed my swearing during the past two weeks, but right now I found myself under the influence of one of those hateful attitudes that's just as sinful as cursing.

"Kim, I feel awful. Please say something."

Before I could respond the way I wanted to, the peace of God flowed through my head and heart, and the negative words I'd planned to say stuck in my throat. God's love was more powerful than my human anger.

"That's okay, Neil. I understand." *Huh? Did I really say that? Things aren't one bit okay; yet they are, and I don't understand why.* Although I'd let God speak for me, my feelings needed to catch up with my words.

"But how can you, Kimmy? I could have taught you everything you needed to know. I could have translated your testimony. I could have taught you the rules of pronunciation before you started reading."

I breathed a silent prayer before responding. I needed to say the right thing. "I think I know why God wouldn't let you help. He wanted me to rely totally on Him. Accepting your

Spanish expertise would've kept me from doing that. Then, too, the villagers wouldn't have gotten so caught up in the reading if I hadn't needed their tutoring."

He nodded, and I smiled about making such good sense to a boy genius. "But didn't God want you to use your Spanish at all? Charlie and Rob must have had a rough time not knowing they had a capable translator in their midst." I hadn't meant to accuse him of negligence, but I expressed my curiosity badly.

"Kimmy, maybe you've noticed I don't fit in well among so many eighteen-year-olds?"

"Mmm-hmm."

Team members had accepted Neil on the surface—he was a well-motivated, hard-working, functional part of the team—but how many people had tried relating to him on a personal level? Who'd really tried getting to know him?

I hadn't.

"I was afraid I'd sound like a show-off if I admitted publicly how good I am in Spanish. If I sound boastful telling you about my expertise, how would the others have taken it?"

"Good point, but—"

"I explained everything to Rob and Charlie after the first morning's meeting. No matter how desperate they were for a translator, they understood and respected my dilemma. I helped assign the villagers to teams and offered to help in other strategic ways. They encouraged the villagers to help them guard my secret."

"And to think Anjelita almost married us off without me knowing how talented you are."

"Bravo." He chuckled. "Haven't you wondered why Anjelita gave up so easily after our lone evening of being sweethearts?"

"Many times."

"I had a little heart-to-heart with Rosa and Anjelita. I

explained that we both had sweethearts back home and didn't want to be disloyal to them. I do, you recall, and I'll bet you have a boyfriend at home yourself. Probably a lot of them."

"Duh!" I thumped myself in the head. *What a great solution.*

"Sounds like a ripe watermelon to me," Neil said, egging me on. He was growing bolder with his elder now, and I loved it. I'd never realized he could be this much fun.

We laughed together, and I heard a little snicker from Aleesha.

We rode in silence for a few minutes.

"Kim, uh, Kimmy. I'm sorry, but I like 'Kim' better. I hope you don't mind. . . ."

He was so cute. If he'd been a puppy or a kitten, I would've tried taking him home with me. *Mom and Dad, this is my new pet kid, Neil. He doesn't eat much, and he's already housebroken. He can sleep on the floor in the basement, and I promise to take good care of him. You'll barely know he's around. He'll be too busy memorizing every book in the public library and doing post-doctoral studies while completing his first year of college.*

"You and Aleesha!" I winked at him. "Me, too." I looked around to make sure Rob wasn't nearby, but he must have been on another bus this time. "I didn't want to admit I disliked the nickname Kimmy. I was afraid of losing some much-needed goodwill."

A grumble came from Aleesha's seat. "You're kidding me." She didn't open her eyes. How long she'd been awake was beyond me, but I doubted that she'd missed one word of this conversation. I would've done the same thing in her place.

Aleesha hadn't finished, though—talking or listening. "Go on, Neil. You were saying, 'Kim. . .' before you both started chasing that ugly rabbit."

"Uh, right." He peeked around me at Aleesha and then looked at me again. "I really admire your ability to learn Spanish pronunciation the way you did."

" 'Uh' is right, Neil," I said, smiling. I didn't want to chance scaring the poor boy any more today. "And thanks."

"Your intensive course was great. I learned to speak the best Spanish anyone can learn in high school, but you learned to pronounce it the way native speakers do. I'll bet God uses that talent of yours again someday."

I buried that seed of encouragement somewhere deep inside my brain, where it might take root and grow.

"Maybe so," I said. "Neil, you know what was so frustrating in Santa María?"

"What?"

I got serious again. "I prayed hard that God would use my reading for His purposes, and I believe He did. But I wanted to see results, and I haven't. Not except maybe the look on Rosa's face when I gave her my Spanish Bible." I sighed and got quiet.

"Kim, God used you in ways you wouldn't believe, and I'm the only one who can tell you the specifics."

The only one? What in the world. . . ? "Tell me! Please."

"The day you started reading, the village men—the women, too, although they were shier—asked what you were doing and why you were doing it. Once you no longer needed constant correcting, the villagers asked more about the content of your reading. They were determined to understand what Lucas was all about. They asked how the Santa Biblia differed from other books they were familiar with, and you'd be amazed at the variety of books they named. Everything from Mexican history to recent secular novels.

"I'm no theologian, but between a lifetime of Sunday school and several online seminary courses I've taken recently, I answered most of their questions. While my pastor might not agree with every detail, I don't think I misled anyone.

"God used you to lead them in some real, honest-to-goodness soul-searching. I'm not saying everyone became a Christian, no matter how much both of us wish—"

"All three of us," Aleesha said, her eyes still closed.

"The seed you planted fell on soil that was more fertile than you could ever imagine."

As anxious as I was to hear the rest of Neil's story, a strange and seemingly unrelated question popped into my head. I wouldn't be satisfied until I got the answer.

"Why did you need to 'confess' your reason for not using your Spanish expertise to help me? I mean, since God told you not to help, it's not like you sinned against me. The whole thing was between you and God. You didn't need to tell me anything about it."

"Interesting you should say that, Kim. I understood how anxious you were to find out whether your reading of Lucas had done any good, but I couldn't reveal that without telling you the whole story."

While I stumbled over my words fishing for a response, Neil reached into his backpack and pulled out a stack of papers—twenty sheets of mix-and-match paper, maybe more, covered front and back with smallish, gently flowing, feminine longhand in a garish shade of red ink.

I'd seen them once before. On top of Rosa's blanket. Before I could say anything, Neil explained.

"Rosa wrote this letter and asked me to translate it for you. I've looked through it hurriedly. It's lengthy—you can see that— and it's quite personal in places. I have a packet of tissues here somewhere. . .all three of us will need them."

Neil was serious about the tissues. He took a couple and handed me the packet. I was already misting in anticipation. "Reading this to you feels weird."

"It shouldn't, Neil. This is between you and me. . ."—I glanced at Aleesha, who was still pretending to sleep—"and old sleepyhead over there."

Aleesha amazed me by remaining silent.

"Go on, Neil."

He apologized for not being able to do a thorough translation without his laptop. After Rosa used up all of his paper, he'd gotten more for her from Geoff. Since she hadn't given him the letter until that morning, he'd only gotten to look over it briefly and would have to translate most of it on the fly.

I assured him that I—Aleesha and I, that is—would be patient and understanding.

"You'll want to take the original home with you," he said, "but we'll find a copier at the airport so I can have a copy to translate properly. I'll e-mail it to you early tomorrow if I have to stay up half of tonight to do it."

"Don't. At your convenience is soon enough." I hoped I sounded sincere, but we both probably knew I hadn't meant it. I wanted it as soon as possible.

His translation on the bus was rough, but comprehensible, and the tissues disappeared faster than either of us had expected.

chapter sixty-one

*M*y dear sister Kim, let me tell you about the
horrifying storm that led to your coming. Then
*you'll better understand why your time here has meant
so much to all of us.*

*I've never seen a windstorm as violent as the
one that demolished the village a month ago. Village
legends tell of such storms; so from the instant we
spotted it heading toward us—it was visible for miles
across the flat countryside—we knew we had little
hope of survival unless it veered in a different direction
before reaching Santa María.*

*The black wind shocked us by going over—over
and around—the building I've heard you refer to as a
"church," whatever that is. In the yard, it spewed filthy
remnants of trash from far away to make room in its
belly for our houses and possessions. You've seen and
helped to clean up that rubbish.*

*We didn't remain in our homes waiting for the
funnel to attack, however. At the first sighting of the
black spiral, we ran hither and thither with no sense of
purpose. No one knew what to do or where to go.*

You poor people. . .

*Observing the chaos, my older daughter, Alazne—
Alazne means "miracle"—yelled so everyone could
hear, "Go to the caves! Take your families and go to the
little caves."*

Everyone knew what she was referring to. Numerous small, underground caves abound in the area behind the church. Everyone who heard Alazne's cry began running toward them.

Her dependence on crutches—she was born with spina bifida—didn't keep her from rushing from house to house to make sure each family heard her warning. I saw her help several older people.

That wasn't safe, though, was it? The twister had to be awfully close by then. . . .

Although I feared for her safety and urged her to hurry to our cave, I couldn't ask her not to help the people of her village. I didn't try to. She seemed far older—more mature and more responsible—than her twelve years.

More mature than me at eighteen. . .

I remained outside our cave watching and waiting for Alazne as long as I could. She still hadn't come to the refuge we would soon claim as our only home. In my heart of hearts, I believed—or at least I tried to convince myself—she was safe in another cave.

We couldn't delay going inside any longer. We cowered at the bottom of the cave as broken pieces of housing flew by at speeds we couldn't comprehend. Some debris fell inside, and the ground vibrated with such intensity I was sure our rocky ceiling would cave in and crush us. If the bowels of the earth didn't open up and swallow us first.

Anjelita and I screamed words we couldn't hear

and shivered with a cold terror nothing could calm.

Why didn't you pray? Duh. And how would you have known to. . . ?

Although I would have given anything to make sure my Alazne was safe, I had no one to place my hope in. I'd heard the word prayer and had a vague understanding of its meaning, but I didn't know how to do it or who to pray to.

As quickly as the black storm came, it departed in an easterly direction, staggering with the intoxication of consuming Santa María. Anjelita and I had to clear away enough debris to reach the mouth of the cave before we could exit.

Other villagers came out of their caves. They wept aloud, imagining what the wind would have done to them and their loved ones if they hadn't found shelter.

Anjelita and I began looking for Alazne. No one had seen her since the twisting funnel struck the first house. Person after person told us they would have died if Alazne hadn't routed them to the caves.

When our cave-to-cave search proved fruitless, our panic level went sky-high. If the storm had carried Alazne off, we wouldn't find her. And we wouldn't know whether she had died quickly but painlessly, suffered a lingering death, or was still alive somewhere, waiting for help that would never come.

From the ground above the caves, we could see that the ancient building you call a church was still standing. Village legends claim that it was the only building to survive a similar storm a century earlier; that's why the villagers were superstitious about it.

Anjelita and I trudged toward it, hand in hand, picking our way carefully among the rubble. We hoped to find some clue regarding Alazne's whereabouts.

Lord, please. . .

Anjelita broke free and ran toward the front of the building, swaying this way and that to keep her balance as she slipped on loose pieces of trash. A moment later I heard her normally small, timid voice cry out in the most piercing and hideous scream I'd ever heard.

Neil, stop! No more! I don't want to hear. . . .

As I turned the corner, I saw Alazne's storm-battered body lying motionless near the door. She must have been unable to open the door because of the debris that blocked the way. She probably would have survived if she'd been able to get inside.
I screamed and ran toward her. The great depth of the rubble made it nearly impossible to reach her. But we persisted. Once we were close enough, I dropped to my knees and tried to turn her over. She lay face down, her arms wrapped around something I couldn't see. It anchored her so securely I couldn't move her.

She wasn't dead. . .was she?

Now that we'd found Alazne, I couldn't—I wouldn't—give up hope. Not yet. Why should she die because she cared more for others than for herself?
She had no heartbeat, no pulse. No! No! This wasn't true! I couldn't accept what my eyes and my

brain tried to tell me. My heart refused to surrender hope.

She had to be unconscious—nothing worse than that. She would regain consciousness any minute.

Suddenly the horrible truth took root in my head and my heart, and I began wailing. A woman in childbirth could not have wept more hysterically.

Anjelita looked up at me with tears in her eyes.

My dear little one, I thought, how selfish I am. I've ignored your loss. No one can take your sister's place, but I still have you. But you have lost your only sister.

After pulling her close, we rocked and swayed together on top of the rubble, our cheeks touching and our tears mingling.

Once the village men removed Alazne's body, they discovered the cross Alazne apparently tried anchoring herself to. The one you've seen fastened to my doorway.

Funerals may be different elsewhere, but we usually burn the body to prevent the spread of disease. No one dared to suggest that we cremate Alazne, however. We do not treat our heroes that way.

The concept of one person dying voluntarily for the sake of many was beyond my ability to grasp. But I thought about it during your reading of Lucas.

Anjelita brought me out of my daze by grabbing my arm and shaking it until she had my attention. "The necklace!" she cried. "Your grandmama's necklace! It's not there!"

I looked at the body again. She was right. The necklace Alazne always wore, the one I'd promised Anjelita she could wear sometimes, too, was missing. I'd watched Alazne put it on earlier that morning. . . .

No one had seen it. Perhaps it had broken off and fallen through gaps in the rubbish to the ground below.

Finding the necklace was not as important as staying alive, however. We couldn't look for it without clearing the churchyard of debris, and no one would have done that just to look for a necklace, no matter how precious. So I didn't tell Anjelita about its probable whereabouts, and she didn't mention the necklace again until the day you found it.

Lord, why did You let an inanimate object survive the storm when precious Alazne didn't?

In the rubble, someone discovered a broken shovel—a dented blade attached to perhaps two feet of a badly splintered wooden handle. It didn't belong to any of us. Someone else found one of Alazne's crutches in the debris. An older man brought out a piece of light rope he had salvaged, and a fourth person fashioned the three materials into an awkward, but usable, shovel.

Each of the village men took his turn at the backbreaking job of digging a grave in the dry, hard earth. Although the men got sweaty and thirsty, none of them complained.

They dug the grave several inches longer and wider than Alazne's slender frame and deep enough to put a layer of pebbles, broken glass, and larger stones over the body to deter predators from digging it up.

Tears filled every eye that afternoon.

I couldn't watch my neighbors throw dirt over Alazne's body, but when I saw them cover her with the layer of stones, I almost passed out. I imagined Alazne

*trying to breathe with dirt and rocks covering her face
like that, and I could barely breathe, either.*

But that's not the end of it, Rosa. What has Lucas
been trying to tell you?

*Anjelita seemed to know what I was thinking,
though, for she said in her simple, childlike way,
"Alazne is dead. She doesn't need to breathe any
longer. But she is dead only here. She is alive
somewhere else. I know it."*

*Although Anjelita spoke with a precious hope that
had no foundation in fact or logic, her words—her
mysterious faith—moved me profoundly. Dead here,
yet alive elsewhere? Where did she think Alazne was
now? How could I prove her right or wrong? How
could I be sure?*

*One moment, I thought my heart would stop
beating. The next, it beat out of control. So great was
my desire to believe Anjelita was right.*

Lucas gave you the answer. Do you believe. . . ?

*The events I have described took place several
weeks before you and your friends arrived in Santa
María. I still cry frequently over my loss, but fighting
to survive took precedence over grieving.*

*We returned to our cave each night to sleep,
for it kept out some of the chilly night air, but the
ground was hard and uncomfortable. We couldn't find
anything to eat at first and knew we would starve if we
didn't die of dehydration first.*

Surviving the storm didn't guarantee ultimate

survival. Many infants, young children, and elderly villagers died the first week after the storm. Whether from starvation or pollution of the only water they could find, they died. Whether from inescapable exposure to the daytime heat or fatigue that zapped all of their strength, they died. Whether from hopelessness that made them quit trying or the paralysis of depression, they died.

Although we noted their deaths with regret, we took them in stride. What choice did we have?

But where will they spend eternity. . . ?

Miss Kim, when you and your friends came, you brought our first real hope of survival. You delivered bedding and clothes, and you helped us build new homes. You brought food, and we regained our strength. You brought water, and we reveled in the pure, fresh taste that assuaged our thirst without causing more deaths.

You brought something else, though. Love. Unconditional love. I knew you were different when I first saw you and Anjelita together, but—because you look so much like Alazne—I couldn't stand being close to you. Seeing you give your all with an unselfishness that reminded me of Alazne was difficult, too.

If only I'd known. . .

But when Anjelita started gaining new confidence and taking greater pride in herself—no longer tormented about the arm she'd been born without—I couldn't turn my back on you any longer.

When I showed you Alazne's photograph, my inability to explain who she was and why I loved you like a new daughter frustrated me. You obviously recognized the similarities in your appearances. I recognized the similarities in your attitudes and actions.

Miss Kim, your reading from the Bible has meant so much to Anjelita and me. To the whole village. You demonstrated great courage and determination reading in our heart language without knowing how. Learning to pronounce our words in the rote fashion the villagers employed must have seemed like a black storm of challenge.

The villagers noticed how much you and your friends differed from us. In such remarkable ways that we realized our lives lacked something more important than the most valuable of our lost belongings. As you read from the writings of Luke day in and day out, getting badly sunburned, almost losing your voice, and yet always eager to begin again the next day, we appreciated the difference even more.

And I wondered if I was doing any good. . . .

We knew nothing about God before you began reading to us, although I'd tried for years to find out whether somebody like God existed. But if our ancestors ever knew about the God of the Bible, they abandoned Him—perhaps after that storm a century ago—and declined to pass the Good News down to us.

So we had no idea of God's existence—not who He is or what He is like. Neither did we know how much He loves us, what He wants to give us, or what He expects of us. Although we've often said and done things that seemed wrong, we didn't possess a standard of goodness or a guide for right living.

Consequently, we failed to understand that our human nature was evil and merited eternal condemnation. More important, we didn't know that God has an only Son who died to make us His Father's children, too.

The more you read to us about Jesus, the more I thought about my precious Alazne. If I wept that much over my lost daughter—a human being—how much more God must have grieved over the death of His Son.

I still have Anjelita, but Jesus was God's only Son. If God hadn't raised Him from the dead, the Father would have become childless.

So profound. . .

I looked through your Bible a number of times while you were eating lunch or supper. God led me to a verse that said a very good man might give up his life for his friends. That is what Alazne did. But it also said no one willingly gives up his own life for his enemies. Yet Jesus did that very thing.

For us.

You sound like you believe that. Do you? Please say yes. . . .

Earlier today, you read a verse John wrote and you repeated it a number of times for Anjelita to memorize. That's when I finally understood the meaning of the cross. I wept for hours because God loved me that much, even though I wasn't one of His children.

I've been pondering these things for hour after sleepless hour, frustrated that I can't ask you more about your God. But we don't speak the same language, and you return home in the morning.

The way you and your friends forgive one another is amazing. Jesus taught that God's forgiveness of us is dependent on our forgiveness of others. I wept aloud over grudges I've held against my fellow villagers for years.

He'll forgive you. Just ask. . . .

John—the John who immersed Jesus in the wilderness, not the one who wrote how much God loves the world—prepared the way for Jesus' coming. I believe God sent you to prepare the way for Jesus to come to this village.

How I hope and pray. . .

This Jesus of yours has become my Jesus, too. I believe in Him with all my heart now.

Neil, pass those tissues. Hey, everyone, wait'll you hear this. . . .

I began talking to Him early this morning as if He were in the cottage with me. I knew He was. I prayed the prayer He used as an example for His disciples, but I needed to talk to Him about other things, too. I didn't know what to say at first, talking on my own like that, but—because forgiveness is so important—I started confessing and repenting of every sin I could think of and asking Jesus to forgive me.

I love you, my sister. . . .

I told Him I'd do my best to avoid doing those things again. That must have been the right way to pray, though, for never has a bath in the cleanest and purest water left me feeling so perfectly clean.

Many villagers are interested in Jesus now, too. Some of them are close to accepting Him. I'll keep reminding them how much He wants them for His brothers and sisters. I won't let them forget what you've read to us, and I'll ask God to bring to mind any details I forget.

I'll keep praying for you and every single one of them. . . .

You once asked your leaders to bring water outside so we wouldn't thirst while we listened. Immediately afterward, you read about Jesus offering living water to the many-times-married Samaritan woman. That was not a coincidence.

Miss Kim, I've accepted that living water. The past no longer haunts me. I do not fear the future. I don't know everything I want to know about this new life, and I don't understand everything I want to understand. I would give up everything I own to possess a copy of the Bible, but I have nothing left after the storm to offer in exchange for yours.

Please come back to Santa María as soon as you can. Bring the others—as many of your friends as you can—and teach us more about Jesus. We can never learn enough. If you bring a Bible for us to keep, I'll be grateful beyond words. I have no right to ask that, though. Bring yours when you return, and I will stay up late every night—all night if I can—reading and memorizing Jesus' words while you sleep.

I will ask you many questions then, but I will also answer your questions. I'm sure you have been curious about things you could not ask about. How I wish I could tell you more, but this much writing has already taken many hours of many nights, copying some of it from a journal I began keeping years ago.

Perhaps I'll turn it into a book someday. I will call it Rosa No-Name because I grew up as an orphan who did not learn her mother's name and identity until adulthood.

I want you to be the first to read it.

By the way, Anjelita has been talking about giving you the necklace that belonged to her sister. It was originally her great-grandmother's. I fully approve, however. You are her sister now, and she thinks you should have it. She may find it hard to part with since it's the only physical reminder of Alazne other than the photograph. But if she offers it to you, please accept it. It will symbolize your relationship as sisters.

I'll keep sharing the Good News with Anjelita until she becomes a sister of Jesus, too. She is close to making that decision, but I do not want to push her. I understand that this decision must be hers.

May you have a blessed life until we meet again, whether it's on earth or in heaven. Blessed is a much nicer word than cursed.

Your sister in Christ, Rosa

chapter sixty-two

A cloud came over Aleesha, Neil, and me. Not a dark, gloomy cloud, but a mystical, spiritual one. Perhaps the Holy Spirit Himself.

I wanted to say something, but I couldn't. Neil of the genius-sized vocabulary couldn't find a single appropriate word to speak, and even Aleesha the Outspoken was unspoken.

What can I say, Lord? Sarah laughed at the idea of old-age pregnancy and I reacted similarly to Your reading plan for the Bible. I couldn't imagine anyone understanding what I was reading, but I couldn't see the whole picture.

You did, though. It was Your picture.

How You must have shaken Your head at my skeptical obedience. Yet You accomplished more through me—through Neil and me—than I'd ever dreamed of or hoped for.

Thank You for Rosa's conversion. That makes this trip worth everything that's gone wrong. Help her to grow in her relationship with You. Give her patience, courage, and wisdom as she continues witnessing to Anjelita and the other villagers. Lord, may they all become Your children.

Only after praying did I realize Neil had grasped my left hand and Aleesha was holding the fingertips of my right hand. We were one in a more special bond of love than ever.

Although I'd reveled in the gorgeous yellow flowers on the cacti of Santa María, I'd overlooked one significant characteristic until that morning. The blooms lasted only for a day. Although the special feeling I'd experienced that morning would wither and die, too, I'd do my best to remember and cherish it.

I buried my face in Neil's shoulder to hide my tears. No matter how scrawny I'd thought of him as being, his shoulder seemed bigger now. Big enough, anyhow.

Oblivious of everyone else, I let go of my emotions. My teammates probably couldn't tell if I was laughing or crying, but I was actually doing both.

I was barely conscious of Neil releasing my hand and placing his right arm over my shoulder. Although many boys had done that, Neil did it in a way that made me feel safe, protected, and cared about.

I remembered a story Dad told me about a flight from Cincinnati to Atlanta. "I was already in my window seat when a very attractive girl in her early twenties sat down in the aisle seat. An empty seat separated us.

"She confided that, after a lifetime of avoiding flying, she was petrified. She would've gotten off the plane, but she was on her way to visit her fiancé and meet his parents. She had to make this flight regardless of the terror that ate at her insides.

"She wasn't exaggerating. She shook like someone with a muscular disease that affects control of the body.

" 'I know this is asking a lot,' she said with a shy smile, 'but would you hold my hand during the flight?' "

Despite his hesitance to hold hands with a nice-looking young woman, he felt sorry for her. She still had a viselike grip on his hand when they landed in Atlanta.

"The girl thanked me graciously—over and over again. How could I deny my pleasure—not from holding hands with a beautiful young woman, but from knowing I'd helped her endure her pain by taking some of it upon myself?"

That story—I'd heard it often enough to remember every detail—revealed a Christlike side of my dad I'd rarely seen any hint of in my relationship with him. Maybe God brought that event to mind because I needed to develop a similar sensitivity. One that might help Dad and me connect better.

I needed him to hold my hand sometimes. And I'd make him understand I was available to hold his, too.

I was vaguely conscious of Neil's left hand reaching across his lap to take my left hand. I didn't notice at first that he'd extended his right arm to touch Aleesha's shoulder. She put one hand on top of his and hummed so softly I couldn't recognize the song.

But it was God's music. Nothing else would have done.

I realized then how much Neil had aged—no, how much he'd matured—during our two weeks in Mexico. No longer conscious of his youthfulness, I squeezed his hand to thank him for what he meant to me now.

chapter sixty-three

I fell asleep again after that and began dreaming. But this dream seemed more vivid and exciting than any vision I'd ever had, and I let it sweep me along. I didn't want to wake up until I had to. I bathed in the details and soaked up as many of them as I could. Although I usually dream in drab generalities and nondescript colors, this dream was rich in such unique, brilliant hues of detail I couldn't have assigned names to them.

Upon waking, most of the details would be beyond my ability to verbalize. Nonetheless, I would never cease being awestruck at what my awesome God revealed during that snooze.

The mission team was in heaven surrounding God's throne. Most of them, anyhow. They were holding hands and singing praise songs in English. But when I looked at their lips more closely, I realized that each person was singing his own song with its own unique melody, rhythm, and lyrics. Yet I didn't hear them separately; they were well-integrated parts of a rich, harmonic whole.

Aleesha's voice suddenly boomed out, "Hey, girl, where you been? Eternity is half over!" Then she giggled and asked, "Guess who else is here?"

Before I could respond, she pointed at the villagers of Santa María.

I counted to be sure, naming each person as I went along. Most of the villagers were present, and they sang in Spanish at the top of their lungs, barely able to take their eyes off Jesus long enough to look my way, smile, and wave. Their faces seemed to question why I'd taken so long arriving. I shrugged.

Maybe I'd lived longer. I hoped that's why several of the villagers and other team members were missing.

Although I'd never met Alazne, recognizing her was easy. She and Anjelita still looked very much alike, although they had an ageless appearance that characterized everyone I saw. I couldn't remember how old I was, and I didn't care.

I was here for. . .eternity.

Alazne, Rosa, and Anjelita stood together hand in hand. Caught up in joyous songs that never ended, they glanced in my direction, smiled broadly upon recognizing me, and motioned with their heads for me to join them. My joy at seeing the three of them together—a family united for eternity—was inexpressible.

I couldn't walk fast enough. The crowds parted to let me through, raising joined hands so I could pass underneath, and I heard myself singing, too.

My heavenly brothers and sisters sang in every conceivable earth tongue. Many of them used unfamiliar musical scales. Yet the diversity of languages and styles enriched the quality of the music.

I hugged Rosa and the girls, and Anjelita and Alazne made room for me between them. Seeing Anjelita's whole right arm, I took their hands in mine and added a loud whoop of praise to the Great Physician who'd waited until heaven to heal Anjelita. Then I whooped again at Alazne's lack of crutches. The villagers echoed my joyful exclamations, which they added to their everlasting songs.

Together we sang, each of us voicing a different song—a song that detailed everything we were personally thankful to God for. Our songs had no end, for we never ran out of blessings to be grateful for.

I caught Anjelita looking at me and trying to suppress a

giggle. I twisted my eyebrows, and she said with a tone of playfulness I'd never heard her use before, "You're singing in perfect Spanish now. It was good you could speak our language so well when you came back."

I awoke from my dream with the awareness I'd spent such a tiny part of my life in Santa María—a mere one million, two hundred and nine thousand seconds—give or take a few. But how that time had changed me.

I knew now what God wanted me to do with my life. At least for the short term. Under His leadership, my plans would always be subject to change.

God's dream for Santa María took such deep root that it became my waking desire, too. Fulfilling that dream would require me to return to Santa María at the earliest possible opportunity.

Now that God had lit that kind of fire in my heart, I knew He wanted me to prepare by majoring in Spanish—not music—and becoming as fluent as possible. And maybe I could work with the migrant children again and practice my Spanish on them.

About the Authors

ROGER BRUNER worked as a teacher, job counselor, and programmer analyst before retiring to pursue his dream of writing Christian fiction full-time. A guitarist and songwriter, he is active in his church's choir, praise team, and nursing home ministry. Roger also enjoys reading, Web design, mission trips, and spending time with his wonderful wife, Kathleen.

KRISTI RAE BRUNER is pursuing a career in management and trying hard to fit college into her busy schedule. Living in the Orlando area, she's a typical twenty-four-year-old who enjoys reading, watching DVDs, playing video games, hanging out with friends, and cooking. During her teen years, she went on a life-changing mission trip to Mexico.

Next in the
ALTERED HEARTS series. . .

Lost in Dreams

Coming Fall 2011